breakaway

AN ACCIDENTAL MARRIAGE HOCKEY ROMANCE

SINNERS ON THE ICE
BOOK 3

ANASTASIJA WHITE

Silka.art

This book is a work of fiction. Names, characters, locales, businesses, events and incidents are products of the author's imagination or are used fictitiously. Any resemblance to actual person, living or dead; events; or locations is entirely coincidental.

The author acknowledges the trademark status and trademark owners of various products, and/or brands referenced in the work of fiction. The publication/use of these trademarks is not authorized, associated with, or sponsored by the trademark owners.

Edited by Caroline Knecht, https://reedsy.com/caroline-knecht

Cover Design and characters art by Anna Silka, https://www.instagram.com/silka.art/

Characters art by Alina Alilyushka, https://www.instagram.com/alilyushka/

This book is intended for an 18+ audience.

For trigger warnings, strongly advised to visit https://www.anastasijawhite.com

ISBN 978-609-08-0447-6 (ebook)

ISBN 978-609-08-0446-9 (paperback)

ISBN 978-609-08-0448-3 (special edition, paperback)

To the ones who have been carrying the impossible weight of grief on their shoulders, and still have found the strength to stand and be present even when it feels like there's not enough air.
This one's for you.

playlist

1. “Never Not Love You” - Thirty Seconds to Mars
2. “Океан” - L’One, Фидель
3. “THE LONELIEST” - Måneskin
4. “think later” - Tate McRae
5. “Fresh Out The Slammer” - Taylor Swift
6. “Оптимист” - Max Korzh
7. “Chemtrails Over The Country Club” - Lana Del Rey
8. “In The Stars” - Benson Boone
9. “Sorry” - Halsey
10. “My Blood” - Ellie Goulding
11. “Hold On” - Chord Overstreet
12. “СИЛЬНО” - MONATIK
13. “Ghost” - Justin Bieber
14. “Beautiful Pain” - Eminem feat. Sia
15. “making the bed” - Olivia Rodrigo

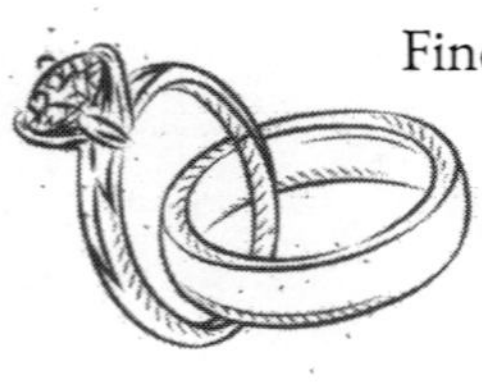

Find the rest of **BREAKAWAY** playlist here:

author's note

Before you begin, I want to say **THANK YOU** so much for taking a chance on Roman and Nevaeh's story. It means the absolute world to me, and I hope you'll love a little sprinkle of Eastern European culture references and Russian words in this book.

BREAKAWAY is full of very different emotions from sadness to happiness, from heartbreak to love. I'd like to say that it's a story with 'right person right time' trope. The timing for these two is everything.

This book contains some sensitive topics, so please check the trigger / content warnings before you continue. It includes: mention of death of a sibling, mention of death of a parent, car accident (off page), motorcycle accident, grief depiction. For a full list of triggers, please visit: https://shor.by/BTCW

There's nothing more important than your mental health.

Enjoy!

With love,
Ana.

Nevaeh

ONE

it's nothing

One Year Ago

"Hey, Trav." I press my phone to my ear, making sure my apartment is locked. "Are you on your way?"

"Sorry, babe. I still have a ton of work to do. Release week is always crazy, and the testers found another bug. I need to fix it."

An exasperated breath springs out of my mouth, and I mask it with a cough. If I'd known Travis wasn't going to be able to join me, I wouldn't have agreed to go. I'm always happy to see my best friend, but going to a club with her and her fake boyfriend is definitely not something I planned on.

"Any chance you can meet us later?" I ask, descending the stairs. The click of my heels echoes in the stairwell.

"I'm not sure, Nev. No one is going to fix my code for me, and with the release on Monday, I have a pretty tight deadline. And—"

"And you're working overtime again?" I huff, tightening my grip around my phone.

"You moved our date twice last week because you had to work overtime too. Did I say anything? Writing that article about the art exhibition was important to you, and I knew it."

Sighing, I close my eyes for a second. He's right. "Sorry, Trav. I know it's not your fault." I walk to the front door and push it open, stepping onto the street. "See you tomorrow then? Maybe we can hang out at my place?"

"How about you come over after the club? Even if it's late. I miss you."

A smile pulls at my lips, and warmth spreads through my body. Who knew that being stuck in an elevator could bring someone like Travis into my life? Definitely not me. It's too much like *Serendipity*, and I don't believe in fate. "Okay, I'll text you later," I murmur.

Once I hang up, I shoot a quick text to Angie. Just to let her know that I'll be third-wheeling with her and Drake.

ME:

I'll be at the club in 40. Alone. Travis is still at the office

ANGIE:

Sucks that he's busy, but don't worry. Drake says he can invite one of his teammates. You won't be a third wheel.

ME:

Tell your fake boyfriend I love him.

ANGIE:

🙄

Chuckling, I shove my phone into my purse and notice my Uber pulling up in front of my apartment building. Well, I can only hope Drake's teammate is a nice guy, like him. I hung out with my fair share of jocks when I was in high school and college, and I can safely say that those guys aren't my type. They are too self-absorbed and too cocky—but not in a good way. I also never seem to have anything in common with them. Spending the night dancing with an arrogant and self-centered ass would be a bummer.

"NEV, OVER HERE!" Angie calls out from the entrance to the club.

She's standing with Drake, whose hand is secured around her narrow waist. Her long brown hair streams down her slender shoulders. She's wearing a red dress that highlights her sun-kissed skin and her flawless body. Big and bulky, Drake hovers over her with his broad shoulders and six-foot-five frame. They are the picture-perfect couple. She's the one who has always believed in magic, making a wish any time she sees 12:12 on a clock. I'm not superstitious like her, but I'm ready to cross my fingers and even my toes for these two to finally get together officially. Their fake dating doesn't make any sense.

"Hey, lovebirds." I smile, stopping in front of them. "Sorry if I made you wait. My Uber was driving so slow."

"Hey, Nev." Angie leans forward and plants a kiss on my cheek. "You're fine; we got here like five minutes ago."

"And we're still waiting for Roman," Drake announces, fixing his dark brown eyes on me. "So, don't you worry. You won't be third wheeling."

"Did you set me up on a double date with your teammate?" I tease, noticing his eyes rounding.

"What? No, I just thought—"

"Drake, I'm joking!" I giggle, glancing between him and Angie. With how she's chewing on her bottom lip, I know she's trying to bottle up her laughter. "I love you two, but I'm glad I'm not going to spend the night feeling like I'm in your way."

"Never." Angie glances at something over my shoulder. "Hi, Roman."

I turn my head; my gaze trails up a male's chest in a tight black tee, and clashes with eyes that are a deep turquoise color. Naughtiness glitters behind his irises, and a coy smirk forms on his clean-shaven face. His eyes slide down my body, and my skin ignites. I'm suddenly feeling hot. This guy is easily the most handsome man I've ever seen.

I blink, breaking the trance I've gotten myself into. Am I really salivating over a guy? Just because of his looks?

Don't you remember Kyle Edwards, Nevaeh?

The prettiest faces often hide the ugliest souls.

Rolling my lips together, I look away and focus my attention on Angie. She frowns as her eyes roam over my face. She didn't miss the way I went from smiling to scowling. Not that it surprises me. Since I met her on my first day of college, she's been the only person in my life who knows everything about me. She gives me everything—love, zero judgment, and unconditional support. And I love her in return just the same.

"Hey, Drake, Angie," the guy says, lining up with me. "Sorry if I made you wait."

"Totally fine, man." Drake shifts his gaze from this guy to me. "Roman, this is Nevaeh."

Glancing to my left, I crane my neck so I can look him in the eyes. Even with heels on, I barely reach his chin. He's probably a good six foot three. I'm not sure if it's his height or the cocky grin on his face as he studies me from under his thick eyelashes, but something about him irritates me.

It doesn't mean anything. I'm not going to be friends with this guy. This can be the first and the last time we see each other.

I extend my hand to him. "Nice to meet you, Roman."

His gaze slips to my outstretched hand, then flashes back to my face. A slight tilt of his head, and he cradles my palm with his. My heartbeat goes pitter-patter, and a breath gets stuck in my throat. Our eyes lock, and he gives my hand a firm shake. His skin is warm and calloused. A billion tingles spread through my body; my whole being vibrates from one simple handshake. It's so weird, it freaks me out. I force a smile on my face and pull my hand away.

"It's nice to meet you, Nevaeh," he murmurs without averting his gaze.

I nod and look away, not meeting Angie's eyes. The last thing I need is for her to start asking questions when I have no idea what's going on with me myself.

"Should we head inside?" Drake suggests, and relief washes over me. A crowded club is exactly what I need to pull myself together. I'm in a relationship, and that's all that matters.

"Do you need a refill?" Hearing the question, I squint at Roman. We've been at the club for three hours, and now we're sitting at the bar to catch our breath. "Nevaeh?"

"No, I'm good," I tell him, returning my gaze to the dance floor. For the last five minutes, I've been eyeing the crowd, into which Angie and Drake disappeared. I don't know how I feel about being left alone with Roman. The number of times he has made me laugh tonight is equal to the number of times I've wanted to strangle him.

"How long have you known Angie?" he asks, and I meet his gaze. There's a glass of whiskey in his hand, and his eyes are glued to my face.

"Since our freshman year." I shrug, my fingers drumming on the bar. "What about you? How long have you known Drake?"

"We met on the ice before he joined the Thunders. Plus, his best friend, Colton Thompson, talked my ear off about him. When Drake walked into the locker room last season, I felt like I had already known him forever," he drawls, bringing his glass to his lips. My traitorous eyes zero in on it. My mouth goes dry, and I pinch my brows together. *Please, not again.* "Angie and Drake look great together."

"He's helping her get rid of her ex. They're just fake dating," I mumble, noticing how his eyes widen. Oh my God! What am I doing? Angie's going to hate me. "Forget I said that—I'm full of shit."

Roman stares at me with the glass still pressed to his lips. Then he lifts one shoulder and says, "*Horosho*[1]."

I sit up straighter and tilt my head to the side, watching him with my eyes narrowed. "You're Russian, right?"

A chuckle escapes his lips as he lowers the glass. "No."

"But that was Russian, the word you said...wasn't it?"

"It was," he deadpans.

"Then how come you speak Russian if you're not Russian?" I hook one leg over the other to sit more comfortably.

---

1. Хорошо. — Okay.

"You do realize people speak Russian in more countries than just Russia, right?" Roman puts his elbow on the bar and props his head on his fist.

"Duh, of course." I look away from his taunting smile. "Teach me something in Russian," I say, peering at him again.

"Like?"

"Teach me how to say thank you."

"That's easy. *Spasibo*[2]," Roman says nonchalantly. "Do you want me to say it slower?"

"*Spasibo*," I repeat after him.

He continues to stare at me, not saying a single word. Suddenly Drake and Angie join us, glancing between Roman and me.

"You're saying it all wrong," he finally mutters, his eyebrows pinched together.

Rolling my eyes, I exhale and say as slowly as possible, "*Spasibo*." I arch an eyebrow and cross my arms over my chest. "What's wrong? I nailed it. Admit it."

His eyes slide to Angie and Drake, and then he brings his gaze back to me. "That was better, but you definitely need more practice."

My jaw unhinges, and my eyes are probably ready to pop out of their sockets. "You're..." I point my finger at Roman. "A jerk. That was my first time trying to say anything in Russian — of course I need more practice."

Without a single care in his voice, he takes his glass from the bar. "Saying 'thank you' in Belarusian would've been way harder, doll."

"Doll?" I echo, snatching his drink and downing it in one go. "Buy yourself another one."

I look at Angie, calculating in my head how to tell her about my slipup. Pulling her away from Drake and his insufferable teammate is my best shot. Without another thought, I jump off the barstool, wrap my hand around Angie's wrist, and announce, "We're dancing."

Angie tries to argue, but I just pull her further into the crowd. Something about this guy makes me act stupid, and I need a break if I

2. Спасибо — Thank you

don't want to end the night doing something more ridiculous. I've already made too many mistakes tonight.

"Nev, what's wrong?" Angie asks, her deep green eyes staring at me warmly. I snake my hand around her waist, silently pushing her to start dancing. "Are you upset we left you with Roman?"

"No. Just..." I trail off, mulling over my next words. "He was teasing me, and I let it slip that you and Drake are fake dating." Angie's mouth forms a little O, and she blinks. "I'm so sorry."

She sighs. "It's fine. I'll talk to Drake. This whole charade is getting out of hand anyway. I should've never asked him to pretend—"

"Are you pretending?" I catch her off guard with my question and can't help but smile when I notice a grin tugging at the corners of her mouth. "He's a great guy, Angie."

"I know." Her eyes roam over my face. "What do you think about Roman?"

The smile drops from my lips immediately. "He's okay. What should I think about him?"

"You've been acting kinda weird tonight, and I can't really put my finger on it, but I think it might be because of him."

"I'm with Travis," I state matter-of-factly. Without waiting for her next words, I turn her around and press my chest to her back. "I'm happy."

Dancing with Angie, I try to push every single thought out of my mind. But then I remember I'm supposed to go to Travis's later, and suddenly, I feel like the biggest liar on Earth.

Heading toward the bar, I let my gaze roam over Roman. He sits with his back to me, and a visible tension in his shoulders catches my attention. His rigid posture is a significant difference from how he was with me, or even when we were all together. It's as if he's uncomfortable being here alone.

I swallow my nerves and slide my palms down the skirt of my

dress, trying to straighten it. Once I'm right behind him, I tap him on the shoulder. For some reason, my fingers linger on his tee, feeling his tense muscles underneath it. Roman jerks in his seat, and his head swivels in my direction.

"Drake said you'd look after me." I pull my hand away and climb onto the barstool beside him. "They left."

He scans me from head to toe, the glint in his eyes turning dark. The tip of his tongue slips out of his mouth, and he slowly licks his lips. I watch him, enchanted, warmth unfurling in my lower abdomen. *The excitement. The longing. The craziest need.* I ball my fists on my lap, my nails digging into my skin. What is so fucking special about this guy? I've never felt like this before. It's utterly wrong.

"Did you tell Angie about you blurting out her secret?" he asks, his voice deep and low. Even over the loud music, I hear him clearly. As if he's whispering right into my ear.

"I did," I confirm. "Did you mention it to Drake?"

"I did." He nods, a smile lifting his lips. "I don't think they will be fake dating much longer. Those two are in love; it's clear to everyone around them. It's time they recognize it too."

Biting my bottom lip, I try to hide my smile but fail. With a big toothy grin, I let my shoulders drop, and the tension I felt disappears. Lightness fills my every pore as I wave to catch the bartender's attention. The guy beside me is not who I thought he was, and maybe that was the reason I was so weird around him. That must be it.

"Do you want to hang out for a bit, or do you need to get home?" I ask, realizing that my heartbeat is calmer now. The lighting dynamically illuminates the place, an ever-changing spectrum that dances to the rhythm. The music reverberates through my skin as I wait for his answer.

Roman runs his fingers through his sandy blond hair, his eyes trained on me. "There's no one waiting for me at home," he tells me as the bartender joins us. "I can stay for a few more hours, if you're in."

I smile. "I'm in."

"ARE YOU ALWAYS SUCH A GENTLEMAN?" I glance at Roman as we make our way to the exit. His hand is on my lower back, guiding me forward and keeping me from swaying.

"I'm not a gentleman," he bites out.

Stopping abruptly in the middle of the crowd, I make him halt in his tracks too. I turn toward him, letting my eyes sweep over his body. The pulsating vein in his neck makes my breath hitch, and I force myself to look up. The second my gaze meets his, I smile, and the heat rekindles in my lower abdomen. "You are. You've been watching out for me all night, making sure I always had a drink, waiting for me outside the bathroom."

Roman dips his head, pinning me with his stare. His turquoise eyes burn into mine. My chest rises and falls, and the rhythmic bass has nothing to do with how my body trembles.

"A real man always keeps his word," he says and steps back, hiding his hands in his pockets. "Let's go."

Without sparing me a glance, he turns on his heel and easily makes his way through the crowd. I gawk at his back as he moves further and further away from me. *Good job, Nevaeh. Was it really necessary to flirt with him again?* The last two hours I spent in Roman's company were completely different than the moment I met him. All my awkwardness disappeared, and I was just myself. Flirty and easygoing. It looked like he was in need of company, and my babbling provided that. Until ten minutes ago, when he finally had enough of me. I lightly slap my cheeks with my palms and follow him.

Outside, I lean my back against the wall and take a deep breath. A cool breeze envelops my body, and I shiver when I notice Roman moving toward me.

"Okay, I need your address." He stops in front of me, his phone in hand. "Nevaeh?"

I focus my blurry vision on him. The alcohol in my system is making my legs wobbly. "I'm not going home."

He sighs and purses his lips in annoyance. "Just give me an address, so I can call an Uber."

I click my tongue and tell him Travis's address, adding, "I'm going to my boyfriend's."

Roman's blues find mine for a moment, and then he looks away. "Okay. I just want to make sure you get wherever you're going safely." He pockets his phone. "We're lucky; we don't need to wait long. The car will be here in five."

I push some strands of hair off my face, tucking them behind my ears. "Why did you stay after Drake and Angie left?"

"Because. It's nice to get a change of scenery from time to time," he replies, folding his arms over his chest. The tattoos on his left arm draw my attention.

His tattoos aren't a sleeve; they're scattered all over his arm. They're chaotic and kinda senseless: numbers, some words, a dream-catcher, a heart on fire. The second my gaze falls on one colorful tattoo, I reach out and touch his skin.

"SpongeBob," I mumble under my breath, leaning forward to get a closer look. There's a word written beneath it, but before I have a chance to figure it out, he steps back, his arms dangling at his sides. "What's wrong?"

"Nothing," he states, holding my gaze, and yet the deep scowl on his face screams otherwise. Even though I know I should keep my mouth shut, curiosity gets the best of me.

"Do you love SpongeBob so much that you got a tattoo—"

"It's just a tattoo." Roman glances over his shoulder, and I swear I hear him sigh in relief. "Our Uber is here." He trains his eyes on me, and literal chills run down my spine. The corners of his mouth drop —there's not even the tiniest shadow of a smile. The heaviness of his stare makes my knees give out, and I tumble forward, barely stopping myself from face-planting.

"You okay?" he asks, and I nod, beelining toward the car in silence. All I want is to get as far away from him as possible. His mood swings give me whiplash.

After thirty agonizing minutes in the car with the guy, who spent the whole ride texting with someone and ignoring my presence, I feel way more sober. The guilt of having flirted with Roman gnaws at me, making me feel terrible about myself. Travis has always been good to me, and he doesn't deserve his girlfriend hitting on another man while he was busy at work. It was disrespectful and stupid. I should know better.

The Uber stops in front of Travis's building, and I climb out of the car. I'm tempted to just slam the door and walk away, but hearing him say my name stops me in my tracks.

"Nevaeh?"

I bend down, my eyes meeting his. "What?"

"Thank you for hanging out with me. You saved me from another night getting lost in my head."

"You're welcome." I shrug and take a step back. "Bye."

"I'll be seeing you." His soft murmur goes straight through me; the back of my neck feels hot. Without another glance, I close the car door and hurry into the building.

Once I hear Travis's voice through the intercom, I relax. Everything that happened tonight stops mattering. A familiar comfort blankets me, and I feel at ease. I have no idea why I reacted to Roman the way I did, but if there's one thing I'm certain of, it's that Travis makes me feel good. Whatever happened at the club is meaningless.

It's nothing.

Nevaeh

TWO

the wrong person

Now

SITTING ON THE COUCH, I STRETCH MY LEGS OUT IN FRONT of me, feeling exhausted. I had the day from hell at the magazine, and I have no desire to move, not even a finger. The slapping sound of Happy's paws reaches my ears, and a second later I lock eyes with Travis's dog.

I pat the couch. "Come on, Happy. Come here, sit with me."

The French bulldog slowly walks closer and jumps on the couch. Huffing, he turns around several times before he finally settles down beside me with his head on my lap. I sigh and close my eyes, gently petting his slick, sandy-colored fur. It calms me down, and I even start to smile. Although I like all pets, I've always been more of a cat person, but this dog and Angie's Doberman really make me reconsider.

Pets keep me company and don't ask questions when I don't want to talk about the things that are bothering me. Like right now, for example. I'm dreading the moment Travis gets home from work. He saw me crying in the elevator when we accidentally met in the office today. He'll want to know what happened, but unfortunately, I don't have an answer for him.

Lately, everything feels off.

My phone dings with an incoming message, and I grab it from the couch. I check my notifications and smile involuntarily when I see my best friend's name.

ANGIE:

Saw your Stories. Why were you crying?

ME:

Stupid drama at work. I was just angry because things weren't going my way.

ANGIE:

That's like a default state for you these days. What's wrong?

ANGIE:

and don't even think about giving me that "everything is fine" bs

ME:

I don't know. Nothing seems to make me happy right now. I got the promotion at work but can't find it in me to be excited about it. Things with Travis are fine but…I feel weird

ANGIE:

I think I chose the worst time ever to go to France with Drake

ME:

You chose the best time ever. You already started showing, there's no way you could've hidden your baby bump much longer. You don't want Drake to find out before the trip

ANGIE:

True, but I still hate that I can't be there for you

ME:

You are there for me, even if you're far away. Wait…isn't it the middle of the night for you?

ANGIE:

It's 2am in Nice

ME:

You're impossible! Get your pregnant ass back to bed!

ANGIE:

😀

Shaking my head, I lock my phone and put it back down on the couch. I need to get going. Travis will be home soon, and I need to take Happy for a walk before that. With a sigh, I slowly move the dog off of me and stand up, hovering over him. His beady eyes focus on me, and a smile curls my lips. He's such an adorable little pup. I'm happy Trav decided to get him five months ago.

"Give me ten minutes, Happy, and we can go." I wink at the dog and head toward the bedroom.

With Travis's place decorated in only white and gray, I've often felt as if I'm the only colorful element in it. It's so sterile and pristine that it's even started to affect my choice of clothes. Black and white, nothing bright or vivid. Nothing revealing or even a little bit provocative. I don't feel like myself here. At twenty-six, I don't feel like I have any control over my life.

But it's not like I have anyone to blame except myself.

My relationship with Travis was a whirlwind. We hooked up for months, no strings attached, and then suddenly we became exclusive. Dates, staying at each other's places, my belongings getting scattered all over his apartment without me even realizing it. I never told Angie, but I think her romance with Drake was something that pushed me to move forward. For years, she's been the only stable element in my life, proof that not everyone leaves when things become a shitshow. Seeing her so happy and in love, I wanted the same. I didn't want to feel left behind, and when Trav asked me to move in with him, I agreed. I thought it was the right thing to do, a logical continuation of our relationship. Almost seven months later...I'm sure I should've waited.

I feel lost most days, and I have no idea how to find myself again.

In the bedroom, I take off my black bodycon dress and put on a white hoodie and black sweatpants. Collecting my hair into a bun, I check my reflection in the mirror and purse my lips tighter. I look so gloomy, I want to cry.

I swear I'd do anything to change this terrible mood I've been in.

Closing my eyes, I count to ten in my head and then focus my attention on myself in the mirror again. "You're going to be fine. It's just a phase, and it'll get better soon. Everything's going to be alright," I tell myself with conviction, hoping that if I say it enough I'll actually believe it.

I take a step back, ready to head out when I remember that I wanted to try out a new leash I bought for Happy. Opening one drawer after another, I start to frown. I'm sure I put it here yesterday, but now it's nowhere to be seen.

I'm rummaging through Travis's sock drawer when my fingers brush something solid. My eyebrows knit together, and I grab a little box and take it out. The second I realize what I'm looking at, it falls from my trembling fingers.

No. No, no, no. He can't be thinking about proposing, right? We're not fucking ready.

My heart beats violently, and my breathing becomes ragged. I press my palm to my forehead, my eyes moving around the room. My body buzzes in a familiar way; a cold sweat breaks out all over my skin. Memories from my past come crashing down like waves during a storm, burying me under all the hurt and fear I felt when the truth about my ex, Kyle Edwards, was revealed. Heaviness makes my chest ache, and my vision becomes blurry. My mouth fills with saltiness, and I unclench my teeth, releasing my bottom lip.

With shaking hands, I take the box from the drawer again. What if I'm overreacting? *Please, I want to be wrong.* Slowly, I open the box and stare at a beautiful diamond ring. It's simple, with a brilliant stone floating over a platinum band. This ring is something any girl would be happy to get, but not me. Tears run down my face, and a sob lodges in my throat.

I close the box and put it back where I found it. Wiping away my tears with my palms, I rush to the bathroom and kneel in front of the toilet. I don't stop throwing up until my lungs start to hurt. Then, unable to move, I sag onto my ass. Something warm presses up against my hand on the floor and I squint, seeing Happy next to me. I scoop the dog into my arms and press him to my chest as silent cries rack my body.

I should've never agreed to be in a relationship with Travis. My parents' divorce, my mom disowning me because I took Dad's side, Kyle's crimes—those things affected me way more than I was willing to admit. All those years back, I recognized the broken pieces of Angie's soul behind her eyes, and it was exactly what drew us together. Two lost souls who found peace in each other's company. She grounded me, giving me solace and fueling my body with confidence and self-esteem. I wanted to be better. With her finding her perfect match in Drake, I was frantically looking for someone to take her place...for someone who would help me build my life. Travis just happened to be there, and I fucking hate myself for leading him on.

Putting Happy back on the floor, I slowly stand up and drag my feet to the bedroom. My movements are slow and robotic; I'm not even thinking anymore. All I want is to get out of this apartment and out of Travis's life. He deserves someone who will appreciate and love him, not someone who throws up at the sight of an engagement ring.

THE FRONT DOOR opens and closes, and I'm still sitting on the couch with Happy's head on my lap. After I packed my belongings, brought the boxes to my car, and took the dog for a walk, I returned to the living room and just sat, waiting for Travis to come home.

"Nev?" Travis calls out, confusion lacing his voice. His steps get louder, and a moment later he walks into the living room. "Why is your suitcase by the door?"

I hold his gaze, chewing on my bottom lip. Taking a deep breath, I say, "We need to break up."

A loud, vibrating laugh bolts from his lips, and he runs his fingers through his blond hair. "Are you kidding me? Did I miss something?"

"Trav, I know how this sounds, and I'm incredibly sorry, but I can't do this anymore." I sniff, looking away.

He moves closer, crouching in front of me and putting his hands on my knees. "Nevaeh, look at me. Please."

I lick my lips and swallow my nerves. Reluctantly, I meet his brown eyes. His brows pull together as he studies my face with a deep hurt behind his irises.

"What's going on?" he whispers. "I saw you crying today at the office, and now you're breaking up with me. Wha...How can I help you?"

A lonely tear trails down my face when I lean forward and cup Travis's cheek. "I was crying because I couldn't deal with my emotions. Because I was angry and disappointed that my coworker botched an assignment I gave her, and I took responsibility for it. No one blamed me, but I felt terrible. It's like...everything is fine, but at the same time it isn't. I don't even know how to explain it to you."

"Let me help you, baby," Travis pleads, his palms running up and down my knees. "Sometimes things stop making sense, and we need a moment to find ourselves in the craziness. I'm here for you, and I will always be here for you. I will do—"

"I saw the ring, Trav." I shake my head. My tears are freely streaming down my face now. His eyes round, and his pupils widen. "I'm not ready..."

Travis leans back, his mouth hanging open. He threads his fingers through his hair, making a mess of his curls. "I wasn't going to propose to you right away. I wanted to wait till your birthday."

"In four months?" I hiccup. "I had a panic attack when I saw the ring. That's not a normal reaction."

His eyes stay on me, making it hard to breathe. Then he pushes away from me, rises to his feet, and starts pacing back and forth. The longer he keeps quiet, the more uncomfortable I feel. I want him to shout at me, to tell me how wrong I am, but instead, when he finally looks back at me—I see tears.

"Travis..." I whisper, my voice trembling.

"So, this is over? We're over? Or you just need a break?"

"I haven't been myself for a while now. Nothing has been making sense. Nothing is bringing me joy." I look down at Happy, and my heart constricts painfully. "I need to get myself together first. To work on my issues. Anything that will make me feel like myself again. You deserve better."

He runs his palm down his face. "But what if I only want you?"

"You don't." I shake my head. "My parents were never happy together. My mom cheated on my dad with his best friend. All I ever saw was pain and hurt. Lies and scandals. Even my first boyfriend turned into my worst nightmare. I have no idea what it means to love someone without holding back, what it means to lose myself in someone without being afraid that I will become a different person. I'm not capable of the love you deserve."

"I'll wait for you. No matter how long, I will." He stomps back to the couch and grabs my hands in his, bending down to look me in the eye. "You're *it* for me, Nev. And I will wait for you to see that I'm it for you as well. The way we met...it was destiny."

It was just a broken elevator. The words hang on the tip of my tongue, but I swallow them down. We were never right for each other...and once he's had time away from me, he will see it too.

I nod, pulling my hands out of his grip. "Okay. Let's talk again in a few months."

"A few months?" he asks, taken aback. I stand up from the couch. "Where are you going? You don't have a place to stay, and it's already eight o'clock."

"I booked a room for tonight. I'll figure out the rest tomorrow."

"You can stay—"

"No," I say and stroll toward the hallway. I don't even allow myself a second glance at Happy. Because if I see the dog, I'll lose it again.

Right before I grab my things, Travis catches my elbow and turns me around. His eyes desperately search my face, his lips quivering. "I love you, Nev."

"I love you too," I lie and wrap my arms around his shoulders, hugging him tightly.

I know this *is* the end. I have no right to continue giving him false hope. This man deserves to be happy...just not with me.

"Bye, Travis," I whisper and step back, taking my suitcase.

Waiting for the elevator, I prop my shoulder against the wall, feeling defeated. The fear of ending up with the wrong person is catching up to me like never before. If I know anything for certain, it's that I don't want to be like my parents. In a loveless marriage. Zero respect for one another. After watching them, I know it's better to be alone than with someone who isn't right for me.

Unfortunately, I let myself be fooled that I could build something with Travis. Something big and full of love. Something that would last forever, even if deep down I knew it was an illusion, I just refused to admit it.

My only regret is that I had to break his heart to realize it...while there's only emptiness in my own.

Roman

THREE

the day is coming

I JOLT UP IN BED, BREATHING HEAVILY. MY BODY IS covered in a cold sweat; my hair is stuck to my forehead. I glance at my nightstand, and five a.m. flashes on the clock. It's the fifth time in two weeks that I've woken up long before my alarm is set to go off. With a groan, I push the covers aside and get up, heading into the bathroom. A shower is the only thing I can count on to help me get rid of the remnants of my nightmares.

It will be seven years next week, but it still feels like it happened yesterday. The void in my chest never goes away, aching more and more with each year that passes. All my achievements, all my victories and losses, my sleepless nights and lonely days during the offseason, I can never share those with him. With the person who deserved all of this so much more than I do...my brother.

Warm water streams down my face and over my body. I shut my eyes tighter, trying—and failing—to hold it together. "*Chert*[1]," I cuss, sliding down and slumping onto my ass in the shower. A single tear leaks out of my eye and trails down my cheek. I catch it with my tongue, tasting salt and feeling resentment toward myself. *A fucking*

1. Чёрт — Shit

crybaby. Tilting my face up, I close my eyes, letting my tears mix with the droplets of water.

My therapist said I shouldn't be ashamed of living. Shouldn't feel guilty, because it wasn't my fault. That's so easy to say, and so hard to do. Especially with the anniversary coming up.

I need to go somewhere, anywhere, just to distract myself and keep from getting lost in my memories. My teammate Dean Crawford's text pops into my mind, and I realize I'm not so opposed to his idea anymore. Going somewhere loud and crowded, with booze and the prospect of finding some random girl for a hookup, sounds like just what the doctor ordered. Anything to soothe this pain. My anger. My night terrors. Anything to make me feel less than I currently do.

Slowly, I stand up, turn the water cold, and let it envelop me. Only when my teeth start to chatter do I get out of the shower, grab the towel from the hook, and dry my body. I stop in front of the mirror, eyeing my reflection wearily. Nothing a few mugs of coffee can't help with. I run a hand down my face, thick stubble tickling my palm. It's not that visible, and it's far from the beard my teammate Colton Thompson is sporting. His looks great, while mine barely grows, and I don't have the patience to wait until it fills in. A clean-shaven face is what I usually go for, but for the past few weeks, I've been slacking on everything, including my looks. I'll fix it soon. Maybe tomorrow...or some other time.

I lower my eyes to my SpongeBob tattoo and trace it with my fingertips. The ghost of a smile curves my lips, and I whisper the word that's written beneath it. "Optimist." The title of my brother's favorite song and his motto for life. I'm not even close to the person he was, but God knows I'm trying. For him. For Mom. And maybe for me, the little Belarusian boy who spent his days dreaming about playing in the NHL with his twin. Inhaling sharply, I shake my head and walk out of the bathroom.

My sleep schedule is definitely out of whack, but with the time difference, this is exactly when my mom's workday is over. Starting my morning by talking to her will set the right tone for the day. At least, I want to believe that.

"It's too early," Mom says instead of a greeting. "Why are you awake, Roma?"

"Just forgot to turn off my alarm. Don't worry."

Mom sighs. "I didn't know I raised a liar."

Sauntering to the window in silence, I look down at the pool. The water shimmers under the barely there sunlight; it's peaceful and quiet, making me think about the house I saw last time I was scrolling through Zillow. Beige brick facade, two stories, with floor-to-ceiling windows and a light brown roof. It had a neat lawn and a pool in the backyard. It's in a good neighborhood; Colton and Ava live nearby. That house is exactly what I want in the future...when my mom is here with me, and maybe my future wife. And yet, I closed the app the second similar thoughts filled my mind. I'm not ready for that. Living in a rented apartment suits me better.

A borrowed life in a borrowed place. The best description of Roman Pashkevich.

"*Synok*[2]?" I blink, pushing away my gloomy thoughts. A note of worry is loud in my mom's voice. "Are they back? Your nightmares?"

"They aren't too bad."

"Roma," she mutters under her breath. "Why don't you start therapy again?"

"I can handle it, Mom. Grief isn't new to me."

"Neither is guilt. It was never your fault, but you let this feeling consume you. Even seven years later, it's still the same. You need to move on," she pleads, her voice shaking. "I'm not telling you to forget. I'm just asking you to stop living as if you don't deserve to be here. Maksim would've been so proud of you."

"I will, Mom. I promise," I say quietly, turning away from the window and heading to the kitchen. "Tell me something good, *pozhaluysta*[3]. I kinda need it."

A soft chuckle follows my words, and then Mom starts talking about her day at work. About her new colleague Olya, a cute redhead

---

2. Сынок? — Son?
3. Пожалуйста — Please

who is twenty-five just like me. I laugh at her not-so-subtle attempt to match me with this girl, even if the chances of me ever meeting her are close to zero.

I haven't been in a relationship since I was eighteen and my life went to hell. And while I'm not opposed to the idea of starting a family one day, for now it's definitely the last thing I'm interested in.

Besides, how can I love someone when I hate myself? It's a road leading straight to heartbreak.

"HEY, DEAN," I say, stopping in front of Crawford.

He immediately wraps me in a hug, clapping my back. "Hey, man. Happy you changed your mind." He steps back, his green eyes twinkling with mischief. "I really thought I'd need to beg you."

"That desperate?"

"I got back from Arizona a week ago, and I'm already so fucking bored." He shrugs. "Thompson is in Michigan with his family. Benson and his girlfriend are in France. Koskinen is still in Finland, just like Couri. And you were trying to bail on me. Not cool, dude."

"Sorry." I grin as we head to the entrance of the club. "I'm not the best company these days, but I'll try not to be a buzzkill."

Crawford squints down at me. "If you need to vent—"

"It's all good. Don't worry. Nothing I can't handle."

"Okay." His plump lips ease into a big smile. "Any goals for tonight?"

I smirk, hiding my hands in my pockets as the bouncer lets us in. "I'm not leaving this place alone."

"Me either." Crawford laughs, bumping me with his shoulder. "Let's go, Thunder Boy."

Rolling my eyes at the nickname, I follow him further into the club. The pulsating beat of the music goes right through my body, sending a gazillion goosebumps over my skin. The sound is loud and pounding, and I start to nod my head to the bass. EDM is definitely one of my favorite genres, especially when I just want to relax and not think about anything. It's exactly what I need right now.

Here's hoping that tonight will be just like the beat. Fun and uncomplicated.

I WATCH Crawford dance with a petite brunette, a smile playing on my lips. It's been three hours, and I don't regret coming here with him. Dean is fun to be around, easygoing and very friendly. Not once has he tried to get me to open up. Instead, we just talked about our time off, our teammates, and his plans to go to Mexico next weekend. The more I listened to him, the more I really feel like I should go somewhere too. To distract myself from my memories and give my tortured mind a break.

Nursing the glass of whiskey in my hand, I let my eyes wander around the place. The dance floor is packed, so many people dancing and chilling to the blaring music. My gaze doesn't linger on anyone as my thoughts swirl in my head. A few girls approached me, but despite my initial plan, I don't want to go home with any of them. My fucked-up mood is a real turnoff to any attraction I might feel.

I raise my glass to my lips as my eyes zero in on a girl with blonde hair cascading down her shoulders and two little buns on top of her head. She's dancing with a guy who has dark, curly, shoulder-length hair and his arm wrapped securely around her waist. Taking a sip of my drink, I frown, racking my brain and trying to understand why the girl looks so familiar.

The whiskey burns my throat, and tears form in my eyes. Realization finally dawns on me as I study her face. It's Drake Benson's girlfriend's best friend, Nevaeh. And I know the look on her face all too well—she's drunk.

Mesmerized, I watch as the guy slides his hand up, grazing Nevaeh's tits until his palm is on her throat. He tilts her face toward him. I down my drink and rise to my feet. My focus is solely on them as I make my way through the crowd. The guy whispers something in Nevaeh's ear, the strobe lights illuminating her face and reflecting in her glassy stare in a way that sends chills down my spine.

After she kept me company at the club the first time we met, we saw each other on several occasions: games she attended with Angie; Drake's birthday party, where she was with her boyfriend. I don't even remember talking to her the last time we were in the same room. I barely know her.

And here I am, an idiot playing the knight in shining armor in order to make sure she's alright.

When I come to a stop, my eyes roam over Nevaeh, and my eyebrows pinch together. Not even a trace of pink remains in her honeyed blonde hair. Her shoulders sag, and the black minidress she's wearing only accentuates the paleness of her skin. The dark streaks of smudged mascara under her eyes make me do a double take. She looks miserable. What the hell happened?

"Can I help you?" Tearing my gaze away from Nevaeh, I focus on the guy she's dancing with. There's a deep scowl on his lips, and his brows are drawn together. He's lean and not really muscular, around five foot nine. He barely hovers over her.

Ignoring him, I step closer and lower my head so my eyes are on the same level with hers. "Nevaeh?"

Her gaze flickers to mine, and her luscious red lips slowly part. "You..."

"What do you want?" The guy tries again, his hand gripping Nevaeh's waist even harder. "She doesn't know you."

I level him with a stare. "She does. Her best friend's boyfriend is my teammate." The guy narrows his eyes at me, pushing his hair off his face with his free hand. "So yeah, I know Nevaeh. What I don't know is why it looks like you're trying to take advantage of how drunk she is."

"It's not like that," he retorts, avoiding my eyes. "She's staying with me, and we decided to let loose a little. I had no idea she would get this wasted."

"So instead of taking her home, you took her dancing?" I don't mention that he was two seconds from shoving his tongue down her throat when I interrupted them.

The guy's bravado slowly dissolves, and he fidgets in place, putting distance between him and Nevaeh.

"This is ridiculous." He steps back abruptly, and Nevaeh's legs shake now that she doesn't have anyone to lean on. "Tell her she can get her stuff tomorrow. Her problems are not my concern. I'm done here."

Hurrying away, the guy disappears into the crowd, leaving me alone with a very drunk Nevaeh.

Dammit. What am I supposed to do now?

Roman

FOUR

unexpected company

"You sure you don't need my help?" Crawford asks, his gaze zipping to Nevaeh. She stands with her back pressed to the wall, her eyes shut and her head hanging low. My hand on her shoulder is the only reason she hasn't fallen on her face yet.

"Absolutely. This isn't the first time I've brought her home," I mutter, noticing his eyes widen. "Though she wasn't *this* drunk last time."

"She's hammered, man," he comments, crossing his arms over his chest. "I've met her a few times with Angie, and when she was at Drake's birthday, with her boyfriend. We never really spoke much with each other, but I definitely didn't think I'd ever see her like this. Why drink so much if you can't hold your liquor?"

"Have you never blacked out?" I ask, getting aggravated by the judgment in his voice.

"No. You?" Arching an eyebrow, I hold Crawford's gaze instead of answering. He snorts, shaking his head. "Shouldn't have asked. How old were you the first time you drank?"

I glance over his shoulder, noticing an Uber pulling up. "Fourteen," I reply absentmindedly. "My friends convinced me to try vodka."

"Vodka?" Crawford bellows. His jaw hangs open. "You tried vodka at fourteen?"

Rolling my eyes, I wrap my arm around Nevaeh's waist and pull her to my side. With a shrug, I meet my teammate's gaze. "I was *so* out of it when my friend brought me home, my mom literally hauled me inside by the hood of my jacket. Never drank vodka again." I take Nevaeh in my arms, round him, and head to the car. Crawford follows, staying beside me. We stop by the car, and he opens the door for me, helping me get her into the backseat. "Thank you, Dean. Sorry for leaving you like this."

"It's fine; I understand. Good thing you noticed her. In the state she's in, who knows what could've happened." We shake hands, and I move to sit in front. "Do you know where she lives?"

"The guy she was with said Nevaeh was staying with him. So, with that option out, I'll take her to my place." I open the car door. "Hopefully, she won't freak out when she wakes up."

Crawford's lips curl into a big smile. "That sounds like a fun morning for you."

"Fuck off," I laugh and climb inside the car. "Bye, Dean."

"Bye, Roman."

I exchange pleasantries with the driver, then pull out my phone and spend the rest of the ride playing Archero and listening to the quiet snoring coming from the backseat.

I OPEN the door of my apartment and slowly walk inside with Nevaeh in my arms. She's still asleep, and I hope she stays like this till morning. The last thing I need is to deal with her in a drunken stupor. I have no idea how she's going to react when she realizes she's at my place.

We aren't friends, just acquaintances. When I met her a year ago, I thought she was stunning, but I also knew she wasn't single. Hitting on women with boyfriends is a line I won't cross, no matter how attracted I feel. And with her…my attraction was through the roof.

"Wh-where...am I?" Nevaeh's voice cuts through the quiet like a knife, and I look down at her. Her eyes are half open, and there's a deep wrinkle between her eyebrows as she surveys my place. "Where is Sam?"

I lick my lips as I sit her on the couch. Stepping back, I hide my hands behind my back and tower over her. My heart suddenly picks up its pace, beating violently against my rib cage. My palms become clammy. She tucks her hair behind her ears, and her lips purse into a slight pout.

"Where is Sam?" She repeats her question and finally focuses on me. Her eyes slowly travel from my legs up to my face; the moment our gazes meet, she gasps. "You!"

It's the second time she's said that instead of my name. With a sigh, I crouch in front of her, my hands on my knees. "It's Roman. You remember me? I'm Drake's teammate."

Nevaeh jerks away from me, hugging herself tightly. "Where is Sam?"

"Is Sam the guy with curly, shoulder-length hair?" She nods, her eyes glued to my face. "He said you would need to get your stuff tomorrow. He left you with me."

I don't say anything else, because I'm sure in her state she would barely understand the gravity of the situation she was in. Her "friend" was taking advantage of her. I wouldn't be surprised if this Sam guy was encouraging her to drink more, to drown her problems in alcohol so he could get her to do whatever he wanted. It's so much easier to manipulate someone when alcohol impairs their judgment and they aren't themselves. Like taking candy from a kid and making them believe they wanted to give it to you.

"Why would he do that?" Nevaeh sobs, tears streaming down her face. "Why did you bring me here? Where am I?"

"Shh, Nevaeh, everything is fine. You're safe. I just want to help you," I reassure her. My palms are burning on my knees. The need to haul her to my chest and calm her down is overwhelming, but I resist it. "You can stay here and leave tomorrow morning. It's not a problem at all. You're not bothering me."

She hiccups, wiping her eyes with her palms. Her shoulders tremble, and quiet whimpers leave her lips as she sobs. Suddenly, she clamps her hand over her mouth, and her eyes go wide. "I think I'm going to puke."

Blyat'[1].

Jumping to my feet, I grab her hand and pull her up. Hurriedly, I tug her to my bathroom, turning on the lights as we go. She kneels in front of the toilet and empties her stomach almost immediately. Taking a deep breath, I go get her a glass of water and sit by her side, gently collecting her hair and holding it back for her.

"That's right. Let it all out," I murmur, trying to distract myself from the sounds by running my hand up and down her back. "Don't hold back."

I don't know how long we stay like this on the floor, but when she turns to look at me, a wave of overwhelming sadness breaks over me. All the color is drained from her face. Her ruined makeup is smudged over her cheeks and under her puffy eyes.

"I'm sorry," Nevaeh whispers, sniffing.

"That's okay. You feel better now?" She nods, and I give her a reassuring smile. Then I hold out the glass of water I brought, and she downs it in what seems like one gulp. Standing up, I pull her to her feet too. "Let's get you to bed. You can sleep in my room, and I'll take the couch."

"But—"

"Shh." I flush the toilet and turn her toward the door. To my relief, she doesn't try to argue with me, just follows my lead. Her small hand rests in mine, and an unexpected warmth coats my palm where our skin is touching.

We stop by the bed, and I let go of her hand and head to my walk-in closet. Grabbing a T-shirt from the shelf, I turn around and return to the bedroom, halting in my tracks when I get there. Nevaeh is already lying on her right side at the very edge of the bed, her hands hidden under the pillow. I smirk, padding closer and noticing her legs

---

1. Блять (cuss word). — Fuck.

dangling from the bed. Putting my tee on the nightstand, I bend down and slowly take off her heels. She pulls her legs to her stomach, curling into a little ball.

Without thinking, I reach out and push her hair off her face. Her eyelashes tremble, but her eyes stay closed. I smile as I cover her with my blanket. Moving as quietly as possible, I get a pillow and a spare blanket from the closet and walk out of the bedroom, closing the door behind me with a muffled sound. I could go sleep in my guest room, but it would take time to make the bed, so the couch sounds a thousand times more appealing. Besides, it's just for one night.

After I finally settle in on the couch, I'm wide awake. Tonight did not go the way I expected. Instead of a hot girl riding my dick, I have a girl peacefully sleeping in my bed while I'm alone in the living room.

I'm broken, and I don't see a way to fix it, but I think I recognized myself in Nevaeh tonight. Drinking my ass off just to forget, just to stop caring. Doing absolutely anything to take my mind off the things that are bothering me.

I don't know what happened to her, and I'm not going to pry if she doesn't want to talk about it. But if she'll let me, I'd like to help her. Focusing on someone else's problems offers a welcome break from my own terrors, and I swear I need it.

Her unexpected company could be exactly what I need to keep me from losing it.

"OH MY GOD! Why are you awake?" Nevaeh's high-pitched voice draws my attention to her. She stands in the doorframe, covering her face with her hands.

"It's eleven o'clock," I say pointedly, my eyes roaming over her figure. She's no longer in her dress. My white tee covers her perfectly, hanging just below her ass. Forcing myself not to stare, I focus on her face. "How did you sleep?"

"Good," she mutters, peeking at me through her spread-out

fingers. "Can we talk after I get cleaned up? I think I embarrassed myself enough in front of you last night."

"Sure. The bathroom is over there." I point to the door on her left.

She nods and dashes to the bathroom without another word. Once she's almost inside, I call out to her, "Are you hungry?"

Our eyes meet as Nevaeh glances at me over her shoulder. "Yes." With a thud, the door closes, and I'm alone again, sitting on the couch with a wide grin on my face. I have no idea where this good mood is coming from, but I'm going to enjoy every second.

"IT'S NOT MUCH, but I hope you like fried eggs with bacon and salad." I put the plate of steaming hot food in front of Nevaeh. She looks up at me with a hesitant grin on her lips.

"I'm so hungry, I think I'd eat anything. And this"—she pulls the plate closer to her and takes a fork in her hand—"looks delicious."

I lower myself into the chair across from her and silently dig into my food. Nevaeh does the same, and for a moment the kitchen is filled with only the rhythmic clatter of our forks against our plates, the subtle sounds of chewing, and the occasional clink of glasses as we put them back on the table after taking a sip. When I'm done with my food, I push away my plate and relax back against my chair. Nevaeh finishes at the same time, but unlike me, her posture becomes tense. Avoiding eye contact, her gaze wanders over the kitchen as she raps her fingers on the table.

"Do you want coffee?" I ask, breaking the silence. She meets my eyes for a second and nods. "Good. How about you wait for it in the living room?"

"Okay." Nevaeh gets up and takes her plate from the table.

"You can put it in the dishwasher. I'll run it later," I tell her, and she does as I say. With a discreet glance in my direction, she saunters to the living room and sits on the couch, hiding her legs under her butt.

After a few minutes, I stop in front of her with a mug of steaming hot coffee. Nevaeh takes it with a grateful smile and lifts it to her lips. I plop down on the couch beside her, keeping a good distance between us. I don't want her to think that I expect anything from her for my help.

We sit in silence, drinking coffee and not looking at each other. As weird as it probably sounds, I feel comfortable. It doesn't bother me for even a second that she doesn't talk. The atmosphere in the room is light and pleasant, making me breathe easily.

A deep sigh comes from my right, and I turn my head to peer at Nevaeh. She holds her mug between her palms, her bottom lip pulled between her teeth. Looking up, she meets my gaze. Her deep blue eyes framed by thick lashes bore into me, and a tinge of pink covers her cheeks.

"What happened last night?" she asks, her voice shaking.

Half turning to her, I sit more comfortably and tell her everything I know.

Nevaeh

FIVE

my friend's friend

The coffee Roman made for me is already cold, but I continue to hold the mug between my palms as if it will warm me up. Or maybe knock some sense into me. Because the things he said about what happened last night make my head spin.

How could I be so reckless? Drinking until I was almost in a blackout...what was I thinking? That my friend would take care of me? I have so many questions for myself, but I don't know the answers. Except one. It was naivety in its purest form. Something bad could've happened if it wasn't for the man sitting next to me on the couch.

"I'm not sure if a thank you will be enough," I mutter, looking up from my lap and focusing on Roman. "But thank you for looking out for me, for taking care of my drunk ass, and for letting me sleep in your bed. Thank you."

He smirks. "Stop thanking me. I didn't do anything special."

"You're giving me a headache." Shaking my head, I look around his living room. High ceilings and big windows fill the room with natural light, accentuating the light colors of the interior. White blends with charcoal and blue tones, making the darker elements stand out—the navy couch we're sitting on with white plush pillows, black shelves with books and some awards, the huge TV covering most of the wall in front of the couch. It looks simple, but special details here and there, like the small wooden coffee table, are proof of a designer's touch. I like it here.

"What are you planning to do now?" His question brings my attention back to him. Those deep turquoise eyes stare at me with such intensity, I really get the feeling he sees right through me. "I mean, your *friend* said you need to get your stuff out of his place."

Prolonging the moment so I don't have to answer him, I finish my coffee and put the empty mug on the table beside his. With a shrug, I say, "Well, it's a good thing I took a week off from work. Otherwise, I'd have to call in sick with a hangover. I guess I probably need to get my stuff out of Sam's place, and then I'll book a hotel. Or call someone else to let me crash with them. Don't worry about it. I'll figure something out. It's just temporary, while I look for a place of my own."

Roman doesn't say anything, seemingly lost in his thoughts as his fingers drum on the back of the couch. I use this little moment to study his face. A strong, chiseled jawline covered in thick blond stubble gives him a roughed-up look, just like the prominent dark circles under his eyes. I notice the paleness of his skin and how drawn-out his features are. As pathetic as it sounds, I've looked for him at every game I attended with Angie, admiring how handsome he is every single time. Now, he doesn't look like someone who gets a lot of sleep, and I can't help but wonder why.

He clears his throat, and I meet his gaze. "Last night, as I listened to Crawford talk about his plans to go to Mexico, it made me realize I want to go somewhere too. Take a little trip," he explains slowly, raking his fingers through his hair. "I was looking at flights and hotels this morning, just before you woke up. I want to leave on Friday and come back on Monday, so if you want, you can stay here while you're looking for an apartment. I don't mind."

My jaw drops, and I gape at Roman in total bewilderment. He can't be serious. "You don't even know me."

"What does that have to do with anything?" He cocks an eyebrow, props his elbow on the couch, and leans his head on his fist. My mind obligingly flashes a memory from the night I met him for the first time, and it causes my heart to gallop and my palms to become sweaty. He's still the most attractive man I've ever seen. "You're my friend's friend."

I chuckle. "Well, yeah, but you found me at the club barely conscious."

"Are you trying to tell me that's normal for you?" Roman asks with an absolutely bored expression. I swear it looks like an emotionless mask; not even a single muscle on his face is moving.

"Of course not!"

"Then what's the problem? I'll leave tomorrow around lunch, and you'll have my apartment to yourself for three days."

I look away and focus on the Thunders jersey with number 24 on the back, hanging on the wall near the window. It's not Roman's number, and why is there an M instead of an R before his last name?

"Nevaeh?" My name leaving his lips envelopes me; it's deep and soothing, engulfing my whole body in warmth and bringing my attention back to him. "I promise I won't bother you if you stay. You won't even notice me."

I tip my head to the side, watching him in silence. With a deep breath, I say, "Thank you."

"Does that mean you'll stay?" Roman asks, and I nod, unable to keep myself from grinning.

His eyes sparkle, lighting up his features like little sunrays peeking through a cloudy sky. A smile lifts his full lips, mirroring mine, and I find myself enthralled by him yet again. Since we met a year ago, he's been distant with me. I don't remember him smiling at me or saying anything except for a little small talk when he couldn't avoid it. I'm not even sure if he finds me attractive. Roman's indifference is something I'm used to, so now I'm cataloging his smiling face deep in my mind so I can revisit it any time I want. Just because I like looking at him.

"So, what are you planning to do now, roommate?" he teases, making me burst out laughing. "I'll get the guest room ready for you, but if you need my help with anything else, just ask."

"First I need to go to Sam's place for my stuff. And then—"

"You're not going to that asshole's place alone." Roman's playfulness instantly disappears as he pins me with his stare. I should probably be annoyed by the commanding tone of his voice, but instead my skin heats up, and the back of my neck feels hot. I trap my bottom lip between my teeth, fidgeting in place and ignoring the fire in my lower abdomen. "I'll go with you."

The air between us becomes charged as I hold his gaze. The atmosphere is closing in on me, but not in an uncomfortable way. This need I feel for him is...madness.

Jumping to my feet, I barely avoid knocking my knee into the coffee table. "We can leave in twenty minutes," I mumble and beeline to his bedroom, where I left my clothes.

Space. Lots and lots of space. That's what I need to clear my head of this man.

"I DIDN'T ASK BEFORE, but curiosity is clearly getting the best of me," Roman says, glancing at me, his hand on the steering wheel of his BMW X4. In the white tee he's wearing, his tattoos are on full display, but I force myself not to stare, remembering his reaction to my question about his SpongeBob tattoo. "How do you know this Sam guy?"

"We were friends in high school, and then we kinda lost touch until I met him at the magazine a year ago. He's a freelancer, writes sports articles for us from time to time," I reply, hiding my fingers in my hair and slowly threading them through it. "We ran into each other in the office yesterday, and I let it slip that I'm staying at a hotel while I look for an apartment. Sam offered to let me stay at his place, since it's close to the office and he has a spare room...and I agreed."

"Did he ever hit on you before?" Roman's jaw is set hard, and his eyebrows pinch together as he peers at me and stops at a traffic light. I put my hands in my lap, silently wishing for the moment when I can change into something more comfortable than this minidress I wore to the club.

"Never. Besides, when we met last year I was already with Travis. I introduced them to each other, and they were always friendly whenever we met. Sam was always respectful to me. I have no idea why it changed last night."

"Maybe because you're single now."

"Well, he knows I broke..." I trail off, cursing myself in my head. My breakup with Trav isn't something I want to talk about with Roman, ever. Damn. "It's complicated, and Sam knew that. I never thought he'd try to take advantage of me."

Roman's eyes coast over my face, and then he looks away and focuses on the road again. "People's lives are full of lies and pretense. So many hide behind fake facades, ones they built to tuck away their demons, and you'll never know what's behind the mask unless they let you see. Trust is overrated, because no one is ever one hundred percent honest. In my experience, I can name like five people who I'd really call a friend. Is Sam really your friend?"

I shake my head. "In school he was. Now? Hardly. I made a huge mistake, and *in my experience*...I should've known better." As I meet Roman's eyes, his words play on repeat in my head. With an arched brow, I ask, "And you? Are you honest with your friends?"

He contemplates me for a moment, and then he shrugs. "I am." He looks back ahead of him as he parks near Sam's building. "But that doesn't mean they know everything."

I KNOCK on Sam's door and take a step back, bumping into Roman's chest. A rush of blinding energy pierces through me, and I awkwardly shift to stand beside him. My cheeks feel warm as I throw him a subtle glance. Hands hidden in his pockets, he props his shoulder against the wall. His legs, in light blue jeans, are crossed at his ankles, like nothing in this world can frazzle him. Our eyes meet, and the ghost of a smile lifts his lips for the shortest moment, and then it's gone. He pulls one hand out of his pocket and knocks again, way louder than I did.

We wait in silence until the door finally opens. Sam's eyes land on me, moving all the way down my legs. A smug smirk forms on his face, and for the first time in a while, I ball my hands into fists. "Nev? I'm so glad to see you. I didn't know what to think—"

Roman clears his throat, and Sam's gaze flicks to him. His smile transforms into a scowl, and his lips purse together tightly. He folds his arms in front of him and sticks out his chest in an attempt to look bigger. "What do you want?" he asks Roman.

"I'm here to get my things," I say. I take a step forward, trying to get past Sam. It's so tempting to tell him that he looks ridiculous thinking he can intimidate Roman, who is bigger and taller than him, but I keep my thoughts to myself. All I want is to get my stuff and be done with this man.

Sam's uncertain eyes run from me to Roman. With a resigned sigh, he steps back. I breeze past him and go straight to the room he showed me yesterday. My suitcase sits by the bed, right where I left it. Thank God I didn't bring any boxes with me. Bending down, I pull out the suitcase handle, walk out of the room, and head back to the front door.

Roman and Sam are facing each other in silence; the only sound comes from Sam's foot tapping on the floor. I step closer, and my eyes instantly find Roman's.

He tilts his chin up. "You good?" I nod, and he switches his attention back to Sam. "You're lucky I got to you before you touched her."

"Fuck off, dude. I didn't force her to drink; it was all her," my former friend exclaims snidely, as I move past him out of the apartment. "Everyone in school knew she was always DTF if she was drinking."

My jaw drops, and I wheel to my right, too stunned to say anything. Sam's smiling face makes me sick to my stomach, and a wave of nausea washes over me. The guy I considered a friend just called me a whore, not even trying to deny what he was after.

"DTF?" Roman asks, the crease between his eyebrows becoming deeper.

"Down to fuck," I whisper, the ache in my chest increasing. The longer I stare at Sam, the harder it becomes for me to breathe. Tears burn my eyes like acid.

The sound of a sharp hit rings through the air, followed by a man's whimpers. I blink away my unshed tears as I watch Sam press his palm to his mouth.

"The fuck did you do that for?" he cries.

"Watch your mouth next time." Roman shrugs, his thumb brushing over his knuckles. "I have a friend who was at the club last night too, and he would confirm that we saw you taking advantage of a drunk girl. I don't think anyone would want to work with a sex offender."

Sam huffs, taking his palm away from his busted bottom lip. Emotionless, I stare at him. Not even pity crosses my mind. What goes around comes around, and he got what he deserves. He glares at Roman for a moment longer, and then he shuts the door of his apartment with a thud, leaving us alone.

I wipe away an unwelcome tear with my thumb and tighten my grip on the the suitcase handle. Turning to my right, I'm ready to leave, but a warm palm covering mine makes me pause. Roman is already by my side, gently taking the suitcase from me.

"Thank you," I say quietly as we head to the stairwell.

"Let's get you out of here, *roommate*." Roman smiles at me, and we start to descend the stairs.

Roman

SIX

why not?

The sun slowly begins to set, a golden glow bathing the streets, casting long shadows, and gradually cooling the air. The water in the pool below mirrors the sky, where soft hues of orange and pink blend together. I sit on a chair on my patio, my laptop on my lap and my phone pressed to my ear.

"How's Michigan treating you?" I ask Colton, as I finish booking a hotel room in Vegas.

"It's good to be home. Michael and Meghan are happy to spend time with their grandparents, because they obviously let them do way more than Ava and I do," my teammate says, making me chuckle.

"Your kids have you wrapped around their fingers, man. You're delusional if you think that's not true."

"I'm not as strict as Ava, but that doesn't mean I let them do whatever they want," he retorts.

"With Michael? Maybe not. But Meghan's got you tied up in knots." I laugh as I remember him dressed up in a *Paw Patrol* costume. "You were the most adorable police dog I've ever seen."

"Remind me to never invite you to our Halloween party ever again," he grumpily scoffs. "What have you been up to? Did you decide where you want to go?"

"Just booked a trip to Vegas." I close my laptop and put it on the small wooden table next to me.

"Vegas?" Colton asks. "Are you going alone?"

"Yeah, why not?"

"Because no one goes to Vegas alone, Roman. It's a place where you go to have fun, let loose, and not worry about anything. You need someone to look after you."

"I think I'll be fine." I shrug, looking down at the pool and seeing two girls sitting on the edge, their legs dangling in the water. One of them is my neighbor, a cute brunette with an inviting smile and tits to die for. We've talked a few times, and last week she invited me to her place for *coffee*. I was teetering on three hours of sleep with a massive headache, so I said no, and I don't think she took it well.

"At least tell me what hotel you're staying at so I can check on you."

"Fuck off, Colt. I'm not a child."

"You're three years younger than me," he counters, laughing, happy he was able to rile me up. "But, seriously, Roman, I wish you'd take someone with you. It would be way more fun."

A light knock makes me jump, and I turn my head to notice Nevaeh standing behind the closed glass door to the patio. I nod, and she slides the door open, stepping outside and slumping down onto the chair across from me. She pulls her legs to her chest and wraps an arm around her ankles. Her sapphire blue eyes focus on me, and a little smile plays on her lips.

"Roman?" Colton's voice in my ear makes me finally stop staring at Nevaeh.

"Sorry, I just spaced out." I glance at the girl across from me. She's no longer watching me; her eyes are diverted to the pool. My friend's words echo in my head, but I push them away. Asking her to go to Vegas with me? She'll think I'm crazy. "Everything's going to be fine. I was pretty wild when I was younger; you don't need to worry about me."

"I remember your stories," Colton says. A kid's voice gets louder on the other end of the phone. "Sorry, man. Meghan wants me to help her find her teddy."

"Of course. Tell the wife and kids I said hi."

"Will do. Bye."

I hang up, put my phone on the table beside my laptop, and peer at Nevaeh. She's wearing a white crop top and gray sweatpants, her hair collected in two braids. *Comfort.* The word comes to my mind, and my body fills with warmth. She's calm, and her skin is glowing in the light of the setting sun. My heart starts to beat faster, my eyes glued to her face. She's so beautiful...I can't even force myself to look away.

"Roman?" Nevaeh says, and I blink away the spell she put on me. "I said I'm sorry for interrupting. It's getting late, and I thought maybe we could order something. I don't really want to eat alone."

"No worries, and that sounds good to me." I nod, standing up and collecting my things from the table. She joins me, and I let her in first, sliding the door closed once we're in my bedroom. I put my laptop on my bed and slip my phone into my pocket, meeting her gaze the second I look up. "What do you usually have for dinner?"

"It's not what I usually have, but I'm really craving pizza." Nevaeh closes her eyes. There's a dreamy expression on her face, and a cute smile adorns her features. "Anything with mushrooms and cheese... God, even thinking about it..." She opens her eyes, noticing me staring at her. "Sorry."

Chuckling, I shake my head and go to the kitchen with her padding beside me. Without her heels on, she doesn't even reach my shoulder. My lips stretch into a big smile; a nickname flashes in my head, and I know it suits her better than anything.

I glance at her, pulling the menu for the closest pizza place out from the drawer. "Let's order some pizza, Malyshka[1]."

---

1. Малышка — Baby girl

"GOD, this is the best pizza I've ever had!" Nevaeh sighs. The nape of her neck rests on the back of the couch, and her eyes are closed.

"Or you were just really hungry," I say, propping my feet up on the coffee table.

She snorts. One of her eyes opens and peers at me. "You're not going to ruin my good mood."

I raise my hands in front of me in surrender. "Your wish is my command, Malyshka."

That gets her full attention, because she sits up straighter with her gaze trained on me, curiosity swimming behind her irises. Arching an eyebrow, she half turns to me. "That's the second time today you've called me that. What does it mean?"

"What does what mean?"

"Ma...something." Her cheeks taint a shade of pink, seemingly embarrassed.

"Maybe I'll tell you one day."

Nevaeh stares at me from under furrowed brows for a moment, then she shakes her head. "As long as it's not 'doll,' you're fine."

"It's not, I promise."

A comfortable silence settles between us, our eyes locked on each other. It shouldn't be a big deal, but the way my body warms and my heartbeat quickens makes me break eye contact. She said it's complicated between her and her boyfriend. Last night at the club is the best evidence of that. She's dealing with a breakup, and making a move on her now? The most reckless idea ever. A ride on my Kawasaki is a way safer adrenaline rush. Risking my heart isn't worth it, especially since it never fully recovered after my brother's death.

"Where did you decide to go?" Nevaeh asks, sitting cross-legged.

"Vegas." I subtly move away from her, putting more distance between us.

With her eyebrows pinched together, she studies me, chewing on the inside of her cheek. "You're going to Vegas? Alone?"

"Now you sound like Colton."

"Well, that's because it's weird. Most people don't go to Sin City alone, Roman. Where is the fun in that? Who's going to stop you from betting all of your money on red? Or from wasting your money at the strip clubs? Or from getting stupid drunk?"

"I will." With a shrug, I glance at my brother's jersey. "I know how to look after myself."

When I return my gaze to Nevaeh, I notice her staring at Maksim's jersey too. The last thing I need is her asking questions. These days, Mom is the only person I can talk to about my twin and have it hurt less and not more. The fear of losing my cool in front of someone I barely know—or, even worse, opening up to someone new —is huge. Not even my teammates know exactly what happened. Just Colton, but he never pushes me to talk about it. He understands.

The pain of losing such a big part of me is never-ending. It lies beneath all the bricks I built up around myself; it's injected deep into my core. I don't really let anyone close to me anymore, because anything can trigger it. Falling deep into the hole of self-destruction isn't new to me...but I'm afraid next time it happens I won't find a way out by myself.

"I hope you have fun," Nevaeh says quietly with a small smile.

"Me too." I shift, slowly calculating how I can retreat back to my room. I don't want to make her feel unwelcome, even if I really do need a moment to myself. Her closeness plays games with my head, and I want it to stop. "Do you like your room?"

"It's perfect. I honestly have no idea how I'm going to pay you back for everything you've done for me."

"Just promise to never drink that much again with someone you don't really know. That will be enough."

Bursting into giggles, Nevaeh leans closer until our eyes are level. "I promise," she says, her gaze darting to my lips. The movement is brief, but I still catch it. Swallowing my nerves, I rear back and throw my hand over the back of the couch.

'It's complicated' girls are taboo.

Thanks, inner voice. As if I didn't already know that.

"What are you planning to do this weekend?" I even out my breathing, putting a polite smile on my face.

Nevaeh frowns, and scrunches her nose. She fidgets away from me until she's out of reach. With her arms folded over her chest, she averts her gaze to her legs. "My priority is to find an apartment. Then I think I'll buy myself some ice cream and watch something on TV."

"So you're *that* kind of girl?" I cock an eyebrow at her. "The kind who eats ice cream to forget about her problems?"

"Nothing makes me feel better than chocolate fudge brownie. You should try it; it's heaven."

"No thanks. I'll take your word for it."

Biting her bottom lip, Nevaeh looks around. She seems lost. What if my behavior confuses her? I'm acting like a jerk, giving her whiplash with how often my mood changes. Not that I can help myself...being attracted to someone I can't have is a struggle. Reasons to stay away flash in my head. Too bad my heart lives a life of its own.

"It's getting late," I say, taking my feet off the coffee table. "I'm going to head to my room. I still have a suitcase to pack."

Her hand flies to her hair, and she tucks a few locks behind her ear, nodding. "Yeah, you're right. I have an apartment to look for."

We stand up at the same time, avoiding looking at each other. With a heavy heart, in an atmosphere that feels like there isn't enough air, I go to my bedroom and don't look back.

BREATHING RAPIDLY, I sit on my bed, balling my fists. My face is wet from tears, and I grit my teeth, angry with myself. I throw my blanket aside, stand up from the bed, and snatch my phone from the nightstand. Two a.m. Wow, is this a new fucking record?

Releasing an exasperated sigh, I wipe my face with my hands and slap my cheeks. Hard. I would've given up on a lot of things if physical pain could solve the ache in my chest. The slap dulls it for a moment, makes the memories quieter, but it never stops it completely. The ache is always with me.

Tiptoeing out of my bedroom, I go to the living room and turn on the TV, launching Netflix. The volume is as low as possible when I turn on the first episode of *Peaky Blinders*. I've watched this so many times, I can quote the characters. It's my favorite show, and it always quiets my disturbing thoughts, letting me lose myself in the world of Thomas Shelby.

I'm halfway through the first episode, when my eyelids grow heavy. Leaning back into the couch, I nestle more comfortably in case I fall asleep. The hand on my shoulder makes me jerk awake, and I barely stop myself from yelling. Glancing over my shoulder, I find Nevaeh standing behind me, an empty glass in her hand.

"I didn't know you were up," she mutters, giving me a small smile. "Sorry I scared you."

"It's fine." My voice sounds hoarse as I run a hand down my face. "Did I wake you?"

Nevaeh shakes her head, rounding the couch and sitting down beside me. She's still in her clothes from earlier. The only difference is her hair, which is pulled into a little messy bun on top of her head, a pencil peeking through it.

"I have an article due in a week, and I decided to work on it." She lifts her glass. "I came out here to get some water. Can't sleep?"

I nod. "I decided to watch something to see if that'd help me."

Her gaze drifts to the TV, her eyes following the people on the screen. "I've heard so much about this show, but I've never gotten around to watching it. Is it worth it?"

"One hundred percent. It's the best show ever. You should watch it."

"I'll think about it." She smiles, her eyes roaming over my face. "You're going to sleep through your flight to Vegas."

Then an idea pops into my head, and before I can think it through I blabber, "Want to come with me?"

Her eyelashes flutter; she's gawking at me, slack-jawed. "I thought you didn't need company."

I need company more than anything these days, even if I don't want to admit it aloud.

"*Prosto*[2]...Sorry, I was just thinking back to what you and Colton

---

2. Просто... — Just...

said, and I guess you're right. It'd be more fun to go with someone," I mumble. "I'll pay for everything; you don't need to worry about anything. I'm sure you'll need a good chunk of money for a deposit on an apartment."

Nevaeh continues to stare at me in silence. The voices of the actors on the TV barely reach my ears, and my heartbeat echoes in my chest so loudly, the sound sears through my skin. With a lift of her shoulder, she smiles.

"Why not?"

Nevaeh

SEVEN

he's just a guy

"So, does Drake know?" I ask Angie, watching Roman from afar as he buys coffee for us.

"Not yet." She laughs heartily, and the sounds of people's chatter become louder on the other end of the line. "Sorry, we're at a restaurant for dinner, and it's really crowded. Drake went to the restroom, so I decided to call you."

"That's fine. When are you planning to tell him?"

"In Paris. We'll be there in two days," she replies. "How are you, Nev? Are you feeling better?"

Twisting my mouth, I bite my bottom lip and stare at the plane that's getting ready to take off. I hate lying to my best friend, but I don't want to bother her with my problems when she's enjoying her time with her boyfriend. I'll tell her the truth once she's back.

"I'm good. Took a few days off to recharge my batteries, and it's really been helpful."

"That makes me happy. I've been worried about you, Nev. Once I'm home, we need to have a sleepover."

"I better go to Layla's then. Your last sleepover traumatized me." Drake's voice reaches my ears. "Who in their right mind watches all of the *High School Musical* movies to feel better?"

"Your girlfriend," Angie deadpans, making me burst out laughing.

"Touché," Drake says.

I turn my head and notice Roman walking toward me with two cups of coffee. "Okay, lovebirds, I gotta go. Have an amazing day. Love you both."

"Love you too, Nev. Tell Travis we said hi."

"Will do. Bye, Angie." I end the call just as Roman joins me.

He extends a cup to me, and once I take it, he lowers himself across from me on the couch. "Thank you," I tell him, and he shrugs.

If someone asked me what I was doing here with this guy, the only answer I could give would be I don't know. My plan for the weekend was simple: find an apartment, hopefully sign a lease, and then throw myself a pity party. Ice cream and movies. Easy and predictable. What better way to cheer myself up than ice cream? What better way to forget about my own problems than lose myself in the worlds of fictional characters?

Apparently, going to Vegas with a guy I barely know.

Roman sips his coffee, his elbow set on the back of the couch, his cheek resting on his fist. His white tee has ridden up, revealing a line of sun-kissed skin and delicious-looking abs. My eyes traitorously zero in on it, and a warmth that has nothing to do with the hot cup in my hand spreads through my whole body. He's a guy I barely know...a guy I'm insanely attracted to, and it scares me to death. Because I don't think he likes me at all.

"How is Benson?" The question makes me stop staring at his abs and brings my eyes to his. He's no longer sporting his thick stubble, and his clean-shaven face looks boyish. The turquoise color of his eyes now holds a darker shade of navy blue, reminding me of the sky on the edge of a storm. A great contrast to his soft features. Only his jawline and cheekbones stand out with how refined they are.

"Good. He and Angie are enjoying their time in France. She is obsessed with that country, and Paris in particular."

"Yeah, Drake mentioned that once or twice. He said it's a special place for her." Roman gives me a quick smile and takes another sip of his coffee. "I'm not surprised that's where he took her."

Bringing my cup to my lips, I mull over his words. With a tilt of my head, I narrow my eyes. "What does that mean?"

With one eyebrow raised, the corner of his mouth quirks up. "You need to be a bit more specific."

"The way you said that...about Drake taking her to France. Do you know something?"

Deep, honeyed laughter bursts out of his lips, and his eyes crinkle with playfulness. "Malyshka, English isn't my second language. There's no hidden meaning behind my words. Angie loves France, and her boyfriend took her there for a vacation. That's all."

I continue to stare at him, as if expecting him to crack and start telling me his secrets, knowing perfectly well he won't. This guy has the best poker face. Like last night, as he was watching *Peaky Blinders*, I couldn't get a read on him. He looked detached, his face expressionless.

The day he lets his mask slip will be the day I finally know who Roman Pashkevich really is. If that ever happens.

"What are you working on?" I glance at Roman, who sits on my left near the window. The moment it was allowed, I pulled out my laptop and continued writing the article I didn't finish last night. We had about thirty minutes left in our flight when I typed the final words.

"An article about the best places to go with your partner if you want a change in routine. You know, instead of restaurants and bars."

"May I?" He cocks an eyebrow, extending his hand. My gaze drops to his outstretched palm, then back to his face. He looks genuinely interested, as if he really wants to know what I wrote. "I kinda peeked a few times, but I think reading the whole thing will be more interesting. Plus, I'm curious."

Fighting a smile that forces its way onto my lips, I push my laptop into his hand. Roman takes it and starts reading my article. I keep my eyes on the seat in front of me. It's never been easy to watch someone reading my work.

Roman hums, drawing my attention to him at once.

"Hmm?" I echo, frowning. He meets my eyes, and his lips suddenly break into the most handsome smile. For some stupid reason, it agitates me. I snatch my laptop back and close it, stuffing it into my backpack. "I should've known you wouldn't like it."

"Nevaeh." His low murmur slides under my skin, causing heat to creep onto my cheeks and the back of my neck. It happens so quickly, it's like he flipped a switch.

"What?" I ask, my voice louder than I intend. "Your 'hmm' was very telling."

"First, I need you to stop making assumptions about my words. Second, your article is really good. It's witty, smart, and entertaining." My jaw drops, and I continue to gape at him in silence. "My 'hmm' was only for one reason—I didn't see any sports-related activities mentioned."

Turning to him, I fold my arms over my chest. "Elaborate."

"Well, art exhibitions and museums are great. It's educational, entertaining, and sometimes awe-inspiring when you just stare at something and can't look away because it's so perfect," Roman explains. "Concerts? Might be loud, but at the same time you can bond over the songs you both love, or just dance together, which is a huge plus. Movies? Clearly a great date; everybody knows that. Escape rooms? A bit extreme if you ask me, but you'll need to work as a team, which is a great test for a relationship, to see if you have a future together."

"So you like my suggestions?"

"I do, but I don't really understand why you didn't include any sports. Going to a game together? The excitement, the adrenaline, the pure fucking endorphin rush when your team wins—it's the best thing ever."

He has a point. A really good one. I groan, shifting in my seat so I can sit straight. "Dammit, and I thought I was done."

"You're welcome." I glare at him, but it quickly disappears

because he puts his hand on my knee. "You wrote an amazing article, Nevaeh. If you add in some sports, it'll just make it better."

"Thank you." I hold his gaze. The feeling of his hand on my skin is intoxicating, setting my whole being on fucking fire and making my body hum in anticipation.

I've never felt anything even close to how this man makes me feel. Even with the guys and girls I was in love with. He's just different.

Suddenly, his hand is gone, and he leans back into his seat. "Sure. Anytime." His reply is clipped and curt, and it makes me set my jaw hard. His attempt to create distance between us when we're sitting next to each other on a plane is ridiculous—so are my reactions to him. I need to get over it.

He's just a guy. And I have an article to finish. With a sigh, I pull my laptop out again. Writing always helps me clear my mind.

ROMAN STEPS OUT of the elevator first, proceeding to his right. I follow him in silence, debating in my head whether I'm making a mistake or not.

A little too late for that, no?

I roll my eyes and twist my lips into a scowl. My inner voice is annoying me. Of course it's too late. Instead of agreeing to come to Vegas on a whim, I should've said no. Right off the bat, because that was the most logical thing—and yet I let my consciousness black out while my heart was running the show.

Dammit, I broke up with Travis four days ago. I should be home, watching rom-coms and eating ice cream. I should be looking for an apartment. And, more than anything, I should feel something when my ex sends me pictures of him and his dog on walks, telling me how much they miss me.

But I don't feel anything...unless it involves the guy walking in front of me. Guess I seriously fucked up.

"This is our room," Roman mutters, glancing at me over his shoulder. I stop beside him right as he opens the door with the key card and lets me in first. "I tried to get them to upgrade what I booked, but this was the only available room with two beds."

Barely listening to his mumbling, I step into the room and look around. It's big, spacious, in warm colors with two double beds, a table and chairs by the window, a big TV on the wall, and a bar underneath it. I walk straight to the window and look down at the famous Las Vegas Strip. Putting my hands on the glass, I close my eyelids and let the sunlight warm my skin.

I don't need to open my eyes to know he's beside me. His arm brushes mine as he stands close. "I've been to Vegas for games, but I never really had the chance to explore," he says quietly. I turn my head to look at him, and our gazes meet. "Thank you so much for agreeing to come with me."

"Don't mention it," I reply, averting my eyes. The longer I look at the city, the stronger the feeling in the pit of my stomach becomes. I don't know his reasons, but I think I need this trip just as much as he does. "Thank you for inviting me. I promise you won't regret it. I'll be great company."

Roman's lips curl into a crooked smile. "I don't doubt it."

Smiling at each other, we stand at the window side by side, watching the city and not saying anything. The moment is peaceful and calm, and for the first time since I walked out of Travis's apartment, I start to believe that everything is going to be alright.

I'm going to be alright.

Roman

EIGHT

my type

I'm sitting on the couch in the lobby, playing Archero on my phone. Nevaeh stayed in the room to shower and get ready for dinner. She said it wouldn't bother her if I stayed, but I decided it would be best if I went downstairs. Just picturing her in the shower fucks up my mood; I'm having a hard time concentrating on anything else.

The less temptation, the better. I'm already walking a very thin line between what is right and what I want. And fucking Nevaeh into oblivion should definitely not be something I consider at all. It shouldn't even cross my mind, but it does...and *blyat'*[1]—I'm thinking about her all over again.

I quit the game and send my mom a text to let her know I made it to Vegas. It's around five a.m. in Belarus, and she should still be asleep, but the last thing I want is to worry her. She's the most important person in my life. Without her, I'm not sure I would've made it through Maksim's death. Everything I have now is because of Mom, and I'd go to the end of the fucking earth for her.

"Sorry," a sugary-sweet voice says, and I look up from my phone. A redhead with wild curls framing her face stands beside the couch,

1. Блять (cuss word) — Fuck

her hands locked behind her. My gaze slips down to her cleavage—her tits are almost spilling out of her black dress. Raising my eyes back to her face, I see a sultry smile on her red lips. "I'm here with my friends." She points over her shoulder at two girls standing near the reception desk. "And I noticed you're here all alone, so I thought maybe I should introduce myself. I'm Zoey."

Tilting my head to the side, I continue to stare at her without saying anything. She shifts in place, crossing her legs at the ankles. My silence makes her uncomfortable, but I don't really feel bad about it.

"It's nice to meet you, Zoey," I finally say. "What are you and your friends doing in Vegas?"

A relieved sigh jumps out of her parted lips. She uncrosses her ankles and steps closer to the couch. "We're here for my friend's bachelorette party. We plan to let loose. Do some crazy stuff, you know? What happens in Vegas, stays in Vegas, right?" She doesn't hesitate to sit down beside me, her leg brushing mine. "What brings you to Vegas?"

Trying to hide from haunting memories is the answer, but of course I keep that to myself.

"Same as you, I guess, aside from the friend who's getting married."

Her face, which has a smattering of freckles, lights up, and she inches closer. "Any chance you'd like to join us? Hang out with me and my friends?"

"I don't think my friend would like that."

Putting her hand on my knee, Zoey turns to me. Her flowery scent mixed with the alcohol on her breath envelops us both. "You think your friend won't like us? The girls and I are nice...very nice."

I hold her gaze as her hand slowly moves up my leg. *Well, this is new.* I don't remember anyone ever coming on to me this hard. The elevator dings, and the click of approaching heels echoes through the lobby. Averting my gaze from Zoey, I see Nevaeh heading over. A white summer dress with little flowers streams down her body, ending just above her knees. A bodice accentuates her narrow waist and pushes up her round tits. Her hair cascades down her bare shoulders, two braids framing her face. She slumps down onto the couch beside me and leans forward.

"What did I miss?" she asks, making Zoey retract her hand from my leg.

"I was making friends with Zoey," I reply nonchalantly. "She's here for a bachelorette party."

"Um...I didn't know you were here with someone...sorry. I better go," Zoey mutters, rising to her feet.

Scurrying away from the couch, she joins her friends, and a moment later they step into the elevator. Unable to keep my face straight, I turn to Nevaeh with a huge grin on my lips. "I think I can use your help with scaring the girls away."

Her slightly narrowed eyes roam over my face. "Was her hand on your knee when I got here?"

"A bit higher, actually," I confirm.

"A bit higher," she repeats, shaking her head. "I didn't take you for a touchy-feely guy, but I guess it depends on the person who's doing the touching." Standing up from the couch, she hovers over me. "Let's go to dinner. I'm starving."

Without waiting for my reply, Nevaeh turns on her heel and strolls to the exit. My gaze slides from her toned back down to her tanned legs in red heels. An indecent image of her on all fours flashes in my head, but I quickly push it away, jump to my feet, and follow her outside.

She sounded pissed, for whatever reason, and making things worse is definitely not on my to-do list. Not today, and not ever. I need this trip to help me survive next week.

"REMIND me again why we're doing this?" I ask Nevaeh as a few more people enter our pod at the High Roller. She glances at me and proceeds to the railing without a word. "Nevaeh?"

I stand next to her, my eyes coasting over the Las Vegas Strip. The glowing buildings and streets spread out before us. The city's energy is full of vivid colors, intensified by the never-ending sounds of nightlife. The night sky creates an astounding background, making the city lights even brighter. My lips stretch into an involuntary smile, lightness filling my body. It feels good to be here, to not think about all the things that usually bother me.

"What do you think?" Her voice is quiet and a little distant. I squint at her, meeting her gaze.

"It's beautiful," I reply as the pod slowly starts to move.

She collects her hair and puts it over her shoulder, combing her fingers through it. "I just thought ten p.m. was too early to go back to our room. And since tomorrow we're planning to go to the Bellagio all day, we might not have time for the High Roller. And you definitely don't want to miss this when you come to Vegas."

"It was a great idea. Thank you."

Lifting her shoulder in a tiny shrug, Nevaeh focuses her gaze on the view in front of her. I take it in too. Other people chat around us, laughing and joking, but it doesn't bother me. If anything, the noise quiets my inner voice, keeps me from focusing on my past. It's good to be here.

"So, was that girl from the lobby your type?"

Blinking, I turn my head and stare at Nevaeh. She's not looking at me; her gaze is still glued to the view outside the pod. "You mean that Zoey girl?"

"If that's her name." Nevaeh sneaks a glance at me and looks away immediately. "Was she?"

Furrowing my brow, I keep silent, racking my brain for an answer. I didn't expect her to bring that up, especially not now. At dinner she was a bit pouty and hostile at first, but once the waiter finally brought her penne basilica with a glass of prosecco, her mood changed. She told me about her work at the magazine and the articles she'd been working on, including a recap of a Taylor Swift concert she went to with Angie, Drake, and his sister, Layla. She even talked about how she loves cats. That was actually hilarious, especially after she started rambling about Angie's dog, Cooper, and how he helped her change her mind and become a dog person too.

The conversation was fun and light, but this question right now isn't.

"She was pretty," I say, and Nevaeh's eyes instantly fly to me. A little scowl crosses her features, darkening her gaze. "I don't really have a type."

"Everyone does," she counters, shifting from one leg to the other.

"What's yours then?"

"It's not about appearances for me." Nevaeh turns around and leans against the glass, staring off into the distance. "I've dated men and women, and I never really defined which I like more or what attracts me to them. It's more about their vibes, and the emotions they bring me."

"And you say everyone has a type?" I turn to my right, propping my shoulder against the glass to get a better look at her. "But you don't?"

A gentle grin dances across her lips, and she cocks her head, meeting my gaze. "You have a point. Though, the more I think about it, the more I believe it's really about attraction on a deeper level. When you just know you both are on the same wavelength."

Before I can stop myself, I ask a question that's been hanging on the tip of my tongue. "Were you and Travis like that?"

Her smile falls. The tension in her shoulders becomes evident. Then she sighs, and her hands slide down the skirt of her dress, as if trying to smooth invisible wrinkles. "Maybe at first..." She shakes her head, her hair veiling her shoulders. "Damn, Roman, you're good. Turning the conversation around without me even realizing. Fine, let's pretend I believe you. You don't have a type."

My gaze coasts around her face, admiring the smooth, radiant glow of her skin. Her little upturned nose and those full, tantalizing lips, the sprinkle of freckles on her nose and cheeks. Her big, sapphire eyes framed by long eyelashes and softly curved eyebrows. She's not wearing a lot of makeup tonight, and still...she's breathtakingly beautiful.

She wants to know what my type is? She just needs to look at herself in the mirror.

"I'm paying for your drinks tomorrow," she suddenly exclaims, and I frown. "I don't feel comfortable having you pay for everything. You promised to let me pay for something, and yet dinner was on you."

A smirk plays on my lips. I push myself off the glass and stop in front of her. Nevaeh cranes her neck, and our gazes smash together. I press my hands to the glass next to her face, crowding her in my embrace, and lower my head.

"I invited you on a trip last minute. You just broke up with your boyfriend and need to rent an apartment, and most landlords require a security deposit. I know you can pay for dinner, drinks, or anything else we decide to do while we're here. That doesn't mean you should have to," I say with a smile. "Besides, my mom taught me that if I invite a girl somewhere, I should be the one to pay. And I hate disappointing my mom."

Nevaeh gazes at me in silence; her chest rises and falls rapidly. Suddenly, a genuine smile breaks across her face, and she dips her head to the side, her hair brushing my hand. "Your mom raised a good man."

"She did. My mom is the best."

Her gaze becomes distant, and her smile slips away. But then she quickly recovers, the corners of her mouth quirking up. Taking a step forward, she grabs my tee in her fist and pulls me closer to her. "I'm still paying for something tomorrow. Anything. Drinks or food." She tugs on my T-shirt, and I lower my head even more, so our foreheads are almost touching. "If I need to fight you on this, I will. Am I clear, Roman?"

"Very." I nod, swallowing down my nerves. Her closeness affects me in the worst—or best—way possible. My skin heats up, the beating of my heart skyrocketing within milliseconds.

Letting go of my T-shirt, Nevaeh steps back. The next thing I know, she's standing with her back to me, watching as our pod starts to descend.

Tomorrow will be...interesting.

Nevaeh

NINE

the source of all my problems

THE BUZZING OF MY PHONE WAKES ME UP. I SIT UP IN bewilderment, squinting to my right and quickly grabbing my phone from the nightstand to silence it. It's only nine a.m., but it's Angie, and she wouldn't be calling if it wasn't important. Tossing my blanket aside, I get out of bed and glance at Roman. He's asleep on his belly, hugging the pillow and looking incredibly cute with his disheveled hair falling into his eyes. A smile curves my lips, and I silently tiptoe to the chair beside the window.

"Hey, Angie," I say quietly, pressing my phone to my ear.

"Hey, Nev. Did I wake you up?"

"Yeah, but it's fine. It was time for me to get up anyway." I slump down into the chair and pull my legs to my chest. "How are you?"

"We're going to Paris tomorrow," she blurts on an exhale. "I'm nervous."

"Why?" Pinching my brows together, I bite my bottom lip. She's been dating Drake for a year, and the guy is the epitome of a family man. He loves his niece, and he always makes time for his friend Colton's daughter, who is his goddaughter. He's kind, loyal, and he adores Cooper, even if he's never really had great experiences with dogs. The guy is perfect, and I can't think of a single reason he'd be unhappy about Angie being pregnant.

She laughs. "I don't know."

"Angie," I chuckle, shaking my head. "Everything is going to be alright. You're going to your favorite city with your favorite person, and you're about to tell him that he's going to be a dad. Trust me, I have a good feeling about this."

"Thank you, Nev. I needed to hear that."

"That's what friends are for, honey."

"You're the best friend in the world," Angie murmurs. "How are you? Any fun plans for the weekend?"

Fun plans? We're definitely going to the Bellagio Conservatory & Botanical Garden, and probably to the casino, since Roman claimed he's never gambled and it's something he needs to experience at least once in his life. But other than that, who knows? When alcohol is involved, it's hard to make any solid plans...and I'm definitely going to drink tonight.

"Not really. I'll probably stay in"—I notice movement to my right, and a sleepy Roman sits up in his bed—"and watch something with Travis."

His eyes zip to me the second my ex's name leaves my mouth; he gives me a quirked eyebrow. I press my finger to my lips, asking him to stay silent. Roman shrugs and looks away, picking up his phone from the nightstand.

"A quiet weekend sounds good, especially after all the stress you've been under."

"Yeah, um, Angie, I kinda need to use the bathroom. Talk to you tomorrow?"

"Of course! Love you, Nev."

"Love you too. Don't forget to send me pictures from France."

"Will do," Angie says. Then she hangs up.

I put my phone on the small table beside me and peer at Roman. He's watching me with an unreadable expression on his face. Again.

"Angie doesn't know you broke up with your boyfriend?" he asks, and I shake my head. "You don't want to worry her while she's away with Drake?" I nod in confirmation. "*Ponyatno*[1]."

Knitting my brows together, I purse my lips. "What does that mean?"

"*Ponyatno*? 'I see,'" he explains, getting out of bed. "We better start moving if we want to have breakfast."

"What do you mean by 'I see'?"

Roman stops by the bathroom door and throws me a glance over his shoulder. "You're a good friend, Nevaeh." With that, he steps inside and closes the door behind him.

I sit still, fiddling with my fingers. Taking a deep breath, I quickly count to ten, stand up and saunter to the closet.

THE ATTENTION to detail is astonishing. Every composition is like a work of art, carefully crafted and arranged to display manicured landscapes and floral sculptures, creating a breathtaking view. The air is filled with the sweet aromas of flowers and foliage, making me forget where I am.

I could stay here for hours and not get bored. The beauty of nature is so simple and so powerful at the same time, my head is spinning.

"You're doing it again." A mocking voice in my ear sends shivers down my spine. Looking up, I find Roman staring at me with a taunting smirk. "Your jaw is on the floor."

Flipping him off, I shake my head. "It's not my fault you can't appreciate beauty."

He laughs heartily, shoving his hands in his pockets. "I never said it's not beautiful. I just don't get why we've stayed here for so long."

I take another picture on my phone and check to see how stunning the pastel pink roses look. There's nothing more beautiful than these flowers, even if Drake's sister, Layla, who is a florist, says that

1. Понятно. — I see.

peonies are superior. I toss my phone in my purse and shoot my gaze to Roman.

"Why did you agree to come? You've looked bored since the moment we walked inside."

"Bored?" He cocks an eyebrow at me, moving to his left to let an old couple walk past him. "This is my usual facial expression."

Rolling my eyes, I head to the last composition. It reminds me of Alice in Wonderland. Dark blues, vibrant reds, and bright yellows make up the scenery. Orchids, daisies, hibiscuses, and of course roses reflect the imaginative world to a tee, making my smile grow bigger. Here and there I notice teacups, pocket watches, and top hats between the flowers, leaving no doubt that I'm right about the theme of this installation.

"Is it...Alice in Wonderland?" Roman stops by my side.

"Looks like it," I reply, pulling out my phone to take more pictures. Once I'm done, I slip it back in my purse and turn my head to look at my companion. "So why did you agree to come?"

Roman stares at me with the ghost of a smile playing on his lips. With a shrug, he shifts a little, and his hand brushes mine. "You wanted to see it."

I blink several times, my mouth twisting as I bite the inside of my cheek. "So we're here just because I wanted to come?"

He nods. "I know we discussed it last night, so I was planning on it. But when I heard you lying to Angie and telling her you were spending today with your ex, I decided it would be nice to act like a boyfriend who would do anything for his girl—including coming here and pretending that I care. To make your lies more believable."

My jaw opens; his bluntness makes my eyebrows reach my hairline. "To make my lies more believable? Are you for real?"

"How could you?" Roman presses his palm to his chest. "I'm playing the role of the perfect boyfriend, and this is what I get in return? You're cruel."

I purposefully trail my eyes around his body, pausing on his groin. When I meet his gaze again, I put my hands on my hips. "Perfect boyfriends give perfect orgasms. Are you up for that part too?"

His mask slips. His intense gaze bores into mine, his jawline clenching. It happens so briefly, I start thinking it was just my imagination. Then his lips morph into a cunning smile, and when he lowers his head, I know nothing good is going to leave his mouth.

"There are certain sacrifices I'm not willing to make, Malyshka," he drawls, taking a step back. "I'll wait for you outside."

Watching him walk away from me, I mentally scold myself. *How many times does this man need to show that he's not interested? When will you finally get it?*

Dammit. Common sense is definitely something I'm lacking lately...especially when it comes to Roman.

I need a drink.

"DARE," I say, putting my glass down on the table. It's my sixth cocktail...I think.

"Again?" Roman asks, dipping his head. "Fifth in a row?"

Shrugging, I scan the crowded bar we're sitting in. It's been hours since we left the Botanical Garden and ended up here—first we went to play slots at the casino. The only thing I can say is, today isn't my lucky day. I'm afraid to think how much money I could've lost if it weren't for Roman, who dragged me away from the machines.

Being stubborn when things don't go my way is my curse.

"What's my dare, Roman?" I insist again.

He runs his fingers through his hair, twirling an empty glass with his other hand, the ice cubes clinking. A sudden burst of laughter from the bar makes him turn his head. I look too, noticing a bunch of girls clearly celebrating a bachelorette party.

"Okay, I've got a dare for you," Roman says, and our gazes collide. "Call your dad or mom and say you're engaged."

The pang in my chest is blinding. The memories of Travis's ring and my reaction are too fresh in my head. Add in my strained relationship with my parents, and this dare is a catastrophe for my not-so-sober self. I try to keep my face emotionless, but the alcohol makes it impossible. The trembling of my lips comes first, and the tightness of my throat follows, my emotions threatening to spill over any second. I sniff, wiping away a traitorous tear with the heel of my palm.

"Nevaeh?" His voice sounds softer and closer. "Malyshka?" Gently taking my chin between his thumb and index finger, Roman tilts my face up. Worry crosses his features, wrinkling his forehead, the corners of his mouth dropping. "*Chert*[2]. I'm so sorry. That dare was stupid. I don't know what I was thinking."

"It's okay." I sniff louder and press my palms to my cheeks to stop the tears from spilling.

Roman's eyes roam over my face, his jaw set hard as he studies me. His nostrils flare as he leans closer and sets his elbows on the table. "What happened between you and your ex-boyfriend? Did he not want to get married?"

He just flipped the damn switch. Uncontrollable sobs lodge in my throat, and tears stream down my face freely. Roman's eyes round, his pupils dilating. Without any hesitation, he scoots over to me and wraps me in his arms. I hide my face in his chest, letting myself cry. The trembling of my body gradually stops, and I lean away and give him a tiny smile.

"I'm so sorry," I hiccup.

A small smile lifts his lips. "Stop saying that. Everything is fine." Cautiously, Roman cups my cheek, wiping away the remnants of my tears with his thumb. "What happened?"

"I'll need another cocktail for that story." It's a little joke to lighten the mood, but it's also the truth. I don't think I can talk to him about me and Travis without alcohol.

"How about you take a second, and I'll order us more drinks?" he says, and I rear back, hiding my face in my palms. I probably look like a total mess. "Malyshka, there's nothing to be ashamed of."

I wave him over to the bar and rush to the restroom the second he stands up. No one is pretty when they're crying their eyes out, but I think I'm taking it to another level. Red and puffy eyes, black streaks

---

2. Чёрт. — Shit.

of mascara on my cheeks. As I lock the bathroom door, the only thought in my mind is that at least I was smart enough to bring makeup wipes with me.

I WONDER what time it is. Like, is it night already? Or just evening? I think the concept of time got totally lost the moment I downed my last cocktail. My tenth cocktail...or was it fifteenth? That Screaming Orgasm was definitely the eleventh, but then...Gah, why do I even care? I promised to never drink that much with someone I don't really know, and Roman is...someone I don't really know.

Stopping in my tracks, I press my palm to my forehead and stare in front of me. The city lights, all the hotels and casinos, mix into some monstrosity, making me nauseous. The music that flows freely from every street corner makes me want to close my ears. I'm so confused right now.

Where is Roman?

"Roman?" I yell, spinning around and immediately realizing it was a horrendous idea. Covering my mouth with my palm, I stand still and hope I won't be puking my guts out somewhere on the Vegas Strip.

"*Slava Bogu, ya tebya nashel*[3]." As slowly as possible, I turn around and stare at a white T-shirt. "Nevaeh?"

Looking up, I recognize Roman.

The source of all my problems.

"Where...where...?" I slur, and he frowns, bending down to me. "Where were you?" I try again.

"Me? I've been trying to find you for the last twenty minutes. Why did you leave the bar without me?"

I shrug, narrowing my eyes to see him better. "You didn't wanna participate in my exre...expermen—experiment."

3. Слава Богу я тебя нашёл. — Thank God I found you.

"Getting married to some random person *ne eksperiment*[4]." He shakes his head. "There are better ways to prove you're not afraid of marriage. Your ex just wasn't your person."

Looking him up and down, I purse my lips. "Screw you." I stalk past him, trying to read the names of the places I pass. *Oh, another bar! Might be a good place to find myself a husband or a wife for a day.*

When my hand is on the doorknob, Roman catches up to me. His big palm sneaks around my waist from behind and covers my belly. My back is pressed to his solid chest.

"Where are you going?" he whispers in my ear, his hot breath warming my already heated skin.

"To get drunk," I slur as I twirl around to face him. "And find myself someone who will help me. A guy or a girl...doesn't matter."

Roman tries to hold my gaze, but his eyes constantly slip to my mouth. At least, I think they do. Or do I just wish they would?

It would've been so much easier if he'd agreed.

"Do it for me," I mewl, pressing my finger to his chest and gliding it down to the waistband of his jeans. "Please."

His hand slides down my ass, squeezing it over my dress. My breath hitches, and I feel a throb between my thighs; my panties are a mess. It really, really, really would've been so much easier if he'd agreed —because the way I want him is insane.

"I don't even know if I can," Roman growls, pulling me closer to him. "I'm from Belarus, in case you forgot."

The silliest smile blossoms on my lips as I realize he's slowly giving in. "Wanna drink some more? And google?" I stand on my tiptoes and whisper as if it's the biggest secret in the world, "Google knows everything."

Throwing his head back, Roman bursts out laughing. When he finally calms down, he looks at me and says, "Fine. Let's go for another drink and see if I can participate in your experiment. If not— we're going back to the hotel."

Without thinking, I put my hand on the back of his neck and pull

4. Не эксперимент — Not experiment

him into me, only to press my lips to his cheek a moment later. "*Saps...Spasibo.*" I smile, then tilt my head. "Is it the same in Belarusian?"

"It's *dzyakuy*[5]," Roman states and sidesteps to let two couples walk into the bar. "Let's go, or there will be no tables for us."

Opening the door for me, Roman lets me go in first and then guides me to an empty table on our right. The place is crowded and loud, but I couldn't care less about that.

Because he's with me.

MY HAND IS SO small compared to his. It's almost comical how his palm engulfs mine. But the smile on my lips has nothing to do with that...the feeling of his warm and calloused skin against mine makes me giddy. If only he would stop for a second, that would be wonderful, because everything spins.

"Roman, where are we going?" I slur. "Can you please stop? Please?"

He halts in his tracks, and I stagger beside him. Looking down at his phone and then raising his face to the building on our left, Roman mutters something in Russian under his breath.

"Roman?" I try again, finally drawing his attention to me. His gaze is heated, his eyebrows etched together as he pulls his bottom lip between his teeth. "What are we doing here?"

"Just like you wanted, we're going to prove that you don't have a *fear of marriage*. Prove that no one cursed you," he exclaims. "*Tvoy byvshyi prosto ne tvoy chelovek. I ty eto znaesh*[6]."

I snort, rising onto my tiptoes and bringing my face to his. "I didn't understand a thing...but you sound so sexy when you talk in Russian, I really don't care."

---

5. Дзякуй — Thank you
6. Твой бывший просто не твой человек. И ты это знаешь. — Your ex is just not your person. And you know it.

Letting go of my palm, he slides his hand under my hair and cups the nape of my neck. His lips hover over mine, and everything around me stops as I anticipate his kiss. I close my eyes, my poor heart thrashing against my chest, beating violently and loudly.

Suddenly, something hot presses to my forehead, and my eyes snap open. The lingering feeling of his lips on my skin makes my breath hitch in my throat. The crooked smile on his face and the mischievous glint in his turquoise eyes cause my knees to give out, and I stumble into him.

He catches me with ease, wrapping his arm around my waist. Dropping his lips to my temple for another quick peck, he turns us both toward the entrance of some building and guides us inside.

"*Poydem*, Malyshka[7]. We have a lot of places to visit tonight."

7. Пойдём, Малышка. — Let's go, Baby girl.

Roman

TEN

please don't let me be married

Inhaling deeply, I nuzzle my nose in silky hair. The aroma of vanilla and probably jasmine slides under my skin, forcing a smile on my face. My hand slowly trails up the soft curve of a hip. The second my mind registers this information, my eyes open.

Chto za khernya[1]*?*

When my vision adjusts to the dimness of the room, I notice sunlight peeking through the closed curtains.

Looks like it's morning already.

Slowly propping myself up on my elbow, I look down at Nevaeh sleeping peacefully in my bed. Her body is up against mine, her ass pressed to my groin and my hand plastered to her hip. The good news? We're still dressed. The bad? I don't remember how we got back to our room.

I take my hand off her hip and move away as carefully as possible. First I set my feet on the ground, and then I push my body up until I'm standing. The moment I turn to my right, a pounding ache spreads across my skull. It's like a marching band snuck up into my head to perform. Gritting my teeth, I shut my eyes tight in hopes that this pain will disappear. No luck.

---

1. Что за херня? — What the hell?

Blyat'[2], this hangover is the worst I've had in years.

As slowly as possible, I turn on my heel and go to the bathroom. Turning on the light is inevitable, but nothing can prepare me for the wave of nausea that washes over me once the room fills with light. My headache intensifies, rages, my temples throbbing. Every muscle in my body aches; I don't have the energy to take off my clothes before I get myself into the shower. Turning on the cold water, I slump down onto my ass and just sit under the pouring water, hoping that the ache will go away.

There's nothing I want more than relief.

I OPEN the bathroom door and creep out. Not hearing any sounds except Nevaeh's quiet snoring, I grab my clothes. My towel falls to the ground as soon as I return to the bathroom, and I pull on a new black T-shirt and black sweatpants. Weaving my fingers through my hair, I blow out a breath, and then I brace myself with my hands on either side of the sink. The cold shower helped to dull my headache, and only a little fatigue reminds me of the state I woke up in. My skin is as pale as fucking chalk, and the dark circles under my eyes are starting to look like a permanent guest on my face.

Why did I do this? I lean forward and press my forehead to the mirror. Drowning my problems in alcohol isn't the answer. My past is my teacher—my father's experience should be my best reason to stay away from drinking. Even Maksim's death...What the hell was I thinking last night?

With a sharp inhale, I step away from the sink. The low grumble of my stomach echoes in the quiet. I know better than to try and eat anything after the night I had, but maybe I can have some coffee? Dark and strong with just one cube of sugar to refuel my body and stimulate dopamine.

Yeah, I can definitely try coffee. Hopefully, I won't regret it.

---

2. Блять (cuss word) — Fuck

Tiptoeing out of the bathroom, I look around for my phone and finally notice it on the floor by the door, along with the key card. *Zaebis*[3]. At least I didn't drop them in the hallway. I grab everything off of the floor, shove it in my pocket, and open the door as quietly as possible. Nevaeh is still asleep, and I don't want to wake her up. Fingers crossed, sleeping in will save her from the hangover I had.

I PLOP down into a chair in the darkest corner in the lobby. Taking the tiniest sip of black coffee, I swallow it and pause, checking to see how my stomach will react. When nothing happens, I allow myself to relax into the plush material of the chair and close my eyes. The bitterness of the coffee lingers on my tongue, and when I take a more generous sip, it slides down my throat, evoking a warmth that spreads all over my skin. The little cube of sugar melts, making it just a bit sweeter. It's exactly what I need right now.

Pulling my phone out of my pocket, I finally check the time, and my brows rise up. One p.m.? I expected it to be at least two hours earlier, but whatever, there's nothing I can do about it. I read Mom's texts about her Sunday plans to visit her sister, and a low chuckle escapes my lips when I read her text saying she hopes I had a fun night. If she only knew. She wouldn't be happy with me. Getting blackout drunk was something I did when I was a teenager. Doing it as a responsible adult? Definitely not something I'm proud of.

I send Mom a few texts, asking her to say hi to my Aunt Lena, and also letting her know that I'm flying back home tomorrow morning. She doesn't know I'm here with Nevaeh, and I'd prefer to keep it that way. The number of questions I can imagine her asking is huge, and knowing my mom, I won't hear the end of it. The less she knows about certain things, the less worried she will be. That's something I've learned throughout the years.

Pressing the cup to my lips, I open my web browser to look for a

3. Заебись (cuss word). — Awesome.

show Nevaeh and I might see tonight. Hot coffee fills my mouth, but the second I see the article that's open on my phone screen, it threatens to spill out. I forcibly swallow, cough, and set my cup on the small table in front of me, my eyes watering. My phone is like a ticking bomb in my hand, making my palms sweaty. There's no way I googled this.

Can I get married in Vegas if I have a work visa?

I click through the tabs I have open, and most of the articles make me want to drop my fucking phone as if it's poisonous.

How to get a marriage license

Marriage license bureau Vegas address

Nearest wedding chapel Vegas

Tossing my phone on the table, I hide my fingers in my hair and dig my nails into my scalp. This is a fucking joke. I remember playing Truth or Dare at the bar, and it was probably just part of that stupid game, right? It has to be, because...no, it's impossible. Why would we get married? It makes no sense.

I lick my lips, my eyes glossing over the lobby without seeing anything. My gaze zeroes in on my coffee cup, and I feel nauseous. Bile climbs up my throat, making it constrict painfully. I inhale and exhale, again and again—anything to calm down my breathing and not let the bile come out. Why am I panicking? I don't even know if my googling means anything.

A clipped memory pops into my head. Just an image, no sound. Nevaeh sits across from me at the bar, her hands on the table as she tells me something, her hair falling into her eyes. She tucks her wild locks behind her ears and meets my gaze. A shy smile graces her features when my palm covers hers.

What the hell were we talking about? *Blyat'*[4]. I don't remember shit about what we did at the bar or afterward.

There's only one way to know what happened. I need to go back to my room and talk to the only person who can help me shed light on

---

4. Блять (cuss word). — Fuck.

last night's events. Or at least try to remember some of the night if, like me, she has zero recollection.

Please don't let me be married.

I CAUTIOUSLY open the door of our room and step inside. The cup of coffee I brought for Nevaeh is in my hand. I walk further into the room and see her stir in bed. Freezing on the spot, I watch her in silence in case she's not ready to wake up.

Groaning softly, Nevaeh sits up in bed. She's pouting, and her eyebrows are pinched together. Her hair flows down her shoulders, looking adorably messy. Stretching, she raises her arms in the air and yawns loudly. Even in my distressed state, I can't hold back a smile. Something about this girl just resonates with me, drawing me to her and causing emotions I've never felt in my life.

"Hey," I say quietly, and she turns her head to me. Her eyes travel from my face down my body, assessing the clothes I'm wearing. "How do you feel?"

"Don't know yet," she grumbles and stands up from the bed, hesitant. Rotating her neck, she stretches again, and a small smile crosses her features. "Well, at least my head doesn't hurt."

"Lucky you. I woke up with a raging headache." I step closer and extend the cup to her. "Here, I brought you some coffee."

Nevaeh lowers her gaze to the cup and then looks back at me, her eyes roaming over my face. "How long have you been awake?"

"An hour."

Becoming pensive for a moment, she continues to stare at me, but I doubt she really sees me. One hand slides down her dress while the other flies to her hair, threading her fingers through and stumbling over some knots. The change in her face is sudden, her cheeks growing a deep shade of pink as her lips part.

Without a word, she hurries to her suitcase, rummages through it, and grabs something. The next thing I know, she's closing the bathroom door behind her.

I take a deep breath, put her coffee on the nightstand, and decide to clean up our room, starting with finally letting in the sunlight.

"YOU SURE YOU don't want to eat?" Nevaeh asks, arching an eyebrow at me from across the table. We've been sitting at the restaurant for twenty minutes, and the only thing I've managed to have was another cup of coffee.

"I'm fine," I drawl, drumming my fingers on the table. Trying to figure out the best way to ask her about last night is giving me a headache all over again.

"God, you're frustrating!" she says angrily, and my eyes snap to her in an instant. Putting her fork on her plate and pushing it away from her, she leans back in the chair, her gaze glued to me. "We haven't known each other long, but I can tell you have something on your mind. What's going on?"

I run my palm down my face. It's like my brain went into short circuit, because for a moment I forget how to speak English. Setting my elbows on the table, I lock my hands in front of me, and, after a long exhale, I finally go for it.

"What do you remember about last night?"

Nevaeh frowns, trailing her fingers over her braid. Her silence is deafening, and I'm slowly losing my shit. *Please, say something.*

"I remember that after the casino we went to the bar, and we were playing Truth or Dare." She trails off, twisting her lips into a little grimace. I wait, praying she remembers more than I do. "I think we went somewhere...but I don't remember where, exactly, or what we were doing. Why? I mean, we made it back to our room, right? Sure, I fell asleep in your bed, which I'm really sorry for. But I was fully dressed when I woke up, so I don't think anything happened between us. Is that what's bothering you?"

"No, of course not. I know nothing happened," I blurt, mentally slapping myself when I notice how her gaze darkens. *Fuck, this shit is messing with my head.* "I'm just worried we did something...extremely stupid."

"Such as?" She arches her eyebrow, crossing her arms over her chest.

Instead of answering, I pull my phone out of my pocket and show her the articles I discovered in my browser. Nevaeh keeps silent at first, but then she bursts out laughing.

"You think we got married?" I nod, and she only snorts louder. "Roman, that's absolutely ridiculous. I broke up with Travis because I realized he was going to propose to me. I'm not ready for marriage; I'm not sure I'll ever be ready. There's no way I would've agreed to get married, even if I was drunk as shit."

Something flashes in my head, a fleeting memory. But no matter how hard I try to catch it, it's gone. The only thing I'm sure about is that I heard her talking about not being ready for marriage.

Leaning back in my chair, I put an open palm to the top of my head, barely listening to Nevaeh's rambling. She goes on and on about her ex, about how she got sick when she saw the ring. Grabbing her purse, she takes her phone out and starts looking for something.

Suddenly, she shuts up; her face becomes pale. My heart drops to my feet, beating loudly.

"What is it?" I ask.

With trembling hands, she puts her phone on the table and pushes it toward me. I look down, gaping at a picture of a marriage license with our names. My mouth becomes dry, and I swallow with difficulty.

"I need a moment." The words rush out as I jump to my feet. Without waiting for Nevaeh to respond, I dash out of the restaurant, desperate for fresh air...because I truly feel like I'm suffocating.

Eto pizdets[5].

---

5. Это пиздец (cuss word). — It's a nightmare.

Nevaeh

ELEVEN

of all people

My gaze is glued to the black screen of my phone. My chest painfully constricts any time I take a breath. This is a joke. That's the only explanation I can find for the picture on my phone. It doesn't make any sense, dammit!

Pressing my palms to my face, I silently scream, cursing myself. Turns out my mother was right about me. I'm a stupid girl who never thinks about the consequences of her actions, making mistake after mistake and always getting into trouble. Apparently, getting too drunk and almost being taken advantage of by Sam wasn't enough. To top it off, I needed to go and get married to a guy who wants nothing to do with me.

Just fucking perfect.

I lower my palms from my face and scan the restaurant. It's packed with groups of friends and a few couples; the clattering of cutlery, the clinking of glasses, laughs and chatter fill the space. Biting my bottom lip, I rap my fingers on the table. The first thing I need to do is figure out my next steps. Or maybe *our* next steps, since I'm clearly not alone in this.

Glancing out the window, I realize that Roman is nowhere in sight. I lean forward, almost pressing my forehead to the glass, and still nothing. Where is the damned man?

The waitress nods when I wave my hand to get her attention and ask for the bill. My foot taps a nervous rhythm on the floor as I wait for her return. My aggravation grows, not allowing me to calm down. From a state of total disbelief, I'm heading straight to extremely annoyed.

Pulling my phone out of my purse, I launch Photos again. If I took a picture of the marriage license, shouldn't I have also taken a picture of the chapel? Of anything that would help me piece together what happened last night? I was so stunned to see the first picture, I didn't even check to see what else there is.

I zoom in on a selfie of Roman and me in front of a wall full of flowers. By how dilated my pupils are and how glossy my stare is, I'm surprised I was still standing, let alone saying "I do." There's text above the flowers, the name of the place. I quickly find the address in Google Maps. It's a twenty-minute walk from here, and it's exactly where I'm going to go next.

As I step outside the restaurant, my gaze wanders around in hopes of seeing Roman. No luck. *Well, screw him*. I'm going alone then. He's already been on my last nerve with his mood swings and how relieved he sounded when I told him nothing happened between us. I swear he makes me feel like the ugliest monster to ever walk the earth...and I'm so over it.

With my phone in hand, I stalk away from the restaurant, checking the directions as I go. So many people pass by, but I don't pay any attention to their chatter. The thoughts swirling in my head become worse and worse with each second. My desire to cry is huge, but I push it down as far as I can. I'll have time for that later. Now, I need to deal with this marriage thing.

"Nevaeh?"

Roman's voice startles me for a second, and I glance over my shoulder to see him running after me. Then I remember how he walked out of the restaurant and never came back. Straightening my shoulders, I speed up and ignore his voice calling my name again.

"Nevaeh!"

Fingers curl around my elbow, halting me in my tracks. Roman stops next to me, not looking out of breath or even remotely worried. His mask is on again, and that tiny glimpse of his real emotions I saw at the restaurant is long gone.

I pull my elbow out of his grip and keep walking, not sparing him a single glance. It doesn't seem to bother him. He just hides his hands in his pockets and follows me.

"Where are we going?" Roman asks after a few minutes of silence.

"*We* aren't going anywhere," I reply snidely. "*I'm* going to the chapel we went to last night. I want to fix this."

"Fix it?"

Stopping, I glare at him. "Yes, Roman, I want to fix it. I'm not sure if you know anything about this since you're not from here, but an annulment is possible. We were drunk as shit, with no clue what we were doing. The lack of consent because of intoxication will be easy to prove." When he doesn't say anything, just continues to stare at me with his deep turquoise eyes, I add, "There's no way I'm staying married to you, of all people."

"Me of all people? What does that mean?" He narrows his eyes. The tip of his tongue darts out of his mouth, and he moistens his bottom lip.

I shrug and take a step forward, bumping into someone's chest. The only reason I don't fall on my ass is because of Roman's hand on the small of my back, steadying me. Looking up, I find myself right in front of an obviously drunk guy, who's swaying from side to side.

"Bitch, why are you standing here? People are trying to walk," he slurs, lowering his head to look me in the eyes. "You better be—"

It happens so fast, I don't even notice. The guy yelps loudly as his back hits the wall, Roman holding him by his collar. "You think it's okay to talk to a woman like that?" he asks menacingly, his voice just above a hiss. "Say you're sorry."

The guy's eyes focus on Roman and then flash to me. "Sorry," he mumbles.

"Do you forgive him?" Roman asks me, and I nod, standing as

still as a statue. He takes a step back and lets go of the guy. "*Molodets*[1]. Have a nice day."

My mouth is agape, my fingers clutching my phone as I squeeze it harder. A hand on my lower back pushes me to start moving, and when I glance to my left, all I see is an absolutely unbothered Roman.

"That was unnecessary," I grit through my teeth, moving away from him until his hand falls off my back.

"He was rude to you."

"And? Didn't you see how drunk he was? That could've escalated into something really ugly. Sometimes it's better to just ignore situations like that."

Roman squints at me, meeting my gaze. "I know how to fight, and I hate when people are rude for no reason. Drunk or not, he should've watched his mouth."

I puff out my cheeks, not allowing the warmth his words caused to spread over my body. It shouldn't turn me on—not with him at least, because he's been pretty clear where he stands, and my attraction to him is starting to remind me of a teenage crush. Unreasonable and hopeless.

"Whatever." Sneaking a glance at my phone, I turn right at the next intersection. "It's not like I can force you to do anything."

"Except marry you," Roman says with a dry laugh, and I swat him in the stomach with an open palm. "Ouch!"

"I'm pretty sure this *brilliant* idea would've never crossed my mind," I state with conviction, keeping my chin up. It doesn't matter how tempting it is to look at him for his reaction; I need to stay focused.

"Of course, because you never would've married *me*, of all people."

Rolling my eyes, I mutter under my breath, "You're twisting my words."

"No, I'm quoting you," he counters, stepping closer to me to let two girls in pink wigs walk past him. His forearm brushes mine, and I

---

1. Молодец. — Well done.

tighten my grip around my phone. The assault of goosebumps scattering over my skin makes me feel hot, and I pout, annoyed with my body's reaction. "Which actually reminds me that before we were interrupted, I asked you what you meant. Why is marrying me such a terrible thing?"

Grumbling, I pivot to my right and stop under a well-groomed palm tree. I'm not risking someone bumping into me again and this caveman getting in trouble because he can't control himself. Being called a bitch by a total stranger is the least of my concerns right now. We're wasting time.

Roman walks over and stops in front of me, dipping his head so our eyes are level. "So?"

"Do you want to stay married?" I ask nonchalantly, trying to play it cool so he won't see how nervous I am.

"Of course not," he says, shaking his head.

"Then why are we talking about what I said? It doesn't matter." I pinch my brows together and purse my lips. "You don't like me; you've made that crystal clear. Why should we—"

"You think I don't like you?" Roman dips his head lower, until he's all I see.

Nervously, I thread my fingers through my hair and shrug. "That's definitely the impression you gave me." Swallowing my nerves, I go for it, even if I hate how needy I sound. "Am I wrong?"

"You're a beautiful girl, Nevaeh, but I'm not interested in you romantically," he states softly, taking a step back and putting more distance between us. "I'm not interested in anyone in that way right now, in all honesty. My life is total shit, and no one should be part of that."

Sometimes all anyone needs is a shoulder to lean on...and I think that's exactly what Roman is looking for. Even if he doesn't want to admit it, his actions prove it with total clarity. My presence here in Vegas is the best evidence. If only he'd let me in, even as a friend...it could change so much.

Mustering a smile, I lock my hands in front of me. "Then I really think we should get an annulment. It's only logical. No one needs to know—because I truly can't even imagine telling Angie that I got married in Vegas. Or, even worse, Travis finding out about it. It would break his heart."

Something flickers behind Roman's eyes, his gaze becoming heavier as he stares at me. "Sure. We don't want to break your ex's heart."

"That was mean," I say, poking my finger in his chest. "Travis is a good guy; he doesn't deserve that. I've already hurt him too much."

"Whatever you say." He turns to his left and bows his head. "Shall we?"

This time, I don't dwell on what to do. Holding my head high, I start walking again, checking the directions from time to time and not letting Roman's presence play with my head. As soon as we figure out how to fix the mess we created, we can go our separate ways. That's exactly what I'm going to focus on.

"Look who's here! Roman Pashkevich, the Thunders boy. I thought I might see you again."

A man in a white suit with short black hair blocks our way the second Roman and I step into the chapel. The fake smile on his face makes me feel uneasy, and I shift, instinctively sliding closer to Roman. "Did you two wake up and realize what you did?"

I frown, eyeing this man suspiciously. I have no idea who he is, but the way he keeps staring at Roman creeps me out. "Sorry—" I start.

"Realize what?" Roman shushes me, not only with his words, but with his arm wrapping around my waist. He pulls me into him, splaying his palm over my belly. "That my girlfriend and I got married last night?"

The man's smile drops, confusion coloring his features. My insides freeze, and my head is spinning. What is Roman playing at?

"I was sure you wouldn't remember a thing with how wasted you two were. The image is engraved in my brain, because I couldn't understand how you could be so reckless three weeks before preseason starts." The man narrows his eyes, a taunting scowl marring his face. His gaze coasts over Roman and me, his disturbing dark brown eyes sending shivers down my spine. "I'm glad I was wrong about you."

And yet, his posture and the look on his face says the opposite.

"Yeah, me too," Roman says, his hot breath fanning over my neck. "We're flying home tomorrow and just wanted to know when our marriage certificate would be ready."

"Usually in ten days."

"Awesome, then we'll need to plan another trip." *What?* "Thank you so much for your help..."

"Emmett," the man says, extending his hand to Roman. After the shortest handshake, the man puts his hands in his pockets. "I was your witness, actually, since you didn't have one."

"Thank you," I say on an exhale, deciding to play along. All my questions can wait till we leave this chapel.

"You're very welcome." Emmett's eyes roam over my face and then linger on Roman's palm on my belly. "Look after your husband, sweetie. Our Vegas team is a strong opponent; the Thunders will need to work hard if they want to win at least once."

I nod, feeling Roman's body tense. He's not the calmest person in the world. I've seen it on the ice, and I've witnessed it myself. Making a scene here? With a douche who is already after him because he plays for his rival team? It's so not worth it.

"Bye, Emmett. It was nice to meet you," I say sweetly, tugging on Roman's hand on my belly. Reluctantly, he steps back and lets me pull him out of the building.

Hand in hand, we stroll away from the chapel, heading back to our hotel. Silence grows heavier between us, and it slowly becomes hard for me to breathe. I have so many questions, but I don't even know where to start.

"I think the Bellagio fountains are starting." His quiet murmur draws my attention. Our eyes meet, and a little smile crosses his lips. "I wanted to go when it's dark, but...I think it might be good to stop and look now. What do you think?"

"Okay."

Making a little detour, we turn left, and sure enough, the fountains come into view. The music is loud, and I quickly recognize the BTS song as we stop at the railing. Though my brain refuses to focus on the astounding view or the catchy music. All I can think about is Roman's body blanketing me from behind as he puts his hands on the railing on either side of me.

"Ever since I watched *Ocean's Eleven*, I've wanted to come here. To see this place with my own eyes. Feel the atmosphere." Roman speaks softly behind me, and the back of my neck becomes warm. "Never in my life would I have imagined getting drunk and married along the way. It feels surreal."

"Do you...do you not want an annulment?" I ask the question that's been on the tip of my tongue since the moment we walked out of the chapel.

"It's not about what I want." He sighs, dejected. Slowly, I turn around and peer at Roman. "The man from the chapel is right, Nevaeh. Preseason starts in three weeks. The last thing I need is for it to start with news about me getting shitfaced in Vegas and getting married to someone I'm not even dating. No way Emmett will keep what he knows to himself if he somehow finds out we got an annulment. I can't risk it...hockey is all I have."

My heart drops, the ache in my chest growing stronger. He looks so miserable, and that tiny pause between his last words... *What are you hiding, Roman?* I swear, he's like the most well-kept secret ever. One I want to discover.

But more than anything, I want to help him.

Weirdly enough, being married to him doesn't trouble me the way Travis's ring troubled me. With my ex, I knew I didn't want to get married to someone who wasn't right for me. With Roman? It doesn't feel like that. I was agitated by his mood swings, with the realization that he didn't reciprocate my feelings. But other than that, it feels right. As if he's—

"I'll totally understand if you want an annulment. It's your life, and I don't want to ruin it for you."

Staring at Roman, I keep silent. The chatter, music, and noise of the busy streets fade into the background. A small smile forms on my lips, one I'm not even trying to hide. Without overthinking or dwelling on the consequences of my answer, I tell him, "You won't. We'll make it work. Don't worry."

Roman's gaze wanders over my face, falling on my lips and lingering there for a moment. I can barely breathe, and my heart beats so loudly. Something happens between us, like the air itself becomes charged. Hot. Powerful. Intoxicating. It reminds me of the anticipation of my first kiss, when all I could think about was how it would feel to be kissed by someone I like. He cups my face with his big palms. Our eyes are glued to each other, as if communicating on their own, in a language we don't understand. Lowering his head, he presses his lips to my forehead, his thumbs gently caressing my cheeks.

"Thank you, Nevaeh," he whispers hoarsely, leaning away and crooking a smile.

A few heartbeats later, he twirls me around gently, so I'm facing the fountains. His arm is wrapped around my shoulder from behind when he inches toward my ear, his lips grazing my earlobe.

"Let's forget about this whole marriage disaster for a few more minutes. We can discuss everything in our room, or at dinner."

"Dinner sounds nice," I say, reveling in the warmth of his embrace.

"Then dinner it is." He chuckles and kisses the top of my head. "Enjoy the show, Malyshka."

Roman

TWELVE

more like a wife

"Are you sure that's everything?" I ask, putting two boxes on the floor beside the bed. Straightening my back, I meet Nevaeh's gaze as she pulls jean shorts from her suitcase on the floor.

"You saw my car," she replies with a shrug. "That's all I have."

My gaze travels around the room, counting six boxes and her suitcase full of clothes. Rubbing the back of my neck, I feel weird. This reminds me of a fucking circus. Except the circus left town, and now only one clown remains...me. What's happening right now still doesn't make any sense. *Chert*[1].

"Do you need my help with anything?"

"No, I'm good." Removing more clothes from her suitcase, she presses the pile to her chest and stares at me with an arched eyebrow.

Right. "I'll be in my room then. Find me when you're ready for dinner." I take a step back, stopping in the doorway of my guest room. "But if you don't want to eat with me, that's fine."

A small grin lifts her lips as she walks to the walk-in closet. "I don't mind your company. Plus, we need to get used to each other. We're going to be stuck together for a while."

"Cool." *Cool?* How old am I?

---

1. Чёрт. — Shit.

Huffing, I turn around and head to my bedroom. I better use this time to unpack and take a shower. My body is too tense and rigid. I don't think I've been able to relax for even a second since Nevaeh and I came to an agreement about *our situation*. And considering that, on top of it, the resurfacing memories about my brother and my horrible sleep schedule are the definition of a shit show, I feel doomed.

I have no idea what I'm doing.

My phone buzzes, and I take it out of my pocket as I step into my bedroom. Smirking, I answer. "I'm alive, don't worry."

"You think that's the only reason I'm calling you?" Colton laughs.

"Of course not." I sit on the edge of my bed, tracing the pattern on my blanket with my fingers. "How are you, Colt?"

"Good. We'll be home on Wednesday. Ava is planning a second birthday party on Saturday, and we want you to come. Do you have plans?"

"No plans. I'll be there. Just tell me when, where, and what to get your wife."

"Books," he replies casually. "I'll send you the link to her wish list, and you can choose which one to get her."

"Got it," I say. My fingers freeze on the blanket. The thought crosses my mind, and before I think it through, I blurt, "Any chance I can bring someone with me?"

There's a pause on Colton's end, and I clearly hear his footsteps and then the sound of a door closing. "You got yourself a girl?"

More like a wife. "Yeah, but it's complicated."

"Doesn't sound complicated if you want her to meet your friends," Colton points out. "But absolutely, bring her with you. I can't wait to meet her."

You've already met her. The words threaten to spill out, but I force myself not to say anything. A phone call is not how I want to tell my friends about what happened in Vegas.

"How was your trip? Did you have fun?"

Plopping onto my back, I stare at the ceiling and start telling Colton about Vegas—without mentioning Nevaeh, of course. That's a secret I'm going to keep...for now.

I PUSH the door open and slowly walk out of the bathroom. A towel is wrapped tightly around my hips, and water drips from my hair down my face and my chest. I spent more time in the shower than I'd initially planned, but the feeling was just too good. The tension in my muscles disappeared, replaced by a warmth that spread over my skin and loosened up the knots in my chest. Hopefully, that feeling will help me sleep through the night.

"Oh my God, I'm so happy for you!" Nevaeh's voice halts me in my tracks. Shouldn't she be in her room? "This is the best news ever, Angie. I'm not only going to be an auntie, but also a maid of—"

The second her gaze meets mine, she stops talking. Open-mouthed, Nevaeh gapes at me from the couch in the living room. I run my fingers through my hair, shuffling uncomfortably. With a dip of my head, I give her a crooked smile and proceed to my room. Before I close the door, the sound of Nevaeh clearing her throat reaches my ears.

"Sorry, Angie. I just saw something, and...um...it's nothing. What matters is your news. Tell me everything."

Shaking my head at my stupidity, I go to the walk-in closet. *Prosto ofigenno*[2]. I made a total fool out of myself in front of Nevaeh. Just because she was busy in her room when I got into the shower doesn't mean she would stay there the whole time. I don't live alone anymore, and I need to remember that.

Thank God I still have three weeks before preseason starts. I can use it to get to know Nevaeh, and we can make some rules so this will be comfortable for both of us. Walking out in nothing but a towel is definitely not on the list.

I should know better.

---

2. Просто офигенно. — Just awesome.

"HERE." I set a plate of mashed potatoes and fried chicken wings in front of Nevaeh. "Hope you like it."

Sitting in the chair across from her, I pull the bowl of salad toward me and put some on my plate. It's nothing fancy, just tomatoes with cucumber and lettuce seasoned with olive oil and a little bit of salt. I would've added green onions like my mom always does, but the look on Nevaeh's face when she saw me taking them out of the fridge made me reconsider it. Maybe next time.

As I start eating, I can't help but sneak glances at my new roommate. My curiosity sizzles inside me, the desire to know what she thinks about my cooking growing with each passing second. What if she doesn't like it?

"Where did you learn to cook like this?" Nevaeh asks, adding some salad to her plate. "It's delicious."

I shrug, trying to act indifferent—and failing, because a smile blooms on my lips. "My mom worked a lot, and she didn't always have time to cook. So she taught me."

She grins at me, taking a glass of apple juice from the table. "I've said this before, but your mom really raised a good man. A guy who knows how to cook? A ten out of ten, immediately."

"She didn't want me to starve to death, that's all," I joke, ignoring the warmth that spreads across my skin, and the unfamiliar feeling that forms in the pit of my stomach. "Ordering in is easier some days, especially when I'm traveling for away games. But if I have time, I'll always choose homemade food."

"So this won't be the last time you cook for us?"

"If you want me to, of course," I say, finishing my dinner.

Nevaeh points her fork at me, a big smile playing on her lips. "I'm definitely going to take you up on that, Roman. I know how to cook, but it's not my favorite."

"Then I'll do the cooking."

"What if I do the cleaning?" she asks, and I cock an eyebrow at her, expecting an explanation. "I thought we could discuss what each of us are going to do since we will be living together."

"Cleaning is all yours." I nod, taking my mug from the table. "Just a little reminder of what I said in Vegas: you don't need to pay for rent or utilities."

She gives me an eye roll. "Yeah, yeah, yeah. I'm your *guest*. I remember." Looking around the room, she slowly moves her finger over the rim of her glass. "I actually forgot...Angie asked me to come over for a sleepover tomorrow night. I'm planning to go there right after work and be back Wednesday evening. Is that okay with you?"

"Of course it's okay. You don't need to ask permission to go somewhere. Just give me a heads-up so I know you're not going to be home," I say. "And while we're on the subject of plans...do you have any for Saturday? My friend Colton invited me to his wife's birthday party, and I kinda asked if I could bring you with me. Only if you're comfortable."

"Did you tell him it would be *me*?" Her eyes round as she gawks at me with parted lips.

"No. I just asked if I could bring someone; I didn't say who."

"God, you scared me." Nevaeh shakes her head. "I'm going to talk to Angie tomorrow. Just the thought of her finding out about my breakup with Travis—not to mention what happened in Vegas—from someone else makes me want to faint."

I watch her silently as she finishes her food. The meaning of her words registers in my brain, and I curse inwardly. If Angie knows, then Drake will know too. I better be ready to have a talk with him; he's going to have a lot of questions.

These thoughts go into a loop, and the phone call I overheard echoes in my mind. If I'm right, then that means..."Is she pregnant?" I ask.

Nevaeh hiccups and starts coughing, covering her mouth with her palm. When she finally calms down, she downs her juice, glaring at me from under her eyelashes.

"It's not nice to eavesdrop on people."

"You were in the living room. That's the only reason I overheard."

"Yeah, I was in the living room, and that's definitely the only reason I saw you half naked, gallivanting around your place."

"Gallivanting? I was on my way from the bathroom to the

bedroom," I deadpan, noticing her pouting. "I'm sorry for bringing it up, and I'm sorry for the towel thing. I promise to never do that again."

"Okay," she replies with a lift of her shoulder.

Standing up, Nevaeh goes to the sink and takes care of our dishes, motioning for me to stay put. I hold my mug between my palms, my eyes following her every move. When she stands on her tiptoes to put a glass away, her crop top rides up, and the bottom of her lacy black bra peeks out from under it. Diverting my attention, I focus on the calendar pinned to my fridge...quickly realizing that was the worst idea ever.

My gaze zeroes in on Friday, the date of my brother's death, and suddenly, that's all I'm thinking about.

IT'S HARD TO BREATHE. My lungs hurt so much, I can't even think straight. I'm suffocating—an invisible leash closes harder and harder around my neck. The tightness in my chest mixes with my heart, which is going absolutely insane. It feels like it's missing its beats.

My eyes are wide open, and darkness envelops me. For a second, I really think I'm losing my vision. And yet, after a moment of sheer panic, my gaze adjusts to the dimness of the room, and I finally recognize where I am.

It's my bedroom.

It was just a dream.

Hiding my face in my trembling hands, I lie still, wanting nothing more than for this fatigue to go away. I'm sweating, and my face is wet from all the tears I cried during my nightmare. I hope I didn't scream...

When my heartbeat finally calms down, the dizziness also goes away. Slowly, I sit up in bed, push the covers aside, and stand up, checking the time on the clock on my nightstand. Three a.m. A humorless laugh springs from my mouth as I creep to the kitchen. It's ridiculous to think that lately, the only time I slept through the night was when Nevaeh was next to me.

It's not like I can ask her to come sleep in my room...*Polnyi bred*[3].

Pouring myself a glass of cold water, I head to the living room and plop down on the couch. Without giving it much thought, I turn on the TV, check the volume so it's quiet, find *Peaky Blinders*, and start the third episode of the first season. I hope it helps like—

"You and your love for this show." A quiet voice behind my back sends shivers down my spine. I glance over my shoulder and see a very sleepy Nevaeh in a loose black T-shirt and tiny shorts. She rubs her eyes, yawning. "Why don't you ever watch it at a reasonable hour?"

"Did I wake you?" I ask as she rounds the couch and sits beside me.

She shrugs. "It doesn't matter. I woke up, and I'm here."

"Nevaeh—"

"Shut up, Roman, and let me watch."

Instead of moving away from her like I usually would, I sling my arm around her shoulder and pull her to my side. She lets me, cuddling close and hiding her legs under her butt. She smells like something really sweet, reminding me of the vanilla marshmallows I used to love so much when I was a kid. Her loose hair flows over her shoulders, tickling my skin whenever she fidgets in her seat. I shouldn't be so comfortable, but I am.

Only because she's here.

---

3. Полный бред. — Complete nonsense.

Nevaeh

THIRTEEN

a random girl

STIFLING A BIG YAWN, I STEP INTO THE ELEVATOR WITH A few colleagues from other departments. They chat about some new club they're going to on Friday, while I just lean against the wall, exhausted. Last night, I got about four hours of sleep, and I could barely open my eyes when my alarm went off this morning. Even if I hoped to feel more productive and awake after I got to work, it didn't happen. Five cups of strong black coffee did give me a boost of energy to make it through my workday. But once that boost was over, I crashed.

"Dammit." I cover my mouth with my palm, yawning loudly.

The elevator comes to a stop on the sixteenth floor, and the second the doors open, I regret not taking the stairs. Travis and one of his colleagues, Viraj, walk inside, talking about some code they're trying to fix. I don't move, silently praying my ex won't notice me.

I have no idea what I'll tell him if he asks where I'm living.

When the elevator stops at the underground parking garage, I linger, waiting for everyone else to walk out first. Purposely dragging my feet, I follow people out, keeping my eyes on Travis's broad shoulders in a white tee ahead of me. *Please don't let him see me.*

The moment he looks over his shoulder, our eyes meet. His

eyebrows hit his hairline as he gapes at me in surprise. I give him a small smile and zip to my car, the clicking sound of my heels echoing through the space. Just a few more steps and I—

"Nevaeh, wait!"

Fuck.

Halting in my tracks, I turn and see Travis hurrying in my direction. He stops a few feet away from me, a gentle smile playing on his lips. He's always been the kindest man, even if things are shitty. His gaze roams over my face and slides down my body; I shift awkwardly, crossing my legs at the ankles.

"Hey, Trav," I say hoarsely. My mouth is suddenly dry.

"Hey." He exhales, hiding his hands in his pockets. "How are you?"

"Good. You?"

"Okay, I guess. Getting used to a new routine has been weird." Travis shrugs. "Did you take some time off? I haven't seen you for a few days...since you..."

I look away, glancing at my car and then bringing my gaze back to Travis. "It's my first day back after a week off."

"Oh, that makes sense. I was worried you decided to quit because we work in the same building."

"That would be pretty extreme, even for me." I chuckle, and his smile becomes broader.

"Did you find an apartment? I've heard the market is tough right now."

"I got lucky. I found something affordable in a good neighborhood," I lie.

"Where is it?"

"It doesn't really matter. It's just temporary."

His face lights up, and I suddenly realize the twisted meaning of my words. At least, I realize how he could've mistaken them. I'm giving him false hope again. Exactly what I wanted to avoid.

"I'm really happy you found a place to stay. I'd have hated if you—"

"Trav, I'm so sorry, but I need to get going. Angie's back from France, and I promised her a sleepover."

"Oh, well, then...tell Angie and Drake I said hi."

"Of course." I take a step back, putting more distance between us. "Bye."

"See you around, Nev." His voice hitches, sounding hopeful, while all I want is to disappear. I certainly didn't think it through when I broke up with him and hoped time apart would help him move on. How is that possible if we work in the same building and, knowing Travis, he'll be trying to see me?

I deserve a master's degree for my excellence in the art of creating problems.

Even once I'm in my car, Travis still stands where I left him. His eyes are glued to me, and the longing in his gaze, one I know so well, makes me uncomfortable. He doesn't look like someone who's ready to forget about his ex. Not even a little bit. Fingers crossed, he'll never find out about my marriage to Roman. It would be a disaster if he did.

"I'M SO, so happy for you!" I hug Angie tight as the aroma of vanilla and cinnamon surrounds me.

Closing my eyes, I let my imagination run wild, trying to figure out what she's been baking. It's a game we've played since graduation. Any time I caught her experimenting in the kitchen, I would guess what new recipe she was trying her hand at. The woman can do no wrong in my opinion, and she always has the most delicious food I've ever tried. Nothing really compares to it...maybe Roman's cooking.

That was the dumbest thought ever, Nevaeh.

"Thank you, Nev," she whispers, moving away and settling comfortably on the couch.

My gaze falls on her little baby bump, perfectly pronounced under her red tee, and I reach out my hand and press my palm to it. An overwhelming wave of warmth washes over me, causing my throat to tighten. Happy tears form, and I wave a hand in front of my face to stop them from spilling.

"I feel like the most extra person ever," I mumble, sniffling.

"You're not extra." Angie laughs, covering my hand on her belly. "You're just my best friend."

"And you're my soon-to-be-married best friend, who's going to have the most beautiful babies in the world," I tease, making her laugh even harder.

"I'm not so sure about the 'soon' part."

"What do you mean?" I ask, picking up my glass of wine from the coffee table.

"The season starts soon, and we won't have time to plan everything before that. I think we'll wait till summer." She shrugs. "It's not a big deal, honestly. If I'm not meant to become Drake's wife before our baby is born, so be it."

Taking a sip of my drink, I look around the room. My thoughts are in shambles. The things I want to share with Angie hang on the tip of my tongue, but I have no idea how to start the conversation. I tap my fingers on my glass, the nervous rhythm echoing the rapid beat of my heart. It's Angie, for fuck's sake—why am I so afraid to open up to her? She's never judged me.

The sound of a door opening and closing brings me back to reality. I tense, listening to paws slapping the tile. A moment later, Cooper appears in the doorframe. The dog tilts his head, watching me, and it feels like he's smiling. His tail is wagging, and I can't help but grin in return.

"Hey, Coop," I say and shift my gaze to look at Drake. He stops beside Cooper, an open smile gracing his features. "Hey, Drake. Congrats on your engagement!"

"Hey, Nev. Thanks." He smiles at me, pushing his curls out of his eyes. "I'll take Coop to wash his paws, and then we'll be in the bedroom. It's girls' night. I don't want to be in the way."

I frown, pinching my eyebrows together. "You're not in the way."

"Okay, okay, I'm not. I just have a book I'm dying to finish, and it'll give you the opportunity to gossip without me around. Win-win situation, if you ask me."

Angie mouths *I love you* to him, and he winks at her. My insides constrict; it's becoming harder to breathe. Their love for each other makes me all dizzy and fuzzy, filling me with love and affection. I'm levitating; my skin ignites with the happiness they make me feel. If I ever have even the tiniest ounce of the love they have, I'll be over the moon.

"How's Trav?" Drake asks, peering at me. His deep brown eyes reflect kindness, and the smile curving his lips is gentle. And yet I feel like I'm center stage under a spotlight, getting ready to give a speech.

I forcibly swallow a gulp of wine and lower the glass to the table. Straightening my back, I glance between Angie and her fiancé, and then just say on an exhale, "We broke up."

"What?" Drake mutters, his eyebrows lifting.

But his surprise is nothing in comparison to the gloomy look on Angie's face. She sighs. "I knew something was wrong."

Drake pushes himself off of the doorframe and heads to the couch, sitting down beside Angie. They both stare at me, making me fidget in my seat. A huffing sound from the doorway diverts my attention to Cooper. He lies down on his belly and puts his head on his paws, as if waiting for me to explain myself. With a click of my tongue, I focus on Angie and Drake and tell them about how I walked out of Travis's apartment after I discovered the ring.

"Well, that sucks," Drake says, patting my knee sympathetically. "But if you weren't happy, then it's for the best."

"Thank you, Drake. But the hardest part is that Travis is dead set on us being end game." I shake my head. "I saw him today after work...and I'm afraid he'll think there's still a chance we'll get back together."

"What are you going to do about it?" Angie takes my hand in hers, her eyes wandering over my face. "What if time apart—"

"Time apart won't change anything for me. Besides, things are way more complicated now. It's better if I keep my distance from him. If Travis knows what happened—he'll hate me."

A loud huff from the doorway makes all three of us turn our heads to Cooper. "Dammit," Drake exclaims, jumping to his feet. "I forgot to wash his paws. Coop, I'm so sorry." Drake bolts out of the room, and the dog happily follows him.

Taking a deep breath, I meet Angie's gaze. She's watching me with a pensive expression on her face. Her dark green eyes remind me of lasers, because I feel like she sees right past my bullshit. She leans forward and grabs an apple slice from a plate. Her silence makes my skin itch. She knows there are things I'm not telling her.

"What happened after you left Travis?" Angie finally asks.

I close my eyes and rest my head on the back of the couch. Without looking at her, I start talking. I tell her about the hotel I stayed at, about Sam and his offer, about Roman suggesting I stay at his place while he goes to Vegas.

"Dammit, Nev." Angie lightly slaps my forearm. "Dammit!" I open my eyes and stare at her, biting my bottom lip. "I'm so happy Roman found you in the club, that he was there and that he noticed you. I don't even want to think about what could've happened if he hadn't been there."

"I know."

She moves closer and hauls me to her chest, hugging me so hard my breath hitches. I wrap my arms around her, clinging to her like my life depends on it. She's my sunlight, always guiding me through the darkness and helping me find my way whenever I feel lost. And it would be a lie to say I don't feel lost.

I need her.

"Did you find an apartment? Or are you still staying with Roman?" she whispers.

"With Roman," I answer, and Angie leans away. "I'll be staying with him for a while."

"Why?"

"Because I went to Vegas with him." I lower my voice, holding her gaze. "We got wasted, and now we're married."

Angie's eyes round into saucers. Perplexed, she gawks at me in silence. Clearing her throat, she blinks several times to get rid of her shock. "You're married to Roman?"

"You're what?" Drake's voice tears us apart. Angie and I turn to see him frozen in the doorway. "You're married to Roman? Pashkevich?"

I nod, my hands becoming clammy. "It's an absolutely insane story, and we still don't remember why we decided to do it. But yeah, Roman and I are married. And if Travis finds out...I can't even imagine how much it would hurt him. I want him to move on because we're not right for each other, not because he hates me."

"Why don't you get an annulment?" Drake comes closer and sits beside Angie again. "I'm sure neither you nor Roman want this marriage."

Shifting, I cross my arms over my chest. The ache in my heart becomes stronger. I like Roman—a lot, actually—and the fact that he doesn't like me is a bitter pill to swallow. I haven't figured out how to deal with it yet, and Drake's words slice right through me, hurting me even more.

With a lift of my shoulder, I explain what happened once we went to the chapel, that we agreed to stay married until the season is over. I tell them how Roman suggested I live at his apartment, and how he told me that whenever I feel like I need a way out, we can get a divorce.

"I don't feel obligated to stay, but...I want to help him. Plus, it works for me." I twirl the stem of my glass between my fingers. "We're like roommates."

"I kinda see his reasoning." Drake shakes his head, pulling Angie to his side. "To have all the attention on you when the season is just starting is a pain in the ass. Especially if that attention is about him getting wasted and marrying a random girl." His eyes zip to me, and he winces. "Sorry, Nev."

I laugh, but it comes out bitter. "You have nothing to be sorry about. He *did* marry a random girl. One he doesn't even like," I blurt and look away, noticing Cooper walking into the room. I beckon him with a hand, and he comes closer, wagging his tail. "Hey, Coop. You're such a good boy, aren't you?"

Angie and Drake continue to stare at me, but I don't pay them any attention. I just focus on petting the dog. I need time to collect myself. Anything to stop them from asking questions about Roman and our arrangement.

There's something I'll never mention to them. One more reason why I want to stay by his side and help him. Hearing him scream and cry in his sleep broke my heart.

Roman

FOURTEEN

ink on paper

Tuesday passed in a blur. I barely did anything, mostly just moped around my apartment and pretended to have a life. When I woke up after only four hours of sleep, I wasn't even surprised. I just went to the living room to watch *Peaky Blinders*, and once it was light enough, I hit the road. Mindlessly. Without any goal or destination. Just to feel something other than resentment and pain. Those two feelings live rent free in my head, intoxicating my mind and body. Guilt that I can't shake off no matter how much I try resides in my heart, making it impossible to enjoy my days.

But the adrenaline rush I feel any time I ride my Kawasaki doesn't fail me. Compared to my sleepless nights when my thoughts are consumed by heartache, the time I spend on my motorcycle is the only time I don't think about my brother's anniversary. The warm air around me feels like freedom, liberating me from my nightmares and depressing thoughts.

Maneuvering, staying in control of every move while also focusing on the road and everything around me. The thrill I feel when I lean into turns causes a smile to spread over my lips. The roar of the engine and the acknowledgment of the power underneath me makes my heart pound in my chest, and the blood in my veins heats up. The smells, the drop in temperature as I get close to the ocean, the sounds.

I feel alive when I'm on my motorcycle...and in the offseason, I need it like I need oxygen.

Hockey is my cure. It's the only thing that makes sense when nothing else matters. I owe everything to this sport, and I miss my time on the ice like crazy. A motorcycle ride is the closest I can get to feeling that high in the offseason. And that's exactly why I still have my Kawasaki, even if my mom has begged me to get rid of it.

Today's ride felt like a blessing. Getting home was like the cruelest joke; parking my motorcycle brought back all the thoughts I'd suppressed on the road. *Da chto za bred*[1]*!* Is there any fucking way to make it hurt less?

"Roman!"

I halt in my tracks, my hand on the doorknob. Looking over my shoulder, I notice Nevaeh sashaying toward me. Her white dress with lacy details on the skirt spotlights her golden skin and the narrow curve of her waist, pushing her round tits up. A high ponytail bounces left and right with each step she takes in her nude stilettos. It's the perfect view except for one tiny detail—the huge bouquet of pink roses in her hands.

"Hey." Nevaeh stops beside me, her eyes crinkling with a devilish glint. Her gaze roams over me, lingering on the helmet in my hand. "You went for a ride?"

I nod, eyeing the bouquet like it's the source of my misery. "What's this?"

Her smile fades immediately. She looks down at the roses and then back at me with her eyebrows knit together. She shrugs, pressing the roses closer to her chest. "They're from Travis."

"The ex," I exclaim as I jerk the doorknob and open the door wide. "I thought you said you wanted him to move on."

"I still do," she says quietly, following me inside the building. "I felt bad saying no to him."

"Giving him hope when you know the breakup was final is bad. Saying no to him giving you flowers shows mercy." I start climbing

---

1. Да что за бред! — What a bunch of nonsense!

steps, not sparing her a single glance. Her footsteps stop, and that's how I know she's taking the elevator instead. Good. Maybe walking to the sixth floor will help me ditch this insufferable agitation. It's like the cherry on top of my already fucked-up mood, and I don't need it.

Stair after stair, I ascend until I'm on my floor. Breathing heavily, I stomp to my apartment door. A drop of sweat slides down my cheek, and I wipe it away with my hand. *Na huî vsyo eto*[2]. Why am I getting so worked up? Because I want her? *Na huî.*[3] It's stupid. She's as off-limits as she was the day I met her.

But she's my wife.

The words flash in my head, and I grit my teeth because it means shit. Our marriage is a joke. Stupid ink on paper. No one in their right mind would want to be married to me...I'm a disease. Destructive and poisonous. I demolish everything around me until there's nothing left but the scorched earth. It makes no difference that we're legally tied together now. When it's time to sign the divorce papers, she'll hate my guts so much, she'll be relieved to be free from me.

It will be so much better if I keep my distance. She doesn't need my mood swings or my jealousy. Especially if I have no right to feel jealous.

I'm just her roommate, after all.

A LITTLE GREEN and yellow cardboard box appears in front of my face. Looking up from my laptop, I find Nevaeh with a Sour Patch Kids pack in her hand.

"What is this?" I close my laptop and put it on the coffee table.

"My favorite. Chewy candy. Really sour chewy candy," she replies, holding my gaze.

"And you're giving it to me...why?"

"Peace offering." She tosses the box onto my lap and plops down

2. На хуй (cuss word) всё это. — To hell with all that.
3. На хуй (cuss word). — To hell with that.

beside me on the couch. "I hate conflict. It makes my skin itch and turns my brain to jelly. I don't want to feel like that at home...sorry, at your place."

I chuckle, taking the box and opening it. "It's your home too," I tell her.

"Your silent treatment doesn't really scream hospitality. And it definitely doesn't make me feel at home," Nevaeh says, watching as I take a candy and put it in my mouth. I extend the box to her; she takes it and quickly tosses a candy into her mouth too. "Thanks."

"I should be the one thanking you. And also apologizing to you." I turn to her, letting my eyes wander over her makeup-free face. This girl is absolutely perfect, with and without makeup. With her hair down or in a ponytail or braids. I'm mesmerized by her, falling deeper and deeper in the river of denial. Soon, convincing myself to stay the hell away from her is going to be very difficult. "I'm sorry for what I said. It's not my place to comment on you and Travis, and I have no right to talk to you like that."

Nevaeh tosses a few candies into her open palm, and returns the box to me. "You were rude, but you were also right. I shouldn't have taken the flowers from Travis. It gives him hope, and that's not what I want."

"Did he come to your office?"

"Yes. No. Not exactly." She dumps the candies into her mouth and chews, while I continue to stare at her. With an exasperated sigh, she turns to me. "We work in the same building. Yesterday, when I was on my way to Angie's, I saw him in the elevator."

They work in the same building? My skin becomes hot, and before I say anything stupid, I stuff my face with six candies. The sour taste fills my mouth, and I close my eyes for a second, wincing. It's better this way though. It's better to chew on these, than say things no one wants to hear.

"I was sure he'd try to see me, so I planned to leave later than usual so I could avoid him," Nevaeh mumbles, sitting cross-legged. "But he showed up at my office with the bouquet when I was about to leave.

He even insisted on walking me to my car, telling me over and over how much he and Happy miss me."

"Happy?"

"His dog. The cutest French bulldog," she explains, a gentle smile blooming on her lips. "Trav knows I love Happy."

"So he's using him to guilt-trip you into getting back together."

"No, it's more about making me miss him, so I'd want to see him."

"And you'd need to go to his place for that." I nod in understanding, putting the empty box on the table. "He's good. Using anything he can to get you back."

Nevaeh meets my gaze, watching me in the quiet of the room. She's nothing like I thought she'd be. At first glance, she's a very easy-going, always ready to have fun kind of girl. But it's so surface level that I'm not really surprised I misjudged her. There's so much more to her, something deeper and unexpectedly darker, and I'm finding it really hard to puzzle her out.

"We'll never get back together. I don't love him, and a loveless relationship isn't what I want for myself. I witnessed enough of that in my childhood. There's no way I'd go back to it as an adult."

"'Never' is a really strong word, Nevaeh. I'm sure you never thought you'd get married on a whim in Vegas, and yet—here we are. Life is full of surprises. No one knows what's going to happen to them for certain. We can only guess, and unfortunately, we're not always right."

"I get what you're saying, but you're wrong."

Silence stretches as we sit on the couch, looking each other in the eyes. A tingling feeling in my fingertips urges me to move closer, to feel her skin against mine, to blanket myself with her warmth and tenderness. But I do nothing...because I don't want complications.

"Do you want to eat?" she suddenly asks, making me blink. "Maybe we can order some takeout and watch something together."

I stand up from the couch and hover over her. "I cooked yesterday. Macaroni with chicken cutlets. There are also tomatoes and cucumbers in the fridge if you want a salad." I extend my hand to her, and she takes it, letting me pull her to her feet. "Though if you want something else, we just need to—"

"Macaroni and chicken sounds good. Especially if you have some grated cheese to add." A smile blossoms on her lips as she looks up at me, curling her fingers around mine. The wave of heat scattering over my skin throws me off, like a sudden cold wind on a scorching day. My heartbeat picks up, and I swallow my nerves and force a smile onto my face.

"I'll trade you some grated cheese for you telling me about your day yesterday. How did it go when you told Angie the truth?" We saunter into the kitchen holding hands.

"Are you asking if Drake knows? He does. And why hasn't he called you? Because I told him not to. But I'm one hundred percent sure he'll bring it up at Ava's birthday party on Saturday." Nevaeh grins, making me snort. "That should give you a bit of time to think about what you'll want to say. So be prepared because I'm sure your friends are going to have a lot of questions."

I let go of her hand and nudge her toward the table. She goes to climb onto the chair, and my eyes zero in on her perky ass in cotton shorts. My mind immediately offers a memory from Vegas, when I woke up with my hand on her hip. And things start to feel a bit too tight in my pants.

Ocharovatel'no[4]. Exactly what I don't need when I'm trying to feed her a delicious meal.

Skirting the table, I move to the fridge. "I'm already terrified."

Her mellow laughter spreads across the room, filling every little space with her presence. I chuckle to myself, choosing to focus on right now instead of torturing myself with all the what-ifs of my future.

I have all night for that.

---

4. Очаровательно. — Lovely.

Nevaeh

FIFTEEN

jealousy doesn't look good on you

My eyes fly open, and I sit up in bed. The room is dark; the closed curtains don't let in even a sliver of light from the street. I rub my palms over my face, feeling my heart galloping in my chest. Waking up so abruptly isn't super healthy, and my head feels heavy. With a loud yawn, I toss my blanket aside and jump to my feet.

I head straight to Roman's bedroom. I tiptoe, but the tapping sound of my bare feet echoes through the quiet space. When I stop in front of his door, my palms are sweating. I feel nervous. Pressing my ear to the door, I listen carefully, silently hoping it was just a dream. What if it's all in my head? What if he just can't sleep and—

A sob bolts through the air and goes right through me. My heart squeezes painfully in my chest, and I clutch my tee, finding it hard to breathe. It's one of those situations I would've been happy to be wrong about, and now I feel miserable because I'm right. Roman has nightmares, and they keep him awake.

I hesitate, debating in my head what to do...or if I should do anything at all. The evening we spent together having dinner and watching *Peaky Blinders* brought some peace between us, something both of us really needed after he snapped at me because of the flowers. And yet, we're not friends. We don't talk about any personal stuff, just share funny stories and discuss the show we're watching. He's reserved and distant, and I have no clue how he'd react if I went into his room.

I better go back—

"*Maks, net, pozhaluysta*[1]." His quiet voice mixed with his sobs makes me freeze on the spot, silencing all the thoughts in my head. "*Pozhaluysta...*[2]"

It would be so much easier if I could understand what he was saying. Him and his Russian, dammit.

Taking a deep breath, I put my hand on the doorknob and push the door open. As slowly as possible. I bite the inside of my cheek, padding into his room and stopping beside his bed. The moonlight coming from the living room through the open door casts a shadow on his face, traces of his tears making me dig my nails into my skin. Roman is lying on his right side, his knees pulled to his chest. His hands are hidden under his pillow. His blanket is on the floor, and the sheets look like a total mess.

My heart beats so violently, like a drum reverberating through my body, I'm surprised he doesn't wake up. Uncertainty engulfs me as I bend down and lift his blanket. There's nothing I want more than to help him deal with the night terrors that torture him. It's like a mantra that resonates in my brain, getting louder and louder with every breath I take.

Fuck it.

Rounding his bed, I climb in from the other side. With calculated slowness, I move closer, cover him with his blanket, and search his face in the dimness of his room. His jaw is clenched hard, and I hear him grind his teeth in his sleep. His usually plump lips are pursed into a thin line, his eyebrows etched together. Even in his sleep I can see the tension in his rigid muscles. Whatever he's dreaming about is still haunting him.

I lick my lips and gradually lower myself onto my right side, moving forward inch by inch until I'm under his blanket too. Closing

1. Макс, нет, пожалуйста. — Maks, please, don't.
2. Пожалуйста... — Please...

my eyes, I snake my hand around his waist from behind until my chest is up against his broad back. My breath gets stuck in my throat from the contact. I wait for him to wake up, to kick me out of his bed, but it doesn't happen.

It feels like time has stopped. Little by little, his body relaxes into my embrace. Roman's no longer muttering or crying, his breathing is deep and rhythmic. Mustering the courage, I slide my hand higher and feel his heartbeat. Steady and slow. His nightmare seems to be gone, and he's sound asleep, quietly snoring beside me. My eyes grow heavier, and I'm trying my hardest to stay awake.

The logical part of my brain knows I should leave. The illogical part of me, the one that rules my heart, wants me to stay. He smells woodsy and powdery. Notes of sandalwood and, strangely, coconut are easily recognizable. His scent injects under my skin, warming my insides and making my head dizzy. It feels good to be so close to him, and it makes it really hard to resist my attraction to him. And yet, I should resist. Using his vulnerable state to enjoy his closeness is wrong.

I force myself up and out of his bed. Back in my room, I hide under my blanket and close my eyes. His scent crept under my skin, igniting a tingling sensation all over my body and flooding my veins with his presence. The beating of his heart still echoes in my ears, even when sleep overtakes me.

He's all I feel...and all I dream about. And I'm not sure that's a good thing.

"ROMAN SAID he already bought a gift for Ava," I tell Angie, holding my phone between my ear and my shoulder while rummaging through my purse. Where are my damn car keys? "Do you think I should buy something for her myself?"

"Well, you're going as a couple, so one gift is enough. But if you want to make a good impression on Roman's friends, I'd suggest you bring something small. Maybe flowers? Or chocolates?"

"I was thinking maybe flowers for Ava and something sweet for their kids, but I'm not sure." I finally fish my keys from my purse.

Angie chuckles softly. "You're taking the role of Roman's wife very seriously. His friends will know what happened in Vegas and why you decided to stay together. You don't need to pretend."

"I'm not pretending," I blurt, instantly biting my bottom lip. *Me and my big mouth.* "What I mean is, his friends have already met me, but we've never really talked to each other. If I'm going to be stuck with him till summer, there's a pretty good chance I'll see them all more often. I don't want it to be awkward."

"It won't be awkward. I promise," Angie murmurs. The distant chatter on her end of the phone becomes louder. "How are things between you and Roman?"

I unlock my car and slide inside, keeping silent. When the door is closed, I relax into my seat and let my shoulders sag. "We're good. He's a pretty awesome roommate."

"Just roommate?"

"Just roommate." I confirm. "Nothing has happened between us. Not in Vegas, not in his apartment. He's made it clear that he's not interested in me, just like I'm not looking for a relationship. I need to find myself before I get back on the market."

"I thought you—"

"Jesus!" I blurt, cutting Angie off. Travis is hurrying toward my car with a huge bouquet of red roses. I grip the steering wheel. I should've left the second I got in my car.

"Nev, is everything okay?"

"Travis is here. Again," I grit through my teeth, faking a smile as he waves at me. "I gotta go, Angie. See you on Saturday."

"See you, Nev. Bye."

My ex stops near my car, and I roll down my window. "Hey, Trav."

"These are for you." He extends the flowers to me, smiling from ear to ear. "I went to your office, but Gigi said you'd already left, so I rushed to the parking garage. I'm so glad you're still here."

"Travis, you shouldn't have—"

"Please, Nev, take them." He bends down and puts the bouquet on my lap. "I know how much you love roses. It's just a little something to make you smile."

"Thank you."

"Do you have plans this weekend?" *And here we go.* "I thought maybe we could do something together. Maybe take Happy for a walk in the park."

"I don't think that's a good idea, Trav. We broke up."

Travis winces, sticking out his bottom lip. "I remember." With a rejected sigh, he hangs his head low. "We were friends before, Nev. Why can't we start by going back to the basics? Spend time together, just walking the dog and talking like in the good old days. Happy misses you."

Tapping my fingers on the steering wheel, I exhale loudly. "Maybe on Sunday?"

"Deal." His face lights up with a smile. "Send me your new address, and I'll come pick you up."

"No need. Let's just meet at Discovery Park at two p.m., if that's okay with you?"

"Sure." Travis leans over and kisses me on the cheek. "See you, Nev. Looking forward to Sunday."

"Bye." I wave curtly, watching him step away from my car. My hands feel clammy, and nausea forms in the pit of my stomach. I broke up with him so he could move on and forget about me, and meeting him for a walk in the park definitely won't help.

I fucked up.

I PARK MY CAR, slowly get out, and take the bouquet from the passenger seat. The smell of roses is strong and pleasant, and I hide my nose in velvety petals. I hope Roman won't notice me bringing home flowers again. I don't want him lecturing me. Especially since I know he's right. I just...couldn't bring myself to throw the bouquet away. It's too beautiful.

I stroll toward the apartment building, holding the roses close to my chest. Despite not getting enough sleep, I feel good. I managed to get ahead of the new article I'm working on, and I also made good progress on next month's issue after I got approval from my boss, Kai. It was a good day, and I hope my evening will be good too.

Loud laughter comes from my left, and with my peripheral vision, I notice two people heading to the front door too. I turn my head, and my eyes zero in on Roman with a tall brunette. Her painted red lips wear a seductive grin, and she bats her eyelashes at him, touching his arm affectionately. He's carrying two grocery bags and nodding his head at whatever she's telling him. I lower my gaze down her body, scowling at the deep neckline of her dress. I swear her breasts look like they are ready to pop out. A gnawing feeling forms in my chest, and my jaw ticks. My fingers start to tremble, and I tighten my grip on the bouquet, hissing the second a sharp thorn pricks my skin.

Jealousy doesn't look good on you, Nevaeh.

"Shut up," I scold myself.

I'm too far away for them to hear me, but Roman looks up, and our gazes lock. Just for a moment, because he drops his eyes to the bouquet in my hands. He smirks, shaking his head in disbelief.

Screw him. He has no right to judge me.

Rushing forward, I line up with Roman and his girl and enter the building without a glance in their direction. The door closes behind me with a bang, and I take the stairs, leaping two at a time. The clicking sound of my heels thunders through the space, but I don't pay any attention to the ruckus. All I want is to be alone, as far from this infuriating man as humanly possible.

Not even his delicious food will lure me out of my room.

I SIT UP IN BED, looking around frenziedly. The darkness in my bedroom doesn't leave any doubt that it's still night. Reaching over to my nightstand, I snatch my phone and check the time. Three a.m. Almost the same time I woke up last night.

My chest rises and falls with my erratic breathing. I know why I'm awake. Just like yesterday, his sobs disturbed my sleep, twisting my gut into a tight knot. I lift my blanket, ready to climb out of bed, but memories of Roman with the brunette, and him coming home thirty minutes after I did flood my mind, keeping me rooted in place.

Plopping down on my back, I cover my head with another pillow to muffle the sounds. The room becomes silent, and I close my eyes.

His nightmares aren't my problem.

Roman

SIXTEEN

please...stay

"Didn't expect you to be up."

I slowly turn my head and see Nevaeh. She stands beside the couch, dressed in light blue jeans and a white tee with the word "Censored" across the chest. Her hair swims down her shoulders, and two little braids frame her face, with makeup only slightly accentuating her eyes.

"Roman?" she says, lowering her head to meet my gaze.

I cover my mouth with my palm to hide my yawn. My mind is all foggy, my thoughts swirling and scrambling at breakneck pace, not letting me focus on anything. My headache is pounding in my temples.

"What time is it?" I ask hoarsely.

"Eight thirty." Nevaeh frowns, studying me with her eyes narrowed. Grabbing my chin between her fingers, she tilts my face toward her. "What time did you wake up?"

I jerk my head, and her fingers drop away. "Around three." When I stand up from the couch, she takes a step back. "Why are you talking to me?"

She scoffs, folding her arms over her chest. "Why do you need to make everything so difficult?"

"You spent yesterday evening ignoring me. Giving me the silent treatment. And suddenly I'm the one who makes things difficult?"

Lifting her chin up, she glares at me. Her teeth are sunk in her bottom lip, her face darkening. She opens her mouth and then closes it again, tapping her foot on the floor. Her agitation rises, and a darker shade of pink tinges her cheeks.

"How long did you sleep?" Nevaeh asks.

"Three hours." I shrug, skirting her and ambling to the kitchen. With each step I take, my head starts to hurt more. It feels like someone is drilling holes in my fucking skull.

"Roman, you need to sleep."

"I'm good," I tell her, pouring some water into a glass. "Go to work. I don't need a babysitter."

"You need sleep," Nevaeh bites out, stomping over to me. "You look like a fucking ghost. Go to bed."

"*Da ne mogu ya*[1]," I yell, halting her in her tracks. My hands are trembling, and I put the glass on the kitchen counter to avoid spilling water. "I can't. Not today."

Nevaeh stands still, her arms dangling at her sides. Her eyebrows knit together as she anxiously searches my face. Licking her lips, she rocks from her heels to her toes, shooting daggers at me with her eyes. Her chest rises and falls so quickly, I have no doubt she's pissed. With a quiet snort, she takes a step back.

"As you wish."

Turning on her heel, Nevaeh storms to her bedroom and then to the front door. Her little black purse is hanging over her shoulder when she walks out of my apartment. The door slams closed, and I quietly slide down to the floor, leaning my back against the cupboard. I'm drained. So empty that I don't even have it in me to fight my demons. Not today, at least.

Today, I let them win.

---

1. Да не могу я — I can't

"Roma, how are you?" my mom asks, her worried voice coming through speakerphone. I lie on the floor in my living room and stare at the ceiling.

"*Nikak*[2]." I sigh, inhaling sharply. "I don't feel anything."

Mom sniffs. "Roma…You shouldn't be alone tonight. *Pozhaluysta, mal'chik moy dorogoy*[3]."

"Everything is going to be alright. I promise, Mom," I whisper. Any time I try to lift my head, it feels like it's going to explode. This headache blurs my vision, and every fucking sound heightens my pain. Even my mom's voice brings me discomfort.

"Maks would be so mad at you if he—"

"He's dead, Mom. For seven fucking years today. Don't tell me what my twin brother would do if he could see me now," I say and cover my eyes with my palm. "Did you go see him?"

"I did," Mom confirms quietly. "I visited your dad too…your grandma said hi."

"That man is dead to me, Mom. I don't care about him or his side of the family."

"Roma," Mom warns, but I just shrug it off. I couldn't care less what she has to say. This is the one thing she and I will never agree on.

"Let's talk tomorrow, Mom. Bye." I grab my phone, hang up, and toss it back on the floor. I need to get up, go to my room, and stay there. I need to avoid Nevaeh while I'm in such a fucked-up state. And yet, I lie still, my eyelids growing heavier.

Just a few more minutes, and I'll go to my room. Just a few more…

"Roman?" Her fingers brush my hair from my forehead and delicately slide down my cheek. "Is everything okay?"

I open my eyes and meet Nevaeh's gaze. She sits on the floor, hovering over me. Her eyebrows are pulled together, and she's staring

2. Никак. — Not great.
3. Пожалуйста, мальчик мой дорогой. — Please, my sweet boy.

at me from under her eyelashes. The corners of her mouth drop, collapsing into a deep frown.

"What time is it?" I whisper huskily. My throat is so tight, it's hard to swallow.

"It's eight p.m.," she replies, caressing my cheek with the pads of her fingers. "I had a meeting with my boss, and it ran late, so I just got home from work. And found you here."

"Sorry if I scared you." I sit up and glance at her. "And sorry for being rude to you this morning. You didn't deserve it."

Nevaeh smiles weakly. "Thank you." Her gaze coasts over my face, and she tilts her head to the side. "How long have you been on the floor?"

"Since this morning."

Scrunching her nose, Nevaeh takes a deep breath. "Did you eat?" I shake my head no.

Exhaling loudly, she gets up from the floor and extends her hand to me. I take it, barely registering what's happening around me. With a hard pull, Nevaeh helps me to my feet. I stagger; standing still is a struggle. Even the floor feels unsteady.

Nevaeh tugs on my hand and makes me follow her. My headache is still there, but it's not pounding so hard anymore. Or I'm just too weak, and the pain stopped mattering. Opening the door to my bedroom, she pulls me inside and stops beside my bed.

"Get in," she orders in a stern voice. "Now."

I do as she says, climbing into my bed and hiding under the blanket.

"Now sleep!" Nevaeh exclaims, taking a step back, ready to flee my room.

When her hand is on the doorknob, I prop myself on my elbow and call out to her. "Nevaeh?"

"What?"

"Can you please stay with me?"

She looks over her shoulder, and the crease between her eyebrows deepens. Then her shoulders drop, and she nods. "I'll just change my clothes and be back, okay?"

"Thank you," I whisper and close my eyes.

This exhaustion is bliss. It silences my mind, banning every little thought from making an appearance. No memories abusing my brain, no emotions causing me distress. It's all gone…and I'm just an empty shell, hoping to make it through the night.

Saying good-bye wasn't the hardest part. It was way tougher to learn how to live without someone who was always there for me. Who shared the same dreams and knew all my secrets. Losing my brother left a hole in my chest, and no matter how I try to fill the void…it's never enough.

The slight shift of the mattress underneath me makes me aware of her presence. She moves closer while still keeping her distance. I open my eyes and turn onto my left side, facing Nevaeh. The tiniest smile crosses my lips when I notice she brought the blanket from her room and is now hidden under it.

"Why can't you sleep?" she asks, watching me intently. My eyes roam over her beautiful face. She's not wearing makeup, and her hair is pulled into a little bun on top of her head. Just looking at her brings me comfort. It calms me down and heals my invisible wounds, stopping them from bleeding.

A little cure for my tormented soul.

"I have nightmares."

Nevaeh hides one hand under her pillow, scrutinizing me. I wait, expecting more questions. And kinda hoping she's not going to pry. Lying to her doesn't feel right, but telling her about Maksim feels even worse.

Sighing, she reaches over and pushes my hair off my forehead. "When I was little, I had nightmares too," she says softly, holding my gaze. "Not because I dreamed about anything bad. But because my parents thought it was a good idea to fight at night. They'd wake me up with their screams, sometimes broken dishes or furniture. Anytime it happened, I'd get so scared I was afraid to move. I'd hide under my blanket for hours, trembling and crying silently. Even after my nanny told them I could hear them, they never stopped. Being at each other's throats was much more important than their daughter."

A sad smile spreads over her lips as she looks at something over my head. "My nanny wanted to help me, so she gave me a plush toy and promised it would protect me. It was Sulley from *Monsters, Inc.*—my all-time favorite movie." Her breath hitches, and she closes her eyes, lying still. "After that, whenever my parents would get into another argument, I'd hide in my walk-in closet with Sulley pressed to my chest. I wanted to be like Boo, the little girl from the movie. To live in a monster world instead of living with my parents."

The sadness drowns me like an avalanche, breaking through my bones and going straight to my heart. I clench my jaw and grit my teeth as another emotion overwhelms me. Anger. So much anger at her parents, dammit.

"Eventually they stopped arguing. After that they just silently hated and barely tolerated each other. There wasn't any love. Just business, because their marriage was beneficial for both of them." She lowers her voice. "My parents got divorced when I was sixteen. My dad caught my mom cheating on him—with his best friend, in their bed. It was something he couldn't forgive...and I couldn't either. I haven't talked to my mom since." A bitter laugh rises from her throat. "Not that I talk to my dad much these days, but at least he didn't disown me."

"Your mom disowned you?" I ask in utter disbelief. Looks like we have more in common than I thought.

"Yeah, and she made sure I knew it. Just to spite me, she threw away everything she'd ever bought me, but even that wasn't enough. One day, I came home from school and found Sulley cut into pieces."

"But..."

"She didn't buy it for me," Nevaeh mutters, understanding my confusion. "She just knew how much I cherished it; she remembered that I'd clutch it to my chest any time I felt sad or scared. I didn't bat an eye when she took back the jewelry she bought for me, but Sulley? I cried my eyes out, and couldn't sleep for days."

"I'm so sorry, Malyshka."

"It's fine. Life has proven to me over and over that not all monsters hide in closets or under beds. Sometimes they give birth to you...and sometimes you date them."

Falling quiet, she gapes at me, her mouth forming a little O. I hesitate, expecting her to say something else but also knowing she won't. She let something slip she wasn't going to share, and the horrified look on her face says it all.

With a sigh, I move closer and haul her to my chest. Resting my chin on the top of her head, I feel her relax into my embrace, and she cuddles into me.

"Seven years ago, my brother died," I whisper, bile clogging my throat. "Most of the time, I can deal with the pain of his death...but not on the anniversary. All the things I'll never tell him. All the stories he'll never share with me. All the dreams and fucking good-byes that will never be said. There isn't a day that goes by without me thinking about him, about how it would've been different if it were me—"

"Roman!" Nevaeh gasps, trying to lift her head, but I just hold her tighter. "Don't ever say anything like that again! You hear me?"

"Okay..." I say, yawning loudly. "It's not like I can help myself. Seven years is a long time."

She wiggles, and I loosen my hold on her, letting her sit up beside me. Staring down at me, Nevaeh bites her bottom lip. Her eyes travel around my face. I yawn again, hiding it behind my palm.

"You need to sleep, Roman," she murmurs. "Your friends will be worried if they see you like this."

"Will you stay?" I ask quietly.

"Roman, I..."

"Please...stay," I beg her, my voice barely audible. "At least until I fall asleep."

Her lips tremble, then form the cutest little smile. She bends down and kisses my forehead, awakening a very strange and unfamiliar feeling inside my abdomen.

"Night, Roman." Nevaeh lies down and rests her head on my chest. "Sleep tight."

"Sleep tight," I whisper back, wrapping an arm around her shoulder. The sensation I feel only intensifies, spreading warmth all over my body.

Are these butterflies in my stomach? Because of her?

Nevaeh

SEVENTEEN

i'm not his sister

Did I really think I wasn't going to fall asleep in his bed? Because if I did, the title of the most delusional person ever would be mine. Or maybe I'm just a hopeless romantic who can't stay away from the man I like. He's a little bit broken, a little bit distant... but nevertheless, he's the man I can't stop thinking about.

The man who might hold all the pieces of his shattered heart, who might fit mine perfectly. I can't even imagine feeling anything like that for someone who doesn't reciprocate it. To have someone constantly on my mind while I don't think I've ever crossed his.

"Malyshka, it's time to wake up," he whispers, gently caressing my cheek. I smile, opening my eyes and peering at him. "You weren't asleep?"

"I wasn't ready to start the day," I correct him.

Roman chuckles, and I turn onto my right side to have a better look at him. His skin is brighter, and the usual dark circles under his eyes aren't so prominent. A long and restful night's sleep was good for him, allowing him to recharge his batteries. And I hope it improved his mood. For his own sake. The way he's torturing himself because of his past isn't healthy. Even if I understand him better now.

"Thanks for staying with me. I needed that."

"What are friends for?" I give him a small smile. "I'm glad I could help. If you want to talk, just know that I'm here for you."

Roman sighs, closing his eyes. "I also wanted to thank you for not pushing me to talk about Maks...about my brother."

"I figured it might be too much on a day like yesterday. Talking opens old wounds and doesn't always bring healing..." I mutter, and his eyes focus on me. "I'd love to know more about your brother though. Whenever you feel like talking about him and what happened. But no pressure. Only when you're ready."

The corners of his mouth lift, lighting up his face. He's so fucking handsome always, but this smile...it makes my heart melt. As if I'm made of snow, and now I'm just a little puddle. "I think he would've liked you. You carry this sunshiny energy inside you. Maks was like that too. An optimist who always saw the good in people."

"And you're a pessimist?" I ask the first thing that comes to mind, because the somersaults the butterflies in my stomach are doing are making me all giddy.

"I prefer the term 'realist.'"

I roll my eyes, sit up in bed, and lean against the headboard. "A realist with pessimistic tendencies. And a sunshine girl who gives great advice to others but never follows it. We make a great team."

"We do." Roman sits up. Our shoulders are brushing, making my body hum in the most pleasant way possible. My skin buzzes, the heat in my lower abdomen sending goosebumps all over my body. The way I want to beg him to touch me is concerning. It's like I can't even trust myself when he's around.

I turn my head to look at him. Roman squints at me, meeting my gaze and smiling gently. Something feels different. It's like we know something that no one else in the world knows. Like we're the only two people who know some secret...one neither of us wants to share with others.

And I suspect that the secret is us. Here in his room, waking up in the same bed after opening up to each other a little bit. It's the best secret I've ever kept.

"Ready for Ava's birthday?" he asks in a low voice. "To meet my friends?"

"Well, I've met them all already, but I can't say I'm not nervous."

"Nervous? Why?"

"It's silly," I mumble, remembering Angie's words. His friends will know our marriage is just a ruse. I don't need to try and make them like me. It's all temporary. Like seasons changing year after year. Once summer comes, we will be divorced.

Roman shifts a little, and I move away from him. Cradling my cheek with his warm palm, he looks me in the eyes. "Tell me."

"I'm just worried they aren't going to like me. They know me as Angie's best friend, but now...now I'll be there with you. And—"

"If someone has a problem with you, then they have a problem with me. That's how it works, Malyshka. And my friends already like you, so being with me won't change their perception. Quite the opposite, actually."

"Even if you tell them the truth?"

He looks at me, and the intensity of his deep turquoise eyes sets my body ablaze. His gaze drops to my lips, and I swear my heart stops for a second.

"Even if I tell them the truth," he rasps, his eyes darkening. "The truth about the most precious and beautiful girl I've ever met, who agreed to be my wife...even if I'm the last person she would've ever wanted to be married to."

Then he presses his lips to my forehead. Swiftly. Barely. But it's still earth-shattering. It's like tomorrow won't come if he's not with me, and I don't know what to do to stop myself from feeling this way. I plaster a smile, trying to hide my infatuation with him, and how him calling me beautiful makes me feel. *Kiss me, please* hangs on the tip of my tongue, but I swallow it down along with my nerves.

"You don't need to flatter me, Roman. All those sweet words won't work on me anyway." I jump to my feet. "Breakfast on you?"

He frowns slightly, confusion creeping onto his face. I pull my blanket off his bed and press it to my chest, as if creating an invisible wall between us. Blinking, Roman clears his throat and nods. "Yes. What do you feel like?"

Rounding his bed, I head to the door, throwing "Surprise me" over my shoulder. The best way to deal with our marriage is to turn it into a joke. To make fun of the situation we've gotten ourselves into.

Fingers crossed it will actually work.

"AND WHY DID you need to buy this? I remember telling you I got something for Ava," Roman says as we walk down the stairs. He's carrying a bouquet of three books mixed with beautiful violet tulips. When I first saw it today, my jaw was on the floor, but all he did was shrug when he noticed my shocked state. He not only bought the books his friend's wife wanted, but he also found a girl who makes book bouquets and ordered one for Ava. It was thoughtful and cute, and it made me like him even more.

"I want your friends to like me, remember?" I beam at him, pressing a big red M&Ms toy to my chest. It's filled to the brim with different candies, with a reading journal on top. The second I saw it yesterday at the bookstore I went to at lunch, I knew it would be perfect for Ava. "It's just a little something. I didn't want to show up empty-handed."

"Did Angie tell you about the Thompsons' love for M&Ms?"

I nod. "She mentioned that Ava and Colt are obsessed, so when I saw this and the girl at the shop told me it could be filled with anything I wanted, I knew I should get it."

"That's very—"

"Roman!" A woman's voice pierces the air, halting us in our tracks on the third floor. Turning my head, I notice the tall brunette I saw him with the other day. She strolls down the steps, her eyes laser-focused on Roman. The salacious smile on her face makes me clench my teeth.

"Claire, hey." He nods in greeting as she lines up with us, forcing me to move a few steps down to give her room. "How are you?"

"Good," she murmurs. "Going out for lunch with my best friend. You?"

Annoyance brews inside my chest, spilling into my veins and ruining my mood. I walk down the stairs with them following me. Shivers run down my spine, and I flex my shoulders in discomfort. This feeling is physically unpleasant. I hate it.

"Nevaeh and I are going to my friend's place. It's his wife's birthday."

"Oh..." The brunette falls silent, and even without turning around, I know she finally decided I'm worth paying attention to. It feels like her gaze is digging holes in my back. "Any plans for tonight?"

"Not really."

"Maybe you want to make a quick detour on your way home? I still have the wine you gave me." The sweetness in her voice makes me want to gag. "We can watch something together. Eat, drink, and... talk."

The pause irks me. I'm tempted to turn around and throw the M&Ms in her face. Why does she think it's okay to hit on a guy when he's with another woman?

"Sorry, Claire. I'm pretty sure we'll be home late."

"I don't care if it's late," she chirps. "I'm sure your sister won't mind if you come over."

I swivel my head around so fast, my neck hurts. "I'm not his sister." I snarl, glowering at her.

Her eyebrows knit together, her eyes dancing between Roman and me. "No?"

"No," I mimic her, scowling.

Turning back around, I hurry down the stairs and storm out of the building. Assuming I'm his sister? This is ridiculous.

Roman and this Claire girl linger behind, and when they finally join me outside, she doesn't look happy. She shoots me a glare full of anger, and then she walks away. Swaying her hips like she's a fucking runway model.

"Ready to go?" Roman sidles up to me, scrutinizing me with an amused look on his face. His trembling lips give away his attempts to hide his smile.

Rolling my eyes, I head toward his BMW. I refuse to give him the satisfaction of teasing me. Once we're in the car, he drives away from the building. He keeps silent, just like me, and it dawns on me that maybe the silent treatment is a bad idea. I want to know what he told her.

"Who's the girl?" I ask, half turning to get a better look at him.

"My neighbor," he replies with a snort. "I thought that was obvious."

"Gah, you're impossible! Who is she to you?"

Roman glances at me, quickly looking me up and down with an open smile playing on his lips. "My neighbor. Claire is my neighbor."

"That's all?"

"Yes."

My knee starts bouncing, as I bite the inside of my cheek. "She's weird. Why the hell did she think I was your sister?"

"She thought you were my older sister."

"What?" My eyebrows go up; his words surprise me to the core. First, she assumed I'm his sister. Second, that I'm older?! I should've thrown the candies at her stupid face. It would've been so satisfying.

"She said she thought we were siblings because we're both blonds. I have no idea why she thought you were older though."

"Because she's an idiot. That's why."

"But you are older," he taunts me, boiling my blood so much I'm ready to scream.

"Did you really need to remind me?" I drawl. I still haven't decided how I feel about him being one year younger than me.

"Kinda. You're cute when you're pissed off."

I rap my fingers on my knee, feigning indifference even though the butterflies in my stomach are performing some sort of ritual, fluttering their wings harder and harder.

"She was obviously hitting on you, so I find it hard to believe there's nothing between you two." I decide to go all in and be extremely blunt. I need to know.

"Claire flirts with me all the time. I don't even pay attention to it." He shrugs, his eyes glued to the road. "She's invited me to her place several times, but I always say no."

"Of course you do," I deadpan snidely. "That's why you got home thirty minutes after me when I saw you with her last time."

Roman stops at a traffic light and turns to look at me. "I helped her bring her groceries up to her apartment, and we chatted a little. What did you think I was doing with her?"

"Hooking up. Thirty minutes is enough time for a quickie."

A burst of laughter pours from his lips. I wait, watching him with my eyes narrowed. When he finally calms down, the light is green. Before he starts driving again, Roman leans over and whispers, "I don't do quickies." He pulls back and focuses on the road. "Thirty minutes is like a pregame for me. I find it nice, but nothing special. If I fuck—I fuck long, Malyshka."

Really looking forward to it.

The words flash in my head, and I feel the lightest throb between my legs. I'm hopeless.

Roman

EIGHTEEN

it won't happen again

Sauntering to the Thompsons' house with Nevaeh beside me, I can't stop myself from smiling. It's been like that since the moment we got into my car. Or even earlier, when she snapped at my neighbor. Her jealousy was so evident, and it's hard not to be fascinated by it.

Even if fascinated is the last thing I should be feeling.

Her ex and his daily bouquets, her story about her parents...all reasons for me to keep my distance. The girl's been through way too much already, and she'll be better off without my shit. Yet convincing myself to stay away from her is becoming almost impossible. Almost... because not letting my selfishness win is one of the toughest challenges I've faced lately.

At this point, I'm genuinely curious how long I'll be able to resist her; I hope at least until the season starts. Away games will be a blessing.

"You think everyone's already here?" Nevaeh asks as we get to the door.

"Maybe." I knock, glancing at her. The skirt of her summer dress flutters in the wind, drawing my attention to her toned legs. Her sun-kissed skin glows in the sunlight, making my mouth water. I move my gaze up her chest. Her dress contours her round tits and hugs her body like a second skin. She is such a beautiful girl, dammit. I can't take my eyes off her.

The door opens, and Colton's voice follows. "Punctuality is definitely not your strong suit."

I shoot my gaze in his direction, instantly noticing his widened eyes as he glances between me and Nevaeh.

"Hey, Colt," I say in greeting. "Didn't think two minutes meant being late. You remember Nevaeh?"

He nods, stepping aside to let us in. "Of course. Come on in."

Nevaeh walks in first, and I follow her every step into the house until I hear Colton close the door. Wheeling around, I stop beside her and meet my friend's gaze. He watches me with his eyes slightly narrowed, a smile still playing on his lips. Thompson has one of the best poker faces, but now it's failing him.

"The girls are in the kitchen," he says to Nevaeh. "My wife, being her stubborn self, refused my help, even at her own birthday party. If you want—"

The sound of approaching steps makes me turn my head, and I see Angie hurrying over from the living room. She's in a floral dress that's wrapped tightly around her waist, showing off her growing baby bump.

"I thought I heard the door opening." Angie lines up with us and wraps her arm around Nevaeh's waist. "Hey, Nev." She gives me the quickest once-over, and my smile dies. "Roman."

Okay, she's definitely not my number one fan right now.

"Hey, Angie." I hide my hands in my pockets, suddenly feeling out of place.

"I need to steal Nev from you," Angie says sweetly, making Nevaeh follow her.

Colton and I stay silent, watching them disappear into the living room. A nudge to my shoulder forces me to stop staring and look at my friend.

"Let's go out back," he suggests, and we head down the hallway. "Everyone's already here, except Xander, Bella and their kids. They're running late."

A burst of laughter rings through the air as Colton and I make our way out to the terrace. I notice Drake sitting at the table and talking to Clay Rodgers, our team's new goalie. Clay and I have met before, not only during games, when he was playing for the Chicago Hawks, but also at different parties at Thompson's house. He's Colton's best friend, and a really nice guy, always funny and kind. Not to mention incredibly talented. I really believe that with him on our team, we'll have a chance to finally win the Stanley Cup.

"Hey, Drake, Clay," I say, lowering myself into a chair across from them. Colton sits beside me.

"Finally, the man I've been waiting for!" Drake puts his elbows on the table and leans forward.

"Wait..." Colton drawls, looking between Drake and me. "Did you know about him and Nevaeh?"

"Of course! Nevaeh came over after Angie and I got back from France, and she told us about her and Roman's drunken wedding in Vegas."

"Their *what*?" Colton turns to me, his jaw is ready to hit the floor. It's probably the first time I've seen him so stunned. It's kind of hilarious. "What the hell happened? I thought you were going to Vegas alone."

I rub my palms over my face as Colton and Drake continue to gawk at me. Clay, on the other hand, looks highly entertained by the whole situation. *Da blin*[1]. Can't they just let it go? With a sigh, I sit straighter and start explaining what happened and why Nevaeh and I agreed to stay married till the season ends. When I finally finish, there is only silence. And it troubles me.

"Damn, man," Colton mutters, locking his hands behind his head. "I understand why, but it's still fucked up. That's, like, almost a year away...What if you meet someone you really like? What if Nevaeh meets someone?"

"There are so many things that could go wrong." I shake my head. "But I...I can't imagine my life without hockey. I can't risk my career."

---

1. Да блин. — Dammit.

"Don't you think that's selfish?" Drake asks. "All I hear is you, you, you. Have you even thought about Nevaeh?"

Frowning, I hold his gaze. "I didn't force her. She had a choice, and this was her decision too. If she'd said she wanted an annulment, we would've gotten one in the blink of an eye."

"Nevaeh likes you," he states angrily.

"You're wrong. She's still not over her ex."

Drake rears back, his lips in a tight line. "Travis?" I nod, crossing my arms over my chest. "Nevaeh doesn't love him. She never did. Why would she want to get back together with him?"

"She said it's complicated," I mumble under my breath, my confidence waving me good-bye. What if I misunderstood everything when it comes to her ex?

"It is," he confirms. "Nevaeh wants him to move on, but Travis still thinks she's the one for him. He's not ready to give up on her. That's why it's complicated, Roman."

The table falls silent. I chew the inside of my cheek, my eyes moving around the terrace. What if I don't need to hold back with Nevaeh? If she doesn't care about her ex, there's no reason for me to stay away. We can get to know each other and see if things between us could work out. What if we try being together for real? The attraction is there; I can't deny it. And it's growing stronger with each day I get to spend with her.

I've never liked anyone more than I like her. That's gotta be something, right?

"I WONDER why no one ever said anything about you liking her. It's so pathetically obvious."

The hand holding my glass freezes in midair. *Kakogo hrena*[2]*?* I turn my head and gape at Clay. He takes a sip of his drink, not bothered by my reaction in the slightest.

2. Какого хрена? — What the hell?

It's been hours since Nevaeh and I got to Thompson's house. Food, drinks, and conversations passed the time. Kids' laughter and jokes about the upcoming season didn't leave any room for boredom or sadness. It's probably the first time in a while that I've felt so good being around people. My friends and their families. And Nevaeh. Even if I have barely seen her because she's keeping Angie company, hanging out with Ava, Bella, and Layla. We don't need to pretend that we're a couple...but I find it extremely difficult not to watch her. Did Clay notice?

"What do you mean?" I ask, playing dumb.

Rodgers downs his drink and focuses on me. "Benson's been roasting you about Nevaeh liking you, insinuating that it's all one-sided. But if he looked close enough, he would know you like her too."

"That's—"

"Cut the bullshit, Roman. Not with me, okay?" he says, furrowing his brows. "I know better than anyone here what it's like to hide your feelings from everyone."

I follow his line of sight and see Layla. Drake's sister holds her daughter, Maya, while talking to Ava. The blonde hair cascading down her shoulders makes a great contrast to her daughter's brown hair, her head resting on her mom's shoulder. The memories of locker room chatter I overheard come to mind, and I look back at Clay.

"You still like Layla," I say quietly, and he shoots me a glare.

"Way to change the subject," he comments snidely, but he doesn't tell me I'm wrong. "All I want to say is...don't let your chances go to waste. Stop spending time doubting all the will-she-won't-she bullshit. If you like her, do something about it."

I keep silent, the thoughts swirling in my head becoming louder and more prominent with each passing second. A smile blossoms on my lips when my eyes land on Nevaeh running after Michael, Ava and Colton's son. They are both laughing when she catches him and tackles him to the ground with him landing on top of her, his back pressed to her chest. She tickles him, the sound of his laughter reverberating across the lawn. Isla, Xander and Bella's daughter, runs up to them, giggling and saying something about Michael losing a bet.

A heavy hand lands on my shoulder, and I shift my gaze back to Clay. He hovers over me, his yellow-green eyes radiating warmth.

"Think about what I said, Roman." He squeezes my shoulder one last time and walks away, joining Colton at the grill.

I didn't expect to get relationship advice from Clay Rodgers. But the more I think about it, sitting at the table on the Thompsons' terrace, the more I realize I should be grateful.

This push is exactly what I needed.

"Did you have a good time?" I ask Nevaeh as we walk into my apartment.

Without turning on the lights, we both stop to take off our shoes and then proceed to the living room. She's been blabbering about Ava and Bella's oldest kids, Layla's daughter, and Angie's pregnancy nonstop, but she never really said anything about whether she liked being at the party or not.

"Absolutely." She pauses near the couch and spins around to look at me. "You?"

"Yeah." I take a step closer to her, my skin igniting instantly, the heat crawling up my neck. The prickling sensation in my fingertips makes my heartbeat throb. A sudden nervousness combines with my growing desire to cross the line. To go all in and see where things take us.

Nevaeh's lips part, and she slowly takes her purse off her shoulder and puts it on the coffee table. "It's only ten o'clock. Do you want to watch something?"

"We can," I coo, taking another step closer. "We can do whatever you want..."

"Whatever I want?"

Cradling her cheeks with my palms, I lower my head to meet her eyes, searching her face, trying to figure out what sort of mood she's in. My heart beats so violently in my chest, even my breath hitches.

"What do you want, Malyshka? Tell me."

"I want..." she whispers as I slide my palms down her throat, feeling her heartbeat pulse under the pads of my fingers. "I want you to kiss me."

I smirk, smugness boosting my ego. With a tilt of my head, I close the distance between us and press my lips to hers. Briefly. Kissing her and moving away as soon as our lips barely touch. Once, then twice. Then over and over, drawing little whimpers out of her mouth any time I lean away. The kisses are just little pecks, but they set my body on fire.

Her fingers clutch my T-shirt; she's clinging to me and pressing her tits against my chest. She stands on her tiptoes, her hand snaking around my neck to pull me closer.

Sliding my hands down her waist, I hoist her up and put her on the arm of the couch, settling between her legs. Covering her mouth with mine, I kiss her harder, forcing my tongue between her lips. The moan she makes is like the sweetest melody to my ears. I'd kiss her a thousand times just to hear her moan...for me.

"Nevaeh..." I whisper between our kisses. Her tongue swirling around mine makes me lose my goddamn mind. My skin is burning hot, and my hard-on strains against my jeans. It's not my first time kissing a girl, but it's definitely my favorite. Every emotion is heightened. Every breath I take is more powerful than the last. Every beat of my heart feels more intense...all because of her. "*Ty svodish menya s uma*[3]. Tell me to stop, Malyshka, please."

"Never," she says breathlessly, clinging to me harder.

We kiss and kiss, our hands roaming around each other's bodies. Until the ringing of her phone startles us. I stop, breathing heavily, and press my forehead to hers.

"I hate my phone," she says, and I chuckle. "It should've been on silent."

---

3. Ты сводишь меня с ума. — You're driving me crazy.

"That would've been nice. Do you need to answer it?"

"Depends on who's calling. Can you...?" Nevaeh points at her purse, and I take her phone out of it as it stops ringing. I don't intend to look, but a missed call from her ex catches my attention anyway.

My chest hurts; it's like I can't take a deep breath. I extend her phone to her as a message pops up on her screen. From him.

TRAV:

> What if after the park we go to that Chinese restaurant you wanted to try? I can make a reservation

"What park is he talking about?" I ask, gritting my teeth. My mood is so all over the place that I don't even try to hide what I saw.

Nevaeh grabs her phone and reads the text. Biting her bottom lip, she peers up at me. Her hand is wrapped tightly around her phone, and yet I notice the trembling in her fingers.

"I...I promised to meet with Travis tomorrow. At Discovery Park. To take Happy for a walk."

"So it's a date," I state, taking a step back from her.

"No. We're going as friends. Travis knows I miss Happy, and—"

"And that's why he wants to make a reservation at a restaurant you wanted to go to? Because you're *friends*?"

What a fucking joke!

"It's not a date. And I'm not going to the restaurant with him. That's what he wants, but it's not—"

"You should say yes," I deadpan. My every word is venomous.

"Roman..." she whispers, pressing her palm to her chest.

"This was a mistake." I put even more distance between us. "It won't happen again."

Turning on my heel, I stalk to my room and slam the door behind me. It doesn't matter what Drake said about her and her ex. Words mean shit; only actions matter. She's keeping him close. Giving him hope. She still hasn't drawn a line.

My brother was in our friend Kirill's car that night because our teammate told Maks he saw his girlfriend with her ex, a football player she used to fuck when she was bored. Maksim died because Kirill was drunk and lost control of the car, I know that. But the reason my twin even got into that car was because he wanted to confront a girl. A girl who couldn't decide who she wanted to be with, who was leading guys on and playing games.

I'm done with all that nonsense.

Nevaeh

NINETEEN

to be mine

I WONDER HOW ONE WOULD FEEL IF THEY WERE GIVEN what they wanted, and then it was taken away a moment later. Disappointed? Angry? Or just sad? All three emotions are raging inside me, and I'm teetering on the edge of a breakdown.

The desire to do something with this energy is destructive. I barely slept, and I left the apartment first thing in the morning. Seeing Roman might trigger something I'm trying to suppress with all my willpower. We're stuck with each other for almost a year, and if things go to shit…I have no idea how we're going to make it through.

Angie's words surge inside my head, and I purse my lips tighter. Of course I can divorce him. It's the easiest and most obvious decision ever. But something in me resists the very idea of it. I've never ignored my best friend's advice before…until yesterday. As soon as she started telling me that I don't owe Roman anything, that I can leave him whenever I want, I zoned out. And, oddly, I didn't feel bad about it.

Probably because I don't think I'm doing anything wrong. It feels all kinds of right…especially when he kissed me.

What happened between us last night didn't surprise me. I saw him watching me at Ava's party. The longing in his eyes was evident, coating my skin like the warmest blanket on the coldest day. All his little smiles, his arm casually draped over my chair, his fingers drawing circles on my skin. His hand on the small of my back as we walked to his car. The flirting, him serving me wine and making me a plate. Something changed, and I was loving every second of it.

I was absolutely obsessed by the time he asked me what I wanted and I told him to kiss me. Indulging my fantasies turned out to be a million times better than I'd imagined. What I thought it would be paled in comparison to what it actually was. Being kissed by Roman was mind-blowing. It knocked me off my feet and pushed me to beg for more. So much more.

The hard outline of his cock rubbing against my pussy turned my panties into a fucking waterfall. I've never been more turned on than I was last night. Not only because of *how* he kissed me, but because *he* finally gave in.

Everything was ruined within one stupid minute. It's like a cruel joke. The man I've been crushing on likes me, but he's not going to touch me ever again...because Travis chose the worst time ever to call me. I could've had a chance to make things right if Roman hadn't read the text. But he did. His jealousy sent a thrill down my spine, exciting me for a second. Until I realized it had transformed into resentment. Toward me.

It's the worst outcome possible.

Sitting in my car, I press my forehead to the steering wheel and close my eyes. Feeling this fucking doomed makes me ill. I'm used to always finding solutions to my problems. Sometimes it takes a long time, and sometimes it's not easy. But eventually I always know what to do...unlike now.

There is a puzzle piece I'm missing. Something that makes him feel so strongly about me still talking to my ex. He's so deep in his own head, he's not even listening to me. He doesn't want to know my side of the story...and it sucks.

The sound of Gavin DeGraw's "I Don't Want to Be" rattles the quiet, and I snatch my phone from the passenger seat. As I answer, I open the car door and climb outside.

"Hey, Nev. Sorry I didn't hear your call earlier. My phone was on silent," Angie explains softly. "How are you?"

"Roman kissed me last night." I pause, leaning against my car.

"And how do you feel? How was it?"

"Everything I wanted and more." Intoxicating but soothing. It's like he took all my worries away and filled me with happiness and calm instead. Men and women I've kissed before...all those memories are a blur. But the memory of his is still there. Vivid and intense. I shut my eyes, chewing on my bottom lip. No longer swollen from his kisses, my lips feel so ordinary.

"What happened after?" Angie asks, gently nudging me to continue.

"Travis called me and then sent me a text, and Roman saw it because I asked him to give me my phone. He said kissing me was a mistake."

"But why was Travis calling you? I thought you were trying to keep your distance from him."

"I am, but he's not making it easy," I snort bitterly. I explain everything about Discovery Park and what happened after Roman read Travis's text. "I don't know what to do, Angie."

"You like Roman," she states matter-of-factly. "I knew that long before you broke up with Travis. Just seeing how defensive you would get when I asked about him, I decided to leave it alone, even if I saw how you looked at him. That attraction was always there. I'm not surprised it's only grown stronger."

"I want this man to be mine," I confess, my eyes watering. "Not temporarily. Not because of our stupid Vegas wedding. I just want him."

"I know, Nev."

"I tried telling him that Travis is my past, and—"

"Roman thinks you're still not over your ex. Drake told me that last night."

A harsh laugh bolts out of my mouth, and I shake my head. "Of course he does. And that text only proved his theory."

"You need to say no to Travis. Make sure he understands that this wasn't a break, but an actual breakup."

"I know. I just feel so bad. Leaving him after I found out he was going to propose was cruel. And I can't even imagine how hurt he'll be if he finds out about me and Roman. About our marriage."

"So you're ready to deprive yourself of a chance at a real relationship with the guy you like so you don't hurt the guy you feel nothing for?" Angie exclaims. "Sorry, Nev, but it's not right. The road to hell is paved with good intentions, remember? And you don't need to tell Travis about Vegas. Just set boundaries."

"I will. Today."

"Good, it's for the best," Angie says softly. The sound of a dog's paws slapping the tile reaches my ears. "When are you meeting him?"

I take my phone away from my ear and check the time. "In twenty minutes."

"Good luck, Nev. Call me later."

"Sure. Bye, Angie. Love you."

"Love you too, bye."

Pocketing my phone, I take a deep breath, close my eyes, and lift my face to the sun. The air is humid, and the wind is nonexistent. It feels heavy, just like my mood. Succumbing to my negative thoughts won't bring me anything good. It will only make things worse. No matter what, I don't want to hurt Travis more than I already have.

Choosing the right words is my specialty, and I can only hope it won't fail me today.

"HEY, NEV." Travis waves at me, coming closer and letting Happy off his leash. The dog rushes toward me, barking loudly in excitement. His tiny tail wags fast, and when he stops in front of me, he starts jumping around.

I smile, crouching down and letting Happy jump into my arms. Closing my eyes, I press the little dog to my chest and hide my nose in his sand-colored fur. The feeling of loneliness slams into me, spreading from my head to my toes. I miss Happy so much. I wish I could've taken him with me.

"Looks like I was right," Travis says, and I look up, meeting his gaze. "You two miss each other."

"Of course we do." I give the dog another squeeze, then slowly set him down and stand up. Trav instantly steps closer and wraps me in an embrace, kissing my cheek. I don't return the hug. My arms just dangle at my sides.

"I'm so happy to see you," he whispers.

I untangle myself from Travis and back away. The smile on my face is a carefully curated mask. I have no right to be angry with him for how last night ended. If I hadn't agreed to go to the park with him in the first place, that wouldn't have happened. But I'm still a little pissed off that he hasn't even tried to move on and forget about me. Or maybe a lot pissed off. Seeing Travis forces all the emotions I've been keeping at bay to the surface, and it's just a matter of time before they spill out.

"How are you, Nev?" Travis asks, his eyes traveling around my face and down my body.

"I'm fine." With a shrug, I wheel around and head further into the park. I'm acting like a bitch, but I don't know how else to get my point across. We are done. The only reason I'm here is Happy.

"Nev, is everything alright?" Travis falls into step beside me, trying to meet my eyes.

"Let's go to that bench over there." I point to a bench on my right. "And we can talk while Happy plays."

"Okay."

"How was your week?" I ask, hoping to fill the silence.

Fortunately, Travis knows me well, and instead of telling me off, he starts talking about work, about some code he's trying to fix and how it is affecting the planned release. Even once we're on the bench, he goes on and on about the work he and his team have done to ensure the quality of the code and avoid bugs. I listen, not interrupting him, enjoying the little break his rambling provides.

"I wasn't sure if you wanted to go to that Chinese place—" I turn my head in Travis's direction, my eyes narrowed to slits. He swallows hard and fakes a smile. "So I booked a table, just in case."

"Wasn't my text clear enough?" I scrutinize him, swinging my foot as I sit with my legs crossed. Sure, my vision was all blurry from my tears, but I remember saying no via text.

"Well, I know you said—"

"Travis," I say sternly, turning to face him. "I feel like no matter what I say, you're not listening. We broke up. That's it. I'm here as your friend, and I'm here for Happy. Us meeting at the park was so I could spend some time with the dog, because I miss him."

Travis's jaw ticks, his nostrils flaring. "Have you started therapy?"

"No."

"Didn't we break up so you could work on your issues?"

I lick my lips. My agitation rises; the beating of my heart becomes thunderous. He's not making this easy at all.

"No."

"What do you mean, 'no'?"

"Yes, Trav, I need to work on my issues. But I didn't need to break up with you for that. I left because I realized I've never been right for you. You deserve someone a thousand times better than me."

"But I only want you!" he argues, grabbing my hand and holding it between his palms. "Nev, please, I'm losing my mind without you. I need you." He sneaks a glance at Happy and then peers at me again. "*We* need you."

Sighing deeply, I hang my head. "Travis, I'm really sorry. But friendship is the only thing I can offer you. We need to keep our distance. No more flowers, no more waiting for me in the parking garage or coming to my office. I want you to see how good you are without me, and that's not possible if I'm always around."

"So you want me to—"

"Start seeing other people. Start going out. Having fun." I meet his gaze, noticing the torment in his brown eyes. "You're an amazing guy, but I'm not *it* for you. I'm not as flawless as you think."

Travis sits with an absolutely miserable look on his face. He keeps locking and unlocking his fingers, chewing on his bottom lip, and avoiding looking at me. Rushing him won't bring me any solace, so I wait patiently, watching him.

"Are you going to start seeing new people too?" he whispers hoarsely.

"Not now," I lie. Or maybe it's the truth, since I'm not interested in anyone except the guy I live with.

"Okay." Travis gives me a tentative smile. "At least we can be friends."

"We can," I confirm.

Sighing, he leans back against the bench and looks up at the sky. "How are you, Nev?"

I mirror him, raising my face to the blazing sun and closing my eyes. After a short internal debate, I start talking. Travis was my friend before things between us changed and we became a couple. I would be happy to have him as a friend again.

I hope it can work.

WHEN I WALK into Roman's apartment at six p.m., I notice how unusually quiet it is. When he's home, he's usually watching something or listening to music. This total silence sends shivers down my spine.

Tentatively, I move down the hallway and step into the living room. It's dark and empty, and a weird feeling forms in the pit of my stomach. Where is he? Did he go for a ride again?

I pull my phone out of my pocket, and my heart sinks. Two texts Roman sent almost three hours ago catch my attention. Quickly unlocking my screen, I read his texts, and the only thing I want to do is to scream. This guy is infuriating.

ROMAN:

Hey, you left early so I didn't have a chance to tell you. Crawford invited me to join him in Cancún. I'll be back in two weeks. Right before training camp starts.

ROMAN:

I have nothing against you having people over. So if you want to, please do. Enjoy your time, Malyshka. The apartment is all yours.

Enjoy my time? Is he fucking kidding me?

Roman

TWENTY

peace offering

"So, how was Cancún?" Colt asks. The sound of the kids' laughter gets louder. "Michael, Isla, can you please go in the house?" he shouts. "Sorry, man. Bella and the kids came to visit Ava. And while they are drinking coffee and talking about books, I'm looking after the kids. Meghan and Ian are fine, but the oldest two drive me up the wall."

"Kids will be kids," I tell him, looking out the window as my Uber stops at a traffic light. "I would be more worried if they were hiding somewhere in silence, plotting God only knows what."

"Well, yeah, you have a point." The kids must go inside, because it gets quiet. "Tell me about Cancún. How on Earth did you end up there with Crawford?"

"I wanted to go somewhere before preseason starts, and it just happened that I saw his post when I was scrolling Instagram. I DMed him, and he invited me to join him. That's all."

"Based on the Stories I saw, seems like you had a lot of fun."

"You're lucky you're on my Close Friends list. Otherwise, you wouldn't have seen anything," I tease him as we enter my neighborhood.

"I'm honored." Thompson laughs. "Is your wife also on your Close Friends list?"

My smile slips away, and I take a deep breath, hoping to get rid of the anxious feeling in my gut. I've been fine most of the time, but Colton's words instantly bring my worries back. They're proof that my whole trip was just me trying to run away from the situation I got myself into and its consequences.

My wife...More like the girl I can't stop thinking about, no matter how off-limits she is.

"No, she's not. I haven't talked to her...since Ava's birthday."

Colton doesn't say anything at first, and I start tapping my fingers on my thigh. Then I hear him sigh.

"What happened after Ava's birthday?" he asks.

"Nothing."

"Sorry, but I don't believe you. You didn't even mention that you were taking a trip when you were at my house, and then suddenly, the next thing I know, you're flying to Cancún."

I prop my head against the window and close my eyes. "I kissed her."

"Was it so bad that you felt the need to run away to another country?"

"Fuck you, Thompson," I grit through my teeth, and he chuckles. "It was perfect."

"Okay, that makes even less sense."

"Her ex texted her. She was planning to see him the next day."

"Was it a date?"

"She said it wasn't, but he wanted to make a reservation at some restaurant she's been wanting to go to," I mutter as the car pulls into my driveway. "I know she's not responsible for his actions, but she kept bringing home flowers he gave her. She was still talking to him, agreeing to see him whenever he wanted. I don't get involved with taken girls, or girls who have no idea what they want."

"Because of Maksim."

I nod, even if he can't see me. "Yeah."

"Sorry to be the bad guy, but I don't think you're being fair to Nevaeh. You know how some people are. They don't take no for an answer. If her ex-boyfriend isn't ready to move on and forget about her, how can she control that?"

"She still—"

"For fuck's sake, Pashkevich. I know how hard it is for you to trust people. How much easier it is to keep everyone at an arm's length, or even farther," Colton says. "I was just like you years ago. If I'd continued to think like that, I would still be alone, without any chance at a happy family. And I can't imagine my life without Ava and my children."

"Just a few minutes ago you were complaining about your kids," I joke, trying to dismiss this nagging feeling of hopelessness his words brought me.

"Very mature, Roman," he retorts snidely. "Just stop making assumptions and talk to her."

"Sorry, Colt. I know you're right," I tell him as the car idles to a stop. "I have no idea what's going to happen once I get home."

"Start with an apology. And maybe flowers. Just don't buy roses."

"Why? Roses are her favorite." I pinch my eyebrows together.

"You know, in case she slaps you across the face with them."

I laugh, getting out of the car and taking my suitcase from the trunk. "I bought something for her in Mexico. I hope she'll talk to me at least."

"I'll keep my fingers crossed for you." Colt chuckles. "Good luck."

"Thank you. Bye, man."

"Bye."

Tucking my phone in my pocket, I thank the driver and head inside my apartment building, straight to the elevator. There's a popular old song that anyone who plays hockey in my country knows; "Cowards don't play hockey," the lyrics go. But I handled the aftermath of our kiss like a coward. Running away, not saying a word to her. Immature behavior at its finest.

When the elevator stops at the sixth floor, my palms start to sweat. I'm a mess just picturing how seeing her will go. I like her so damn much, it's maddening. The feeling I get when she's around is a thousand times stronger than it was with any other girl I've been with. Even in Cancún...there were always girls, making small talk and flirting. Beautiful girls. Hot girls. But I couldn't care less about any of them.

They weren't her.

I open the door, and the first thing I hear is the sound of the TV. The *Peaky Blinders* theme song is playing, and my lips lift into an involuntary smile. She's watching my favorite TV show, even without me, and it makes me unreasonably happy.

Taking a step forward, I psych myself up to see Nevaeh. But a loud bark makes me freeze. I blink, stupefied, as a small French bulldog barrels out of the living room.

What the hell is this?

"Happy!"

Nevaeh runs out of the living room and catches the dog in her arms, lifting it and pressing it to her chest. Our eyes lock, but I'm unable to say even a fucking word. The barking is high-pitched, and I grimace at how unpleasant it sounds.

"Why is there a dog here?" I ask in a low voice.

Her eyes roam over my face, and she pouts, lifting her chin. "Hi. Nice to see you back home."

I shift, clutching the handle of my suitcase harder. "Um, yeah, hi." Pointing at the dog in her arms, I ask again, "Why is there a dog here?"

"You said I could invite some guests over." She adjusts her hold; the dog is probably too heavy for her. "This is Happy, and he's my guest."

"I didn't mean dogs."

"You don't like pets?" She arches an eyebrow, her eyes narrowing.

"I do! I have a dog and a cat at home. That's not the point."

Nevaeh stares at me for a long minute, then wheels around and disappears into the living room. So, we're done talking? Really? I stand in the hallway like a fucking statue. Hiding my fingers in my hair, I huff, trying to make sense of all this.

It's just a dog. Why am I reacting like this? Would it have been better to walk in on her spending time with her ex in my apartment?

Of course not. I should be grateful it's just the dog. But it's her ex's dog, dammit!

Taking a deep breath, I take off my sneakers and pad into the living room, pulling my suitcase after me. Nevaeh sits on the couch, petting the dog, who lies beside her. Not paying me any attention, she continues to watch *Peaky Blinders* with an unreadable expression on her face. Except maybe anger. That is clear, given how quickly her chest rises and falls. I pissed her off. Again.

Voz'mi s polki pirozhok, Roma[1]. *You deserve it.*

AFTER PUTTING my things into the washing machine and taking a quick shower, I get dressed and walk out of my room, holding my hands behind my back. My hair is still wet, sticking out in all different directions no matter how many times I try to tame it. I need a haircut.

Nevaeh is on the couch, watching TV and holding a mug with something steaming between her palms. The dog lifts its head, its beady eyes following my every step.

Coming closer, I stop in front of the couch and extend a box of Sour Patch Kids to her. "This is for you."

She looks up, her lips twisting in a scowl. "It's kinda small for a peace offering."

"Then how about this?" I show her the plush toy I bought for her. A Sulley.

Nevaeh's eyes grow wide, her pupils dilating. Slowly, she puts the mug on the coffee table and takes the toy in her hands. A smile quirks up my lips as I watch her in silence. Looks like I was able to surprise her...in a good way.

"Roman..." She peers at me. "Thank you."

"I hoped you'd like it."

---

1. Возьми с полки пирожок, Рома. — Pat yourself on the back, Roma. *Not the literal translation.*

"Like it? I love it. It looks exactly like my Sulley." Nevaeh grins at me, the toy pressed tightly to her chest.

"Am I forgiven?"

Her melodic laughter fills the room. "For now."

Chuckling, I glance at the dog, who's standing on the couch, his two front paws on her knee. "Think you can introduce us?"

Nevaeh meets my gaze, her teeth sinking into her bottom lip. It's simple eye contact, but everything in me comes to life. I'm so attracted to her, it's like an obsession. No one else matters. Nothing else matters. Only her and what she wants. And damn if I don't want her to want me.

"Happy, this is Roman," she tells the dog with an adorable little beam on her lips. I extend my hand to the dog and let him smell me. He studies me with a very serious expression. "This is his apartment, Happy. He's a good guy."

The dog tilts his head to the side, as if trying to figure out what she just said. The quickest glance in my direction follows, and he starts wagging his tail.

"Good boy," Nevaeh says, petting the dog. Looking up at me, she smiles, fire dancing behind her irises. "I think he likes you."

"I think he does." I put my hand on the dog's fur; its softness forces a smile onto my face. "My mom has a Pomeranian. I gave it to her for her birthday two years ago because she wanted one so badly. Not sure our cat was happy about it though."

"You never said you had a dog and a cat back home." Nevaeh shifts a little to let me sit down beside her on the couch.

"Didn't think it was important." I shrug as Happy starts licking my fingers, making me ticklish. "The dog's name is Adele, because my mom loves Adele's music."

"And what's the cat's name?"

"Mickey. My niece suggested it, and my mom agreed." I lean back against the couch, and the dog climbs onto my lap and puts his paws on my chest. "You're quite a resourceful little fella, aren't you?"

"Oh, he is. He knows all the ways to make you do whatever he wants."

"Talking from experience?" I arch an eyebrow, and she gives me the cutest smile. She's still clutching Sulley to her chest.

"Maybe."

"How did he end up here?"

"After I met with Travis in the park, he promised to keep his distance," she says, holding my gaze. My fingers absentmindedly move along the dog's fur. "And he has. But it just happened that I ran into him in the elevator after work on Friday. I was lonely, and I told him I missed this little furball. So Travis let me take him home."

"When do we need to bring him back?"

"We?" Nevaeh asks, fighting a smile.

"We. I'll go with you."

Her tee rides up, barely hiding her tits. She takes her mug from the table and presses it to her lips, holding my gaze. "Whatever you want, Roman." She looks me up and down with a seductive smile. "We need to take him back tomorrow."

"Awesome," I say, right as the dog nestles on my lap and lies down. "Do we need to take him for a walk tonight?"

"In two hours. For now can we watch *Peaky Blinders*? Is that okay with you?"

"I'll never say no to Tommy Shelby and his family."

Nevaeh laughs. "You and your love for this show." She shakes her head. "In all honesty, I understand. I thought *Game of Thrones* was good, but this one is a masterpiece."

"Wait till you watch *Vikings*. That one—"

She presses a finger to my lips, silencing me. "Stop. One show at a time, okay?"

I raise my hands in front of me in surrender. "Sure."

We sit in silence for a few minutes, watching the fourth season. Suddenly, she leans over, her hot breath fanning over my skin. "Don't think you're off the hook. I still have questions about your trip to Cancún."

I turn my head, meeting her gaze. The tension between us is palpable, and it takes a lot for me to not touch her.

“Looking forward to it,” I whisper, fully acknowledging that the dog is the only reason why I haven’t kissed her.

And probably why I haven’t done more than that.

Nevaeh

TWENTY-ONE

some secrets are worth keeping

Sitting on a chair in the kitchen, I watch Roman put a plate stacked with pancakes and a little bowl of sour cream on the table. Our eyes meet, and a smile rises on my lips. Big and open. I just can't help myself when he's around.

"How did you sleep in Cancún? Are your nightmares…" I fall silent, suddenly unsure if I should've brought it up.

"I sleep better when other people are around," he says, placing two glasses and some apple juice on the table. "Crawford and his friends rented a villa. It was all good."

A pang in my chest quickly erases the smile from my face, and jealousy flares in my heart. I twist my lips and squint at Happy, quietly snoring on the floor beside me. The feeling is all consuming, I can't even find the words to fill this awkward pause.

I saw the pictures from his trip. All the beautiful girls who were there with him. The Stories he posted for his Close Friends list. I wish I hadn't asked Angie to show them to me. Seeing them didn't do me any good, only brought me distress and made me feel miserable.

He thought I wasn't over my ex. No surprise he'd want a rebound.

"Good to know." I force the words out of my mouth and avert my eyes to the pancakes, avoiding looking at him at all costs. "Okay, can you tell me again what this is?"

"*Draniki*. Potato pancakes. Nothing fancy, but still delicious."

"Is it, like, a national dish?" I raise my eyes and see him studying me with a gentle smile on his lips.

"Kinda. Potato pancakes are something you'll also find in Polish cuisine, in Lithuanian, and in so many others. I've tried them in all those countries," he says with a shrug, setting his elbows on the table. "And I simply love them."

I place a pancake on my plate, cut off a little piece, and put it in my mouth. It's savory, with a little bit of salt and probably some onions. The longer I chew, the closer he inches to me. His eyes are glued to my face.

"I'm going to choke on my food if you keep staring at me like that," I tell him, pouring some apple juice in my glass.

Roman laughs, leaning back in his seat. He puts four pancakes on his plate, adds some sour cream, and instantly takes a bite. Closing his eyes, he chews with an absolutely satisfied look on his face. I shake my head, add more pancakes to my plate, and start eating.

"Add sour cream," he suddenly says. "It's better that way."

"Really?" I arch an eyebrow but do as he says. Curiosity has always been my Achilles heel, and I'm not sure that will ever change. If this ends up ruining the taste— "God, it's so good!" I exclaim loudly. "Why didn't you tell me about the sour cream from the start?"

"I didn't get the chance," he says with humor in his voice.

"Next time you treat me to something new, tell me how I should eat it." I point my fork at him. "Deal?"

"Whatever you want, Malyshka."

The words leave his mouth sounding nonchalant, ordinary even. Yet I'm immediately transported back in time, to our moment in the living room. Sadness surrounds me, clouding my mind.

"When we do whatever I want, it doesn't end well," I mutter hoarsely, not thinking twice about what I'm about to say. "I end up all alone in your apartment while you fly to another country and spend time surrounded by tons of stunning girls."

The kitchen pitches into a booming silence. It's like I turned off all sound with my words. I hate this. The way he affects me is overwhelming; it knocks all rational sense out of me. We're not even a couple, but I feel like I'm losing myself in him. And the stupidest thing is...I think I like it.

Because it feels right.

"Nevaeh."

I look up, my eyes clashing with his. So many emotions flash through me, replacing each other at an unbelievable speed. I'm tired of this hopelessness, of this overpowering feeling of jealousy whenever I think about him with other girls. And I'm so tired of him not wanting me back.

"Tons of stunning girls might've been around, but I couldn't care less about any of them," he says, looking at me from under his eyelashes. His gaze is so intense and penetrating, it feels as if he's looking right through me. I smirk, shaking my head. As if I'm going to beli— "I couldn't stop thinking about the one I left at home."

"Really?" I blurt, feeling close to fainting from happiness. It's so not like me; I should be worried, but all I care about is the hope that rekindles in my chest. The warmth that is coursing through my veins, setting my skin on fire.

Roman nods, grinning his beautiful, crooked smile. "Really, Malyshka. I'm sorry for hurting you that night, and I'm sorry for leaving without saying a word. I'm not a coward, but I acted like one for sure."

"You're not—"

"Nevaeh," he groans. "If you keep defending me when I clearly don't deserve it, I'll have to teach you a lesson."

"Are you going to punish me?" I ask, biting my bottom lip.

He picks up his glass from the table and presses it to his lips, holding my gaze. "Maybe," he murmurs, before sipping his juice.

I beam at him, glancing at Happy, who's on his back, quietly whimpering in his sleep. Bending down, I pet his belly, butterflies fluttering their wings in my stomach. Around Roman, they're never calm. They fly around and make me all giddy and hopeful. And maybe horny. Definitely horny, based on the wetness between my thighs.

"My brother...Maksim died in a car crash." I sit up straighter, my eyes glued to his. The pain in his gaze is evident, shuttering all my giddiness and horniness at once. "He got in the car with our friend Kirill, who was so drunk he lost control of the car."

Roman pauses, and I notice his knuckles turning white, tightly wrapped around the glass. Holding my breath, I wait, my heart pumping nervously in my chest.

"Kirill only broke his leg, but Maks died on the spot. His side of the car struck a traffic pole and got wrapped around it." His voice is monotone and emotionless. His glassy stare focused on the wall behind me. "At least he didn't suffer. No pain. No agony. He probably didn't even realize he was about to die."

"I'm so sorry, Roman." I cover my mouth with my palm.

He meets my gaze, and I feel like I'm drowning in his sorrow. His blue eyes remind me of the deepest ocean, one full of pain and hurt. His grief knots my stomach; my heart aches, and his pain makes it bleed. For him. "Kirill was sentenced to five years in jail, even though my mom and I were asking for less. Maks knew he was getting in the car with a drunk driver. He knew and still asked our friend to give him a ride. All because of her."

I frown, eyebrows pierced together as I lower my hand. "Her?"

"Alisa. My brother's girlfriend," he hisses. His lips purse into a tight line, and his jaw ticks. "Our teammate saw her with her ex, and told Maksim. My brother got in Kirill's car that night because he was worried the girl he loved was cheating on him. It wasn't anything new, unfortunately. She'd been leading both guys on for months, playing both of them. It was all a game to her, and Maks paid for it with his life."

The air is stuck in my lungs; my heart constricts painfully. I press my palm to my chest, tears filling my eyes. "Oh my God...I'm so very sorry. That's horrible."

"After his funeral, I promised myself I'd never get involved with anyone if they were in a relationship. That I wouldn't even look twice at a girl who wasn't over her ex or was keeping him close," Roman says. "Taken girls and 'it's complicated' girls are off-limits for me."

"I told you it was complicated between Travis and me," I whisper, the picture becoming clearer by the second. "And then all the flowers, and that text..."

"Yeah."

"Travis and I broke up. I don't see myself ever getting back together with him. For me, that relationship was over the second I got sick after seeing the ring he bought for me." I give him a weak smile. "When I met with him two weeks ago, I made sure he knew where I stand. He hasn't tried to see me once since then. There have been no flowers or texts. He's keeping his distance, just like I asked him to." I look down at Happy and then return my gaze to Roman. "I was lonely here, so when I saw Travis in the elevator, I asked him if I could take Happy for the weekend. He said yes."

"I'm glad he let you take him," Roman says, putting his glass on the table. "I've been thinking about getting a cat or a dog, but with my away games, it's not possible."

"Cooper always saves Angie from boredom when Drake is away."

"I bet he does." He tilts his head, scrutinizing me. "Did Angie show you my Stories? Or Drake?"

Embarrassment heats my cheeks and my neck. I rap my fingers on the table, silently scolding myself for my big mouth. With a sigh, I nod. "Angie. She didn't want to, but...I was a little desperate." I lower my gaze to my lap. "Or a lot."

Roman doesn't say anything. He stands up from the table, takes our empty plates, and goes to put them in the dishwasher. I wait, not knowing what to expect. Turning around, he leans against the kitchen counter, his arms crossed over his chest.

"I think I like this about you. Your possessive side," he murmurs, lighting a fire within me with his words.

As slowly as possible, I stand up and strut toward him. My eyes devour every inch of him, from his legs to his handsome face. His hair is messy, and all I want is to run my fingers through it.

"Possessive me is jealous me. Do you like that too?"

He licks his bottom lip, unfolding his arms and winding his hands around my waist. My chest is up against his, and a puff of air leaves my mouth. Roman lowers his head, his eyes holding enough fire to burn us both.

"No. Jealousy isn't something I want you to feel. Ever," he whispers, making me breathless. He takes my chin between his thumb and index finger, tilting my face up to him. "Just like I'll never get involved with someone taken, I'll never pursue someone else if I'm in a relationship. Or if I like someone." His lips press to mine, briefly, like the touch of a feather. Fleetingly. And still…it's everything. "And I like you, Nevaeh. A lot."

"I would've never guessed if you hadn't kissed me that night," I tell him, wrapping my arms around his torso.

His head lolls back, and he laughs heartily. "I've always liked you. Since the moment I first met you."

"Really?" I lean back, searching his face with my eyebrows pinched together. It feels so surreal, I'm having trouble wrapping my head around it.

"You weren't single, remember? I didn't want you to know how I felt. I didn't want anyone to know."

"You're so good at keeping secrets." I stand on my tiptoes. The desire to feel his lips on mine again is clouding my judgment.

"Some secrets are worth keeping." His lips hover over mine, and I can almost taste them. Soft and luscious. So fucking addictive I can't even stand straight; my whole body is trembling. A shiver of anticipation rolls down my spine, and I run my tongue over my bottom lip.

"Nevaeh…"

He says my name like a warning. In a low growl, thick with his accent, because he's not controlling himself.

"Kiss me," I demand, sliding my hand under his tee and feeling his abs contract under my touch.

He smirks and presses his lips to my forehead instead. "Happy needs to go home, Malyshka. I won't be able to stop if I kiss you now, and fucking you on my kitchen counter in front of your little dog isn't going to happen."

A loud gasp springs from my lips when he turns me around and my back crashes into his chest. His hot breath on my skin sends a jolt of electricity all over my body, one that nestles in my lower abdomen. So fucking hot.

"Even if the view would be absolutely fantastic," he whispers in my ear. Then he pushes me to start moving toward the living room. My whole being is vibrating from our closeness.

And dammit if I don't want him to do exactly that...spread me open on his kitchen counter and fuck me till I can't walk.

I hope he will be up to it after we take Happy back.

Roman

TWENTY-TWO

not with me

"I still don't think this is a good idea." Nevaeh purses her lips and pets Happy, who sits on her lap.

Glancing at her, I reach over and ruffle the dog's smooth fur. "There's no way I would've fit in your car."

She rolls her eyes. "You make it sound like you're so big."

"I am."

Her gaze darts to me, and an adorable pink hue spreads across her cheeks. Why am I not even surprised that she's thinking about my dick?

With a clipped exhale, she starts to grin. "Sorry I don't believe you, Roman. I need proof."

"Don't worry. You'll get it," I tell her, knowing it's a bad idea. Fucking her would complicate everything, open the door for inevitable heartbreak. It would be another brick in my wall of reasons to hate myself. As if that wall's not high enough already.

"Looking forward to it," Nevaeh murmurs, a seductive smile lifting her lips. Looking down at Happy and then out the window, she turns to me. "At least stop the car away from Travis's building. Please."

"Fine."

Once my BMW is parked, I put my hand between Happy's ears

and pet him tenderly. He's a good boy, playful and friendly, and it was really nice having him around, taking him out for walks and just playing with him.

"I think you should get a pet," Nevaeh blurts out, and I meet her gaze, looking at her skeptically. "I'll be home when you're at away games."

Something happens to me when I hear her call my apartment home. A long-forgotten warmth envelops my whole body. I haven't felt that in quite a while, even at my parents' apartment. Everything changed when Maks died. The word "home" lost its meaning, and the apartment turned into just a place I spent time between hockey and sleep.

Nevaeh makes it feel different. Brings up emotions I thought I'd never feel again.

"Roman, what do you think?" I blink and squint at Happy, still perched on her lap.

Is her suggestion tempting? Yes. Will I go for it? No. Our marriage is only temporary. When summer comes, she'll leave me, probably hating my guts and cursing the day she agreed to go to Vegas with me. I'll be lucky if she's still talking to me after this.

Making her fall with me into the pit of my self-loathing isn't something I plan to do. She's so much better than I'll ever deserve.

"Nah, I don't think I'm ready for the responsibility."

Nevaeh narrows her eyes, studying me in silence. With the quickest shrug, she unbuckles her seat belt and opens the car door. "I'll change your mind."

As if I don't have enough problems without any pets.

Getting out of the car, she holds Happy close to her chest. "Say bye to Roman, Happy," she chirps, raising the dog's paw and waving it at me. "Who knows, maybe next time we'll have a little kitten for you to play with."

My jaw drops, and I just blink at her. This girl...I swear, she drives me crazy. Not only with her beauty, but with her wit and her smart mouth. Laughter spills from her lips, and she winks at me, closing the door and putting Happy down on the sidewalk. They stroll away from my car and head toward her ex's building.

Realization dawns on me. Before now, I hadn't really thought about where she's going. Memories from the first time we met flash in my head, when I watched her walk to this building and disappear behind its closed doors. Venomous jealousy finds its way under my skin, fueling my veins and poisoning my thoughts. It's not like I don't believe her when she says she's over him...I just don't trust him.

I don't think someone can turn off their feelings like magic. I never could. No matter how much I tried.

To distract myself, I take out my phone and send a message to my mom. I need to tell her about my marriage. Once the season starts, I'm sure the news will get out. Maybe even earlier, as soon as preseason rolls around. I'm running out of time, and the longer I wait, the more disappointed she will be. And I truly hate making Mom upset; she's been through enough with Maksim's death and my father's. I don't want to add more worries onto her already full plate.

ME:

I have some news :) any chance we can talk today?

Instead of an answer, my mom decides to FaceTime me. *Ochen' v maminom stile*[1].

"Hey," I say, plastering a smile on my face.

"What news?" Her eyes, the same color as mine, are narrowed, a deep wrinkle between her brows.

"Gotta love your approach, Mom. *Srazu k delu*[2]. No excuses," I joke, my cheeks suddenly feeling hot. Okay, I don't think I've ever been this nervous...not even when Mom caught me and Maks smoking our grandpa's cigarettes one summer, when we were ten.

"It's your fault. I'm still recovering from your teenage years, so

1. Очень в мамином стиле. — It's very much like Mom.
2. Сразу к делу. — Straight to the business.

messages like that one give me an instant headache." Mom laughs heartily. "What's going on?"

"Remember how I went to Vegas?" She nods, tucking her curly blonde hair behind her ears. I take a deep breath and confess on an exhale. "I got married there."

Mom is staring at me, unblinking. Pressing her palm to her forehead, she twists her lips in a scowl. A trickle of sweat slides down my spine, and I shiver uncomfortably. I prefer the yelling version of her over this one; her silence makes things a thousand times worse.

"Mom?"

"Roma..." She sighs, shaking her head. "*Ty chto s uma soshel*[3]?"

"Definitely not. I'm just...I went to Vegas to distract myself, to get a break from my nightmares. When I asked Nevaeh to join me, it was just to keep me company. And everything was fine until we got drunk and got married. I still don't know why we did it. Like, I have a few ideas, all of them are based on her ex, but they're just a guess. Neither of us can remember shit from that night."

"And you're still married?" Mom asks, and I nod curtly. "From all the Hollywood movies I watched, I know it's possible to get an annulment. Why didn't you do that?"

I put the phone in its stand and rub my face with my palms, mulling over my answer. Lowering my hands to the steering wheel, I peer at Mom and explain to her my reasons. Slowly, without any rush. I need her to understand.

"Hockey. It's always about the damn game," Mom states once I stop talking. "Have you even thought about this girl? What is her name again?"

"Nevaeh."

"Have you even thought about Nevaeh? Or are you just thinking about hockey and your career?"

"Mom, she agreed. I didn't—"

"Trust me, Roma, if I would've been told that someone's future depends on me agreeing to stay married to them for a year, I would've

3. Ты что с ума сошёл? — Are you out of your mind?

agreed too. That's what good people do." Mom purses her lips, glaring at me from under furrowed brows. "Does she like you?"

"Yeah, but—"

"Do you like her? And I swear, Roma, I'll know if you lie. Do you like your wife?"

My wife...The words light up my skin like a burning match; a sizzling heat spreads from my cheeks down my neck. I wrap my hands tightly around the steering wheel, clenching my teeth.

"I do. I like her a lot."

Mom watches me, puffing her cheeks out in anger. I wait. Every second of her silence makes me more and more nervous.

With a loud sigh, she tilts her head, her eyes softening. "Then don't fuck it up. Please." She smiles gently. "Sometimes we get something we desperately need when we least expect it. Maybe Nevaeh is that for you."

I swallow down the words that are threatening to spill out. About me being a fucking disaster, how I can't be anything more than Nevaeh's worst nightmare. That I'm like King Midas, but instead of turning things into gold, I poison every good thing that has ever happened to me in my entire life. I'm something no one can cure...not even the girl with the most beautiful smile.

"I know that look," Mom says. "You deserve the world, and it's time you realize it. Live. For you and for him, Roma."

"Did you miss me?" My head swivels right, and I gawk at Nevaeh, who's climbing into my car. "Sorry it took me so long, I..." She falls silent, glancing between me and my phone.

"Is that Nevaeh?" my mom asks, switching to English and bringing my attention back to her.

I reach over to my phone and adjust it so Mom can see Nevaeh.

"Yeah," I confirm. Nevaeh's eyes round, her cheeks sporting an adorable pink shade. "Nevaeh, this is my mom."

"Hi," she whispers, waving her hand awkwardly. "It's very nice to meet you."

"You too. I'm Iryna. Sorry, it looks like my son forgot how to introduce people," Mom says, and Nevaeh giggles, her features relaxing. "I'm really sorry Roma dragged you into his mess, but I'm also grateful. Thank you so much for being there for him. The past few weeks haven't been easy for him."

Nevaeh sneaks a glance at me. "I'm happy to be there for Roman." Then she peers at my phone, smiling affectionately at my mom. "And he didn't drag me into anything. It was my decision, and I don't regret it."

"I'm happy to hear that," Mom says with a broad smile on her lips. "What are you two up to, anyway? Isn't it your last day before training camp starts?"

We talk some more until Mom says that it's time for her to take Adele for a walk. After I hang up, my whole body feels light. It's easier to breathe, and my mood is good. I don't think there's anything in the world that can spoil it. I not only told my mom about my marriage, but I also introduced her to Nevaeh...and it went a thousand times better than I could've imagined. They seemed to like each other.

"Ready to go home?" I start the engine and peek at Nevaeh. She's still smiling, looking absolutely irresistible with her blonde hair spilling over her shoulders and her makeup-free face.

"Your mom seems like an amazing person," she says. "I didn't expect to meet her like that, but...I'm glad I did."

"I'm glad you did too." Without giving it much thought, I reach over and take her hand. "Thank you, Malyshka."

She threads her fingers through mine and squeezes. "Always."

I'd be lying if I said I don't enjoy having her hand in mine.

Opening the door to the apartment, I let her in first. My hand is on her lower back. It's like I haven't been able to keep my hands to myself since the moment she got in my car. Touching her, talking to her, making her laugh. Anything to see that gorgeous smile on her face, the one I know she wears only for me.

"I have something for you," I tell her, leaning down to her ear. "I wanted to give it to you yesterday, but I forgot because of Happy."

"Another gift?" Nevaeh turns around, walking backward and holding my gaze.

"I wouldn't consider it a gift."

"Then what is it?" She arches an eyebrow, her hands on her hips, drawing my gaze to the perfect curve of her body.

"Wait for me in the living room," I mumble and bolt to my room, quickly pulling the plastic folder from my drawer and retrieving the document.

When I'm back in the living room, I see Nevaeh sitting on the couch. Phone in hand, she types something, chewing on her bottom lip. My eyes roam over her body, her white cotton dress sticking to her like a glove and emphasizing her narrow waist, and round tits. A need forms in my lower abdomen and hardens my dick in no time.

This is a terrible idea, Roman, my inner voice warns me. I know it is, but I never have been super rational. Especially when it comes to the most stunning girl I've ever seen.

"Here it is," I say, plopping down beside her and almost groaning with discomfort. Sitting with a hard-on hidden behind my fly is not pleasant at all.

Nevaeh locks her phone, puts it on the couch, and takes the paper from my hands. She reads it as I prop my head on my knuckles, watching her reaction. Lifting her eyes, she sweeps her gaze over my face, a little crease between her eyebrows.

"So it's really official. I'm your wife now," she mutters quietly. "How did you get our marriage certificate?"

"Made a quick stop in Vegas on my way home from Mexico."

"How quick?" Nevaeh asks, placing the certificate on the coffee table.

"Just long enough to get the certificate and head back to the airport for my flight home."

The room plunges into silence the second I shut my mouth. We stare at each other, the tension becoming heavier with each breath I take. My heartbeat skyrockets, and I ball my hand tighter to stop myself from reaching out to her.

"You know..." Nevaeh scoots closer to me. Her sweet scent

envelops us both, and her hot breath warms my cheek. "It's still not real, even if it's official."

Forgetting my better judgment, I wrap my arm around her waist and pull her to my lap. "What do I need to do to make it real?"

"Fuck me, for starters." She presses her forehead to mine. "And to make it *really* real, give me an orgasm."

I smirk, hauling her up from the couch. "One isn't possible without the other."

"You'd be surprised—"

I catch her bottom lip between my teeth, silencing her. "Not with me," I state and head to my bedroom.

If this is a mistake, I'll deal with it later. For now, my wife needs attention.

A lot of attention.

Roman

TWENTY-THREE

anything for you

When I kiss her lips, I feel drunk. My mind is so hazy, I barely understand where I'm going. Her hands roam over my shoulders and down my back. Desperately. Frantically. Almost as if she can't stand the idea of anything between us at all.

"Take it off," she orders, her lips leaving mine for just long enough to do it. "Take this damn T-shirt off."

I suck her bottom lip into my mouth and roll it between my teeth. She whimpers when I lean away, a tiny red mark fresh on her bottom lip. Her lips look puffy already, a little bit swollen, and I'm only just getting started.

She won't be able to fucking leave my bed once I'm done with her. Not that I am opposed to that. Waking up with her would be everything—just like finally dipping my cock deep inside her pussy will be. Nevaeh is all I can think about, and even if I don't want to admit it... the lines started to blur a long time ago, mixing what's right and what's wrong together, until I can't tell the difference.

When my feelings twist together like that, all I can do is surrender.

In my room, I put her on my bed and stop beside it. I grab the hem of my tee and take it off, flinging it to the floor. Her eyes darken, her pupils dilating as she slowly slides her gaze from my face to my chest. The heat behind her irises is familiar to me, because it's exactly how I look at her. "Desire" is not even the right word to describe what I'm feeling right now.

I'm fucking obsessed.

"Better?" I ask.

Nevaeh doesn't answer. Instead, she lies on her back, slips her hands under her skirt, and the next thing I know—her panties land on the floor. Bending her legs at the knees, she spreads herself open for me, and the view of her wet pussy is all I want to look at.

My mouth waters, and I swallow hard. The need to bury my face in her precious cunt is insane. I have no idea what stops me from pouncing on her...probably the fact that I want my first time with her to be perfect. It's what she deserves.

"Better?" she teases, trailing her fingers from her neck down to her tits.

"So much better," I whisper hoarsely, dropping to my knees in front of her.

I place my hand on her belly, sliding it down her lower abdomen to her sweet pussy. The second I rub her clit between my fingers, Nevaeh lets out a loud moan and lifts her hips for me.

"So eager to feel my tongue in your pussy?" I murmur, firmly taking hold of her hips and drawing her to me.

"Yes..."

"Good, because I'm fucking starving for you, Malyshka."

Flicking my tongue over her clit and down her folds, I taste her slowly. With each move, I go deeper, stroking her smoothly and adding a little bit more pressure. She's so sweet, and so addictive. Going down on her could easily become my favorite routine, being on my knees for her and giving her pleasure.

"Just like that...You're so good..." Nevaeh moans, lifting her hips up and down, rubbing her pussy over my face. "Please don't stop, Roman."

I suck her clit into my mouth, and she digs her fingernails in my hair. Smiling, I add one finger inside her and then another one, curling them so I can reach her sweet little spot. With how loud she starts moaning, I can't help but feel smug. She'll be coming in no time. All over my face and my tongue. And I can't wait to see her come undone...because of me.

"Your fucking tongue..." she breathes, her fingers tugging my hair harder.

Thrusting my fingers inside her, I fuck her deep and slow. My tongue laps over her clit faster and faster, driving her to her release.

"I'm coming...Roman, please!" Nevaeh cries out, her ass in the air as she comes. Her walls squeeze around my fingers, her juices exploding all over my tongue. Delicious. The best I've ever tasted.

I lick her clit and lazily pump my fingers into her, prolonging her orgasm. Only when her legs stop trembling do I move away and stand up. The tightness in my jeans makes me shift, trying to find the best posture when my boner is threatening to burst.

Nevaeh props herself on her elbows, breathing heavily. Her hair sticks to her sweaty forehead, her eyes hooded with lust as she watches me. Licking her lips, she pushes herself up and sits up straight. I hold her gaze, telling myself to wait. Today, it's all about her and what she wants. All my dirty fantasies about her tied to my bed are on hold... for now.

"Take off your jeans," Nevaeh whispers.

Shaking my head and laughing quietly, I do as she says, but I keep my boxers on. She needs to be more specific if she wants me out of my clothes.

"Get naked," I tell her with a smile.

Mischief flickers behind her irises, her eyes sparkling. But she doesn't argue, just takes off her dress and unclasps her bra. When her clothes fall to the floor, Nevaeh climbs further into my bed. My gaze coasts over her face, her hair splayed over my pillows and down her body, and I start to wonder if I've ever seen anyone more perfect than she is. Her smooth, tanned skin. Her round, perky tits with pebbled nipples. Not too big, and so damn flawless. Her flat stomach rising and falling with her erratic breath. Those hips...and her fine ass.

If I was attracted to her before, when I hadn't had the chance to see all of her, now it's on another level. *Ya real'no teryayu golovu ryadom s ney*[1].

I put one knee on the bed and pause. "Are you on the pill?"

"I am," she confirms, circling a finger over her pebbled nipple. The motion has me transfixed.

"Can I fuck you bare?" I ask. My voice is thick and low. "I just got tested; I can show you the results."

"You can. You don't need to show me anything." Nevaeh spreads her legs wide, dipping her fingers inside her. "I trust you."

"Well, then..."

I quickly take off my boxers, and my dick springs free. Hard and so fucking ready, a drop of pre-cum on its head. I get on the bed and curl my hand around my cock, pumping it slowly. Moving toward her, I keep my gaze trained on her face.

"Oh my God, Roman!" Nevaeh exclaims, her gaze glued to my dick. "There's no way you're going to fit!"

It's not the first time I've heard that, but with her it hits different. It's a fucking billion-megawatt boost to my ego.

"Don't worry, Malyshka, you can take it. No one's complained before."

Her mouth forms a little O, her eyes narrowing in an instant. She pushes herself up and hooks her finger around my little cross necklace, forcing me to bend down to her.

"Did you really mention other women you've been with while you're in bed with me?" she hisses, her gaze dancing between my eyes and my mouth.

"What women?" I say and smash my lips on hers, making her moan the second I pull away.

"I hate you right now..." Nevaeh whispers as I position myself and push my cock inside her. Little by little. Inch by inch. Moving slowly in and out, I wait for her to adjust to my length.

"Hate me? Why?"

"Because you make everything perfect." She moans, her eyes

---

1. Я реально теряю голову рядом с ней. — I really lose my mind around her.

falling closed. "Your tongue in my pussy? Perfection. Your fucking dick hitting me so deep I feel like coming after just one thrust? Perfection."

"How about this?" I ask teasingly, circling my hands around her ankles and placing her legs on my shoulders. I sink more inside her until I'm finally balls deep. I groan, closing my eyes and fucking her faster. "*Kak horosho*[2]."

"Oh God..." Nevaeh exhales between loud moans, her legs trembling. "I'm going to come..."

I grin, open my eyes, and look down at her. Our gazes meet, and the most alluring smile crosses her features. Her fingers are playing with her nipples as I start pounding into her harder, driving us both to orgasm, one I know will be our first...of many.

Staying away from her now that I've got a taste? *Nevozmozhno*[3].

"NEVAEH," I whisper, tracing her cheek with the pad of my finger. "Malyshka, it's time to wake up."

"But I don't want to." Her hands sneak around my torso, and she presses herself closer to me. Her pebbled nipples rub against my skin, even through her tiny T-shirt, and my dick slowly gets harder. *Chert*[4]. A boner is definitely not something I need when she has to work and it's my first day of training camp. Especially when her alarm has gone off four times in the last twenty minutes.

Bending down, I press my lips to her nose. "You're going to be late for work."

"It's your fault for fucking me so good that I don't want to move." She nuzzles her face in my neck. Her soft lips travel down my throat, and I groan, feeling a rush of energy spread through my veins and right to my dick.

---

2. Как хорошо. — So good.
3. Невозможно. — Impossible.
4. Чёрт. — Shit.

Dammit, I have it so bad for her. I need to do something about it. As soon as possible.

Tossing the blanket aside, I scoop her into my arms and get us both out of bed. Nevaeh wraps her arms around my neck, and a bright smile plays on her sleepy face. I carry her to the bathroom, tightening my hold. As if she's the most treasured thing in the world.

It feels so good, just like being inside her felt last night. *So fucking good.* I can see myself wanting to do it again and again, and fucking again. Though even then I'm not sure it will be enough.

I put her on the bathroom counter and take a step back. Or at least, I try. Her hand snakes around my wrist, and she forces me to stay put. With a crooked smile, I inch forward until I'm between her legs.

"You need to get ready for work," I tell her.

"And you need to get ready for your first day back. So what?"

"I still have time." I tuck her hair behind her ears, gently sliding my fingers down the delicate column of her throat. "It's not my alarm that woke us up."

Nevaeh bites her bottom lip, her teeth grazing it slowly. Her hands slip down my hips, and she pushes my boxers down, releasing my already hard dick. Our eyes meet, and I'm a goner. She's won me over, and I didn't even realize we were playing.

"Looks like my alarm didn't just wake us up," she murmurs, wrapping her palm around my cock. A few light strokes, and I brace myself on the counter on either side of her, closing my eyes. "I want you." Her voice is just above a whisper, but I hear it clearly. "I always set my alarm two hours before I need to leave. Gives me enough time to get ready." Her strokes become rougher. "Roman, please..." she begs.

Hauling her to me by her hips, I pull down her panties, ripping them in the process. My impatience got the best of me.

"Guess I'll need new panties."

"Whatever you want, Malyshka," I say, driving myself inside her. "You'll never hear no from me."

"Promise?" She winds her hands around my neck. Her lips are an inch away from mine.

“Anything for you,” I breathe and kiss her, losing myself to the feeling of her in my arms.

Nevaeh

TWENTY-FOUR

i swear

I SIP MY COFFEE AND STARE AT MY LAPTOP, A GIDDY SMILE playing on my lips. It's been like this all day. Even this unexpected meeting my boss scheduled at the end of the day hasn't ruined my mood. I'm happy. Ridiculously happy, actually, and it doesn't even weird me out.

What exactly happened that caused me to feel like this? It's obviously not the first time I had been fucked so good I couldn't even move. Wasn't my first time passing out from toe-curling orgasms. And it definitely wasn't the first time I spent the night with a guy I was crushing on...and yet, I've never been *this* happy.

"Nevaeh?" I blink and set my mug on the table, raising my eyes to my boss, Kai. "Can you please tell us about the materials your department prepared?"

"Sure." Daydreaming at work? During a very important meeting? *A pat on the back for Nevaeh Lawrence.*

"NEVAEH, can you please stay for a few minutes?" Kai asks, looking up from his laptop.

I nod and slump back in my chair, putting my laptop and notes on the table. The meeting ran late. It's past seven p.m., and I want to go home, but I know better than to argue with my boss when he clearly has something on his mind.

"You wanted to discuss something?"

"I did." He nods. His brown eyes focus on me, emitting warmth. "What are you planning to write for our special edition in December?"

I shrug. "My usual. Just need to figure out a theme."

Running a hand through his hair, Kai watches me. His easygoing smile is still on his lips, but by the way he wrinkles his nose, I know he's not happy with my answer. I sweep my gaze over the conference room and then bring my eyes back to my boss. His white shirt clings to his brown skin, highlighting his broad shoulders and toned chest. Kai is an incredibly handsome man, and I know quite a few colleagues who would want to get to know him in a much more intimate setting. For me, he's always been a mentor, someone I can go to for advice if I need it. He's also been a friend.

When I agreed to sing karaoke with my boss at the holiday party, I didn't expect to gain a friend. But it happened; we just clicked.

"Do you remember our conversation a few months ago? When I put you in charge of your department?"

"How could I not?" I ask sarcastically, and he snorts. "You told me I was wasting my potential, and that I needed a more challenging job."

"Correct." Kai smiles. "You listened. You nodded. You said 'got it' several times...and since then, everything has stayed the same."

"I thought being in charge was the more challenging job."

"It is. And you're doing great as a manager. But what about you being a journalist? About you finding joy in writing?"

"My last piece, about the best places for a date, did great. It got a lot of buzz on social media," I argue. "And I enjoyed writing it. I promise, Kai. I love what I'm doing."

He sighs and leans forward, placing his elbows on the table and locking his hands in front of him. "Nevaeh, I hired you because I saw potential in you. Your article about bullying in schools, the one you submitted when you applied for this job, is still my favorite. It's powerful. It has a soul. Why don't you want to go back to writing things like that? Moving stories are what you do the best."

It's so much more taxing to write about my personal experiences. About things I've witnessed myself. About things I've done myself...even if I'm not proud of them and won't ever be. And writing those "moving" stories also makes me incredibly vulnerable. Opening up, letting people see me for who I am, judging me? It's terrifying.

"Nevaeh, look at me." I meet Kai's gaze, biting my bottom lip in annoyance. I'm not annoyed with him though, only with myself. This isn't the first time we're having this conversation, and I always backtrack like a coward.

Instead of putting in the effort and pushing for more, I settle for the options that are within my reach.

"How about we do this," Kai says. "For our special edition, I want you to write something different than what you're used to. Something that will leave people in awe. Something that will leave an impact on them." I open my mouth, but he tilts his head in warning, and I close it again. "I'm not going to tell you *what* to write about. I want you to figure that out on your own. To choose a story you want to tell and work your magic. Because even if you've forgotten, I remember how beautifully you can write."

I turn my head and look out the window, following the cars driving down the street with my eyes. So many daring and ambitious thoughts swirl inside my head, it makes me dizzy.

Kai always keeps me on my toes, testing my abilities. He always encourages me and tries to motivate me to do more, to *be* more. He knows I'm hiding my true self behind lighthearted articles about art exhibitions, new restaurants, and local events. He's giving me the chance to show what kind of journalist I can be. To prove not just to anyone, but to myself that I can be the person I've always aspired to be. Someone who can make people feel every emotion with just my words.

That I can be an author one day.

Bringing my gaze back to Kai, I nod. A smile breaks over his lips, and he leans back, relaxing into his seat. "Fucking finally."

I laugh, shaking my head. "What happened to your 'no swearing in the office' rule?"

"My best journalist finally agreed to do what I've wanted her to do for months. I'm ready to do a happy dance right now, Nevaeh."

"That would be quite a sight. I'm sure some of the girls would do anything to see it."

Kai arches an eyebrow, and that's all it takes for me to understand that I'm walking on thin ice. He acts like my friend on so many occasions, but he's still my boss. I better remember that.

"Sorry, I got carried away." I start collecting my things and slowly stand up from my chair. "Can I go now?"

"Of course. Sorry for keeping you late." Kai stands up as well, grabbing his laptop from the table. "I've been meaning to ask, but haven't had the chance: Are you and that developer still together?"

"Why?"

"He usually waits for you after work, bringing you flowers or coffee at lunch. I haven't seen him in a while."

Kai and I walk out of the conference room and stroll down the hallway. I peer at my boss, craning my neck a little. I swear, every man in my life lately makes me feel short...because they are all so darn tall.

"We broke up."

"Why? If you don't mind me asking."

"Travis is a good guy; he's just not the one for me." I stop at the door to my office and put my hand on the doorknob. "It's for the best."

My boss pauses too, looking at me calmly. "If you think so, then I'm happy for you." Kai nods and walks down the hallway to his own office. "Bye, Nevaeh."

Walking to my car, I keep my eyes glued to my phone. I've been texting with Angie about lunch tomorrow, trying to decide where to go. She wants to know everything about Roman and me, and I've avoided talking about it at all costs. At least until I see her.

Roman isn't some dirty secret. He's not a conquest either. Whatever this is between us it feels larger than life. And I'm here for it...as long as he is too.

I quickly slip my phone into my purse and take out my car keys. Looking up, I freeze in my tracks. Travis is leaning on my car, his hands hidden in his pockets.

"Travis?" I mutter, clearing my throat. "Hey. What are you doing here?"

My ex pushes himself off of my car and pads over to me, stopping within arm's reach. I frown, shifting a little to create more distance between us. For some reason, seeing him now makes me anxious. A chill runs down my spine, and it takes a toll on me to force a smile on my face.

"Another late meeting?" he asks with a bored expression on his face.

"Yeah, um, Kai wanted to discuss our December edition."

"Your boss has always been *awfully* fond of you," he remarks, his eyes boring into mine.

Pinching my eyebrows together, I tsk, feeling anger overwhelm me. I don't like his implication. "He's not just my boss. Kai is my friend. We just talked about my assignment." I cross my arms over my chest. Travis was never like this when we were together, and it's confusing me. I didn't think he was the jealous type. "Why are you here?"

Travis narrows his eyes, scowling. He shuffles his feet, the sound rattling around the parking garage. He's aggravated, and it shows. His body language is tense and stiff.

"Whose car did you get into yesterday?" he blurts.

My mouth opens, and no sound follows. With how far away Roman parked, there's no way Travis could've seen him. Unless...he followed me outside.

"A car?"

"A BMW X4," Travis states. "Whose car is it? And please, Nevaeh, don't tell me it was Uber. I won't believe it."

"It wasn't an Uber." I fake a laugh. "My car wouldn't start, so I asked a friend to give me a ride."

Travis furrows his brow, his eyes full of distrust. "I've known you for over a year, and none of your friends have such a fancy car." He tilts his head, his teeth are deep into his bottom lip. "Maybe Drake, but he drives a Lexus..." Travis mumbles.

"It's—"

"One of Drake's teammates? The one you always watched during the California Thunders games we went to?" He steps closer, hovering over me. "That Russian dude. I don't remember his name. Was it his car?"

"Of course not. Why would Roman give me a ride?"

Silence hangs between us. I stand my ground, trying to act nonchalant. But the tiniest doubt forms in my chest, and the longer Travis keeps quiet, the bigger it grows. I always knew if the truth about my marriage to Roman came out, Travis would be hurt. But lying to his face would make it a thousand times worse.

When he finally breaks the silence, hurt drips from every word. "Did you leave me because you met someone else?"

"Travis, no, please don't think that." I take a step closer and let my hands fall to my sides. "I broke up with you because I realized that we're very different. I'm not the right person for you. But there wasn't anyone else. I swear."

His gaze drifts from my face to something behind my back, and then he focuses on me again. "What about now? Are you seeing someone now?"

"No," I lie, hating myself for how easily the word slips out of my mouth.

Travis sighs and lowers his head, staring at his feet. "I'm sorry, Nevaeh. This is wrong. I'm acting like a jealous ass, and I have no right to. Waiting for you, demanding an explanation..." He looks up, and our eyes meet. "I guess our breakup affected me more than I thought.

It's messing with my head, and I act like a damn stalker. Sorry. It won't happen again. I promise."

"Thank you, Trav."

"I better go. Happy is all alone, and...Bye, Nev."

Storming past me, Travis hurries away, disappearing behind a corner. I stand still, my heart beating violently against my rib cage. With trembling hands, I unlock my car and quickly slide inside. I can only hope my lies won't come back to bite me in the ass.

Roman

TWENTY-FIVE

lying to myself

"God, I hate this!"

I close the front door of my apartment and slowly walk toward the living room. I fix my gym bag's strap hanging over my shoulder. The muscles in my back are stiff, and I'm fucking dying from how sore my whole body is. Practice was awesome, but what I lifted in the gym after is the reason I feel like shit.

I'm craving a hot shower with all my soul.

I stop in the doorframe, watching Nevaeh on the couch. She pouts, her eyes glued to her laptop. Stepping further into the room, I put my gym bag on the floor and pad over to her. Her gaze darts to me just as I lower myself on the couch beside her.

"Hey," I say with a smile. "What happened?"

"Hey." She leans over and gives me a quick peck on the lips. "Remember I told you about that assignment my boss gave me two weeks ago?" I nod, draping a hand over her shoulder and pulling her to my side. "Well, I still haven't figured out what to write, and he keeps asking about it. At the office. Over the phone. In emails."

"That's very boss-like behavior, no? Coach always roasts us if we promise something and then don't do it."

Nevaeh laughs heartily. "You're right, and I know that about Kai. He's always like that. Very persistent when he wants work to be done. It's just...the third email this week, and like the sixth in two weeks."

"What do you mean?" I frown, dipping my head to get a better look at her face.

"I started replying to an email from Penny, my coworker. And then I saw an email from Kai, from yesterday...already opened, but I never read it." She huffs, her bottom lip protruding. "It's so weird. Like I'd ever open an email from Kai and forget about it. It's not annoying spam; it's an email from my boss."

"Does anyone have access to your email?"

"No."

"Then maybe it's a glitch?" I offer, and she bursts out laughing.

"A glitch that doesn't want me to read emails from my boss?"

"Something like that."

Nevaeh relaxes into my embrace, a happy smile on her lips. She looks up, her eyes meeting mine. "How was practice?"

"Awesome. As usual." I lift my shoulder in a shrug. "I love being on the ice. Even if I feel like a bulldozer ran me over after."

"Is that how you feel right now?" Her eyebrows pull together, and concern crosses her features.

"A little bit. I've been dreaming about a hot shower."

Tilting her head to the side, she bites her bottom lip. Her fingers are rapping over her closed laptop. Something is on her mind, and I secretly hope it's showering with me. It would be perfect. A hot shower with this insanely hot girl. I'll be one hundred percent better the second her warm pussy wraps around my cock.

"Tell you what." She pushes her laptop across the couch. "I'm tired, and my workday technically ended two hours ago. I'm all for taking a shower together if you are."

I jump to my feet and extend my hand to her. Nevaeh takes it, entwining our fingers as I pull her up. I wrap my arm around her waist and haul her toward me, her chest pressed tightly to mine. In her crop top and cotton shorts, with a messy bun on top of her head and a pencil peeking through it, she looks so comfortable and so fucking cute. My lips stretch into a big smile.

"I would never say no to something like that."

Nevaeh giggles as I head to my bathroom, pulling her along behind me. I don't know how to describe what's happening to me. It's like my muscles aren't so tight anymore. My lungs are full of air. And even my heart beats steadily, pumping blood into my veins and warming my skin.

I look over my shoulder, my gaze dropping to my SpongeBob tattoo. Optimistic. That's how I feel. It's so unusual for me, but it reminds me of my brother. Easygoing, music always in his earbuds, ready to have fun whenever. And always berating me for being so grumpy, especially with new people.

"Roman?" I raise my eyes to Nevaeh as we enter the bathroom. "You look so lost in thought. Is something on your mind?"

"Just memories." Whirling around, I face her, my hand secure around her waist. "What are we going to do first? Fuck or shower?"

"Fuck," she whispers, standing on her tiptoes. "Then shower, and then...I'm going to give you a massage."

"Massage?" I lower my head, my lips barely touching hers.

"The best in the world. And exclusively for you."

"I like the sound of that, Malyshka," I say. Then I crash my lips on hers, my whole body humming from just one kiss.

It's official, I found my new fix...it's her.

THE MORNING LIGHT peeks through closed curtains, the shadows it casts moving over the ceiling. I inhale, hiding my nose in Nevaeh's hair. She's still asleep, and I don't want to wake her up. It's early; even her alarm hasn't gone off yet. Plus, it feels incredibly nice to have her warm body pressed against mine, her head resting on my chest.

I'm getting used to falling asleep and waking up with her in my bed. It feels natural, normal. Her presence helps me sleep through the night, and not just because I'm exhausted after sex, but because she calms my storm. With her around, my disturbing thoughts are quieter. The pain of losing Maks dulls. It's not like it doesn't hurt anymore—of course it does. It's just that more and more memories resurface in my head. Happy, precious memories, ones I've been trying to push away, afraid I couldn't handle my grief. Remembering my brother, cherishing the time I got to spend with him, protecting all the little things I have that remind me of him.

Something I wasn't able to do until she stepped into my life.

Nevaeh stirs. I tighten my hold on her, pressing her closer to my chest. It feels so fucking good, I don't want to leave my bed. Unfortunately, my selfish wishes mean shit. The team is flying to Texas today to play our first neutral-site preseason game tomorrow. My excitement mingles with my disappointment. I want this sweet girl to come with me.

Tol'ko eto nevozmozhno[1].

"What time is it?" she whispers, moving her palm across my chest and resting it on my heart.

"Six a.m. It's too early. You can sleep some more."

She props herself up and rests her chin on my chest, her eyes traveling around my face. I reach over and push a few strands of hair off her face, gently caressing her skin. A smile spreads over her lips, and I smile back. *It's so easy with her.* So familiar. As if I've known her for years.

"Where did you get this scar?" Nevaeh asks, her index finger tracing a scar on my chin. It's an old one, barely visible, and still she noticed.

"I had a very eventful youth."

Wriggling out of my embrace, she slowly sits up and straddles my legs, her hands on my chest. I drag my eyes down her naked breasts and her toned stomach, feeling sizzling heat spread over my body. My tongue darts out of the corner of my mouth, and I lick my bottom lip. I want her. Just as much as I did before, if not more. *Hotya zachem ya vru sebe*[2]*?* My desire is definitely stronger now.

"What happened?" she asks again, a playful smile on her lips.

---

1. Только это невозможно. — Just it's impossible.
2. Хотя зачем я вру себе? — Though why am I lying to myself?

"I got into a fight after a school dance when I was fourteen. Some guy didn't like that his girl was flirting with me. Somehow, it ended up being my fault." I shrug, gripping her hips with my hands. "I broke his nose, and he cut me with his keys in return."

Nevaeh shakes her head and glances to her left, grabbing my right hand and lifting it. "Where did you get these ones?" She points at the scars on the back of my right hand. Three tiny, white lines.

I chuckle. "I was home alone, and somehow, when I went out on the balcony, the door locked behind me. The weather was mild for early December, but I was only in shorts and a tee. After a short debate, I decided that it would be more expensive for my parents to replace the front door, since it was locked from the inside, than glass on the balcony door."

"You smashed the glass?"

"I did," I confirm. "Though I made a mistake. Instead of hitting the glass at the top, I smashed it right in the middle. The shards of glass cut my skin, and my father had to come home and take me to the hospital. I needed stitches."

With a dip of her head, she knits her eyebrows together. "Your father? That's the first time you've mentioned him. I kinda assumed he wasn't a part of your life."

"He's dead."

Nevaeh squeezes my hand. "I'm so sorry. What happened?"

I close my eyes, clenching my jaw. How do I explain to her that my father was so unhappy that I was the one who didn't die that he drank himself to death? His words are still fresh in my head, even after four years. *It should've been you*, he said. *Maks had such a bright future ahead of him, and now it's you...living his dreams and getting everything he deserved.*

Eto dolzhen byl byt' ya...[3]

"Roman." Her soft voice is quiet. Opening my eyes, I see Nevaeh's beautiful face. She towers over me, bending down to wipe away the tears from the corners of my eyes. "I'm really, really sorry.

3. Это должен был быть я... — It should've been me...

Just know that I'm here for you. Whether you want to talk about it or not. I'm always here."

"I'll tell you about him...just not today, okay?" I say hoarsely. My throat is dry. "It always messes with my head, and I don't think I can handle it. Not when I need to play."

"Whenever you're ready." Nevaeh kisses my lips, then leans away and tucks her hair behind her ears. "I wish I could go with you."

"Me too." I extend my hand and catch a lock of her hair between my fingers. "When I first met you, your hair had pink in it. Why did you change it? It suited you."

Nevaeh's eyes widen, and her mouth opens slightly. "I didn't think you remembered."

"About you? I remember everything," I tell her. "Even the conversation you tried to have with me at Drake's birthday. About Cooper's favorite toy. How you unintentionally threw it away, and you thought he hated you."

Her head lolls back, and my bedroom fills with her melodic laughter. "I wanted to talk to you, and you kept ignoring me. Coming up with something quick after we accidentally ended up in Angie's kitchen together wasn't easy."

"It was hilarious. Though you confused the hell out of me because it was so random." I snort, twirling her hair around my index finger. "Why did you stop dyeing your hair, Malyshka?"

"I didn't just get rid of the pink in my hair. I fundamentally changed my entire wardrobe. It's all black and white now."

"Why?"

Nevaeh takes a deep breath, holding my gaze. "I was unhappy. Lost. I didn't know what to do to make things better, so I changed my style...completely."

I sit up and wrap my arms around her waist. Our eyes lock. "Are you happy now?"

"Yes."

"Do you feel lost?" I ask, moving my hands up to gently massage her tits.

"Not anymore." Nevaeh sighs loudly, winding her hands around my shoulders.

"Good."

I put my hand on the back of her neck and draw her to me for a kiss. There's definitely a silver lining to waking up so early—even if I need to fly halfway across the country, I still have time to fuck my gorgeous wife.

The thought sizzles right through me, causing my heartbeat to go insane. This marriage isn't real. It's temporary. *I don't want this to turn into something more.*

Another lie I'm telling myself.

Nevaeh

TWENTY-SIX

next time, wear mine

I THROW A BALL TO COOPER AND WATCH HIM RACE AFTER it down the hallway. I smile; the joy I feel makes my body buzz with excitement. Today is the first game of the season, and I'm going, but not just as a hockey fan. Not just as Angie's friend either. I'll be there cheering for my man, and I hope with all my might that the California Thunders win. I know it will make Roman happy, and that means I'll be happy too. For him.

At this point, I'd sell my soul to the devil if it would bring my favorite grin to his lips. The one where the corner of his mouth quirks up, a barely visible dimple on his cheek. It's a half smile. Hesitant. As if he's afraid to be happy, as if it's a crime. He's so wrong about that. Roman deserves to be happy, to have more reasons to smile. If only he could see himself the way I do...

"Coop," a child's voice says, and I look down to see Layla's daughter, Maya, stop beside me. Her tiny arm wraps around my leg. My insides feel fuzzy and warm, and there's a cheerful beam on my lips. Giddiness fills me to the brim. I never really hung around kids until Angie and Drake started dating. I preferred the company of adults and kept my distance from people with children. That changed pretty quickly after I got to spend time with Maya, and later with Ava's kids, Michael and Meghan. I'd been missing out on so much fun.

"You want to play with Coop?" I ask. Maya looks up and nods, her little ponytail bouncing up and down.

Kneeling to her, I wind my hands around her and lift her, pressing her close to my chest. Her tiny palm rests on my collarbone, and she smiles at me shyly. Her chocolate brown eyes peer at me from behind her pink-framed glasses. She's such a cute girl, with puffy lips and an upturned nose. She reminds me of her mom, with the exception of her brown hair, which she got from her father. At least, that's what Layla said once, or more like let slip, because "that man doesn't even deserve to be talked about."

It hurt to hear her say that. Not only because Maya is wonderful and that douchebag is a fool for abandoning them, but because it resonated with me…and I felt seen. My parents never needed me. I had everything I wanted except their attention. Damn if I wasn't yearning for them to notice me. For them to love me and be proud of me. It felt like I was a necessary step in the progression of their marriage, a milestone to be achieved, but never truly their daughter.

So, afraid of opening old wounds, I avoided people with kids. I'd see the parents' love for their children and regret how my own family treated me. Maybe that's why I'm so attached to Maya now, because in a way I see myself in her.

"Coop!" I call out, and the Doberman runs toward me, the ball between his teeth. He lets me take the toy from him, and I give it to Maya. "Throw the ball, baby. He'll bring it back to us."

Her small fingers curl around the ball, and she takes it from me. Maya smiles as she throws it. It lands pretty close to us, but it still has Cooper fumbling as he dashes to catch it. Maya's giggles reverberate through my body, and I can't help but laugh too.

We play some more and only stop when Angie comes to remind me that we're leaving in twenty minutes. I pet Cooper, patting the fur between his ears, and then go to the living room. Maya is still in my arms, her fingers playing with my locks.

"You look so cozy together. Any chance I can convince you to work as my nanny?" Layla jokes. She's sitting on the couch, a mug of coffee between her palms.

"Sorry, but I love my job a little too much." I glance at Maya and start smiling from ear to ear. She's so adorable. "But I wouldn't mind watching her for a weekend. I'm sure it would be amazing."

"Oh, I'll definitely take you up on that offer. I haven't gone out in an eternity," Layla says, her gaze sliding to her daughter. Her features soften, and she leans over and places her mug on the table. "Did she try to take her glasses off?"

"No. We were too busy playing with Coop."

"Thank God." Layla sighs, looking up at the ceiling. "Some days, it's a nightmare. I put them on, and she takes them off. Over and over and over. Dr. Reece said it's the only way to help her without surgery. Too bad she's too small to understand how important they are."

"But if she were older, surgery would've been the only way," Angie says, returning to the room. She's in a black dress with red flowers that flows freely from her waist. Her baby bump is still noticeable, and she looks incredibly cute with her hair collected into a high ponytail, a red ribbon securing it. She has always given me a feeling of comfort, but now it's a thousand times stronger, surrounding me with warmth and peacefulness.

"I know." Layla stands up from the couch and takes Maya's sippy cup from the small wooden table. "I just love to complain from time to time—or more like always." She comes closer and extends the cup to her daughter. "Do you want to drink your juice, baby? We're going to your uncle's game soon."

Maya takes the sippy cup and starts to drink, her eyes dancing between her mom and me. A big, open smile blooms on her lips, and she points her cup at me. "Nev."

"Yes, this is Nevaeh, sweetheart," Layla says. "And she's going to the game with us."

"I wanna sit with her." Maya clutches my T-shirt, grasping my hair in her little fist along with it. I wince and jerk slightly to my left. Her hand holding the sippy cup shakes, and the next thing I know, her juice spills all over my tee.

"Jesus!" Layla exclaims, grabbing the cup away from her daughter. "Nev, I'm so sorry."

"It's fine, don't worry." I let her take Maya from me and look down at my chest. It's nothing serious, and it'll be easy to get rid of the stain, but it's so stinking wet.

"You can take something from my closet. Anything you want." Angie walks over to me. "A dress, another tee, or maybe a hoodie."

I pinch my eyebrows together, biting the inside of my cheek. An idea of what I want to borrow from her closet sparks in my head. It's kinda risky, but at the same time, it's exciting. Possessive Roman is my favorite.

"Can I borrow one of your jerseys?" I ask.

Angie stares at me for a moment, and then wholehearted laughter springs from her lips. "You do realize your man will be pissed if he sees you in Drake's jersey?"

"Counting on it, actually."

"You're a bad girl, Nev. Distracting your man at his first game of the season," she giggles. "It'll be fun to see how Roman reacts."

Winking at the girls, I turn around and head out of the living room with Angie in tow. A delicious thrill forms in my abdomen, and I can't help but think about what Roman is going to do to me once we're home.

His dominance in the bedroom is something I've only seen glimpses of, but I want to experience it firsthand. He's been holding himself back, but I want him to let loose. And soon.

Roman might be surprised how well my wild side fits his.

THE ARENA IS BUZZING with excitement. Thunderous music echoes off the walls and spreads through the crowd. People are talking and laughing, discussing the teams' starting lineups. I hear the chatter, but it doesn't hold my attention. The teams are on the ice for warm-ups, and my eyes instantly find Roman as I go down the stairs to our seats, holding hands with Maya.

She hasn't left my side since we got in the car. The moment we stepped into the arena, her mom was on my back, reminding me to stop carrying Maya everywhere. She's two, and she walks just fine on her own...but that doesn't mean she should. I'm enjoying my time with her to the fullest.

"Mom said you're Roman's wife." I still a little, glancing to my right and seeing Michael catch up with Maya and me. Ava and Colton's son is a combination of them both, but the deep brown eyes that are studying me now definitely come from his dad.

"I am."

Michael's eyebrows pinch together, and his lips part as if he wants to say something. "But you were..." he mutters, and then he meets my eyes. "Roman is awesome, and you're kinda cool too."

"Thank you." A compliment from a six-year-old? Priceless.

Michael nods and looks away, his cheeks reddening. With a look of concentration on his face, he rushes down the stairs and straight to the plexiglass to watch the teams warm up. Chuckling, I follow him, not even trying to listen to what Angie, Layla, and Ava are talking about behind me. My gaze is glued to the ice, and I easily find Roman. The number 21 on his back makes me think back to the jersey hanging on the wall in the living room. Now I know it's a tribute to his brother; the M letter means Maksim. But why 24 and 21? Was there some meaning behind those numbers? Or were they just random?

I make a mental note to ask Roman about it. He's like a riddle. One I'm trying to solve, figuring out more and more details about him. It's exhilarating and exciting. Because every new revelation opens doors to more secrets, to more things for me to discover. And I can't get enough of it. Or him.

Stopping behind Michael, I take Maya in my arms and look around the ice. The Vegas team is warming up on the opposite side of the rink. They are one of the best in the league, and I've read articles saying that the Thunders will have a very difficult first home game. The odds aren't really in our favor either, but I still hope for the best.

"Dad!" Michael yells, waving his hand to catch his dad's attention. Colton's head snaps in our direction, and I see a smile creep onto his lips as he nods to his son.

I spot Drake near Colton; they're taking turns shooting pucks into the net. I point at Drake and tell Maya, "Look, baby, there's your Uncle Drake."

Maya leans forward and presses her palms to the plexiglass, a giddy smile on her face. "Drake!"

I cuddle her to my chest. Her hair smells like strawberries, and I hide my nose in it. Happiness overwhelms me, like the waves of a tsunami, and a big smile crosses my face as I continue watching Colton and Drake. Michael blabbers about the players from the Vegas team, explaining their strengths and weaknesses. I listen absentmindedly, lost in the moment.

But then someone races right in front of the plexiglass where we're standing, and I'm momentarily distracted. It's Roman. He skates incredibly fast, a puck dancing on his stick.

"He's practicing stickhandling," Michael says to me, a lopsided grin on his face. "But he's also showing off."

"Is that so?" I ask, and Michael starts laughing, looking absolutely pleased with himself.

"Hundred percent."

"Good to know," I murmur, my eyes trained on Roman, who's coming closer to us again.

His gaze finds mine, and I see a fire spark behind his irises. Letting his eyes coast over me, he frowns. Tilting his head to the side, he raises his hand and makes a twirling motion.

He wants to see whose jersey I'm wearing.

With a smirk, I turn around and show him my back, which has Drake's number and last name on it. I look over my shoulder, and before Roman hurries away again, I get a chance to notice how his lips purse.

Looks like my plan is working.

For the next ten minutes, we continue watching the players warm up. More and more people fill the arena. Layla comes over and stands beside me, while Angie and Ava with her daughter, Meghan, sit in our seats and talk.

"It's time," Michael says, and I realize he's right. The teams are starting to leave the ice.

I'm ready to go to my seat, but in my peripheral vision, I notice Roman skate toward me. My heart instantly goes pitter-patter, my pulse pumping so hard I'm worried my veins are going to explode.

Layla sees Roman too, and with a smile, she takes Maya from me and turns to look at Ava's son. "Let's go, Michael. Roman and Nev need a moment alone."

Even without Layla, Maya, and Michael, I'm surrounded by so many people. There's no place to hide so Roman can tell me what he wants to tell me in private. But, strangely, it doesn't matter.

"Shouldn't you be heading to the locker room?" I joke once he stops in front of me.

"Shouldn't you be wearing my jersey?" he counters, not wasting a minute of his time.

"This one looks—"

"I dare you to say it looks good on you, Malyshka. Say it. You'll find out what it means to be on my bad side." Roman glances to the left and realizes he's the last one on the ice.

"It looks good on me," I taunt, not giving a damn that the woman beside me is listening to our conversation.

Roman shakes his head and backs away. "You better pray we win tonight, Nevaeh. I won't be in the mood for games if we lose. And next time—"

"What?"

"Next time, wear mine," he says in a low growl. Then he rushes off the ice without glancing back.

And now I'm not sure I want the Thunders to win anymore. *Getting punished by my husband sounds way too intriguing*, I think to myself as I sit down beside Angie.

It's something he hasn't done before.

Roman

TWENTY-SEVEN

a coward

WE LOST.

We fucking lost our first home game of the regular season.

We were losing two to one until Colton had a moment at the end of the second period and scored a perfect snap shot, tying the game. It gave us all a great boost of confidence, and made the fans go berserk. The arena was so loud, I didn't even hear what my teammates were saying as we celebrated. We had a chance to win—until Järvinen from the Vegas team scored again. Two minutes before the third period ended, making the final score three to two.

I'm fucking furious.

"Were you trying to break the record for most minutes in the sin-bin?" Drake asks me as we finish getting dressed.

I ignore him. It's better if I keep my thoughts to myself. No one is going to like it if I run my mouth and say things I'll regret later. It's not the first game we've lost. Not the first loss in my whole damn career. It's just that some hit harder than others, and this one hit hard.

In Minsk time, it's already my father's birthday, and I desperately wanted to win tonight. To prove to him that he was wrong about me. Wherever he is, I wanted him to know that I was a talented player after all. Someone he always underestimated. The feeling of anxiety he induced in me, constantly pitting me and Maks against each other, never leaves my fucking head. Even though he's dead.

A dead man plays on my nerves. His memory makes me doubt myself. A fucking ghost has power over my emotions, and the only feeling I have for him now is hate.

Grief, guilt, and self-loathing. The pillars my whole personality is built upon.

"You busted Karlsson's lip pretty good." Drake tries again, stepping closer to me. "He deserved it for checking Crawford into the board."

"*Ya znayu*[1]," I grit through my teeth, buttoning my shirt.

"Benson." Colton's voice sounds stern. "Leave him alone."

I glance to my right and meet Thompson's eyes. He's watching me with his eyebrows pulled together. I mouth *thanks*, and he nods. We're different, but we're so alike in some ways it's scary. Broken people always see each other in a crowd. It's like a sign we wear on our foreheads. *Come and say hi; I'm fucked up just like you are*. A sign I would love to ditch, to find something constant that would mend my heart and ease my pain. Someone who will embrace my chaos and bring peace to my exhausted soul, just like Ava did for Colt.

Just like Nevaeh does for me.

Her name flashes in my brain, and I ball my fists. I didn't tell her about my father's birthday and what this game means to me...and she fucking came dressed in Benson's jersey. I have no right to be angry with her for that, but damn if it didn't make my blood boil even more.

"It was still a great game." A voice from my left reaches my ears, and I turn my head to look at Clay. He's sitting on the bench, fully dressed and juggling a bottle of water. "And you played really well, Roman."

Am I suddenly in some sort of support group?

"Thanks," I reply curtly. I close my eyes, cringing at how bitter I sound.

---

1. Я знаю — I know

Hockey is a team sport, and I shouldn't act like a sore loser. I don't blame my teammates, because Clay is right—we did our best. It just so happened that our opponent was a bit stronger and a bit luckier. And we can all act like crybabies, like I am now, or we can suck it up, let our loss soak in, and do better next time. It's not the end of the world.

I turn around and look at my teammates. The corner of my mouth lifts into a crooked grin. "Sorry, guys; I'm acting like an asshole." Chuckles of approval follow my words, and my lips ease into an open smile. "We played well tonight no matter what."

"True," Coach says as he steps into the room. He looks worn out, and I feel sympathetic toward him. Doing the postgame interview after the team lost at home isn't pleasant. "We did a great job. Vegas used their opportunities in some key moments, and that's something we will work on." His gaze drifts to me, and his crystal blue eyes bore into mine. "And maybe keep our tempers under control, eh?"

With a jerk of my head, I hide my hands in my pants pockets. "Sure..."

"What was that, Pashkevich? It was like you nodded in agreement but also shook your head no."

"Kinda." I shrug.

Coach rolls his eyes. "At least you're honest, *da*[2]?"

"*Da*," I confirm, and the locker room erupts into laughter.

Coach keeps talking about the team's performance tonight, about his expectations for our next game, and also what he wants us to work on during practice. I fold my arms over my chest and listen absentmindedly. Looks like I still know how to pretend to be okay. My teammates and coach don't even realize I'm hiding demons behind this carefree demeanor.

It's better this way. My problems are mine alone; no one else needs to deal with them.

---

2. Да — Yes

I GET in the car and turn the volume up, and my brother's playlist starts playing. I haven't listened to it a lot since I moved to the US, mostly because sometimes it's harder for me to remember English words if I spend hours with Russian music in the background. But today it's the only thing I can count on to bring me some solace.

Max Korzh's "Optimist" blasts through the speakers, and I smile involuntarily. This was Maksim's favorite song, and the reason for my tattoo. Another dedication to my twin.

God, our father hated that we'd watch *SpongeBob SquarePants*. He'd tell us that it was the stupidest cartoon he'd ever seen, and that we would be just like its characters if we continued wasting our time on it. Little did he know how much that show helped us, relaxing our brains after practice and keeping us from worrying about anything. It was fun, light, and really ridiculous, but I think that was exactly why Maks and I loved it. We only stopped watching it when Alisa came into his life.

A wave of memories unexpectedly smacks me in the face. Horrid memories, ones I've tried to keep under wraps, are flooding my brain. It's like one second there's a light rain, but then it turns into a thunderstorm, flooding everything in its wake. My brother's image pops into my head, and my chest constricts. I see him so clearly, it's like he's right beside me in the car. My words from that night zip through my mind, and I clutch the steering wheel tighter.

"Maks, it's not worth it. Why can't you wait? If she's gonna spread her legs for him again, what can you possibly do about it? Just talk to her tomorrow."

He pales. His eyes, which are just like mine, stare at me as if I just slapped him across his face. He sets his jaw hard. "I want to see her."

"Polnaya huinya[3]*." I shake my head. "Why? Alisa's been using you and her ex for months. She tells you one thing and does the other. There are so many other girls who are more beautiful and way better than her. She's just worthless—"*

---

3. Полная хуйня (cuss word). — Total bullshit.

Maks steps into me, grabbing my tee in his fist. "Another word, and I won't care that you're my brother."

I stare at him, anger filling my every pore. "Whatever," I tell him and break free from his hold. "If you want to be an idiot, be an idiot. I'm done here."

Turning on my heel, I stalk away from Maksim. Disappointment slips into my veins, and I ball my fists hard. My knuckles are itching to hit something. Or someone. Anything to keep from bottling up these emotions.

"Roma," my brother calls out to me. I stop in my tracks and wheel around to look at him. "Poydem so mnoy? Pozhaluysta[4]."

I purse my lips in a tight line, my annoyance growing stronger. He's become such a pussy since they started dating. I hate it. "You'll be fine."

My eyes roam over his face, and I notice how tense he looks. How miserable. But I ignore it. I'm too damn furious with him. He's in charge of his own life, and if he wants to spend it running after a girl who doesn't give a damn about him, that's his problem.

Without another word, I walk away. So proud of myself that I'm not like him.

"You know, I really hope you fall in love one day, so you can finally understand how I feel," Maks yells after me. "And I hope she breaks your fucking heart, because that's what you deserve."

I laugh out loud and continue walking toward the club where our friends are. He can say whatever the fuck he wants. I'll never be like him.

Ever.

The sound of tires screeching brings me back to reality. The black Range Rover to my left is trying to stop the car and avoid hitting mine. *Blyat'*[5]. I step on the gas with all my might, speeding up and avoiding the crash by a hair.

Without stopping or even slowing down, I drive away from this damned intersection. The honking of cars grows more and more

---

4. Пойдем со мной? Пожалуйста. — Come with me. Please.
5. Блять. — Fuck.

distant until I don't hear anything except the music still booming in my car.

My heart is going crazy, and I can barely breathe. *It's back.* The ugly truth of what really happened that night between Maksim and me. Something I've tried for seven years to forget, and something that will always be the reason why I can't let go. The reason I feel guilty for living. The reason I hate myself to the fucking core.

I turned my back on the most important person in my life simply because I didn't like the girl he loved. Because I didn't think his feelings were valid and his hurt wasn't reason enough for me to drop everything and support him. She was just a girl. One I didn't think was a good match for him. Why bother?

The answer was so obvious, but I was too ignorant to see it then. He needed company, and he asked me to go with him. Maybe he needed support in order to finally put an end to their relationship. I didn't fucking know what was on his mind, because I left him on his own. I betrayed him, and he turned to the only person who was always there for both of us. To Kirill. Even if Maks knew how drunk our friend was.

Something hot leaks down my cheek, and I wipe it away with my fingertips. Tears. Fucking tears spill out of my eyes, blurring my vision. I hurriedly park my car, unbuckle my seat belt, and start to bawl. The music drowns out my sobs, my shoulders shaking. I hide my face in my hands and let the tears flow.

Ya trus[6]. A coward. I never told my mom about that conversation. No one knows. Not even the fancy therapists I saw. I was too scared Mom would be just like Dad, that she would despise me for what I did once I opened up to her.

And I couldn't stand another parent hating me...so I started hating myself. For her and me both. Because that's what I deserve.

Today. Tomorrow. Always.

Broken people carry their problems like a shield, hiding behind their trauma. I know, because that's who I am.

---

6. Я трус. — I'm a coward.

Day by day, I've been mentally destroying myself, until it became my whole personality. My hurt buried itself so deep that even carving into my flesh won't help to get rid of it. The pain became a routine. And there's nothing I can do to change it.

Part of me died that night. My heart broke, and it was the loudest sound I've ever heard. It still echoes in my head, because I never recovered.

These broken pieces will never heal, and they'll cut anyone who gets too close. They're always there, pushing everyone to keep their distance, since it's safer...

I sit up straight and lower my hands from my face. My eyebrows draw together as I look out the window. With a surprise, I realize that I'm in the parking lot of my apartment building. I didn't even notice how I got here.

The thought begins to pulsate in my head. My brother's last words sneak up on me, and I'm unable to stop myself from falling down the rabbit hole.

There's someone who refuses to back down. Someone who thinks she can fix me. She's waiting for me at home...and I'm so fucked up.

Nevaeh

TWENTY-EIGHT

never

Where is Roman?

The question is like an annoying ad that keeps popping up. I mentally close it and try to distract myself by watching *How to Lose a Guy in 10 Days*—but then it's back again, flashing in my head like a freaking strobe light. It's been three hours since the game ended, and he's still not home.

Did something happen?

I take my phone from the couch, check it again, and put it down. No messages, no calls. Sure, I could call him myself, but wouldn't that seem needy? I don't want him to think that I can't spend even a few hours without him. Because I can...just not now.

Something about the way he looked as he left the ice made my heart clench in my chest. His features were dark, like the sky on a stormy day. I didn't even see a ghost of a smile, but what weirded me out was how he avoided eye contact with anyone from his team. Anger was bubbling inside him, it was so clear and so disturbing. Yet there was more, and I'm not sure I interpreted it right.

Was it resentment?

I tense as I hear the door opening and closing. Biting my bottom lip, I glue my gaze to the TV. My plan is to act as nonchalant as possible, to not let him see how much I'm worried about him.

His steps are slow. I bite my bottom lip, wincing from the pain that strikes right through me. For the life of me, I can't concentrate on what's happening in the movie.

"Hey," Roman says, sitting down beside me on the couch. I turn my head to look at him and instantly notice that he's keeping his distance. His elbows are on his knees, his hands locked together in front of him. "What are you watching?"

"*How to Lose a Guy in 10 Days*. It's an old rom-com," I tell him, plastering a smile on my face, even if I don't feel like smiling. "Layla watched it recently, and it made me want to rewatch it too."

"Never seen it."

"I didn't figure you'd be a rom-com lover, so I'm not surprised. It's good. I can restart if you want—"

"No." Roman stands up, slides his hands down his legs, and then pats his thighs. "I need a shower, and then I'm going to my room. I'm just going to crash. You can watch the movie. The noise won't bother me."

Pinching my eyebrows together, I gape at him in silence. Since he got back from Mexico, I haven't spent a single night in my own bed. Even while he was away I slept in his bedroom. And now he's telling me I'm not allowed in there?

"Um, Roman—"

"Night, Nevaeh." He nods and heads to the bathroom. I stare at his broad shoulders under his jacket and his narrow torso—irritation rises in my chest and climbs all the way up my neck and into my cheeks.

What the hell is going on?

The click of the door closing rips me out of my daze. I look down at my hands, noticing how my fingers are trembling. He's pissed me off big time, and this is probably the first time I've felt so angry at him. When he went to Mexico after kissing me, my anger was mixed with hurt and disappointment. It was a cocktail of emotions, but I knew how to explain what happened between us and what led him to flee to another country. Now? I have no fucking clue.

When I glance at the TV, one of my favorite moments of all time, when Matthew McConaughey's character sees Kate Hudson's character walking down the stairs in that gorgeous yellow dress, is displayed on the screen. Usually it makes me swoon, but now I'm too agitated to care.

Grabbing the remote, I quickly turn off the TV and toss it onto the coffee table. I stand up, and my eyes instantly fly to his bathroom door. It's such a bad idea, but I know myself too well. I'm not going to listen to my reasonable side. With him, there's nothing rational about how I feel. It's all pure emotion, and it consumes me like nothing ever has before.

In a few strides, I'm standing at the closed door. He might kick me out, but right now that's the least of my concerns. I want to know what's going on. I want to help.

With a deep breath, I put my hand on the doorknob and open the door wide. My gaze immediately meets his. Roman is standing in front of the mirror, his hands on either side of the sink. He's shirtless, his pants low on his hips. I'm momentarily distracted, but it fades pretty quickly. The anger flashing behind his irises sobers me up fast.

"What are you doing in here?" Roman asks.

"What happened?"

"You were at the game. We lost," he bites out, pushing himself off of the bathroom counter.

"What happened after that?" I step further into the bathroom, closing the door behind me.

"Nothing. I'm just in a bad mood."

I move forward tentatively, holding his gaze even though it's hard. The heaviness of his glare makes my steps feel like it weighs a ton. "Are you angry with me because I wore Drake's jersey?"

Roman clenches his teeth, his nostrils flaring. "I didn't like it, but it's fine; you don't owe me anything." He crosses his arms over his chest. "I'm telling you, everything is okay. My mood is just fucked up, and I want to be alone."

Swallowing the ball of nerves that climbs up my throat, I step closer and look up at him, studying his face and hoping to see my

Roman. That broken boy I've grown to like so much, it makes me wonder if it's actually love.

"Why are you pushing me away?" I whisper.

His face contorts; his carefully placed mask is dropping. His eyes darken, and his features become narrower. "Because this is wrong."

A pang of sorrow pierces my heart. He doesn't mean that. I might be delusional, might indulge in wishful thinking from time to time. But I know what we have is real. People can't control how they feel all the time, and neither can he. Especially not when he's in such a vulnerable state, with his walls down and his damaged soul exposed for me to see. I know he cares, and that he craves my company just as much as I crave his. This is stronger than anything I've ever felt, and I refuse to give up on him. On us.

"It doesn't feel wrong to me." I press my palm to his chest, right above his heart. Its violent beat echoes in my ears, sizzling through me. "It feels all kinds of right."

Roman watches me with his eyebrows pinched together. His emotional turmoil is written all over his face, and it makes my heart ache. I'd do anything for him.

Lifting his hand, he cups my cheek. His eyes are trained on my mouth as he tilts my face up to him. With a slowness that sets my body on fire, he slides his hand down my throat and wraps it around the nape of my neck.

"I don't want to hurt you," he whispers hoarsely.

"You won't."

"Nevaeh..." Roman growls, his lips hovering over mine.

"Don't call me that. I'm your...Malyshka." A smile spreads across his lips, and his hold on my neck tightens. "Talk to me, Roman."

He bends to my ear and sucks my earlobe into his mouth. "I don't want to talk now. I want to fuck...but I can't promise to be gentle."

"Who said I want you to be gentle?" I taunt. Then I press my lips to his, closing the distance between us. I'm tired of his games.

We kiss, his lips moving with mine. It's anything but slow. It's raw and passionate, consuming me completely. I'm losing myself in him, fading into this man without any regrets.

My tongue slips out of my mouth, and I trace his bottom lip with it. The saltiness I taste makes my eyes snap open. I pull away, gawking at Roman from under my furrowed brow. Has he been crying?

"Roman..." I whisper, cupping his face with my palms. "What happened?"

His eyes search mine, the crease between his eyebrows only deepening. Suddenly, he takes a step back, and my hands drop to my sides. My lips part, but my breath gets stuck in my throat when he snakes his hand around my waist, turns me around, and pulls me to his chest.

Guiding me toward the sink, he stops when my legs hit the bathroom cabinet. Our eyes meet in the reflection of the mirror, and all I see is animalistic need. His usually deep turquoise eyes look like a starless sky, dark and endless. Roman places his hands on my hips and pulls my cotton shorts down to my ankles, taking them off. I'm still in my panties, but he gets rid of those by ripping them apart. Again.

"You need to stop doing that," I scold him, breathing heavily. "Soon I won't have any underwear left."

"Maybe I don't want you"—he puts his hand on the small of my back and pins me down—"to wear any underwear around me."

His hands move gently over my sides, sliding to my hips and lower, to my thighs. The moment he bends my right leg at the knee and lifts it, placing it on the countertop, I gasp. My nipples rub against the marble, ramping my desire up to an impossible level. I got high once, in high school, and damn if being with him doesn't feel just like that.

"Be a good girl for me, Nevaeh," Roman orders, sliding his palm between my thighs and feeling how wet I am for him. "Look at yourself in the mirror while I make you come."

He gets on his knees, and all I see in the reflection are my flushed cheeks and my disheveled hair falling into my eyes. My anticipation grows stronger, and when he finally drags his tongue down my slit, I let out a loud moan. Fuck, this is everything.

Digging his fingers into my ass cheeks, he spreads me open wider. His tongue swirls around my clit, then he sucks it into his mouth and releases it with a pop. When he blows on it, it clears my head from thoughts altogether. This man...his tongue in my pussy is all I want. His strokes are long, like he's doing it on purpose, licking my pussy and fucking me with his tongue as slowly as possible. I have no idea how he expects me to look at myself in the mirror, because the pleasure is so good, I'm fucking levitating.

Roman licks and sucks, speeding up one moment and then slowing down the second I start to clench around him. He's depriving me of my orgasm, making me desperate.

"Roman, please."

"Please what, Malyshka?" he taunts. His tongue is lapping my clit so good, my eyes roll back in my head.

"Let me come," I beg. "Please, Roman."

"Will you ever wear anyone else's jersey to my game again?"

"No. Never!" I cry out. My body goes rigid for a moment, and then my orgasm takes over. It's intense, and my legs are quivering. He doesn't stop though. Fucking me with his tongue, circling his lips around my clit even through my release. He makes me see stars, and I swear it's never felt so good.

His tongue is fucking magic.

"I'm spent," I tell him as he rises to his feet and hovers over me from behind. A smile that would put the Cheshire cat to shame crosses his lips.

He unbuckles his belt and pulls it off. "Hands behind your back," he commands. I do as he tells me, obeying him without question. I feel leather wrap around my wrists, tying my hands together. "Does that hurt?"

"No." A thrill of excitement rolls down my spine; every nerve in my body comes to life.

I watch him through the reflection, my eyes locked on his handsome face. Roman takes off his pants and boxers, and once he's completely naked, he steps into me. His hard dick presses into my ass and makes me lose my mind. He rubs his cock between my ass cheeks, and I go feral for him. My mind becomes so hazy, I don't think I'd even be able to tell him my name if he asked.

Adjusting himself, he slowly pushes his hard dick into my pussy.

Inch after fucking inch. I'm full even before he's completely in. He finds a rhythm and starts pounding into me with a slowness I didn't expect. It's like he's controlling his every move, letting my pussy get used to his size.

"Fuck, Nevaeh, I love how tight you are," Roman coos, his hands firmly wrapped around my waist. "Thrusting into you till you take me whole is my favorite."

"Oh my God," I whimper when his hips slam into mine. He's balls deep inside me, and my eyes flutter closed for a second.

"You keep calling for God, Malyshka, but I'm the one who's fucking you," Roman incites me, smiling at me in the mirror. "Fuck, the way you're clenching around me...Give it to me...*Davay*[1], *Nevaeh*, come for me..."

Railing me harder and faster, he wraps his hand around my hair and lifts. My wrists are burning, but it feels so perfect everywhere, I don't even pay attention to it. A loud growl scatters from his parted lips, and his eyes close. He's coming inside me, triggering my own orgasm, and my pussy spasms around his dick.

"You feel so good," I praise him. My breaths come in ragged bursts. "You give me the best orgasms...I don't think I'll be able to walk."

When Roman stops moving, he steps back and pulls me up. Gently, he unties my wrists and drapes a hand around my waist, making me face him. Our eyes are glued to each other, locked in a world of their own. His gaze drops to my heated cheeks and down my chest, stopping at my wrists.

He frowns, curling his hand around my wrist and lifting it to his face. "You said it didn't hurt."

"It didn't." I smile, but he doesn't return it. "I was desperate to touch you, so I kept twisting my wrists. You didn't hurt me."

"Promise? You're not lying to me?" Roman lowers his head, pressing his forehead to mine.

"Never."

---

1. Давай — Give it to me

His gaze roaming over my face, he takes my chin between his thumb and index finger, making me look him in the eye. "Take a shower with me."

I nod, and he gives me the sweetest kiss.

"Will you tell me what happened?" I ask as he pulls me toward the shower stall.

"Once we're in bed," he replies. He glances at me over his shoulder. "First, I want to take care of you."

Yes, please.

Nevaeh

TWENTY-NINE

that escalated quickly

Roman's arms are wrapped tightly around me, my head resting on his chest. The pounding of his heart resonates with mine. My eyes are tearful, and I bite my bottom lip hard, hoping to stifle my sobs. Him telling me about his last conversation with his brother broke my heart. Bearing that much guilt is unimaginable. It's self-destructive and gut-wrenching. Even just the thought of him walking away from Maksim, not realizing that it would be the last time he'd see his brother alive, makes me want to cry. All over again.

I understand him better now.

"I know that no matter what I say, it won't be enough. Losing someone you love is always hard, but the guilt you carry is even more devastating. I wish I could do something to help you."

"You're already helping me," he whispers, pressing his lips to the top of my head. "I haven't talked about my past so openly with anyone before. Just you."

"That makes me so sad," I confess, sniffing. "We all need someone in our corner. Someone who will guide us and help us overcome our problems when we're struggling to do it on our own. Your mom could've been that for you, and you could've been her safe place too. Your trauma is—"

"If she knew what I said, how I turned my back on my twin, she'd never forgive me."

His words register in my head. Their meaning sinks in, and I abruptly sit up. "Your twin?"

Roman nods, his red-rimmed eyes focused on me. "I'm the older... I *was* the older one. Just three minutes older, so that's the reason for our numbers on our jerseys. I was born at 3:21 p.m., and Maks at 3:24. I always joked about it, about him being my little brother. As if he were someone who needed my support and protection, while in reality he was the mature one. More reasonable and a thousand times nicer than me. People loved him, Nevaeh, and they all have been left with me."

I scoff. "Don't say that. You make it sound as if everyone wanted you dead instead of Maksim."

"My father did." He shrugs. My jaw drops, and I don't even know what to say. "He told me it should've been me."

"What kind of father says that to their child?"

"Mine." Roman turns his head and stares at the wall, his eyes veiled with unshed tears. "Some parents love their children the same; they don't favor one over the other. My mom is like that, but my father wasn't. I was a mama's boy, and Maks was our father's son. We were fucking twins, but my dad treated me like I wasn't his. Always nitpicking. Always criticizing. The comparison game? It was the worst. By the time I was a teenager, I believed my brother was a true-born talent, while everything I had was the result of hard work, nothing else. Our father always said Maks would be the one to make him proud. That he would be an NHL legend, while I would be lucky if any KHL[1] team would want me."

"That's terrible."

"Nothing I wasn't used to."

"But it's still terrible! I know people can get used to absolute shit if it happens to them constantly, but that doesn't make it fucking right. You wouldn't say 'nothing she isn't used to' about a woman

1. Континентальная хоккейная лига (КХЛ) — Kontinental Hockey League

suffering from physical abuse, would you? Why are you trying to justify it?" I'm fuming. My neck feels hot, and I ball my fists tighter. "What about your mom? Did she think it was okay?"

Roman peers at me. The corner of his mouth lifts; his signature crooked smile plays on his lips. He slips his hand around my waist and makes me straddle his legs. "You're so cute when you're angry." His eyes slide to my chest in my new pink PJs and down to my cotton shorts. "And I'm happy to see you going back to your roots and adding more color to your wardrobe. It suits you."

I smile and tuck my hair behind my ears. "Thank you, Roman." Then I narrow my eyes and lower my face to his. "But you're changing the subject, and I don't appreciate it."

"My mom was always arguing with my father, always telling him how unfair he was to me. She filed for divorce a few months before Maks's death, and my brother and I both supported her. He didn't like how our father treated me either." His gaze becomes distant. He's looking at me, but I know he doesn't really see me. "He was a good guy, Malyshka. In every sense of the word...He was a *good* one, and he died."

"If bad things only happened to awful people, life would be so much easier," I whisper, caressing his cheek with my fingertips. "I know it doesn't feel fair, and I know it's hard for you. But you're destroying yourself, and—"

"And you sound just like my mom. *Ne nado*[2]." Roman winces, clicking his tongue loudly. He frowns and gazes at me from under furrowed brows. "You can't fix me. The sooner you understand that, Nevaeh, the better."

Let me help you. The words are tethered to the tip of my tongue, but I swallow them down and force a fake smile onto my face. "I understand," I say. "You can't save someone who doesn't want to be saved."

His pupils dilate, and his jaw hangs open. We sit here in the quiet of his room, our eyes trained on each other. I want to say so many

2. Не надо. — Don't.

things to him, but I know now is not the time. He's not ready to listen. I don't think he's ever going to let himself heal unless he finally understands that moving on doesn't mean forgetting his brother.

"My father hated me so much that he drank himself to death. He couldn't stand that I was still living, breathing...fucking existing. I was in a dark vortex after Maks's death. It was just a black hole, with no hope. No happiness. And no love. This thing"—Roman takes my hand in his and places it over his heart—"is broken. There's nothing left except grief and hate. Whatever you're trying to pour into it will leak out instantly."

I bite my bottom lip, my tears threatening to spill. "You're letting your father win."

"I'm not." He groans and hides his face in his hands. When he looks at me again, I see agony lurking behind the mask he's trying to wear. Why can't he just stop pretending with me? "I don't want to argue with you, Nevaeh. That's who I am, and who I always will be. Not every broken piece is meant to be mended."

Nodding, I slide off of his legs and plop onto my right side, hiding my hands under my pillow. I close my eyes, begging myself to stay indifferent. Reading between the lines, I know what he's been trying to tell me. He'll never love me because he's incapable of love. He will never give me what I want, will never be the man I need.

The most ridiculous thing? I don't believe him.

"Malyshka," Roman murmurs, his voice sending shivers down my spine. His hand lands on my hip as he inches closer to me, pressing his chest to my back. He hugs me tight from behind and hides his nose in my hair, nuzzling my neck. "Don't be angry with me. I hate it."

"I'm not angry. I'm disappointed."

He chuckles softly. "I still hate it."

"I know." I cover his hand on my belly with mine and thread my fingers through his. "It's late. Let's sleep, okay?"

"Okay."

I lie still, the warmth of his body lulling me to sleep. Yet my mind is agitated, and it keeps me awake. His demons aren't new to me. They are my old companions. I know better than anyone how much hate someone can hold in their heart. I've been just like him, so sure I'd never get out of the vicious circle I was in.

If it weren't for Angie, maybe I'd still be that bitter and petty version of me. She helped me when I was sure my battle was lost. She believed in me, and she never gave up on me.

And that's exactly what I'm going to do to him…even if we aren't meant to be.

"KNOCK, KNOCK." The door opens, and Kai strolls into my office. He's in a pastel pink tee and light blue jeans, his Armani watch sparkling in the rays of the setting sun. "Can I come in?"

I snort, shaking my head. "You're already in, boss."

He shrugs, unbothered. "Still needed to ask. Personal space, you know?" Kai lowers himself into the chair across from me, sets his elbows on my desk, and connects the pads of his fingers together. "I thought we were friends."

I rear back in my seat. Confusion clouds my mind as I try to figure out what he means. What could I have possibly done for Kai to come into my office when my workday is almost over and ask questions like this?

"We *are* friends," I tell him. "Why?"

"Well, you know, if I got married, I would've told you."

My face falls. I blink, opening my mouth and then closing it. Kai looks absolutely calm, studying me with his deep brown eyes. With how his lips twitch, I'm sure he finds this amusing. Unlike me. How the hell does he know?

"What do you mean?" I ask hoarsely.

Kai rolls his eyes, reaches over, and grabs a few Sour Patch Kids from the bowl on my desk. He tosses one into his mouth and says as he starts chewing, "There are a few articles going around on social media about you and someone named Roman Pashkevich. A right defenseman for the California Thunders." A big smile spreads across his lips. "And there are very cute pictures of you talking to him at the arena. A girl in her man's jersey and him skating to her before his big game starts."

"It wasn't his jersey." Goodness, why am I talking about that? It's meaningless right now.

"You went to your husband's first home game of the regular season wearing someone else's jersey?" I nod, still processing the news. How does everyone know we're married? "That's why I love you, Nevaeh. You're wild. I don't think I would've had it in me."

"Why? You would look great in a jersey," I tease, finally feeling the knots in my stomach loosen up.

Kai sticks out his tongue at me. "I didn't think you'd be into younger guys. Even if he is exactly your type: blond hair and blue eyes. Except maybe his height. Isn't he a little too big for you?"

"He's big, but it's fine," I say and notice Kai's eyes rounding. He leans forward, his mouth agape. Dammit. I cover my face with my palms, my cheeks burning hot. "I meant his height."

"Sure. His height is the reason you're as red as a tomato." My boss laughs, relaxing into his seat with one hand on his belly. "There's one thing that doesn't really make sense to me though. One of those articles quotes some anonymous source who said you got married in Vegas at the end of August. Weren't you still with Travis?"

Fuck, that escalated quickly. Though the mention of the anonymous source and our Vegas wedding make it clear how everyone found out. It must be that Emmett guy. He probably saw the pictures of me at the game and decided to spill the tea, maybe spoil the beginning of the season for Roman.

"It was after I broke up with him."

Kai arches his eyebrow, a question in his eyes. "So you broke up with your boyfriend and got married to a hockey player? Did you leave Travis for this guy?"

"Yes and no. My breakup with Travis had nothing to do with Roman. This marriage...it just happened, okay? We got married in Vegas and decided to see where it would lead us. So far, so good." I give Kai a weak smile.

My boss's gaze roams over my face, and then he starts grinning.

Clapping his hands together, Kai stands up from his seat. "You definitely look happy. I've noticed it for a while now, just thought it was from you living the single life."

"No. It's all Roman," I confirm despite my heart still aching from our talk last night.

"Does he speak to you in Russian?" Kai asks, heading to the door. "I looked him up before I came to you with questions."

"Sometimes. He calls me 'Malyshka'; I still need to google what it means." I giggle.

"I think it's 'baby'...or 'baby girl,'" Kai muses, looking thoughtful. *How does he know that?* He meets my gaze, noticing my bewildered look. "I had a few friends from Russia back in college, when I was studying in London. Still remember some of the swear words they used, but I won't try to repeat them. They're too hard to pronounce."

"You're full of surprises, Kai."

"So are you, Nevaeh." Kai winks and opens the door, heading out of my office. "You're more famous than me now."

Laughing, he closes the door behind him. I continue smiling as I pull my laptop closer to me. My fingers hover over the keyboard, but I don't move. Kai's words make their way to my brain, and panic washes over me.

Travis.

Roman

THIRTY

my fault

The ringing of my phone rips me out of my sleep. Slowly, I sit up in bed and grab it from the nightstand. Nevaeh's smiling face flashes on my screen, and I can't help but laugh. That's why she asked me to give her my phone last night? To add a picture to her contact? She's adorable.

I press my phone to my ear and fall onto my back. So much for getting a nap in before the game.

"Hey," I say.

"Hey, Roman." Nevaeh speaks in a hushed voice, and something about her tone makes me tense. Usually she's all bubbly and cheerful. "What are you doing?"

"I was taking a nap, but I have to leave for the arena soon. Today is the last game before our five-game road trip, as you know. It should go smoothly. I'd hate it if we lost after two wins."

"Um, yeah, I'd hate that too."

"Everything okay?" I ask, mentally preparing myself for her reply. I think I'm still recovering from when the news of our marriage broke six days ago. I answered so many questions, I'd love to stay silent for a few days.

"Some people will do anything for their fifteen minutes of fame," she breathes, sounding dejected.

I instantly sit up in bed, my grip on my phone tightening. "What did Travis do?"

"Travis? No, no, no. It has nothing to do with him. He's been ignoring me ever since the articles were published. I'm sure he read them." The invisible string around my throat loosens, and I take a deep breath. *Slava Bogu*[1]. With how hung up on her he was, I really thought I'd need to have a word with him. "He saw me yesterday in the elevator, and he just turned his back on me. It's not him."

"Then who?" I get out of bed and go to the bathroom. A quick shower will do, and then I'll need to get ready for the game.

Nevaeh sighs. "My mother."

I stop in my tracks, one hand gripping the collar of my tee. "What did she do?"

"She talked to the media. About me, about my years in school. And Kyle."

"Kyle?" I've never heard her mention a Kyle.

"I dated him in high school."

"And what did she say?"

"He went to jail because of what he did to a girl. And when he did it, I was still with him." Nevaeh sniffs. My beautiful, messy girl...I would do anything to be with her right now. To hold her and help her get through this. "My mother made it sound like I had something to do with it," she whispers.

"How?"

"She said I should've said something about the way he treated me. That I should've alerted her or someone about what a prick he was... that I could've saved Lyn and the other girls he sexually assaulted."

"If you didn't feel comfortable opening up to her, isn't that on her? Doesn't that speak volumes about what kind of mother she is?"

"Mom said she tried everything to have a relationship with me, and I never let her in because I was tight-lipped and introverted," she says. "I'll explain everything about Kyle after the game. It's...not an

---

1. Слава Богу. — Thank God.

easy conversation, and I don't want to talk about it over the phone, especially when I'm at work."

Nevaeh falls silent, and I stay silent too. As my gaze roams over my bathroom, I bite the inside of my cheek. Then an idea pops into my head. I hope she'll go for it. It might help her move on and never look back.

"Malyshka?"

"What?"

"Did you ever figure out what to write for that special edition in December?" I ask.

"Not yet, and I'm running out of time. Kai keeps asking about it."

"Write about Kyle," I say. "Write about your experience. Tell your story."

"It's an ugly story, Roman."

"But it's yours."

Shuffling sounds from her end fill my ear. I wait, hoping she'll agree. She needs this, even if she doesn't realize it yet.

"I'll think about it, okay?"

"Sure," I tell her and finally take off my tee.

"I'm so sorry, Roman. This was the last thing you needed before your game," Nevaeh mutters. "I just wanted you to know, because I'm sure people will be talking."

I snort quietly. "I'm sure they will, but I don't care." Stepping closer to the shower, I start the water and pull down my sweatpants and boxers. "Sorry, Malyshka, I really need to get rolling."

"Sure. See you at the game."

"See you." I hang up, toss my phone onto the marble surface of the bathroom countertop, and step into the shower.

A clear head. That's what I really need...because she's right. People will be talking.

Sitting on the bench, I follow my teammates around the ice with my eyes. My teeth are clenched so hard, my molars could be fucking dust by the end of the night. And not just my molars if Nathan Tucker doesn't learn how to keep his mouth shut.

We started off strong, dominating on the ice. The steady number of pucks we were able to sneak behind Boston's defense in the first period helped us a ton, giving us the motivation we needed to score.

Benson getting the puck in the left circle from Boston's player when he was midway through our zone was priceless. He sent the puck into the board, and it ricocheted to a wide-open Thompson. With a precise wrist shot into the top-right corner, Colton scored our first goal in the first period. Seeing one to zero on the Jumbotron made me extremely happy.

After we cut Boston's defense apart, our team got the chance to make it a two-goal game just six minutes after Colton's goal. I slid a pass under the stick of Nathan Tucker to unlock Crawford. And damn, Dean didn't disappoint, sending the puck into the net with a backhand shot. Leading two to zero by the end of the first period gave the whole arena hope.

How the fuck we went from leading to losing two to three is beyond me. It's like Boston just had a slow start, adjusting to our game and opening up new possibilities after the first period. When we got back on the ice during the second period, they decided they were done letting us win. They have clawed back like fucking beasts, and we haven't had a single chance to score again.

Every moment we have created has fallen short. Even the ones that were successful, when we were able to send the puck toward Boston's net, didn't lead to another goal. Schneider, Boston's goalie, has secured his net every fucking time, making us restless.

My mood only worsened when two to two flashed on the Jumbotron. I want to win. My teammates want to win. Too bad Boston has had no desire to fuck off and let us move forward.

Tucker chirping me was another level of fucked up. Hearing him talk about Nevaeh sent me into a rampage. If it hadn't been time for me to get off the ice, I would've smashed his fucking face in.

At the start of the third period, our first line created the perfect chance to score. Colton finished off Drake's full-ice pass from our team's crease. But the happiness was short-lived. The Boston bench made a quick challenge to overturn the call, and it was ruled that Koskinen was well offside. And, unfortunately, it proved to be a damned demotivator for the entire team. Exactly four minutes after that, Boston made the score two to three.

I glance at the Jumbotron. Six minutes till the end of third period. God, I hope we get the chance to turn the game around and tie it again—and maybe even score one more so we can win.

Jumping to my feet, I get on the ice and enter the game in a rush. I block Tucker, stealing the puck from him and sending it to Colton. A glance to my left, and I see Tucker glaring at me.

"Really think you're going to win?" he says snidely. "Not going to happen, asshole. Just like no one is going to forget who your wife is. Making her boyfriend ra—"

I don't even think. I just turn around and block his path. A smirk forms on his lips, and I'm determined to wipe it off his smug face. I read all the shit that Nevaeh's mom spewed about her on my way to the arena, and it made my blood boil. Only my need to be one hundred percent focused on the game helped me stuff away all those thoughts. Talking to Nevaeh will give me the whole picture, but it's clear to anyone with even a shred of logic that her mom's insinuations are nothing but lies. Even the journalist who wrote the article mentioned that Nevaeh was a victim too.

I toss my stick and gloves on the ice and charge at Tucker, hitting him in the face with my fist. His head flies back, and before he has the chance to punch me in return, my fist connects with his chin. My knuckles start to bleed, and I flex my fist several times.

"Shut the fuck up. Don't you dare talk about my wife. Ever again."

"Don't like hearing the truth?" Tucker laughs, spitting blood onto the ice.

Someone grabs me from behind, pinning my arms to my sides. I try to break free, and that's when Tucker's fist slams into my face. My vision goes black as I shut my eyes. Another blow follows, busting my bottom lip. The commotion around us becomes louder, and someone pulls me away from Tucker, even though I wriggle as hard as I can.

"Let me fucking go!" I roar.

"Calm down, Pashkevich." Colton's voice in my ear sounds furious. "He's not worth it."

"He's a coward!" I yell, finding Tucker with my eyes. He's glaring at me; his face is bloody. "You're a fucking coward! Hitting me in the face when I was held back?"

The referee puts himself between us and pushes me backward. In the penalty box, I slump down onto my ass and stare in front of me. My heart hammers, deafening me and turning all other sounds into white noise. It's like the whole arena has gone silent, even if I know that's not the case.

"*Ublyudok*[2]." I wince from the pain of my split bottom lip. I can only imagine how my face looks. I'll definitely be sporting a black eye tomorrow.

I grab an ice pack from the off-ice official and hold it to my eye, begrudgingly watching what's happening on the ice. Tucker continues cursing from the opponent's penalty box, but I ignore him.

The five-minute penalty for both of us makes my heart drop. I won't be able to help my team. I look up at the Jumbotron, and my jaw ticks. Seeing two to three makes me ball my fists.

The noise of the arena is meaningless. Twelve thousand people slowly dissolve into the background, because I feel her gaze on me. I meet Nevaeh's eyes from across the ice and instantly know she's been crying. Her hands are pressed to the plexiglass, and she's not paying any attention to the game. Only to me.

I jerk my head and watch the ice instead. Hockey. That's the only thing I should be focusing on. Only the game matters right now. I already made a terrible mistake letting that jerk rile me up and starting a fight.

My temper is my weakness. It always has been.

And so I sit in the penalty box, watching my team lose the game.

---

2. Ублюдок. — Bastard.

The final score stays two to three when the horn signals the end of the game, but it feels like we lost by way more than one point. Because I know it's all my fault.

Nevaeh

THIRTY-ONE

in love

THE LIVING ROOM IS DARK, BUT I DON'T TURN ON THE lights. My phone is beside me on the couch, and I continuously glance at it. I hug my Sulley to my chest tightly, hoping to find at least a little bit of comfort. It would be so much easier if this plush toy could silence my worries like it did when I was a kid. Unfortunately, it's not working right now. I'm a mess, and I don't know what to do to make it easier.

Even one single thought about Roman leaving on a five-game road trip pushes my anxiety level to its peak.

The screen of my phone flashes; another message from Angie pops up. Biting my bottom lip, I debate whether or not I should reply. I've been avoiding her and everyone else since the game ended and I fled the arena because I couldn't stand being there. Roman's bleeding bottom lip and perfectly visible black eye have engraved themselves in my brain, and they're all I can think about.

Why did he hit that Boston player? That fight seemed personal, not like others I've witnessed on the ice. What could've pushed him to do that? I can't get rid of the feeling that it was because of me, because of my mother's interview. Chirping happens all the time in hockey, but not everyone plays fairly.

Pushing Roman over the edge is easy, considering how hotheaded he is.

With a deep breath, I take my phone from the couch and unlock it. Swiping away Angie's messages, I type one quick text to the person who's caused me so many tears in the past. The person who continues causing them now, just because she's vile.

ME:

If you ever talk to the media again, lying about me and spitting your hate, I will sue you for defamation.

Once I hit send, I stand up and go to the kitchen. I haven't eaten anything since breakfast, but I don't feel hungry at all. My nerves are my food, fueling me with gloomy thoughts and making me nauseous. I wish I could do something to stop it, but for the last hour, I've been falling deeper and deeper into my own pit of despair.

I pour myself some water and down it in one go. Then I turn around and lean on the kitchen counter. The talk I'm about to have with Roman is the only thing that keeps me sane. I just need him here with me. The warmth of his skin, the gentleness of his fingers when he tucks my hair behind my ears and caresses my cheeks, his strong arms wrapping around me and holding me tight—simple gestures that have the power to make me forget about my worries and my heartaches.

The sound of the door closing sends goosebumps all over my skin. Pushing myself off of the kitchen counter, I slowly stroll out of the kitchen. Our eyes meet the second I step into the living room. The crazy things my heart does in my chest whenever I see him don't surprise me anymore. They scare me, because I know he is *it* for me, but he doesn't see me like that.

"Hey." I walk toward him and stop a few feet away from him. His face looks even worse now. His busted bottom lip and black eye are dead giveaways as to how brutal that hit was.

"Hey, Malyshka," he says. Distress worms its way into my head, and my hands become clammy. Stepping closer, Roman puts his finger under my chin and raises my face to him. His gaze roams over me, and a faint smile crosses his lips. "Everything's fine. I'll be good as new sooner than you think."

The corner of my mouth trembles as I fiddle with my fingers. "Why did you get into a fight with that player? Was it some—"

"He thought it was okay to talk shit about my wife. I just taught him a lesson," Roman replies, unbothered, while my heart skips a beat. His words only confirm my suspicions. He got into a fight because of me. "Let's go for a ride," he suddenly says.

"A ride?" I repeat, a tornado of emotions brewing inside me.

"Fancy a ride on my Kawasaki?"

My lips part, and I watch him in silence. Then, swallowing my nerves, I nod. "I'd love to."

"Good. Then go change." Roman steps back and turns to go to his room. "I'm going to change too. The collar of this shirt feels like a noose."

I don't ask questions, don't let myself overthink his desire to get out of the house. Wheeling around, I go to my bedroom, where I still keep my clothes. I wonder what I should wear for a motorcycle ride. It will be my first.

"HERE." Roman hands me a black helmet with pink stripes. I take it, studying it quizzically. "I got it for you," he says, and my heart starts to pummel in my chest, bringing heat to my cheeks. He got a helmet... for me.

"Thank you so much."

Roman nods, takes my hand, and makes me follow him to a black motorcycle that's parked beside his BMW. He climbs onto it and glances at me over his shoulder. "Have you ever ridden a motorcycle?" I shake my head no, and he crooks a smile. "I'm honored to be your first."

I roll my eyes, and he puts his helmet on. I put mine on too before climbing on behind him. I take a deep breath, trying to calm my nerves. I trust Roman, but it's a bit nerve-racking anyway.

"Wrap your arms around me and hold on tight," Roman says, and I instantly do as he tells me.

He leans forward and starts the motorcycle. I don't have time to fully comprehend what's going on before he's driving away from the parking lot. My whole body is trembling as excitement mixes with something really close to fear. There's so much energy under me, the engine roaring. Little by little, Roman picks up speed. I hold on to him. The heat of his body radiates through his checkered shirt and sets my skin on fire. With a surprise, I realize that after a few minutes on the motorcycle, all my thoughts about the article, about his fight, are no longer bothering me.

All I can think about is the man I have my arms around and the freedom that this ride gives me. It's a blessing.

When Roman stops, I unwrap my arms and climb off his motorcycle. My legs are shaking so much it's hard to stand. I take off my helmet and instantly find myself face-to-face with my favorite turquoise color. His crooked grin and amused gaze send a delicious thrill down my spine. He's still the most handsome man in the world...and he's mine.

"How do you feel?" he asks, reaching over and taking my hand in his.

"Good." Roman glances at me, arching an eyebrow. "The ride was amazing."

"Happy to hear that." He pulls me toward a bench a few feet away. It's perched at the top of a hill; the whole city comes into view, all city lights and dark blue sky. It's magnificent, and I can't take my eyes off of it as I sit beside Roman.

"I love this spot," he says. "Found it a year ago, on a ride. I try to come here once in a while; it helps me sort out my thoughts."

"That's why we're here? So you can sort out your thoughts?"

"We're here to talk and enjoy the view." Roman gives me a pointed look. "I think the secrets we are keeping from each other will keep biting us in the ass if we don't get them out in the open."

I fold my arms over my chest, not saying anything and just staring in front of me. He's right, and I'm kinda surprised he's not angry with me. We've talked about his past so many times, while I never said anything about mine except for a brief mention of my parents.

I wanted him to open up, but I never really did the same in return. It's hypocritical.

"My mom doesn't know I still have this motorcycle," he says. "I told her I got rid of it."

"Why?"

"Mom worries about me." Roman shrugs. "She already lost one son in a car crash, so it was hard for her when I told her I got a car. She accepted it, obviously, but with my Kawasaki? That was probably the first time in my life she yelled at me. I didn't know my mom could cuss so much."

I chuckle. "We all curse when we're angry."

"Not my mom."

"So why did you keep it? I thought you hate disappointing your mom," I tease him, and he bursts out laughing.

"I don't know. I don't really have a logical explanation." We look at each other, and I smile. "It's probably my rebellious side taking over my responsible one. What Mom doesn't know won't hurt her."

"A bad boy at his finest."

Roman smirks at me, wraps his arm around my shoulder, and draws me closer. "Girls love bad boys, don't they?"

"They do," I say, meeting his gaze. "I do."

Roman bends down and presses his lips to mine. The kiss is slow and gentle at first, but the longer it lasts, the more I want. I sink my teeth into his bottom lip, and he groans. My eyes fly open, and I move away slightly, breaking our kiss. I totally forgot about his busted lip.

"I'm so sorry, Roman. I got carried away."

"It's okay," he says, pulling me tighter against his side. "Tell me about Kyle, Malyshka."

"Kyle Edwards was a linebacker on our high school football team. A popular kid with rich parents and good looks. We started dating when I was sixteen. Not because I was in love with him—not at all—but because I was flattered that a guy like him wanted to be with me. Status meant everything to me in those days," I mutter under my breath. "I'm not that person anymore, and I'm proud of myself for changing my life so much, but back in high school, I was stuck-up and self-centered. I was desperate for my parents' attention, and since they didn't give me any...I looked for it from other people. It didn't even matter what kind of attention it was, positive or negative, I didn't care. The more I got, the more I wanted...You wouldn't have liked me if you'd met me back then."

"Even though you're my type?" Roman asks, and some of the tension loosens its grip on my body.

I give him a small smile. "My personality would've been a huge turnoff."

"Then I'm glad I met this new version of you, because you're incredible." He kisses my temple. "What did Kyle do? I mean, I skimmed the article, but I didn't want to make any assumptions. I wanted to hear it from you."

"Kyle was constantly groping and harassing girls at school, but one day he took it too far. He raped a girl at one of the parties at his parents' house. I was there too, and Kyle and I were still together at time." I fall quiet, struggling to find the words to explain what happened. Roman turns to look at me and gently tucks a strand of my hair behind my ear, his long fingers brushing my skin softly. I lean into his touch, closing my eyes for a brief moment, just to collect myself before I finally tell him the whole story. "This girl...Lyn...she ended up committing suicide," I whisper hoarsely. "If you read the article, you know my mom tried to make it sound like I had something to do with it. Because everyone at school thought that too, at first."

"Why?"

"Lyn and I were both cheerleaders. We had sort of a rivalry, but she was so much better than me—more talented, more gracious. Some people thought I asked Kyle to do it because I was afraid I'd lose my spot on the team." I hide my face in Roman's chest. "Anyone who knew Kyle well enough would've never thought that. He was selfish and arrogant. He couldn't care less about anyone except himself. We didn't love each other and..."

"And what?"

"And he was never gentle with me," I say quietly. "After the pictures of my bruises were displayed during trial, no one thought I had anything to do with his crimes. You don't do that to the girl you love."

"I want to kill him." Roman is seething, rage dripping from his words, his posture tense.

"He's dead. Killed himself after serving two years of a ten-year jail sentence."

"Serves him right. *Takiye urody ne zasluzhivayut zhit'*[1]," he growls. "Your mom is fucking disgusting. Blaming you for his crimes? This is beyond me."

"She just wanted to hurt me."

"I think she would've been a great match for my father. They would suit each other well," Roman remarks, and I snort. "The last thing he told me was, 'Your brother is rotting in his grave while you live his life. The NHL would've never even looked your way if Maksim was alive.'"

"I'm glad he's not in your life anymore. Even if that's a terrible thing to say."

"It's fine." Roman falls quiet, and we just sit, enjoying the view of San Jose under the cover of darkness. When he shifts, I turn my head to look at him, my eyes meeting his. "What about your father?"

"I stopped talking to him when I went to college. If you think he ever tried to reach out to me, you're wrong. He was happy I took his side after we found out about my mom's affair with his best friend, but I stayed with him when she left, and he didn't really appreciate that. I was a burden to him, and he was happy to be rid of me when I moved out. He even bought me an apartment in my hometown to keep me from coming home. A generous gift from a loving father..."

"More like an attempt to buy his way out of being your dad."

"Exactly," I confirm, cuddling closer. "When I went to college, I wanted to do things differently, and Angie's friendship helped me. She

1. Такие уроды не заслуживают жить. — Jerks like him don't deserve to live.

brought happiness, love, and hope into my life, and I'll be forever grateful to her. She's my light."

Roman presses his lips to the top of my head, and I think I hear him say, "And you're mine." But it's barely a whisper, so I push it away, because it's probably my mind playing tricks on me.

"Want to stay a little longer?" he asks.

"Yes, please," I say as I put my head on his shoulder.

The sounds of the city get quieter. The sky grows darker as night falls. The wind becomes chillier, but I don't care about any of it. Because I'm here with him. Because he holds me close, and it feels like nothing will ruin this.

They say with the right person, even hell feels like home. And that's how I know Roman is the right person...and that I'm in love with him.

Roman

THIRTY-TWO

my wife

ME:

When are u going to be home?

MALYSHKA:

Around 7? Kai scheduled another meeting about the special edition and it's running late

MALYSHKA:

What time will u be home? I miss u so much

ME:

Same as you. And I miss u more

MALYSHKA:

Wanna bet? I'm going to blow ur mind tonight

ME:

I'll never say no to you blowing me

MALYSHKA:

I AM AT WORK! Stop giving me ideas

ME:

Why? Wet for me already?

MALYSHKA:

Yes. And I hate u

LAUGHING, I GLANCE AT THE HUGE BOUQUET ON THE passenger's seat. There are one hundred and one pastel pink roses, and the scent is heady, making me a little dizzy. I really hope Nevaeh likes them, because I spent quite some time yesterday trying to arrange everything with Layla so the bouquet would be ready by the time our plane landed in San Jose.

I look out the window, my gaze glazing over the parking garage of her office building. Her convertible is parked beside my BMW. After the plane landed, I rushed home to take a quick shower and change my clothes. Not even twenty minutes later, I was already out the door. After I picked up the bouquet, I drove here, silently hoping for her to still be at work, because my surprise would've been ruined if she'd already left.

I climb out with the bouquet, close the door, and lean against my car. I'm glad we won last night. Now my mood isn't marred with gloomy thoughts, and I can simply enjoy my time with my wife.

My wife...

Back in August, I would've never thought I would be calling Nevaeh my wife and meaning it. Now, in the beginning of November? I catch myself thinking about her that way all the time. The feelings I have for her are growing stronger, and it scares me...but I'm also secretly enjoying it. Being happy isn't something I'm really used to—or more like *wasn't* used to. Nevaeh turned my life upside down, helped me see that the world isn't all black and white. That I can actually enjoy my days while remembering my brother and cherishing the time I got to spend with him.

Grief for me is like the deepest waters, when no matter where I swim - I can't see the shore. Nevaeh is my lighthouse, the guiding light that helps me find my way out of my sorrow.

Maksim will always be with me. In my heart. In my mind. And I will never forget him. My brother is a part of me, and that won't change...no matter how happy or sad I am. I finally know that.

The sound of approaching footsteps makes my ears prick. When I look up, I instantly recognize her. Nevaeh heads in my direction, her eyes glued to her phone as she's typing something. My gaze travels down her body, and an elated smile forms on my lips.

Her short leather skirt sashays with each step she takes; her legs look absolutely mouthwatering. The clicking of heels echoes with her hurried steps, and a thrill of excitement rolls over me. *She will notice me soon*. I raise my eyes to the light blue sweater. It must be new; I haven't seen it before, and she told me she went shopping with Angie the other day.

Takaya krasivaya[1].

My phone dings in my pocket. The sound rings out through the quiet, and Nevaeh's eyes fly to me in an instant. She halts in her tracks, her jaw dropping. This reaction is why I'm waiting for her here and not at home. I smile, tilting my head to the side and mouthing, *Hi*.

With a squeal, she runs toward me, and I catch her, wrapping my arm around her waist and lifting her. Her hands are around my neck, and she's peppering my face with light kisses. Her hair tickles my skin, but I only hug her tighter, losing myself in the moment. It's exactly what I've been dreaming about. Her in my arms, and the rest doesn't matter.

Setting her on her feet, I lower my head and swiftly kiss her lips. Control is something I lack around her, but fucking her in the parking garage of her office building isn't in my plans...not tonight, at least.

"This is for you," I tell her, and she takes the bouquet from me. Nevaeh's eyes are dancing between my face and the roses, and the happiest smile plays on her lips.

"My favorite...They're so beautiful," she says on an exhale. "Thank you so much, Roman."

---

1. Такая красивая. — So beautiful.

"Anything for you." And I steal another kiss, just because I'm shit at restraining myself. "Do you mind leaving your car here? I'll drive you to work tomorrow."

"How can I say no after you gave me these?" Nevaeh presses the bouquet to her chest. "Are we going home?"

"Not exact—"

"For fuck's sake! Could you at least not bring him to where I work?" A furious man's voice shuts me up. I see Nevaeh's ex standing a few feet away from us, arms crossed over his chest, his face contorting in anger.

"This is a parking garage, Travis," Nevaeh says, pursing her lips. "Should we not go out in public because we might run into you?"

"Yeah, that would be fantastic. You should! Out of respect for me —if you even remember what that word means."

"What's your problem?" I ask, stepping forward and shielding Nevaeh from him.

"I was just going to my car after a very long and exhausting day at work. Sorry if I didn't expect to see my ex and her new boy toy here."

"Where's your car?" I tilt my head, watching him. He points at a Nissan parked two cars away from Nevaeh's. "Um, sorry, and why were you so surprised to see Nevaeh? You parked so close to her, and now you're acting like she did something wrong."

Travis's nostrils flare, and his hands drop to his sides. He balls his fists as he takes a step toward me. "It's called decency. Basic fucking respect. Though I'm not surprised you know nothing about it. Jocks are always dumb as rocks," he spits, glancing over my shoulder, trying to see Nevaeh. "I shouldn't be surprised by her either. She's not who I thought she was."

"And who am I?" Nevaeh's voice trembles in fury as she comes to my side and glares at her ex.

"A gold-digging slut, apparently."

I rush toward him and grab his collar. His eyes widen, and he digs his fingers into my skin, trying to break free. I just fist my hands harder, making him walk backward until his back hits the concrete wall.

"If you ever call my wife that again, I'll fucking smash your face into this wall." I shake him once, hard, and the back of his head hits the wall. "You have no idea what happened, how we even got together. Keep your assumptions to yourself, and keep your fucking distance. Move on."

Stepping back, I watch him breathing hard. When he looks up and meets my gaze, I notice unshed tears. It's like a flashback—I see my brother in him. This is how Maks probably felt when he found out about Alisa and her ex. The hurt written all over Travis's face makes my heart ache, bringing memories to the surface.

"I'm sorry," I say, surprising myself, and probably him too, given how his pupils dilate. "Nevaeh didn't leave you for me, and this marriage wasn't planned. It just happened."

Travis straightens his back, pushes himself away from the wall, and strides past me. Not a word, not a single glance at me or Nevaeh. He just acts like we're not here anymore. Holding his head high, he gets into his car, and then he's gone.

An uneasy feeling forms in the pit of my stomach, and I can't shrug it off. Him calling her names pissed me off, but at the same time I understand his hurt. He loved her. He wanted to marry her...and then she left him and married someone else in the span of two weeks.

If I knew how to love, I would feel crushed too if someone did that to me.

Turning on my heel, I stalk back to my car. Nevaeh stands completely still, the bouquet pressed to her chest. She meets my gaze, probably recognizing my turmoil with how her eyes soften. I need a distraction. Something strong that will stop me from spiraling, stop me from comparing what happened to Travis with what happened to my brother.

"Roman?"

I don't say anything, just take her hand in mine and pull her toward the backseat of my car. After I open the door for her, I extend my hand, and she gives me the bouquet without question. Once the roses are on the front passenger seat, I join her in the back.

"I want you," I say. "Now."

"You want a distraction," Nevaeh replies, looking skeptical with her eyebrows pinched together. "Why can't we go home?"

"Because we have a dinner reservation in an hour, at that Italian restaurant you told me you wanted to try." I snake my hand around her waist and make her sit on my lap. "I want you."

I put my hand on the back of her neck and pull her mouth to mine. Her scent. The softness of her luscious lips. Her warm skin. It's maddening how easily she makes me forget about anything that isn't her.

My tongue pushes through her lips, curling around hers in slow circles. It's the right kind of kiss, the kind that makes me feel emotions I never thought possible. It's slow and fast. It's gentle and rough. It's carnal, and I'm loving every fucking second of it.

"Roman..." Nevaeh moans as I slide my lips down her throat. "It's a parking garage. People will see."

"Who cares?"

"You're a public...oh God..." I nibble on her skin, my teeth sinking into her flesh. "You're a public figure."

"Malyshka, I haven't seen you in ten days. I haven't touched you." I slip my hands under her sweater, cupping her tits with my palms. "I haven't tasted you in ten fucking days." I bring her bra down, my fingers caressing her breasts, playing with her pointy nipples. Her eyes fall closed, and a loud moan escapes her parted lips. "Do you really think I care about anything except burying my tongue in your pussy?"

With that, I lay her onto the seat, my hands sliding under her skirt. I don't do quickies, and she knows that better than anyone. But I love eating her out. Her tight cunt tastes better than anything, and I swear I'd want her pussy to be my last meal before I died. So fucking delicious.

Nevaeh watches me; her hair is a mess as it falls in her face. Her eyes though? Sparkling sapphires hooded with desire, and I'm so here for it. Dragging down her panties, I slowly position myself between her thighs. Her right leg rests on my back, and she props her left leg against the front seat, spreading herself wide for me.

I smile and dive in, sucking her clit into my mouth, not wasting any time. Her hips jerk forward, and her head rolls back. She moans softly as her fingers thread through my hair. I play with her clit, swirling my tongue around it as I leisurely trace her folds with my fingers, building her anticipation, making her dripping wet for me. I push one finger inside her and pull it out almost immediately. She whimpers and then groans; the loss of friction frustrates her.

"Roman!" Nevaeh scolds me, the heel of her shoe poking in my back. "I want—" I plunge my finger back inside her, adding another one a second later. "God, please don't stop."

"I don't plan to," I murmur against her clit, fucking her steadily with my fingers.

Sucking and licking, twisting my fingers inside her and curling my tongue around her clit, I drive her to her orgasm, and the closer it gets, the harder it becomes for Nevaeh to stay quiet. She's panting, her fingers tugging on my hair. I wince but don't pull away, only doubling my efforts.

She lifts her hips up and down, shoving her pussy in my face and rubbing it against my mouth. I obey, eating her out and thrusting my fingers inside her rougher and faster, to match the movements of my tongue. When I curl my fingers upward, I feel her clench around me. She's coming, her eyes closed and her mouth open. Her legs are shaking, and the loudest moan fills my car.

Her orgasm is racking her body, waves of pleasure spreading through her skin. Even touching her, I can feel how she's burning from the inside out.

"So fucking sweet, Malyshka," I coo, sitting up and lightly slapping her pussy. "So fucking mine."

Nevaeh stares at me for a second. Then she props herself up and sits up too. A pinkish hue covers her cheeks and a pretty big hickey shines on her neck—I'd be damned if I said her look doesn't scream sex. The energy she radiates makes my dick so hard, I feel pre-cum leaking.

"Let's go home...Please." She leans over to my ear, her lips wrapping around my earlobe.

Dammit. This is going to be harder than I thought.

Turning my head, I kiss her lips but move away just as quickly. "No."

I climb out of the backseat and go to the driver's side. Then I start the engine and glance at Nevaeh through the rearview mirror. She's already fixed her sweater and is now trying to comb her hair with her fingers. Her pouty lips make me smile.

"You've been talking about this restaurant for two weeks," I explain. "I had to call in a favor to get us the reservation because they're so booked. We're going to dinner, and then when we get home...I'll let you do whatever the hell you want with me."

"Promise?" Nevaeh grins, braiding her hair.

I wink at her. "I swear."

Nevaeh

THIRTY-THREE

always

"I HAVE NO IDEA HOW YOU DEAL WITH DRAKE'S AWAY games," I mutter. "I feel like Roman spends more time on the road than he does at home. He just got back, and now he's leaving again."

"My dad was always gone a lot." Angie shrugs. "I'm used to it, though of course that doesn't mean I like it." She gives me a small smile. "Drake and Roman love hockey; it brings them joy. All we can do is to support them."

"I do support him," I blurt, making Angie burst into giggles.

"Everyone who knew Roman before you sees it. He's very different, even from when I first met him. You're a good influence on him." Angie dips her head, her dark brown hair falling over her shoulders like a heavy curtain. "Just like he is on you. He's changing you too, Nev, and I love it."

I cover her palm with mine and squeeze it gently. "I told him everything about my past, and he didn't judge me. He's been supportive of me ever since. Just like you. You two are my guiding lights...even if he's more like a rainy cloud on some days."

"As long as you're happy, I'm happy too." Angie puts one hand on her growing belly. "How is your article going?"

Instinctively, I grab my phone from the couch and check my notifications. Getting a phone call from Kai on my day off wasn't something I anticipated—nor him asking me why I even have an email address if I never reply to him on time. I've missed a lot of his emails recently, so all my mornings have started with me going through my inbox to check for anything from my boss. I checked the settings and talked to our tech department. No one seemed to know why it was only happening to Kai's emails, so I kinda gave up. I have way more important things to worry about, and my article is one of them.

"It's almost ready. Just need to go through the part about Kyle one more time," I tell Angie as I squint at my phone once again. "The part about Roman is done though. It was the easiest to write; the words just poured out of me. I even had to stop myself so I didn't go over my word count."

"Does he know you're writing about him?"

I shake my head. "I want him to read it once it's published," I say quietly. "When I'm ready to know what he thinks about me being in love with him."

"Nev..." Angie curls her hand around my shoulder and pulls me to her side.

She doesn't say anything, and I'm grateful for that. Having any sort of expectations when it comes to Roman's feelings is a lost cause. I'll be so disappointed if he doesn't feel the same way. I prefer to just bet it all on red, tell the world about my past and how my present healed me, and hope that the man I love will want to be a part of my future.

Even if he says he's not capable of love.

"I'll be there for you no matter what," Angie whispers, and I cuddle into her, closing my eyes and relaxing into her embrace. "You can count on me. Always."

"I know," I whisper back. I wrap my arms around her and hold her gently. "Love you so much, Angie."

"Love you too." She kisses my temple and leans her head against mine.

We sit quietly in her living room, and the feeling of comfort overwhelms me, the way it always does with her. Drake went for a run, taking Cooper with him and giving us some privacy. He's a good friend, and he wouldn't say anything to Roman about me, even if they're friends too. But I'm glad I was able to talk to Angie without him around. I needed perspective. Needed to get things off my chest and talk about the article I'm working on with someone who isn't Roman.

Because my desire to confess my feelings is getting the better of me lately, and I know he's not ready. Not ready to believe that he deserves to be loved. Not ready to admit that he wants to be loved too. Thinking about it makes my little heart flutter in my chest like a wild bird thrashing against its cage, desperate and scared of what's going to happen next.

And him breaking my heart is a possibility I can't ignore...even if I want to.

THE FIRST THING I hear once I close the door of Roman's apartment is his mom's voice. She giggles, telling him something in Russian, and he laughs too. A warm and cozy feeling forms in my belly. I love the sound of his laughter, so genuine and joyful; it always brings a smile to my face.

Padding into the living room, I find Roman sitting on the couch, holding his phone in front of him and smiling from ear to ear. He notices me, and his grin becomes softer, gentler. Beckoning me with his head, he tells his mom, "Nevaeh is home."

Nevaeh is home. A simple sentence, just three words, but it makes my knees weak. My legs are all unstable as I walk over to the couch and sit down beside him. Roman drapes his hand over my shoulder, pulling me into his side and kissing my temple. His gestures are full of affection, and they lack even an ounce of pretense. And, despite how much I'm trying to forbid myself, I still feel hopeful. Hopeful that he loves me too.

Not as much as I love him, because I try to be a realist, but at least a little bit. The way I feel about him is larger than me, larger than anything I know in this world. It's unique and endless, and even if it might take him time, my love will be enough for both of us. Because nothing has ever felt this right.

"I hope Roma isn't giving you any trouble," Iryna says, smiling gently at me.

"He might be a handful, of course, but most of the time your son is wonderful."

"Wonderful?" Roman leans away and looks down at me. A false scowl plays on his lips. "That's not what you should call your husband."

"You're my husband, so I know better than you what I should call you." I give him a pointed look and switch my attention to his mom. "How are you, Iryna?"

We talk some more, and I enjoy the conversion to the fullest. With one exception. Roman's fingers drawing circles on my skin makes me fidget in my seat, but no matter how much I try to scoot away, he only holds me closer. His hand continually slipping lower brings heat to my cheeks.

By the time we say good-bye to his mom and Roman tosses his phone on the small table, I'm a puddle. Melting, blushing, and panting. My mind is foggy, and I'm trying my best to distract myself. Surely we can't spend the whole evening fucking, can we?

"Why does your mom call you Roma?" I move away and turn to face him.

"Because that's my name." He gives me a crooked smile. "The short form." His hand snakes around my waist, and he pulls me back into him. "Come here."

"Short form? I kinda thought it was a term of endearment," I mumble, biting the inside of my cheek. His palm cups my tit over my clothes, massaging it gently and adding just a little bit of pressure to my nipple.

"Mom used to call me 'Romochka,' and I fought with all my might to make her stop using it. Though my granny calling me 'Romashka' tops it all. In English, the literal translation is 'chamomile.'"

"Chamomile? 'Romashka' is 'chamomile' in English?" I blink and start giggling, loud and contagious. Roman cracks a smile too.

"I'm the last person you'd think of calling that, but my granny doesn't care. She says she's an old woman and I should respect her wishes."

"You should." I playfully push him away and stand up from the couch. "Listen to your granny, Roman."

Heading to the kitchen, I don't look back to see if he's following me. Because I know he is. The warmth of his body cages me, clouding my mind and skyrocketing my arousal to its highest level possible. I think we should spend the whole evening fucking. It's a great—

A knock on the front door stops us both. I look over my shoulder and meet Roman's gaze. Arching an eyebrow in question, I see him shake his head. He has no idea who it might be.

Wheeling around, Roman strolls to the door as I continue to the kitchen. Even with how curious I am, I don't want him to feel like I'm always snooping. This is still his house, and I'm still his guest. And this...

I pause, my fingers curling around an empty glass. A woman's voice reaches my ears, and I recognize it instantly. It's his neighbor Claire, the tall brunette.

Despite how much I want to go to the hallway and listen to their conversation, I stay put. After pouring myself an orange juice, I prop my hip against the kitchen cabinet and stand still, nursing the glass in my hand. No more than two minutes later, Roman walks into the kitchen.

"What did Claire want?" I ask.

"To invite me...*us* to her birthday party. She's turning twenty-four."

"Us?" I cock an eyebrow, and a lazy smile appears on his lips.

"Well, she invited me, but I told her that these days I don't go anywhere without my wife." Roman saunters closer, moving slowly like the predator he is. "Can't say she was happy to hear that."

"Of course she wasn't." I jerk my head in annoyance. "What is she even doing here? I thought she left you alone after Ava's birthday."

His hand slips around my waist and slides down, splaying over my hip bone. "I see her from time to time, on my way home or out and about. Mom taught me to be nice unless I have a reason to be mean, so all I can do is small talk."

I know he's riling me up. Taunting me out of my mind. I know that, but I still fall victim to my jealousy.

"I'd prefer you didn't talk to her." I push past him and scurry to the living room, intending to go to my bedroom and change my clothes. And also calm down, because I don't want to argue with him before his next stretch of away games.

His steps echo behind my back, and the next thing I know, my back collides with his chest. "You and your jealousy," Roman whispers, his tongue licking the length of my earlobe. "I need you to start trusting me, because not trusting me will grow old real quick."

"I trust you."

"Doesn't really feel like it," he states. "I only have eyes for you, Malyshka. Claire, and all those other girls who come around the team, mean nothing to me."

"Those other girls...What are you talking about?"

"*Blyat*[1]," Roman curses.

In one swift motion, he turns me around and puts my back against the wall. His hand curls around my throat as he brings his lips to mine. "If you only knew how much power you have over me." His tongue traces my bottom lip before he sucks it into his mouth and releases it. "If I could, I would spend every fucking day of my life with my head between your legs, making you come and worshipping your sweet little cunt."

His lips cover mine, taking my breath away and turning all my thoughts into jelly. I slip my tongue inside his mouth, fisting his tee and pulling him into me. It's wild and passionate. Nothing has ever felt this good. I swear he feels like heaven on Earth. Roman is just... perfect.

---

1. Блять — Fuck

Without holding back, I kiss him with everything I have until he breaks the kiss and presses his forehead to mine, breathing heavily.

"Malyshka...if it's still not clear how I feel about you, I'll gladly spell it out. You own me. You and no one else," he tells me, his eyes burning into mine. I know it's not "I love you," but it definitely feels like it. With him, it does.

And I know what I want to do for him.

As slowly as possible, I get on my knees in front of him and look up. His hand cups my chin, gently lifting my face. "The most beautiful girl in the world is on her knees for me," he murmurs huskily, and I lean into his touch, his words injecting deep into my core. "Will you let me fuck your mouth?" I nod. "Good."

Roman pushes his sweatpants down, and his hard erection stands in front of my eyes. Wrapping his hand around his dick, he pumps it several times, his gaze never leaving mine.

"Open your mouth, Nevaeh." I do as he tells me, and he slides his cock into my mouth. My lips close around his dick, but I don't move; I'm waiting for him to say it. Roman smiles, his fingers running down my chin. "Suck."

Swirling my tongue around the crown of his cock, I wrap my hand around his length. I suck, teasing him with my tongue, my teeth grazing the sensitive skin of his dick. My hand moves back and forth, jerking him slowly.

"Such a good girl you are." Roman puts his hand on my head, forcing me to take more of him. "Gag on my cock, Malyshka."

Tears spring to my eyes as his cock almost hits the back of my throat. I gag, saliva drooling out of my mouth, but I refuse to stop. Tightening my grip around his shaft, I start pumping him harder. He groans; his other hand slaps against the wall as he balances himself. His hips move, the length of his dick sliding inside my mouth till I'm full of him.

I reach for his balls with my free hand, massaging them gently and then roughly tugging them down. When I do, his breath hitches in his throat, and he groans loudly. My panties are a mess, my wetness coating my thighs.

"You feel so good," he praises me. "Don't stop, Nevaeh. Don't fucking stop."

He's fucking my mouth, his hand on top of my head keeping me in place. With how his movements quicken, I know he's going to come in no time. I continue stroking his cock, sucking the head of his shaft when his cum fills my mouth. I swallow it, feeling my cheeks burning. My lips are swollen, but the euphoria is overwhelming.

Roman steps back; his cock pops out of my mouth. Grabbing my wrists, he hauls me to my feet, and his mouth crashes onto mine. I can barely breathe, so many emotions are mixing together. Our tongues dance around each other, fueling my lust for him. His hands move feverishly over my body as he pushes my legs apart and slips a hand under my skirt.

"So fucking wet," he growls between our kisses, his fingers playing with my clit. "God, you're hot. Hotter than any fucking woman on the planet. You're everything, Nevaeh."

His praise...it sends me closer to the edge with each word he says. He doesn't even need to be inside me to have me coming. The need I felt for him when we first met in the club is a faint ghost of what I feel now. It swallows me whole, and I don't even remember how I lived without him.

Roman pulls his hand out of my panties, puts both hands on my hips, and slides them to my ass. His palms are full of me when he lifts me, and I wrap my legs around his hips. Our lips are inseparable, devouring each other. His tongue is exploring my mouth, making me cling to him harder. I never want him to leave, never want him to stop touching me.

"Oh God, Roman," I moan into our mouths. My skin is scorching; I need to get rid of these clothes.

I have no idea where he's taking me, but when he slams the door behind us I know we're in our bedroom. He lowers me onto the sheets, the weight of his body pinning me to the bed. Nestling between my legs, he rubs his cock over my entrance as I writhe under him. Roman's lips trail down my chin and to my neck, his hot breath sending goosebumps over my skin. When he digs his teeth in my collarbone, I gasp from the pain that he instantly soothes by licking the mark he left on me.

"*Tvoy zapah*[2]...You smell so fucking delicious, Nevaeh. Everything about you makes me so fucking high. It's like I'm constantly drunk. On you," he whispers, his hands slowly undressing me piece by piece.

When I'm fully naked, Roman turns us around and makes me straddle him. I rise, wrapping my hand around his cock to guide it inside me, but he stops me.

"No. Not like that," he orders, moving until we're in the middle of his bed. "Turn around."

And again I obey. Turning around, I find myself in front of the mirror. I lick my lips, my gaze roaming over my body. My breasts are rising and falling with my erratic breath, and my nipples look like bullets. My ponytail has come loose, my wild locks falling into my face. My cheeks are flushed, and my eyes glisten in the darkness of a room lit only by moonlight.

"Take my dick in your little cunt." Roman slaps my ass, and I rise a little as I feel his dick press into my pussy. "That's right, Malyshka."

I sink onto his cock, taking him fully. I'm so dripping wet, he slides right into me to the hilt. *Oh my God*. My lips part as I stare at my own reflection, captivated by how good it feels to have him inside me.

"Ride me, baby, and don't look away...See what I see in you. Your beauty, how hot you are..." I start slowly bouncing on his cock, and he falls quiet, taking a deep breath. "And how good you are for me..."

A smile blossoms on my lips, one I have no control over. All the things he says play with my head and make me lose my sanity. Then I start riding him. Slowly at first, but eventually picking up speed and chasing my own orgasm. I rotate my hips, circling his cock more roughly. He groans, slapping my ass hard.

"Again," I whisper, arching my back and glancing at him over my shoulder. Roman smirks, lifts his hand, and catches my ponytail in his fist. He tugs, and my head rolls back. "Again."

---

2. Твой запах... — Your scent...

Roman digs his fingers into my ass cheeks right as I start losing control. His hand is fisted around my ponytail, his other hand slapping my ass harder and harder with each move of my hips. My moans are so loud they surprise even me. My approaching orgasm makes me fucking scream, and I come more powerfully than I ever have in my life.

"Oh fuck..." Roman groans. My walls are suffocating him. He lets go of my hair, wraps his hands around my wrists, and starts fucking me, lifting his hips higher and higher. Wave after wave crashes over me, the pleasure sliding so deep into my core, I think I feel it in my bones. He comes too, his hot cum shooting right inside me.

I have no idea how long it lasts, but it feels like forever. Multiple orgasms, one after the other, wreck my body. My legs are shaking so hard as I slide off his cock and sit between his thighs, I think I'm going to be spending all day in bed tomorrow.

Sitting up, Roman wraps his arms around my waist from behind. Our eyes meet in the reflection of the mirror. I smile, and he smiles back, gently pushing my hair off my face. Then he presses his lips to my shoulder and rests his chin on it.

"You're so stunning, and so beautiful, Nevaeh. I've never wanted anyone more than I want you," he confesses. "One simple thought about you when I'm away, and my balls turn fucking blue. Do you really think I care about Claire or any other girl at all? They aren't you...and I'll never be interested."

"Promise?" I ask.

"I swear," he says, taking my chin between his thumb and index finger and tilting my head toward him. "Ready for round two?"

I laugh heartily, pressing my forehead to his. "Always," I whisper before I turn around and connect my lips to his.

Apparently, we can spend the whole evening fucking and it still won't be enough.

Roman

THIRTY-FOUR

damaged goods

I HATE LOSING.

It's part of the job. Part of every sport there is. And still, I fucking loathe it.

We won four games, one after the other, but now it's our second game in a row that we've lost. It's our second away game, dammit. It's one to five with only four minutes left in the third period, and it makes me mad.

I grab my water bottle and drink, my hand tightening around it. My eye twitches when I see Seattle leading another charge at our net.

"*Da chto za...*[1]" I mutter, falling quiet and gritting my teeth instead of cursing louder. My fucked-up mood is all over the place. Thankfully, this time Rodgers makes a brilliant save, and I release the breath I was holding.

Jumping to my feet, I rush on the ice and go after Carter, Seattle's winger. I cut around him in the left circle, ruining his chances for a clear pass and sending the puck in Colton's direction instead. Realistically, I don't think we can win, but we can try to score at least one more time while making sure Seattle doesn't score again. I'll take it as a fucking personal offense if they end up scoring six goals.

---

1. Да что за... — What the...

When I notice Seattle's winger, Svensson, dashing toward our net, I speed after him. He hits the puck, making a diagonal pass to his teammate in the right circle. *Fuck*. I grit my teeth, pushing as hard as I can to intercept the puck. Pavel Bure's speed would come in fucking handy right now.

Leaning forward, I extend my stick as far as I can, catching the puck at the last moment, literally grabbing it right from under Seattle's nose. I glance over my shoulder, noticing Drake, and send the puck flying into the board so it'll land right where he is.

The second he has the puck, he skates behind the net, Seattle's players stalking him. With a short pass from behind the net, the puck ends up right in front of Colton, and he doesn't waste even a moment, just lifts his stick and fires a goal into the left corner behind Seattle's goalie.

Thank fucking God. At least we scored two.

When the game ends, the final score on the Jumbotron gives me an expected rush of anger. Five to two isn't the best way to end a game, but at least we didn't let them score more, and we got that second goal. I'm not super proud of myself, but, like Drake always says—it's just another lesson. Take in the loss, mull it over, learn from your mistakes, and do better next time.

"I WATCHED the Champion's League game with Thompson last night, and you fucking reminded me of Rüdiger from Real," Clay says, looking at me with a lopsided grin. "The way you sped up in the third period was awesome. I can't wait to check the highlights."

I roll my eyes and look out the window. We're heading to the airport for our flight home, and, strangely, the atmosphere on the bus is super calm. Obviously, no one is happy that we lost, but it doesn't feel bitter. Or maybe it's just me. I think I'm getting better at accepting defeat.

Mom watches every game, most of the time recorded because of the time zone difference, and she says I'm not as brutal as I used to be.

She's sure it's all Nevaeh's influence. And no matter how much I want to argue with her and prove her wrong, deep down I know she's right.

It's all because of my wife.

Nevaeh sees my flaws and knows damn well how imperfect I am. She's witnessed my broken parts, and instead of running away she holds them close, feeding my soul with her warmth and affection. Even when I'm falling into the abyss of my own darkness, she stays with me. Being with her is easy. Effortless. Right. And she's not trying to change me...I'm changing for her myself.

"Any plans for tonight?" Clay's voice rips me out of my thoughts. I turn my head to look at him, and a half smile plays on his face. "Or maybe your only plan is your wife?"

I smirk. "My only plan is my wife." I pull my phone out of my pocket and unlock it. "The article she's been working on was published today. I think I'll take her out to celebrate. Or maybe we'll order in and stay home. I haven't decided yet. It depends on what sort of mood she's in."

"Must be nice to have someone waiting for you at home." Clay's gaze becomes distant. Shaking his head at himself, he looks out the window. "All I plan to do is play Xbox until I pass out."

"That kinda—"

"Sucks, I know," he says with a shrug. "I just know what I want, and I don't want to settle for something that isn't right for me."

I keep silent, holding my unlocked phone and just staring at my teammate. "Layla is great," I blurt, and Clay's eyes flare at me, and then at Drake, who's sitting with Colton in the next row over.

"You probably want to make that reservation, Pashkevich," he drawls, diverting his attention to the window. Laughing, I open the last message Nevaeh sent me, read it, and quickly reply.

ME:

On my way to the airport. Plan to buy your magazine so I can read your article on my flight

MALYSHKA:

Hope you like it 🤞

MALYSHKA:

And I can't wait to see you

ME:

I have no doubt I'll like it. I'm so proud of you, Nevaeh

Slipping my phone in my pocket, I notice the airport ahead of us, and my lips stretch into a big smile. I'll be home soon.

WITH MY EARBUDS IN, I nestle comfortably into my seat and open the magazine I bought. A few of my teammates start throwing curious glances my way, but I don't care what they think about me reading a magazine with Olivia Rodrigo on the cover. I would read a fairy tale about a princess if Nevaeh wrote it, simply because I want to support her. If it matters to her, it matters to me. It's the kind of logic I believe is right. Because I'd do anything for the people I care about.

Nevaeh doesn't deserve anything less.

> “*I think we all learn from a very young age to be compassionate. To be respectful and merciful to those who need it. A homeless man, an orphaned child, a grieving family. It's so easy to feel sorry for them. For most of us, our desire to do something to help, to support, is powerful. Listening to their stories, crying with them about the tragedies of their past, feeling happy when we see how their lives are changing for the better. It feels all kinds of right, and we never question it. Never think there might be others who desperately need help too...but some people just do a good job of hiding it.*
>
> *We see them in crowds. In the faces of our classmates. In our colleagues. In our friends. In a woman who passes us hurriedly on the street. These people are everywhere, and the only thing that unites them is a lack of love.*

And I was one of them.

Tightness in my chest prevents me from breathing freely. I wiggle in my seat, as if hoping that if I change my posture it will be better. Of course it won't. The feeling isn't physical; it's all emotional. It's suffocating me, forming a lump in my throat. My eyebrows are pulled together, and I start chewing on the inside of my cheek.

Moya devochka...[2]

> *More than anyone, kids look up to their parents. Especially when it comes to their professions, looks, or behaviors. I was no exception. Growing up, I'd watch my mom and think she was the most beautiful woman in the world. The most elegant and stylish. I wanted to be just like her. She was my role model, and more than anything I wanted her to notice me. To hear her praise me for my achievements. I desperately needed her, but she never cared.*
>
> *Neither did my dad, who thought money would fix my loneliness.*
>
> *By the age of six, I knew I was an unwanted child. A burden that my parents carried as they both drowned in their own misery. We were a wealthy family that lived without love in a house filled to the brim with hate and indifference.*
>
> *Unfortunately, little by little, it poisoned my heart.*

I keep reading, learning more and more about her childhood and her years in school. How she sought approval from others, tried to replace the emptiness she felt with a feeling of belonging. Some things I already knew, but some shake me to my core, enraging me and making me hate her parents even more than I already do.

Never showing up to events. Never supporting her in her desire to

---

2. Моя девочка... — My girl...

become a writer. Never telling her that they loved her. Indeed, she had financial support, all the toys she wanted, expensive clothes and electronics. But she didn't have the thing that everybody needs...unconditional love and support.

> *Bitterness became my last name when I grew older. I was hurting inside, and I wanted to make others hurt too. I'd use my status, my parents' money, and even my body. I did anything I could to replace the lack of love with sick adoration from people who simply feared me.*
>
> *Nevaeh Lawrence was the meanest girl you could've imagined. The Queen B who thought she ruled the school and everyone around her. I deserved to be knocked off my high horse. To pay for all the tears and hurt I caused... and Kyle Edwards was my punishment.*

Pressing my palm to my forehead, I scowl as I read about her relationship with Kyle. A girl who lived without love met a narcissistic guy who was spoiled by the love of his parents. The most popular kids in school, they looked like the perfect couple, with only one flaw—neither of them loved the other.

What started as a beneficial relationship for both of them quickly turned into something Nevaeh couldn't control. Kyle used her for sex and his sadistic games, not giving a damn how many bruises he left on her body. He knew she wouldn't say anything, because of the image she was trying to uphold, and he used it in his favor, to justify his own behavior more and more. It was only a matter of time before he tried these things with other girls while also maintaining the image of a loyal boyfriend. Lyn was the one with whom he crossed the line.

> *Knowing that someone died because I was too ashamed to talk honestly about my boyfriend was heartbreaking. Finding out that everyone in school thought I had something to do with it because Lyn and I didn't get along was devastating. Shame became my constant companion.*

My self-confidence disappeared as if it hadn't ever been there to begin with, showing me what a miserable person I was, someone who used other people's pain and hurt to make myself feel better. I deserved every bad word said about me. Every insult. All the hate. It was my punishment for being silent, for being indifferent. For being a coward.

I still remember the questions I was asked during the trial. After all the pictures I took of my bruises were displayed on the screen for everyone to see. "Why didn't you talk to your parents about it? Didn't they notice your bruises?" the prosecutor, a woman in her forties, asked... and I laughed. I laughed so hard I couldn't stop until I realized I was crying.

Dad was always busy with work; Mom hated my guts for taking my dad's side after her affair was revealed. I couldn't remember the last time I saw them, let alone talked to them. They didn't care to listen.

For years I had no one in my corner. Until I finally met her. My best friend.

A smile forms on my lips for the first time since I started reading. The story of her friendship with Angie warms my insides and makes me feel happy. Two lost souls who met on the first day of college and have been inseparable ever since. Nevaeh and Angie saved each other; they've been there for one another through thick and thin. Their friendship is pure, and their love is unconditional. They are family.

> *After meeting Angie, I know how important it is to have someone who's always there for you. Someone who will always support you. Who will always stand by your side, even when things get rough. Someone who will help you without questioning whether you deserve it or not.*
>
> *Knowing firsthand what it means to live without love, I always notice people who are just like me. I see*

through their masks and the walls they build around themselves. People who hate their own existence and don't believe they deserve anything good. I recognize their demons, because in the past they were my demons too.

And that's who my husband is. My broken boy. My Roman.

Everything in me freezes. My hand hovers over the page, not turning it. I stare at the magazine, but all I see is a blank space. She never told me she was writing about me. Never even asked if I wanted my story to be told.

Swallowing down my nerves, I feel my body tensing. My hand curls into a fist as I force myself to continue reading. Word after word, fury overwhelms me. The music in my ears is loud, but I can't hear any lyrics. It all mixes into one word, sounding thunderous in my head. *Predatel'stvo*[3]. It's the only feeling I have, and it makes my blood boil. She betrayed me.

Maksim's death. My struggles with alcohol and my first team threatening to kick me off of it if I didn't do something about my problems. My father dying from a heart attack after months of severe drinking. All the assumptions about me getting into the NHL only because my twin died and I took his spot since I was always second for consideration.

My temples pulsate, my headache intensifying with every breath I take. This can't be happening. Why would she do this to me? The beating of my heart becomes shallow, the pain in my chest blinding me.

> “*Seeing myself in Roman, noticing his hurt, I knew he needed saving. Needed my help, even if he was afraid to ask for it. His broken pieces were longing to heal, and I was the only one who could do that for him. And that's why I decided to stay.*

---

3. Предательство. — Betrayal.

Because people who live without love deserve our help and support.

I close the magazine, gripping it so hard my knuckles turn white. Even tearing it apart wouldn't be enough. Nothing would be enough to make me forget what I just read. I can't ignore the betrayal of her spilling my secrets.

She lied to me. All this time, I was no more than an experiment. Damaged goods she tried to fix, to prove her own theory about people who live without love. People like me, who hate their own existence because of the trauma of their past. People who have no one in their corner until someone like her walks into their lives and suddenly changes their world.

I am a project. A failure she's trying to repair. A disease she's trying to cure.

I stand up from my seat and head to the back of the plane. The magazine is still in my hand. I pass Clay, and he gives me a questioning look, his eyebrow raised.

"You alright?" he asks as I march past him.

"Yeah." I smile as I throw the magazine in the trash. "Better than ever."

Not sparing a glance at Clay or my other teammates, I return to my seat. Slumping down into it, I turn the volume up as loud as it will go and close my eyes. I want to fucking laugh at how delusional I was to think that this girl might mean something to me. *Stupid motherfucker.*

As for my wife, I have a surprise for her. Her little project is about to fail.

Nevaeh

THIRTY-FIVE

he doesn't love me

"You think it's possible to die from hyperventilation?" I ask Angie, pressing my phone to my ear.

She laughs wholeheartedly. "You're fine. Stop worrying."

"Easy for you to say. You're not the one who decided it was a brilliant idea to write about your past, baring your soul for everyone to read." I huff and cross my legs, reaching over for the remote and turning on the TV. "And, as if that wasn't enough, I decided to confess my feelings for my husband...also for everyone to read."

"Aww, that's actually my favorite part of your article. It's so raw and genuine. It gives me all the feels," she murmurs. "I'm sure Roman is going to like it."

"I thought the part about our friendship would be your favorite," I tease her, quickly looking up *Vikings* and turning on the first episode of the third season.

"The part about our friendship is not even comparable. I loved everything about that article because your personality shines through your words, making it perfect. You should be proud of yourself."

"I'm trying," I tell her honestly. "Kai texted me and said the feedback is overwhelming. The reactions from readers online are positive, and there is a lot of buzz from people who are reading the print issue too."

"Ugh, I hoped to buy a hard copy when I took Cooper for a walk, but my bladder decided 'not today'! I had to run home because I had to pee so bad. Being pregnant is so fun," Angie jokes, making me giggle. "But I'm honored you let me read it before it came out. It means more than you know, Nev."

"You're my best friend. How could I publish something so important without letting you read it first? It's just not realistic." I sigh. "I haven't checked anything. Not the website, not social media. I can't even bring myself to read it...not until I talk to Roman."

"I wish I could come over to support you."

"It's okay. You promised Layla you'd watch Maya while she's working. Besides, our men will be home soon. Roman texted me on his way to the airport about two hours ago."

"Yeah, Drake texted me too." Angie falls quiet, and I hear Maya's voice say something about one of her toys. "Sorry, Nev, I need to lead a rescue mission. Skye from *Paw Patrol* was stolen by my very pesky dog."

"Of course," I say with a little laugh. "Tell Maya Nevaeh says hi."

"Sure. Text me if you need anything," Angie says. Then she hangs up, but not before I hear her yell, "Cooper Jones-Benson, get back here now!"

And I burst into giggles, my body shaking and tears forming in my eyes. This is everything.

I'M SO immersed in *Vikings* that I don't even hear the door opening. Only when it slams shut do my eyes fly to the hallway.

It's not a good sign when someone slams the door, right?

Taking the remote from the couch, I quickly pause the show, and that's when Roman comes into view. The first thing I notice is his mask. It's on again. Emotionless and indifferent, he stops in his tracks, his eyes holding mine. Something isn't right. Even the butterflies in my stomach, usually so happy to see him, are still now.

"How was the flight?" I ask the first thing that comes to mind before my throat closes up. My voice sounds groggy and unnatural.

"Same as always," Roman says, hiding his hands in his pockets.

The air in the room becomes charged, and I swallow my nerves. The silence hanging between us makes my skin itch. The guy who left this apartment four days ago was full of life and affection. But now, I don't even recognize him. This blank expression and cold gaze. It's just a shell of the man I love, and I don't understand what happened.

Except...that this might be his reaction to my article.

"I'm—"

The buzzing of his phone quiets me. I watch him pull it out of his pocket, check it, and put it back. Not a single emotion passes over his vacant face, and I feel like we're back to how it was in the very beginning. I have no idea what he's thinking.

"Great article." He doesn't mean it. "You must be proud of yourself."

"Everyone seems to love it," I mumble weakly.

His eyebrows hit his hairline as he shoots his gaze to me. With the way his lips twist into a grimace, I'm sure he doesn't share the sentiment.

"Good for you." Another clipped answer. Another sharp thorn pierces my heart.

Turning on his heel, Roman stomps to his bedroom, leaving me alone. I sit, unmoving, jaw clenched. Should I let him calm down? Wait for him to cool off so we can talk? Because I'm lost right now. Hearing him say that he doesn't feel that way about me yet. Maybe that he will never love me. Those possibilities were loud in my head, and I was silently preparing myself. But I didn't expect this.

I glance around the room, and my gaze falls on the plush toy he bought me. With trembling hands, I reach over and take it into my arms, pressing it hard to my chest. *Please, Sulley, I really need the comfort your presence brought me when I was a little girl*. The monster world would be so much more welcoming than this apartment right now.

Loneliness spreads over my skin, injecting itself deep into my veins. Every bone in my body is filled with the feeling of rejection.

He doesn't love me.

The guy who told me countless times that he's not capable of love doesn't love me.

What a surprise, Nevaeh, right?

I sit on the couch and shut my eyes hard, trying my best not to cry. The sound of the door opening sends shivers down my spine, and I'm surprised to discover Roman in the doorway. He's still in the same clothes he wore when he came in, but now a gym bag is hanging over his shoulder.

Forgetting how to breathe, I follow him with my eyes as he walks over and sits down on the coffee table in front of me. The bag drops to the floor with a thud, indicating how full it is. Roman puts his elbows on his knees, locking his hands in front of him and lowering his chin onto them. Our eyes meet, and it feels like my world is crumbling down. The anger behind his irises kills my last hope.

He doesn't love me.

"What's going on?" I ask in a hoarse whisper.

"I'm moving out," he deadpans, and I press Sulley harder to my chest. "I'm taking some stuff with me, and once I find a place, I'll get the rest. You can stay here. I've paid for the apartment for the rest of the year."

"You can't be serious." My breath hitches in my throat, and my hands become clammy.

"I am." Roman shrugs, his eyes shallow. "The apartment is yours now. I won't take anything except my clothes and personal belongings."

"Roman, if this is a joke, please tell me. Because I—"

"Why would I joke about something like this?"

"Because it doesn't make sense!" I yell and jump to my feet, towering over him. "When you left, you told me you were going to miss me. Every time we talked or texted, you told me how much you couldn't wait to see me. We were happy together, and now this? What fucking happened, Roman?"

The way his facial expression doesn't even waver makes my legs unsteady. He looks bored, almost like this conversation doesn't interest him.

"You betrayed my trust," he replies nonchalantly.

"What?" I slump back onto the couch, my eyebrows knitting together.

"You heard me. You betrayed my trust, and now I have nothing to say to you." My mouth falls open, and I gawk at him. What is he talking about? "Though there's something I actually do want to know." He cocks his head to the side, his eyes narrowing. "Please, enlighten me; why did you think it was a good idea to write about my past?"

What's going on? I'm so lost right now, even my vision darkens. "I didn't—"

Roman lifts his hand, silencing me. "I read the article, Nevaeh. From start to fucking finish." Every word is like a nail that stabs my little heart deeper and deeper. "Who gave you the right to write about me? About Maksim? About my family? I sure don't remember telling you I was okay with it."

"Roman, I don't know what you're talking about. I didn't write anything—"

"*Ty izdevaesh'sya*[1]?" he asks, letting his mask slip for the first time today. "Are you kidding me, Nevaeh?"

"I swear this is some kind of mistake. I never—"

"Stop!" he roars, and I rear back in my seat, instinctively grabbing my Sulley from the couch and holding it close. "I was excited to read that article because I knew how important it was for you. I knew how much you struggled with writing it and how much you were..." Roman pauses, gritting his teeth. "*Blyat*[2], I can't fucking talk in this language." Running his palm down his face, he meets my eyes again. "I knew how vulnerable you felt sharing those parts of your past, and I was so proud of you. Hell, I was planning to take you out so we could

---

1. Ты издеваешься? — Are you kidding me?
2. Блять — Fuck

celebrate. To make you smile because you deserve it for all your hard work. I felt all that, and then I read it, feeling so fucking bad for you when I read about your parents, enraged when I read about Kyle, and so happy when I reached the part about Angie...but then there was the part about me."

"I wrote about my love for you." I hiccup, feeling fat, hot tears stream down my face. "I'm in love with you, Roman."

Roman frowns. His knuckles turn white with how hard he balls his fists. "No." He shakes his head, and I feel my heart break in two. "Everything I told you about my past, about Maksim, about my father...it's all there. You didn't leave anything out. Even my drinking problems. You aired my dirty laundry for everyone to see. To fucking pity me." He clicks his tongue, looking away. "I'm a project you're working on. The broken boy you're trying to heal. It has nothing to do with love."

He stands up and hovers over me; his gaze is full of resentment.

"I told you you couldn't fix me." Roman takes a step back and lifts his bag from the floor. "You should've listened to me."

With squared shoulders and a straightened back, he strolls away from the couch. I cry, my tears streaming freely down my face. My hold on Sulley loosens, and the toy falls to the floor, lying there and proving that not every story gets a happy ending. Especially when the story is mine.

Nevaeh

THIRTY-SIX

come home, roman

Did someone just knock? I sit up on the couch and listen. The quiet of the apartment feels suffocating, as if all sound disappeared when Roman walked out the door a few minutes ago.

Another knock, and this time I hear it clearly. I go to the door, dragging my feet. I'm trembling like a leaf, my teeth clattering as if I'm cold. My broken heart is doing this to me, and also my tears.

God, I want to pretend nothing happened. That this is all a nightmare. That I'll wake up soon, and he will be with me. Will love me...

Pressing my palm to my chest, I wince from the stinging pang in my heart. My eyes well with tears again. I want them to go away.

With shaking hands, I open the door without checking who it might be. The moment my eyes slam into those familiar dark green ones, my knees give out. Angie rushes inside, hugging me tightly and running her hands up and down my back.

"Nev...what happened?" she asks. Like a fish out of water, I try to breathe fully, but I'm too hysterical. "Let's sit down."

Angie closes the door and guides me to the living room. She leads me to the couch, and I climb onto it, pulling my legs to my chest and wrapping my arms around my ankles.

"Oh my God, Nev! You're shaking!" Angie exclaims, pressing her palm to my forehead. I look up, studying her through clouded vision. "Well, at least no fever. Do you want something to drink?" I shake my head no. "To eat?" I shake my head again. "When was the last time you ate?"

I shrug and hide my face in my knees, not looking at Angie anymore. She huffs, clicking her tongue loudly. Her irritation rises, but she doesn't say anything. Instead, she wheels around and leaves the living room. Her steps sound distant at first, and then after a minute she returns. A glass of water materializes in front of my eyes when I look up.

"Drink." She presses it to my knee. "Drink, Nev."

Reluctantly, I grip the glass and press it to my lips, taking a sip. Angie sits beside me, her fingers gently brushing my hair off my face. Silent sobs still rack my body, but gradually, I start to relax. Little by little, the trembling stops, and I can take a lungful.

"What are you doing here?" I ask, staring ahead of me.

"Drake told me you needed me." My head bolts in Angie's direction, my eyebrows knitting together. She looks at me. Her eyes are full of pity, and a clenched half smile plays on her lips. "Roman said something to him at the airport." There's a little pause as she takes a deep breath. "I saw him getting on his motorcycle as I parked my car."

Even though he's furious with me...he cares about me enough to ask my best friend to stay with me. But not enough to love me.

I focus my gaze on the TV screen. The episode I was watching when Roman came home is still on pause, but I can't bring myself to turn it off. It reminds me of him...because Roman suggested I watch it once we finished *Peaky Blinders*. I'm not sure I'll ever have it in me to finish *Vikings* now.

"What happened, Nev? Drake said Roman wouldn't say anything else, just asked me to come over and keep you company."

"He left me. Packed some of his stuff and left."

"What? That doesn't make any sense. Did he read the article?"

"He did. It's why he left. He said I betrayed his trust," I mutter. Then I explain what happened after Roman got home. "I have no idea what he meant when he said I spilled his secrets. You read the article before I even sent it to Kai; you know there was nothing personal in there about him...it was all about how he makes me feel, how much I love him." Letting go of my legs, I lower them to the floor and lean the back of my head against the couch, my eyes glued to the ceiling.

Angie taps her foot on the floor, her fingers rapping over her belly. Suddenly, she stands up. "I was in such a hurry to get here that I totally forgot. Drake brought the magazine home," she says loudly, but I don't pay her any attention. I'm wallowing in my misery.

I know he's *the one* with all certainty. From the first time we met, I think my soul knew it. Even before he said a single word to me. It already felt different when our eyes met that night at the club. Something in him called out to my heart, and it felt right. Like our souls were made of the same material, fitting each other perfectly and filling one another with happiness and a sense of belonging. It's a connection I can't even explain. No logic, no rational thought. I saw all of him—happy, sad, and even shattered—and it only made me fall for him more.

But now I wonder if it was just me?

"Nev." Angie's voice pulls me out of my thoughts, and I sit up with a soft groan.

"What?" I stare at my best friend, who's standing in front of me with the magazine in her hands.

"This is not the same article I read," she says, and my eyes widen. "Like, it's the same, but it's also different. The part about Roman is rewritten."

"What are you talking about?" I snatch the magazine from her hands and skim it. The more I read, the harder my jaw clenches. What I wrote about my parents, Kyle, and Angie is here, but not what I wrote about Roman.

The last third of the article tells the story of his life in Belarus, including parts I didn't even know about. He never mentioned he had problems with alcohol after his brother's death, just like he never said that his dad died of a heart attack. He told me he drank himself to death.

What the hell is this?

"I don't understand." I raise my face and peer at Angie.

"Someone rewrote your article," she suggests, sitting beside me.

"I know that, Angie." I instantly cringe at how I sound. She doesn't deserve my anger; this is not her fault. "I just have no clue why someone would do this. If Kai thought my article wasn't good enough, or compelling enough, he should've told me." I shake my head, my heartbeat racing. "Plus, you know, this"—I point at the article—"requires a lot of digging. And I didn't know about some of those things from Roman's past. He never told me about them."

"You think Kai asked someone to dig up dirt on Roman? To rewrite your article?"

"It seems like that, but...it doesn't make any sense." I close the magazine and toss it onto the coffee table. "Kai came to my office the second he finished reading it and said he loved it. He praised me for writing so openly about my past, about my trauma and my feelings for Roman. He said I was very delicate with what I put in there."

Angie bites her bottom lip, her palm absentmindedly caressing her baby bump. "Roman is very reserved; he doesn't like talking about his past. I'm honestly not sure anyone but Colton knows much about him. So I understand why he saw this article as a betrayal."

"So do I." I stand up and start pacing back and forth. "Roman struggled with opening up to me. And...and he said no one knows about some of the things he's told me. He really trusted me, Angie, and now he thinks I used him to write this story. He doesn't believe I love him."

"He's pissed off and hurt. Before he can really listen to you, he needs to calm down. If there are things in there he didn't tell you about, it will be easy to prove that you didn't write that."

"I need to talk to Kai first. I need to know how this happened and who is responsible." I grab my phone from the table. "Fuck, it's eleven p.m."

"Wait for tomorrow, Nev."

"But—"

"You can't change anything right now. Plus, Roman needs time to cool off—give it to him. He'll listen to you. I'm sure he will."

"What if you're wrong?"

Angie stands up from the couch and takes my hands in hers, holding my gaze. "Roman was angry and hurt, but he still asked Drake to tell me to come here. That speaks volumes. Your husband loves you, even if he doesn't realize it."

"I'm so scared I'll lose him forever," I confess. My heart flutters weakly in my chest, afraid to beat stronger because of the pain it's in.

"You're the girl who makes his bad days better. The girl who makes him the happiest I've ever seen him." Angie smiles softly, her fingers rubbing my wrists with affection. "Sometimes to get to our happy ending we need to go through some shit, to fight against all odds, but that only makes it more worth it. He was yours before you knew it. Even before he knew it." She lets go of my hands and cups my face. "The way you met, him saving you that night at the club, letting you stay here, asking you to go to Vegas with him...it's destiny, Nev. It can't be anything else."

"I hope you're right." I smile at her in return. Her words plant seeds of hope inside my chest, waves of warmth that spread through my veins. "Will you stay with me?"

"Like you even had to ask," Angie laughs.

Listening to her melodic laughter, I feel the tightness in my chest loosen a bit. A familiar comfort blankets my body, and I know it's all because of her. She's my family. My home. And with her around, I start to believe that all is not lost.

This man is mine, and I'll do anything to get him back.

"Hey," I say, walking into Kai's office without knocking. "You got a minute?"

Kai's eyes roam over my face, deep wrinkles bracketing his mouth as he frowns. "Is everything alright? You don't look so good."

"I look like someone who spent all night crying, so 'don't look so good' sounds like a compliment." I slump into the chair across from him and fold my arms over my chest. "What happened to my article?"

Kai rears back in his seat and presses an open palm to the top of his head, confusion written all over his face. He pokes his tongue into his cheek, studying me in silence. "What do you mean? It's doing amazing. All the comments are positive, praising you for being brave enough to speak up, thanking you for sharing a story so many can relate to. It only proves what—"

"I don't care about any of that, Kai." I cut him off angrily and lean forward, setting my elbows on his desk. "What happened to my article? Who did you ask to rewrite it?"

"Rewrite it? I didn't ask anyone to rewrite it," he states with conviction. "You sent me a draft, I read it and told you how much I loved it. Then, a day later, you sent me another draft, saying you thought it would be more powerful than the first and I should use that one."

My jaw falls, and I gawk at my boss, unblinking. *I did what?*

"I-I sent you another file?"

"Nev, are you okay?" Kai asks quietly. "If you're having problems, just tell me. I'll do what I can to help."

The buzz in my ears intensifies. Kai says something, but I don't hear it. A fog clouds my mind, and my heart suddenly feels so heavy, it's preventing me from being able to take deep breaths.

"Can you...Kai, can you show me that email?"

"Of course." He nods, clicks his mouse a few times, and then turns his screen to me. "I was surprised you decided to revise it, honestly. It went from you talking about your feelings for Roman to you telling his story, but I thought you decided to add more drama. To drive your point home about people who live without love."

"I didn't do that. This is not my article, and I didn't send you this email. Someone else did."

"But..." Kai glances sideways, scowling and looking lost in thought. "You said something was happening with my emails to you.

That it looked as if you'd read them when you didn't." I nod, swallowing my nerves. "Did you talk to our tech team?"

"They said they didn't know why it was happening. That it didn't look like anyone had hacked my email."

"When was the last time you changed your password?" I shake my head signaling that I don't remember, and Kai's face darkens. "Someone must've had access to your email. Maybe they were reading my emails to you, checking your emails to me. Whoever it was probably replaced the article too."

"Access to my..." I trail off, the picture slowly becoming crystal clear. How could I've been so stupid? The explanation was right there. "I'm such an idiot."

"You know who did this?"

I nod, standing up from my chair. "Travis."

"Your ex? He hacked your email?"

"He didn't need to. A few months ago, I forgot my laptop here at the office, so I used his. I logged in to my email, sent the article I was working on to myself, and closed the laptop. I didn't even check to see if I logged out; I never thought it would be a problem." I stalk to the door, anger bubbling inside of my body.

"You want me to come with you?" Kai rises in his chair, but I shake my head no.

"It's fine. I can handle him." I open the door but pause in the doorframe. "Can you please replace what's online with my original article?"

"Of course," my boss says. "And take the day off. I'm guessing your husband wasn't happy with that article."

"He wasn't, but I'll do anything I can to fix it," I reply and walk out the door. "I love him, and I refuse to give up on us."

"Attagirl." Kai's voice follows me as I head down the hallway.

If someone had told me that Travis would do something like this, I would've never believed them. He wasn't malicious or scheming. He was a good guy through and through. Until he wasn't.

Because I broke his heart.

VIRAJ, Travis's colleague, sees me first. There's a cup of coffee pressed to his lips. He lowers it and smiles, waving at me.

"Nevaeh, hey. It's been a while," he says as I stop beside him, sweeping my gaze over the office's open floor plan. "How did you get in?"

"Rosie let me in." Joining my ex and his coworkers for drinks a few times definitely came in handy today. Rosie, a nice girl from reception, let me in right away. "Where is Travis?"

"On a call in the conference room." Viraj points to a room with tinted glass walls.

"Thanks, Viraj. It was nice to see you." I veer to my right, saunter over to the door, and knock loudly.

I'm absolutely fuming. It takes a lot not to show how furious I am. But I don't want to be kicked out before I can talk to Travis.

The door swings open, and Travis's face comes into view. He steps back, surprise coloring his features. I push past him, and he lets me, closing the door once I'm inside. Squinting at his laptop, I know his call is over. The code editor is launched, and the lines of whatever code he's working on are displayed on the screen.

"What are you doing here, Nevaeh?"

"Don't pretend you don't know," I grit, plopping myself down into a chair.

"You *finally* figured out I've been checking your emails. Took you long enough I must say. I kinda hoped you'd realize it sooner." He smirks, sitting down across from me. "I could've marked them as 'unread' and you would've never even known something was wrong, but I wanted you to know...and you disappointed me."

"Why did you even care about what was in my work emails?"

"I saw you with *your husband* in his car after you brought Happy back, and you lied to my fucking face when I confronted you about him." Travis shrugs. "Hurt people hurt people, isn't that what they say?"

I shake my head in disbelief. "Did it make you feel better? To spy on me? To replace the article I wrote? Did any of it make you feel better about yourself?"

"In fact," Travis says, relaxing back into his chair, "it did. How does your boy toy feel now? Not so powerful, I assume?" The smile that forms on his face makes me nauseous. "I swear, all that time I spent googling him paid off and it came in very handy when I realized I could use it for your piece. If you only knew how many articles I read in Russian, how many Facebook and VK groups I scoured for inside information. Did you know they have a Russian version of Facebook? It was created by—"

"I don't care!" I yell, shutting him up. "What you did is horrible! Didn't you see what kind of life he had? His twin died and—"

"People die every day, Nevaeh. I don't see you crying about any of them."

I ball my fists, glaring at him. I'm not a violent person, but I swear I want to strangle him. "*I* broke your heart. *I* left you. It had nothing to do with Roman. Why are you targeting him?"

"It had everything to do with him," Travis seethes. "I read your article, Nevaeh. You wrote about your feelings for him. About how you were crushing on him even when you were with *me*." He slams his hand on the table. "I loved you. I wanted to marry you, and you left me the moment you found the ring."

"Because I didn't love you, and I thought it was more honest to leave you then instead of continuing to lead you on."

Travis jerks back in his seat; his upper lip curls into a sneer. "What do you even see in him?"

"Everything you don't," I state, my cheeks heating up. "Roman is loyal, caring, and kind, and you ripped him apart with that article. You have no idea what it means to live with the guilt he's carrying. How hard it is for him to open up. And you made him believe that I betrayed him."

"Did he leave you?"

"He did."

Travis smirks. "Good. Now you know how it feels to have your heart broken. I hope you like it."

His last words hang in the air, and the atmosphere in the room becomes heavier. On my way to his office, I googled what I can do to punish him, and apparently, there's not much. I can't press charges. He didn't hack my email or steal my identity. I gave him access to my email, albeit unknowingly, so it's my fault he even had the opportunity to do this. I could try to sue him for emotional distress, but that would mean putting myself and Roman in the spotlight. And I don't think I want that.

I stand up, keeping my eyes trained on Travis. "I felt terrible about how I broke up with you. You were nothing but good to me, but I had to break your heart because I didn't feel the same way about you. After Roman and I got accidentally married, the only thing I worried about was you. I didn't want you to find out, because I knew it would only make things worse. I didn't want to hurt you more than I already had," I say quietly and round the table, stopping next to him. "You were a good guy, Travis. A good guy with his heart in the right place... but not anymore. To be so cruel? So vindictive toward someone who didn't do anything to you? Who you knew suffered from unimaginable pain? Good people don't do things like that."

Travis looks up, meeting my gaze and licking his bottom lip. "I didn't think about what it would be like for him. What it would be like to have everyone know about his past. I just wanted to hurt you for hurting me," he says with conviction, and I don't see a single sign of regret on his face. His eyebrows are pierced together, the corners of his mouth dropped.

"Well, now you have to live with what you've done, Travis."

I turn around and pad out of the conference room, down the hallway and straight to the elevators. Wasting even one more minute of my time on my ex-boyfriend seems pointless. I have way more important things to do.

ME:

I know you're angry with me, and that I'm the last person on the planet you want to see, but I really need to talk to you. That wasn't my article you read. I would never betray you like that. I swear, Roman.

I hit send, and then I type another one.

ME:

I know what happened, and I can explain everything. Please, come home, Roman. Come back to me.

Roman

THIRTY-SEVEN

because i love her?

I park my Kawasaki in the driveway of a two-story house, then I hop off it and look around. Clay lives in a very nice neighborhood, not very far from Ava and Colton's house. His house is white with a red tiled roof, large windows, and a spacious lawn—looks like something I would want for myself if I decided to settle down and start a family.

That was an incredibly dumb thought, Roman.

"What do you think?" Clay asks, climbing out of his Mercedes-Benz G-Wagon. "You like my little house?"

"I wouldn't call it little," I counter and strut to the backseat of his car, opening the door and taking out my gym bag. "Thank you again for letting me crash. Really appreciate it."

"It's fine. What are friends for if you can't ask them to stay at their house for a few days?" Clay smiles, takes his own bag from the back-seat, and locks the car once the door is closed. "Besides, I figured you couldn't ask Thompson or Benson, because they'd both have a ton of questions. Drake even more than Colt since Nevaeh is his fiancée's best friend."

I roll my eyes but don't say anything, following him into the house. The ride on my motorcycle helped me to calm down a little, emptying my mind of the thoughts that have been troubling me since the moment I read the article. The only question I still have is why. Why would she do something like that to me?

And why the hell did she look so surprised when I asked her about it?

"Want something to drink? Or eat?" Clay looks at me over his shoulder, but I just shake my head. "Okay, let's show you to your room then. But in case you change your mind, the kitchen is over there." He points to his right. "Don't have much in the fridge, but I'm sure you'll find something."

"Thanks, Clay."

We go upstairs, and Clay opens the third door on his left, turning on the lights and stepping inside. I follow him in and sweep my gaze over the bedroom. It's a big room, beige in color, with expansive windows and dark blue curtains. There's a queen-size bed, a desk with a chair, a mirror, and a closet. There's also an en suite bathroom. Simple yet thoughtful. I would've done a guest room the same way if I had a house like this. *Fuck.* What's wrong with me tonight? A borrowed life in a borrowed place is my destiny. There's no need for stupid fantasies that I can have something more.

"It's not much, but I hope you like it."

"It's more than you think," I say, walking to the bed and putting my gym bag on it. "I'll try to find an apartment as soon as possible so I can be out of your hair—"

"You can stay as long as you need, Roman." Clay shrugs. "I actually don't mind the company. Living alone in a house like this can be... well..."

Lonely. That's what he wanted to say, and I can relate. It was exactly how I felt in my apartment. Everything was good and all, but something was missing. Until I brought Nevaeh home after finding her at the club. She filled my place with comfort and warmth...and now I'm running away like a coward because she hurt me.

"Make yourself at home." Clay saunters to the door, clapping me on the back on his way out. "And Roman?" I turn my head to look at him as he pauses in the doorframe. "If you need to talk, I'm here."

I nod, my throat closing up, and Clay walks out and closes the door behind him. Alone, I stand unmoving, my arms dangling at my sides. The strong persona I tried to maintain around Nevaeh and Clay is collapsing, and the pain in my chest becomes stronger. It's hard to breathe fully, hard to think rationally. I'm full of volatile emotions, and I've bottled them up and silently hoped that they wouldn't explode.

Opening the bag, I quickly rummage through the clothes I brought with me. After finding black sweatpants and a white tee, I grab them and go to the bathroom. I put my phone on the bathroom counter, strip naked, and step into the shower, turning on the cold water. Goosebumps rise on my skin, and my hair slowly becomes damp as I raise my face to the water and stand still. The cold is helping me to stop worrying about my feelings, and I desperately need it. I have never hurt like this before because of a girl.

The ringing of my phone snaps me out of my trance. Shivering and with trembling hands, I turn off the water and step out of the shower. Then I dry my hands with a small towel, pick up my phone, and press it to my ear.

"Hey, Mom." My teeth clatter so hard that I clench my jaw tight.

"Hey," she sighs. "How are you?"

"I'm okay," I lie.

"Roma, can you please stop pretending? You're thousands of kilometers away from me, but I know when you're not alright. Always," Mom says. "I woke up this morning to an avalanche of messages from your aunt and cousins. I read the article."

"Unfortunately, I read it too." I climb back into the shower stall and sit on the floor, staring in front of me and not seeing anything. "I'm so sorry, Mom. If I'd known Nevaeh was going to reveal everything I told her, I would've never opened up to her. She betrayed me just to gain more traction on her little article."

Mom is silent, and my eyes veil with unwelcome tears. I press my fist to my mouth and wait for my mom to say something. Is she disappointed in me? Does she resent me for being such a pussy that I couldn't keep my mouth shut?

"I'm glad you opened up to her." What? "It was killing you inside,

Roma, and you didn't even see it. You were allowing darkness to consume you, keeping everything to yourself. Nevaeh helped you let it out, to let go of some of your grief. Your guilt. Your hate for yourself. She helped you."

"Mom, did you even read it?"

"I did, and honestly, I couldn't care less about it. It's our tragedy. It's our family's past. There's nothing to be ashamed of."

"People pity me," I hiss. "I don't deserve that. They should despise me."

"Why?"

"What do you mean 'why'?"

"Why should they despise you? You lost your brother. Your father was terrible to you, but you still—"

"Because you don't know what I said to Maks the last time I talked to him. If you did, you would hate me too."

"I would never hate you, Roma! Stop talking nonsense."

I laugh bitterly. "That night, he asked me to go with him to see Alisa. He told me he needed me. Do you want to know what I told him, Mom? I laughed in his face and said he would be fine on his own. I was so angry with him for running to see that girl that I ignored how miserable he looked. I walked away and went back to party with our friends while my brother climbed into the car with Kirill and fucking died." The words spill out of my mouth, no longer hidden, and my chest tenses. "That's what I did, Mom. I betrayed my twin, and I deserve this life."

"Roma..." Mom mumbles. "Why did you never tell me about this before?"

"Because I knew you'd hate me, just like my father did. And I just...I couldn't..."

"I could never hate you," Mom says, her voice cracking. "I can't. You're only human, and we all make mistakes. We all say things we don't mean, believe that we've made the right decision and then discover we were wrong. It's all a part of life." A sob bolts out of my throat, and I cover my mouth with my palm. "You were an emotional teenager who thought his brother was making a mistake. You wanted the best for Maksim, and you never thought that was Alisa. I finally understand what's been gnawing at you all these years, but it's not your fault. Maks didn't die because of you. Your words didn't lead him to get into the car. He would've gone to see her anyway. It's not your fault."

"Mom..." I choke on my words, tears streaming down my cheeks.

"It's not your fault, Roma. Please, Synok, listen to me. We're not responsible for other people's actions, even if they are our family. You loved your brother. Maks was your entire world, just like you were for him. My beautiful boys, always standing up for each other and being best friends, sharing the same goals and dreams. It's unfair and absolutely gut-wrenching that he died so young, and I know you'll never fully recover because losing him was like losing part of you. But I need you...I'm begging you, Roma, please live. Please stop exhausting yourself with this guilt. It's not your burden to carry. It never was."

Sitting on the shower floor, I cry. My tears are hot and bitter. I bite the inside of my cheek, pressing the phone harder to my ear. "Nevaeh said I should've told you about it a long time ago. She was sure you would understand."

"She's a good girl, Roma, and she makes you happy. I haven't seen you so full of joy in years. You started to heal because of her. You smiled so much more, laughed and joked around whenever we talked."

"It hurts so fucking much that she betrayed my trust." I pause; my shoulders are shaking uncontrollably. "Why does it hurt so much, Mom?"

"Because you love her," Mom murmurs. "And it's not just a silly infatuation; this love is real, Roma. It can even mend the broken pieces of your soul. You need to hold her close and never let her go."

I chew on my bottom lip. "I left her. I took my things and left her."

"Roma!" Mom gasps loudly. I can just imagine her clutching her heart, something she always does when she's nervous. "That was wrong. You need to learn how to forgive—yourself and others."

"How can I forgive her if she can't even explain why she did it? I asked her, and she pretended to be surprised. As if she had no idea what I was talking about."

"Did you give her a chance to explain?"

"I asked her—"

"No, Synok, I'm not asking you what you said to her. I'm asking what she told you."

I tell Mom what happened after I came home, and how stunned Nevaeh was when I accused her of spilling my secrets. The image of her on my couch with the toy I gave her pressed to her chest won't leave my mind. She looked so damn confused; those blue eyes full of tears were staring at me with so much hurt. It aggravated me more than anything. Instead of admitting what she'd done or even trying to justify it somehow, she kept acting like she did nothing wrong.

"At least she didn't say anything about Alisa, or about my talk with Maksim. Instead, she just exposed my problems with alcohol and how my father died," I mutter. Then I instantly fall quiet. Something about what I said catches me off guard, but my mind is too fucked up to think clearly now.

"You can't cut people out of your life just because they made a mistake. Especially not Nevaeh."

"Because I love her?" I smirk. My voice is still hoarse.

"Yes, because you love her and because you'll regret not giving your relationship another chance," Mom says softly. "Some people deserve a second chance, Roma, and you deserve one more than anyone I know."

"I'll think about it," I promise, meaning it with all my soul.

"Good. Now, where are you staying?" Mom asks, and I tell her how I asked Clay if I could stay at his house and how he said yes without trying to interrogate me about what happened.

Talking to my mom calms me down, and when I finally hang up, I don't feel as hopeless as I did before. I put my phone back on the bathroom counter, get back into the shower, and turn on the hot water. Standing under the stream, I let it envelop me, warming my skin and my insides.

Tomorrow's a new day. I hope it's a better one.

I STARE AT MY PHONE, rereading Nevaeh's texts over and over. She says that wasn't the article she wrote, that she knows what happened and can explain it. And my stupid heart gets full of hope in an instant. It beats stronger, reminding me of a steady drum rhythm.

She asks me to come home, and damn if I don't want to rush there immediately. God, I got it bad. So fucking bad, I want to laugh at myself. I'm hopeless.

Pocketing my phone in my jeans, I pull on my hoodie and glance at myself in the mirror. I ruffle my hair with my hand, trying to tame it and instantly giving up. Only a haircut will fix this mess. Grabbing my leather jacket, I leave the room and head down the stairs. The noise of something that sounds like a football game catches my attention, and I walk into the living room.

Clay sits on the couch, a controller in his hand. On his huge TV screen, there's a football pitch, and players in Real Madrid and Barcelona kits are moving around.

"You play FIFA?"

"Going somewhere?" he asks, not even bothering to reply.

"Yeah, I need to meet someone."

"Just out of curiosity, is this someone a blonde girl with big blue eyes and puffy lips? Petite and super hot?"

"I'd really appreciate it if you kept your eyes off of my wife," I grit, and Clay bursts out laughing.

"Aw, I played you like a kid, Pashkevich," he says between fits of laughter. "Go, meet your wife. Looks like you'll be moving back home in no time"

"Fuck off, Rodgers," I huff, turning on my heel and sauntering to the front door. And yet, a smile blooms on my lips, because he might be right.

THE SOUND of the engine reverberates through my body, making my skin hum as I move faster and faster through traffic. The ride brings me joy, a happy smile plastered to my face. The freeway isn't overloaded with cars, and I think I might be home in less than fifteen minutes. It's sunny out, and I speed up even more, leaning forward as I near another turn.

The screeching of tires makes me tense. I dip my chin slightly and notice a car heading straight at me after another one slammed into its right side.

Well...fuck.

The revving of the engine becomes deafening as I speed up, praying with everything I have I'll make it out of the path of the vehicle. My body is rigid as I concentrate all my attention on the road ahead of me.

Barely escaping the oncoming car, I speed up even more. And just when I think I'm safe, I realize that it's an illusion. Losing control of the motorcycle, I try my hardest to stay seated. There's only one way... and fuck, I hate it. My nerves are like chords when I manage to lay my Kawasaki down and slide along with it. The scraping sounds of metal and the screeching of tires are all I hear, but when my body drags along the bike, a pained groan comes out of my parted lips.

Fucking hell, it hurts everywhere.

My motorcycle comes to a controlled stop, and I rise to my feet, pressing my palm to my ribs. I'm breathing hard as my eyes roam over the road. Cars are stopping, and people are running over to check on me and the driver of the car that was coming at me. Its hood is wedged into a pole. There are skid marks on the road from my Kawasaki, and broken glass from one of the mirrors, but other than that, it seems fine. I feel okay. Except for my ribs, but that might be a simple bruise.

I turn my head, and everything in me stills. Even my heart stops beating. With shaking hands, I take off my helmet and peer at the space between two cars, where I just saw my brother. No one is there, and my knees give out. I take a few steps forward, then slump onto my ass on the curb.

Did Maksim save me?

Nevaeh

THIRTY-EIGHT

everlasting

When I hear the door close, I quickly put my mug on the counter and walk out of the kitchen. The sound of Roman speaking Russian sends shivers down my spine, my anxious heart thrashing against my rib cage. But the fact that he read my texts and didn't reply doesn't give me much hope.

I halt in my tracks the second my eyes land on Roman. He's holding his phone to his ear, and...Colton Thompson is standing beside him with his hands hidden in his pockets.

"Hey, Nevaeh," Colton says, his dark brown eyes coasting over my face.

"Hey," I mumble weakly, watching hopelessly as Roman stomps past me to his bedroom. He's still on the phone when he closes the door behind him.

Sigh. His behavior definitely doesn't indicate a readiness to listen to me. Quite the contrary, actually. Forcing a smile onto my face, I focus my attention on Colton instead. "Is everything okay?" I blurt.

"Yes." He nods, shifting his weight from his heels to his toes. "Everything is fine."

Silence stretches between us, and my skin starts to itch. It's so uncomfortable, I want to scream. I glance over my shoulder at

Roman's closed bedroom door and then return my gaze to Colton. "Are you guys going somewhere?"

"No, I gave him a lift home," he tells me, his eyes softening. "Roman crashed his motorcycle, and he was in the hospital—"

"What?" I yell, my hand flying to my mouth.

Colton instantly steps closer and puts his hands on my shoulders, dipping his head to look me in the eyes. "He's alright. He has some cuts and a nasty bruise on his right side, but that's all," he says confidently. "I'm his emergency contact, so I came to the hospital as soon as I got the call and brought him here once he was cleared...Your man is a lucky guy, and a very skilled driver."

"Is he really alright?"

"Yes," Colton says with a small grin. "Trust me, if that wasn't the case, I would've never let him leave the hospital."

His calmness transfers to me, and my heartbeat slows down. Colton has no reason to lie to me. With a curt nod, I take a step back, right as the door to Roman's room opens. My eyes snap in his direction, roaming around his body, trying to see if there are any visible signs of the crash. When I bring my gaze to his face, I see a soft smile on his lips as he saunters over to me.

God, it's been less than twenty-four hours since I've seen him, but it feels like an eternity passed. My longing for him takes a hold of my throat, and I'm struggling to produce even a single sound.

Roman stops by my side and looks at his friend. "Thank you, Colt. Again."

"No worries," Colton says, his gaze dancing between my husband and me. "You're home safe, and you're not alone, so I'm going to go."

Turning on his heel, Colton walks down the hallway, and Roman follows him. Without thinking, I call out to Thompson.

"Colton?"

"Yeah?" He glances over his shoulder, meeting my gaze.

"Thank you."

With a nod, he gives me a smile and proceeds to the door with Roman in tow. I step to the couch and plop down on it, breathing in and out and rubbing my sweaty palms over the skirt of my dress. So many emotions. So many feelings are brewing inside my chest. But the most overwhelming one is love...one I was so sure I wasn't capable of.

Love that doesn't know any restraints. Doesn't see obstacles or accept any rules. But I love my husband without holding back. With an open heart and a burning soul. It's when I lose myself in Roman, only to find my true self in the reflection of his eyes.

And I swear, never in my life have I felt more...beautiful, smart, desired than I feel with him.

I found my person in him.

"Hey." His voice is quiet as he lowers himself beside me. His shoulder touching mine makes my body buzz. Then he covers my palm with his, on the skirt of my dress, and a jolt of electricity goes right through me. I look at him, and he smiles, threading his fingers through mine and lifting my hand to his mouth. His soft lips press to my palm, awakening the butterflies in my stomach—or more like making them go absolutely insane, because I swear I even feel ticklish from what's happening in my stomach.

I ask the first thing that comes to mind. "Were you talking to your mom?"

Roman chuckles, nodding. "Yeah, needed to apologize for lying to her. And I promised that I'm not going to fix my Kawasaki." I arch an eyebrow, not sure if I really believe him. "I swear, Nevaeh, I'm really not going to ride it ever again. That was the last time."

"I'll pretend I believe you," I say with a smile. Then I fall quiet. I feel like we're tiptoeing around the conversation we really need to have. Or maybe I'm tiptoeing, since I was the one who decided to ask him who he was talking to.

Ugh, I should've kept my mouth shut, because now the room is irritatingly silent. I have so many things to say to him—hell, I've been practicing what I was going to say to him since I left the office, but now the words hang on the tip of my tongue, and nothing happens.

"I'm sorry," Roman and I finally say at once, and we both laugh.

"Can I go first?" Roman asks, and I nod. "Yesterday, when I read your article on the plane, I was so furious that I didn't even question how some of those things got in there. I never told you about my first team, and how my future with them was in danger because I started drinking so much after Maksim's death. I never told you about my father and how exactly he died. But so many things that I did tell you about mixed with the things I didn't, and they went overlooked. I saw only the picture as a whole, and I instantly assumed you betrayed me. Because of my trust issues. After that, I didn't think at all. All I felt was rage. I didn't even try to understand why you looked so surprised when I told you about the article; that only aggravated me more and pushed me to run away from you.

"I'm so sorry for walking away, Nevaeh. I'm sorry for not listening to you. For not trying to talk things through. I should've never left you the way I did. I should've never hurt you. I...I was a coward, hiding behind my pain and feelings of injustice." Roman hangs his head low, looking at my palm resting in his. "It's like a breakaway in hockey—a mistake by a defense. When an opponent is left alone with the goalie, with no defense in sight. That's exactly what I did... defending only myself, I left you alone instead of staying and trying to figure out what happened. You didn't deserve that...and I honestly don't deserve you."

"Remember I told you about the strange things happening to my emails?" I ask, clearing my throat. "It was Travis. A few months ago, before we broke up, I logged in to my email from his laptop and forgot to log out. He had access to it, and he replaced my original article with the version you read. He became a jealous, pitiful man. He wanted you to leave me because he knew it would break my heart. He wanted to hurt me for the pain I caused him. You were collateral damage, no more than that."

"The dedication that it took..." Roman shakes his head in disbelief. "You'll probably think I'm crazy after everything that has happened, but I'm grateful to him." My lips part, and I blink, not sure I heard him right. "I finally don't have any secrets from my mom, and she doesn't hate me for what I said to Maks. She said she understands, and that she never would've blamed me for his death. You were absolutely right."

"I'm really happy you talked to your mom, and I hope it helps you move on." My eyes are welling up with tears when I put my head on his shoulder and sigh deeply. "Moving on doesn't mean forgetting Maksim."

"I know that now."

We smile at each other, and my chest doesn't feel so tight anymore. And yet, there's something I really want him to do...something I've wanted him to do since yesterday.

Grabbing my phone from the coffee table, I pull up my article and hand it to Roman. "This is what I wrote about you."

"Nevaeh..." he mutters, staring me in the eyes. The intense turquoise color entices me.

"Please, Roman, read it," I insist, and he obeys.

> *People who hate their own existence and don't believe they deserve anything good. I recognize their demons, because in the past they were my demons too.*
>
> *After years of being in the dark, being broken and not believing I deserved to be loved, I never really let anyone get close to me, except for Angie. I was attracted to my partners. I was even in love, but I always held myself back. It didn't feel right to open up, and I didn't feel comfortable enough to share my secrets. Until a man with the most beautiful eyes swept me off my feet.*
>
> *My Roman.*
>
> *The night I met him changed everything for me, even though I didn't know that then. I wasn't single, and I never acted on my attraction, but whenever I was around him, my eyes involuntarily looked for him. On the ice at his games. At the parties our friends would throw. I wanted to be close to him, but I kept my distance because it was wrong.*
>
> *Even after I finally found the strength to break up with the man I was in a relationship with because I didn't want to continue leading him on, I never thought anything would happen between Roman and me. I*

ended my relationship for me, and for my boyfriend, because he didn't deserve to be with someone who didn't love him.

I wanted to find myself after the breakup, but instead...Roman found me. Everything that has happened since the moment he stumbled upon me at the nightclub led us to where we ended up—at that chapel in Vegas. With me becoming the wife of the man I was crushing on, all while being unsure if he even liked me.

What were the odds that something like that would end well? I didn't know, but I was willing to risk it all. And dear God, how glad I am that I decided to stay.

Broken people know how to love. They went through hell and saw the face of darkness looking right at them, and it still didn't dim their light. Being with Roman taught me that. Even all the hardships and sorrow he went through didn't destroy him. All he needed was someone to be there for him, to help his brightness shine through the broken parts of his soul.

I saw all of him, and I've never loved anyone more than I love him. He's everything I've ever dreamed of. Everything my heart has ever craved. Whatever my soul is made of, it matches his in the most beautiful way. And, what's more, it feels right to be with him.

Real love isn't perfect. It has ups and downs to face and overcome. It needs a lot of work, and it rarely looks like a fairy tale or a romance novel. It's a four-letter word, but its meaning is bigger and more significant than we know.

Everyone defines love in different ways, because no two loves are the same, and that's the beauty of it. That's exactly what makes it worth it.

Mine is the man with the unruly hair and the deep turquoise eyes, who loves the hardest even when he doesn't think he can. He helped me find parts of me that I didn't know existed. He healed me even when I thought I was the one healing him.

He's mine, and I'm his for as long as he wants me. And, selfishly, I hope it's forever.

I know he's done reading when he locks my phone and sits quietly, his fingers wrapped tightly around it. The storm inside me that I expected doesn't come. I'm calm, and warmth spreads over my skin. It's a feeling of hope that fills my every pore and stretches my lips into the biggest smile. I'm happiest when I'm with him, and something tells me it's the same for him.

"When I stood up after my motorcycle finally came to a stop, I looked around, still in shock. I was unscathed. I couldn't wrap my head around why, and then I saw him...I saw Maksim, Nevaeh. He was standing there, between two cars, smiling at me and shaking his head in disbelief at what an idiot I am." His voice cracks with emotion, his eyes finding mine. "I think he saved me. Maks was the reason I was able to lay my Kawasaki down instead of crashing it at full speed. My little brother showed me that I need to live, and...fuck, you probably think I've lost my mind—"

"Not at all." I take his hand in mine, moving my thumbs in slow circles on his skin. "I think your brother saved you because he needs you to live. For you and for him. Please, Roman, be happy. Live life to the fullest. Love as hard as you can. You owe it to Maksim. He will live on through you."

Roman smiles and presses his forehead to mine, inhaling deeply and closing his eyes. "Somewhere in my chest, I have a heart. It's probably not as big as most people's, especially after years of me hating myself and forbidding myself to feel. But it's full of love for you," Roman whispers and opens his eyes, a gentle smile playing on his lips. "Ya lyublyu tebya[1], Nevaeh. I love you. Only you, and I hope you want to stay with me. Because I can't imagine my forever with anyone else."

---

1. Я люблю тебя — I love you

"And I can't imagine mine without you," I say, happy tears leaking down my face. He kisses me without hesitation, his lips moving slowly with mine. It seems like just another kiss, but it feels different. Like the whole world stopped moving, like time froze and there's only us. A man and a woman who accidentally married in Vegas...not knowing then that it was their destiny.

We were always meant to be, even if at first it didn't look like it.

Roman entwines our fingers and pulls me into his side. "I'm so happy to be home with you, Malyshka," he whispers, kissing my temple, and I feel an immense happiness spilling all over my body.

In the past, I was afraid that one day I'd lose myself in the person I love. It scared me and prevented me from really opening up to my partners, so I always kept them at arm's length. Until Roman came along. He found a vacant spot in my heart and decided to stay.

Our love feels better than anything else in the world. Because it's real, and because this kind of love is everlasting.

just married

epilogue

ROMAN

Closing the door to the apartment, I'm met with total silence. It's not what I expected after getting home from our seventh win in a row. Excitement bubbles inside me, and pride warms my veins and makes me feel good.

Where is my wife? I didn't think she had plans tonight.

I walk further inside, taking my phone out of my pocket and dialing Nevaeh's number. Right as I'm about to press the phone to my ear, I hear her phone ringing in our bedroom.

Okay, she's definitely got my attention.

"Malyshka?" I say and push open the door to our bedroom. The view my eyes land on makes my mouth water and all decent thoughts vanish.

"What took you so long?" Nevaeh asks breathlessly, fucking herself slowly with one of her toys, a pink rabbit vibrator. We got it for her a few weeks ago, before I left for my away games. She said she felt lonely without me and needed something new to try. Little did I know that trying new things also meant me getting a call on FaceTime while she pleasured herself. I never came harder from watching than I did that time with her.

"Well, we won." I walk into the room and close the door behind me. "The guys wanted to celebrate."

"I wanted to celebrate too," Nevaeh murmurs, driving the vibrator deeper into her pussy. "Had to be creative, since my husband wasn't here."

I swallow my saliva, because damn if she doesn't remind me of the most delicious dish on the menu at some fancy restaurant. With her round, perky tits and pebbled nipples and her beautiful cunt glistening with her wetness, she drives me absolutely insane, making me reckless. Unhinged, even, if I think about all the things I've done and want to do with her.

As I get rid of my clothes, I keep my eyes on the prize. On my wife, who continues fucking herself with her toy, moaning louder with each new thrust. When I'm fully naked, I climb onto the bed and sit in front of her with my hand wrapped tightly around my dick. Enchanted, I watch her give herself an orgasm, drinking her in from her beautiful face to her toned legs. My heart thumps so violently in my chest, it's keeping me from breathing properly.

"Are you going to come for me again?" I whisper, slowly pumping my cock. "Let me watch, Malyshka."

Nevaeh looks at me, her eyes hooded with desire. Her parted lips call out to me any time I hear the sweetest moan escape them. Reaching between her thighs, I cover her hand with mine and flick the button. The rabbit ears start to massage her clit as I urge her hand to move faster.

"Oh God, Roman!" she cries out, her legs closing in an instant. But I press my other hand on the inside of her thigh and hold her open for me. Relentless, I drive her vibrator deeper and faster inside her. I don't even need to pump myself; my dick grows so hard, even my balls tighten. "Don't stop...please, don't stop."

A few more minutes, and she's a goner. Arching her back, Nevaeh closes her eyes and comes, her body trembling. As slowly as possible, and mostly just to mess with her, I pop the vibrator out of her pussy and turn it off.

"I'll never get tired of this view..." I say, crawling closer and nestling between her legs.

Dipping my head, I take her nipple into my mouth, twirling my tongue around it and then biting it. Again and again. I cup her tit with my palm and play with it, stroking it as I continue my assault on her rosy buds.

Moya devochka[1]. So fucking mine.

Slipping my dick through her slit, I slowly push the tip of my cock inside. Inch by inch, I let her get used to it. Her wetness makes me slide deep quickly, and when I feel her clench around me, I pull out.

"No, baby, not so fast," I taunt her, grabbing her legs and raising them up to her ears. She gasps as I spit on her pussy. "You didn't want to wait for me; that's fine. But I'll make you wait for your orgasm."

I tap her cunt with my dick, making her jerk forward. Gliding it up and down her folds, I let it slip inside her and start thrusting, picking up my pace little by little. Nevaeh moans, chanting my name louder with each dip of my hips. I'm powerless against her charms, my dick feeling hotter the further it slides into her.

"Look at you, Nevaeh. Taking me so good, so full of me," I praise her, my balls slapping against her skin as I bury my dick to the hilt. "Perfect."

My own release is looming, but I refuse to give in, and I pull away again the second her walls squeeze around me.

"Roman, please," Nevaeh whines as I let go of her legs and sit on my ass. "I want to come."

"Good," I tell her, smiling. "I want you to come too."

She scowls, narrowing her eyes at me. Pushing herself up, she sits up and then climbs onto my lap, guiding my dick inside her pussy.

"God, you feel so good," she whispers, winding her arms around my neck. I palm her ass, digging my fingers into her flesh. A faint smile crosses her features when she bends down and seals my lips with hers. Pushing her tongue inside my mouth, she kisses me ravenously and slowly starts to ride me.

---

1. Моя девочка. — My girl.

I slide my hands up her sides until both of my palms are full of her tits. Playing with her nipples, I squeeze and tug on them, making her whimper and then moan in pleasure. Hiding my face in her breasts, I flick my tongue over her puckered nipple, sucking it into my mouth and then moving to the other. Her head lolls back as I sink my teeth into her sensitive skin.

Nevaeh moans, moving up and down on my cock, rotating her hips each time her pussy sinks deep onto my dick. I grip her waist, helping her move faster.

"Just like that, Malyshka," I coo, my eyes falling closed as I feel my release approaching. "Come all over me..."

Riding me harder, Nevaeh rubs her clit against my pelvis. She's so desperate in her desire to come that it makes me smile. My girl is craving my dick, just like I crave her pussy. Day and night. Every day of every fucking week. If I didn't love hockey as much as I do, I would spend all my time fucking her. It's my favorite thing in the world.

"Oh my...Oh my God, Roman; I'm gonna come."

"Fuck...Your pussy..." I'm out of breath. Nevaeh groans, and the next thing I know, her nails are dragging down my back, probably leaving marks all over my skin. "Oh fuck..."

Her cunt clenches around me, pulsating hard over my dick, choking it. She comes, her orgasm crashing down on her, but I don't let her stop. With my hands on her hips, I keep pushing her to move faster for me. Up and down, even breathless, she continues to ride me, her body becoming sweaty.

My lips are ravishing her neck, licking and nibbling on her skin. My release is so close that my mind becomes foggy. "I love your fucking pussy, Nevaeh," I confess in her ear, and I swear I feel her tighten around me again. "Give it to me. Come with me..."

I lift my hips up and down as she continues lowering herself deeper and deeper on my cock. With her name on the tip of my tongue and her walls suffocating me after her third orgasm, I shoot my load inside her.

A minute later, breathing hard, we both fall onto the covers. I turn my head to look at her, and she does the same, a blissful smile on her lips.

"I came four times in an hour," Nevaeh whispers, her fingers tracing my bottom lip. "I need to use the bathroom."

"Of course you do." I catch her index finger in my mouth and suck on it. "We're going to fuck again so I can make you come a few more times before I fall asleep with your tight little ass pressed to my groin."

"My little ass...your groin," she murmurs as I kiss her fingers. "Do you want to try anal?"

"With you, I want to try everything. I want to own every fucking part of you. Including your ass."

"I'm all yours, Roman." Nevaeh smiles as she sits up, her fingers combing her hair. "Sorry, the bathroom can't wait any longer."

She jumps off the bed and strolls to the door, swaying her hips on her way out of the room. I prop my head on my knuckles, my eyes glued to her figure. The image of her hand pops into my mind as I hear the bathroom door closing. She's all mine, and she's my wife, but there's no ring on her finger. And that really doesn't mean anything, because a ring doesn't define a relationship. But I quickly realize that I want her to have one.

Because she's my happy ending.

Hate is always louder than love. Whether it's coming from other people or something we impose on ourselves. It has the power to destroy everything good, leaving only ruins of self-doubt.

Banishing hate is really fucking hard, because it's so much easier to let it consume us. To believe what others say, to let it dim our light. Or, in the case of self-loathing, to just let it win.

But sometimes fighting is worth it. Especially if we have someone special who loves us no matter how sharp the broken pieces of our hearts are. No matter how much darkness we carry inside. They stay, fueling us with light and giving us a reason to live...and to fight for our happiness.

Only love can conquer hate.

And Nevaeh proved that to me when no one else could.

My love for her is wild. It's unpredictable and unexpected. She gives me all the feels, and there isn't a day that goes by when I don't think about her. Like the sweetest oblivion, she makes me lose myself in her and with her.

Ona moya Malyshka[2].

Moyo Solnyshko[3]*, who's always ready to share her warmth with me, especially on days when grief takes a hold of my heart.*

My Nevaeh.

She's the only one I'll ever need.

NEVAEH

"Where are we going?" I ask Angie as we get in the backseat of Drake's car.

"It's a surprise," she says and meets her fiancé's gaze in the rearview mirror. "We need your help with something."

"My help?"

"It's impossible to do this without you," Drake chimes in, looking over his shoulder. "Just relax and enjoy the ride. It won't be long."

Furrowing my brow, I glance between Angie and Drake and start to chew my bottom lip. It's January, the season isn't over yet...Are they getting married? It seems like a possibility. Why else would they say they couldn't do it without me? But where is Layla? And Maya? No way Drake would want to get married without his sister and his niece. Ugh, guess I'm totally wrong.

"What is Roman doing?" Angie half-turns to look at me, both of her hands resting on her baby bump. She's seven months along, and she's as beautiful as ever. Her dark brown hair spills over her shoulders, her deep green eyes sparkle, and a sinful smile plays on her lips.

"He's with Colt at Clay's place, playing FIFA. They have some

2. Она моя малышка. — She's my baby girl.
3. Моё солнышко — My Sunshine

sort of tournament, from what I know." I smirk and peer at Drake. "Why don't you ever join them?"

"Waste my time on video games? No thanks. I'd rather read."

"And what are you reading now?" I hook one leg over the other, listening to Drake tell me about the new detective series he just started.

He's incredibly sweet and kind, and I'm so happy Angie met him. He's her perfect match, and she blossoms with him by her side. They're just so cute, I always feel like a little girl when I'm with them. A fairy-tale princess and her Prince Charming.

When the car stops and we climb outside, I frown. What are we doing at Thompson's?

"And where is this surprise?" I ask, knitting my eyebrows together.

"Inside," Angie replies and takes my hand in hers. "Come on. You're gonna love it."

"Right now I don't," I mumble, letting her guide me. I'm more skeptical than anything, but when Layla opens the door, my jaw drops. "What is this?"

The first thing my eyes land on are rose petals. Pink, red, and beige, they cover the floor, paving a path from the front door to the patio. Arching an eyebrow, I look at Angie, but she only smiles broader and urges me further into the house. Layla and Drake's voices become quieter as Angie pulls me into the bedroom on our left.

"Angie, what's going on?"

"Surprise!" she exclaims and nods her head to my right.

I turn to look, and my breath hitches in my throat. A pale pink wedding gown lies on the bed. A fitted bodice with twisted rose detailing and a beautifully layered tulle skirt draw my attention, and I can't look away. It's the one I noticed in one of the magazines Angie bought when she was looking for her own wedding dress two months ago. I told her that if I ever had a wedding, I would want to walk down the aisle in something like that.

"How...?" I sneak a glance at Angie, and she just smiles. "Is this for me?"

"For you," she confirms. "You're getting married today, Nev."

Tears spring to my eyes, and I bite my bottom lip hard, trying not to let myself cry. Angie notices it, steps closer, and hauls me to her, hugging me as tight as her baby bump allows. I wrap my arms around her and hide my face in her neck, inhaling her perfume and feeling warmth flow through my body, her energy fueling me with happiness.

"Your husband thinks you deserve a real wedding, with your closest friends surrounding you and a beautiful dress that makes you look like a princess," she whispers. "Roman planned everything; he just asked us to help him with a few details. He's amazing, Nev. That man has it *bad* for you."

"He is," I giggle, and she leans away with one eyebrow arched. "And I have it bad for him too. We are hopelessly in love."

"I'm so, so happy for you." Angie steps back, taking my hands in hers. "Let's get you ready; your husband is waiting for you."

Hearing her say that sends a thrill of excitement down my spine. The thought that Roman did something like this for me makes my heart go wild. Every day I think it's not possible to love him more, and every day he proves me wrong.

He's the lyrics I hear in every song about love. He's the words of affirmation I read in romance novels. He's not the thought that crosses my mind on occasion—he's all I think about during the day and in my dreams. He's my entire world, and instead of being scared, I welcome my feelings and let them guide me.

Because I know it's exactly what I am for him too.

STEPPING out of the house with Angie by my side, I can't stop smiling. Colton and Ava with Michael and Meghan, Layla and Maya, Drake and Clay, and even Kai. They are all here, clapping and cheering, but the second my eyes meet Roman's—everything else disappears.

Such a handsome man. My husband stands under an arch covered with roses from top to bottom. He's in black pants, and a white shirt hugs his broad shoulders tightly. A crooked smile lights up his face, and he runs his fingers through his hair, his eyes never leaving mine.

Once I get close enough, Roman extends his hand and takes mine in his. My eyes water as I stop by his side. A sudden nervousness washes over me, and my legs become wobbly. Getting married when I was blackout drunk was so much easier, because right now I'm ready to faint.

"I know that we're technically already married. And I know that maybe this is all unnecessary. But...I really wanted to see you in a beautiful gown." Roman leans into my ear. "And more than that, I really want to see my ring on your finger. It was kinda bugging me that you didn't have one."

"So technically this is all because of a ring?" I ask jokingly, the butterflies in my stomach making me all giddy.

"It's all because of you, Malyshka," he whispers. "For you, I'd do absolutely anything. No limits, no rules. You and your happiness are all I care about. So please, be a good girl and let me put the ring on your finger."

"Anything you want, Roman," I say, and we turn to the wedding officiant, ready to get married all over again.

LAUGHING TO MYSELF, I walk down the hallway, a bit light-headed from all the champagne. It's been several hours since Roman and I got married again, and a platinum wedding band with a full circle of diamonds sparkles on my finger. The atmosphere is light and full of happiness, and yet I can't wait to get home.

I've waited far too long to thank my husband for this surprise. My desire just keeps growing, and soon I don't think I'll have it in me to keep it to myself. He's way too addictive. I can't stay away.

I pass the living room, automatically glancing inside. I take two steps forward, and then I stop abruptly. Astonished, I gape at two people kissing in the darkness of the room. A smile lifts my lips, and I quickly tiptoe away, heading straight to the patio. I feel like a little kid who just discovered a secret she wasn't supposed to know about.

Roman notices me first, a raised brow and a half smile gracing his features as he watches me head toward him. I let him pull me to his chest, his arms wrapping around my waist and holding me close.

"What is it?" he asks quietly.

I inch toward his ear and whisper, "I think I saw Layla and Clay kissing."

His smile grows bigger, his eyes glimmering with mischief. "If that's true, I'm happy for them."

"You think I should—"

"No. I know Angie is your best friend, but please don't tell her. It's not your secret. Let them figure it out on their own." Roman glances at Drake and Angie, who sit at a table with Ava. "Without Drake's involvement."

"Fine, you're right." I sigh, relaxing into his embrace.

Standing here, with Roman's strong arms wrapped around me, I feel content. Happy and loved. Without really knowing it, he made one of my childhood dreams come true. I never wanted a big fancy wedding with lots of guests and an expensive venue. A small, secluded one, with just my closest friends in attendance, was something I always dreamed about.

And Roman made it reality. For me.

He's my favorite place, where I want to be on good days, and even more on bad ones, because being with him makes everything bad go away. He makes the impossible feel possible, and I just know that I can achieve anything with him by my side.

My husband is the most beautiful man, with the most charming smile and eyes so alluring I never know how to stop looking. I love everything about him—his looks, his voice, and his mind, but more than anything I love his soul, in all its brokenness and imperfection. Because it makes him perfect for me.

A long time ago, I thought a perfect love story was what I wanted, but it turns out the imperfect one is exactly what I need.

Because this love story is ours, and I wouldn't want it any other way.

Nevaeh

bonus chapter

Sitting in the car beside Roman, I look out the window. The ride to the airport is incredibly quiet. Not because we don't have anything to talk about, but because I can't hold a conversation. My heart beats wildly in my chest, and my palms are sweaty. Iryna has been nothing but nice to me every time we have talked. When she asks me how I'm doing, I know she's really interested, that she wants to know about my days, about my job and how her son is treating me. A couple times, I have even talked to her without Roman, and it was an absolute delight.

So why am I so nervous?

"Mom likes you," Roman says, putting a hand on my knee and squeezing lightly. "You have nothing to worry about, I promise."

I smile hesitantly. "Thank you." I cover his hand with mine. "I have no idea what's going on in my head, honestly. Like...what if she thinks I'm not smart enough? Or tall enough? Or—"

"Malyshka." Roman snorts, shaking his head. "Mom reads all of your articles, and she always says how talented you are. How powerful your words are. There is no way she'd ever think you're not smart enough." He stops at a traffic light and leans closer, lifting my face with his fingers under my chin. "You're amazing. Don't ever doubt that."

My lips ease into a broad smile, and I inch forward, pressing my mouth to his for a light peck. "Love you," I whisper, leaning away.

"And I love you."

Roman starts driving again, looking quizzical. "What was that about your height? Why would my mom or anyone else care how tall you are?"

"I had...a bad experience."

"Like what?" He arches an eyebrow, my favorite crooked smile on full display. "You have to tell me now, or I'll die of curiosity."

"In my sophomore year of college, I had a boyfriend who was a basketball player. We only dated for two months, and it just so happened that his parents came to watch a game during that time. Wade introduced me to them, and it was fine, but a few days later, he said his mom thought I was too short for him. I don't think I need to tell you how fast I broke up with him..." I trail off, noticing a playful grin on Roman's face. "Why are you smiling?"

"It's hilarious and ridiculous that he lost you because of that. All I can say is, 'His loss.'" His eyes roam over my face and down my chest, and I feel tingles spreading all over my skin. "My win."

"You're way too cocky, mister."

"Maybe that's exactly why you married me."

"I'm pretty sure it was because of the alcohol," I tease him.

"*Nyet*[1]." Roman shakes his head. "You were sober the last time you said I do, so our marriage officially has nothing to do with alcohol."

"Maybe I was just drunk on my love for you."

He pretends to think, but it doesn't last even a minute before he grins at me. Reaching over, he places his hand on my knee again. "Then we were both drunk on our love for each other."

"We sure were." I entwine our fingers.

As my husband focuses on the road, I realize that I no longer feel nervous. Warm and cozy feelings unfurl inside my belly, making my smile grow bigger. I'm content and calm, and it's all because of him.

---

1. Нет. — No.

"Do you see your mom?" I ask, looking around. My hand nests securely in Roman's.

"I...I do." He heads to the right, making me follow him. "Looks like this time she didn't try to bring her whole wardrobe with her. This bag...*Chert voz'mi*[2]."

"Spoke too soon?" I joke, finally noticing his mom.

Iryna stands with her palm pressed to her cheek, studying the people around her. She's wearing a simple white T-shirt, light blue jeans, and white sneakers with pink stripes. Her casual look isn't what I expected, considering how my own mother used to dress, yet it suits her. Roman's mom looks nice, and I can't help but admire how beautiful she is.

"Hey, Mom," Roman says as we stop in front of her. Her deep turquoise eyes, the same color as her son's, dart between us, and a smile lights up her face. He steps closer, letting go of my hand, and hugs her tightly. "So glad you're here."

"Me too," she says and leans away, her gaze sweeping over Roman's face. "*Bozhe*[3], how much I missed you."

"I missed you too, Mom." My husband takes a step back, and his mom's eyes instantly land on me. "Well, this is my Nevaeh."

My Nevaeh...I swear it gets me every time. That and "Malyshka." I'm not even sure which one is my favorite.

"Hi," I mumble, wondering if I should shake her hand or hug her. "It's nice to finally meet you in person."

"Hi, Nevaeh. It's really nice to finally meet you, indeed." Iryna steps toward me and hugs me tightly. My breath hitches, but then I wrap my arms around her too and hug her back. When she leans away, she's smiling from ear to ear. "You're even more gorgeous in person."

"So are you," I tell her, realizing with a surprise that she's just a bit taller than me. "I'm really happy you decided to visit."

---

2. Чёрт возьми. — Dammit.
3. Боже — God

"My son is in the playoffs. How could I miss it?"

"Last time it didn't bother you." Roman rounds her, grabs her suitcase, and lifts the bag from the ground.

Iryna snatches a backpack from the suitcase and puts it on, turning to look at her son. "Last time I didn't come, and you didn't win. Maybe this time will be different." She glances at me and winks. "Besides, this time you'll have two women who love you cheering for you. That's worth something, right?"

"It's worth everything," Roman says, and he starts walking toward the exit. His mom and I follow him, talking about her flight and the last game the Thunders won. It's easy and really pleasant, and I'm happy she's here.

Roman has missed her way more than he let on.

THE NEXT FEW days are a whirlwind. Work, games, sightseeing—so much sightseeing that by the end of the day my legs hurt, although the smile on Roman's face when he watches his mom means everything to me.

I often give them space, leaving them alone so they can talk without me around. Without needing to speak in English. Just a mom and her son, talking about anything and everything. Reminiscing about their past and Maksim. It doesn't make me feel left out. Quite the contrary; it makes me happy. For him and for Iryna. They went through so much, but they still have each other, and it's precious. Their little family is something I admire, and something I belong to.

Even if sometimes it still feels unrealistic. After so many years, to finally have a family who loves me unconditionally and cares about me in ways I couldn't even imagine...

"Nevaeh, honey, can you please help me?" Iryna's voice rips me out of my thoughts, and I turn to look at her. She's standing behind the kitchen counter with her hands covered in flour.

I join her, staring at a bowl that has something white in it. Iryna's laughter fills the kitchen.

"You look so...puzzled," she says between fits of laughter.

"I just have no idea what you're doing." I smile at her.

"Roma will be home tomorrow, and I just want to treat him with something he loves. Syrniki are especially delicious for breakfast."

Biting my bottom lip, I look around the ingredients she has out on the counter: a tub of cottage cheese, eggs, and wheat flour. "What is it? Is it some kind of dessert?"

"Kind of," she says and points to a little plate with raisins. "Can you please bring that here? I forgot, and now my hands are covered in flour."

I nod, quickly grab the plate, and bring it to Iryna.

"Can you please toss them into the bowl?"

"Sure," I reply, and I do as she asks. "What's next?"

"Next I'm going to mix it all together, make the syrniki, and then fry them."

This time, I don't go back to my chair. I stay by her side and watch her shape the mixture into small crumpets and then fry them in the pan. It smells like vanilla, and I can't help but smile.

"Is this typical Belarusian cuisine?" I ask Iryna as she hands me a syrnik.

"Not really; people all across Eastern Europe love them. They're very tasty." I take a bite, and the sweet taste spreads all over my tongue. "What do you think?"

"It's so delicious," I say with my mouth full, making her chuckle.

"And they're easy to make. Roma always loved them, so I thought it would be a good idea to make some. He needs something to cheer him up after that game."

We both fall silent, lost in our thoughts. Iryna and I watched the game at home, yelling at the TV when we thought the referees were unfair, cheering for the Thunders when they scored and when Clay secured the net, booing when Colorado scored. If the Thunders had won, they would've gone to the second round already. They put up a great fight, but in the end they lost four to three. It was a bitter loss.

"When Roma and Maks were little and their team would lose, they were inconsolable. Like, literally, for them it was the end of the world. Instead of two smiling boys, I'd get two thunderclouds. Broody and frowning," Iryna says. "The fact that their father always lectured them after their losses didn't help either. It drove me insane; I wanted to help my boys learn how to accept defeat and turn it into something valuable. No matter how many times I told their father to leave them be, reminding him that hockey is a team sport and they didn't lose because they played badly, but because the team as a whole wasn't effective, or because luck simply wasn't on their side, he never listened."

I hold my breath, devouring every word she says about Roman's childhood. It's fascinating and fulfilling. It gives me all the feels and makes me understand my husband even better.

"I know Roma told you that my ex-husband was always more hostile toward him than his brother. He would find good things to say to Maksim about his performance, but never to Roma. It was exhausting and terrible to hear him ripping apart his son, blaming the team's loss on him." Iryna purses her lips and looks away, staring at the wall with her eyebrows knitted together. "Maks always tried to defend Roma, but it didn't really work, and one day he came up with a plan. He came to me and said that we needed our own ritual for the games they lost. And we figured out one—whether it was an away game or a home game, I would take my boys to the movies. We'd eat popcorn and not talk about the game at all. It really made a difference for Roma, and for Maks too, because he couldn't stand his brother being unhappy."

A smile breaks out on her lips, but when she turns to me, I also notice unshed tears. I move closer and wind my hand around her waist, wanting to give her comfort. Iryna puts her head on my shoulder and sighs.

"They were so alike, but so different. Maks was always softer, gentler, while Roma was moody, more closed off. I do think it's because of his father and his constant desire to pick up fights with him. Not leaving my ex-husband sooner is my biggest regret, a burden I carry because I deserve it." She leans away and peers at me, smiling warmly. "I'll be forever grateful to you for helping Roma, for being there for him and for loving him as he is. You saved my boy, Nevaeh. Just took him in, not paying attention to his scars or his broken heart, and instead fueling him with love and warmth. His darkness is no longer there because you healed him."

"He saved me too," I whisper, and she wraps her arms around me and hugs me tight. "He put my broken pieces back together and glued them with his love. He's my biggest supporter, and I want to be the same for him."

"You already are, Nevaeh. You already are." Iryna smiles, tucking my hair behind my ears. "How about we watch something before bed?"

"With popcorn?" I ask, stepping back from her.

"That would be nice."

"Awesome," I say and busy myself with making the popcorn. The warmth in my body plants a smile on my face, and I just know that tomorrow is going to be great. Because my husband is coming home.

STRONG ARMS WRAP around me from behind; my back is pressed to a solid, muscular chest. My eyes flutter open, and I instantly feel hot breath fanning over my cheek.

"Shh, Malyshka, it's way too early."

Wiggling, I turn around and find myself face-to-face with Roman. He grins at me, his fingertips pushing my hair off my face. I move closer and hide my face in his chest, inhaling the scent of his cologne mixed with mint.

"I thought you'd be home closer to lunch."

"It was always supposed to be early morning. I just never corrected you." He presses his lips to my forehead. "Wanted it to be a surprise."

"I love surprises when they're good."

"Is this a good one?"

"The best," I whisper, feeling my eyelids grow heavier. "What time is it?"

"It's only seven." Roman tightens his grip around me and buries his nose in my hair. "Sleep, Malyshka; we have the whole day ahead of us."

Relaxing into his embrace, I start to fall back asleep, pressing myself into him harder. With him by my side, I feel safe and content, like I've never felt before. He takes everything to the next level, heightening my feelings and making me feel like I can do anything with him by my side.

Because he's my Roman.

Roman

bonus chapter

"It's a surprise," I say, answering Nevaeh's question for the third time since we left our apartment.

"Where are you taking me?" Nevaeh asks, half-turning to me. One of her legs is bent at the knee and hidden under her butt.

"Somewhere."

"Roman, do you want me to strangle you?"

"Definitely not. Who would show you my surprise if you killed me?" I wink at her and put my hand on her knee. "Stop worrying. Everything's fine."

"You and your surprises lately..." She lowers her gaze to the word "Malyshka" tattooed on my arm. "I have no idea what to think anymore."

"Just remember that I'll never do anything to make you upset. That's all you need to know about my surprises."

Nevaeh sighs, shaking her head. "I have a surprise for you too, but now you'll have to wait for it. You messed up all my plans."

"I'm patient. I'll wait," I tell her. Then I focus on the road for the next twenty-five minutes.

When I park in the driveway of a two-story house made of beige bricks and a light brown roof, I glance at Nevaeh, who sits with her arms crossed over her chest. Her puffy lips are smacked together in a pout. God, she's adorable.

"Why the face?" I ask, opening the door and getting out.

"I don't really get what we're doing in Colton and Ava's neighborhood."

"Actually, it's closer to their friends Xander and Bella. They live two houses away," I explain as I help her out of the car. "You don't like it?"

"It's a nice neighborhood." She shrugs. "Never really thought about it. Why?"

A cold sweat breaks out over my back, my tee clinging to my skin. What if I'm making a mistake? Nevaeh never said she doesn't like living in our apartment, never said anything about wanting to live in a house.

Fuck, I should've asked.

"Roman?" Nevaeh steps into me, wrapping her arms around my torso and looking up at me. "Is everything okay?"

I dip my head, my hands cupping her face and sliding to her nape. Her blonde hair with pastel pink highlights shines in the sun, the hot July wind blowing lazily, spreading goosebumps over my skin.

"Remember I told you that one day I'd love to have my own house? A place for my family?" I ask, and she nods. "This is the one... but only if you like it. Only if it's something you want, because we can keep living in our apartment. It's not a big deal. I didn't sign anything yet, so—"

Nevaeh pinches my side, and I fall quiet, watching her without blinking. The beat of my heart grows faster, thundering in my ears and silencing all the sounds around us.

"You done rambling?" At her question, I chuckle, smiling at her tenderly. "I spend a lot of time at the office, and once the season starts, you basically live on the ice and on the road. We can go the whole day without seeing each other, but nights? They belong to us. All my midnights are yours, because even if you're away, I fall asleep with your voice saying the sweetest things in my ear through the phone." She tilts her head, her hair spilling over her bare shoulders. "Having a whole house just for us? Without being afraid that I'm too loud? Without prying neighbors? It would be a blessing...on one condition though."

That makes me laugh. Wholeheartedly and loudly, with my head thrown back and my eyes closed.

"And this condition? What is it?"

"I want a cat. Or a dog. Or both." A cheeky grin forms on her lips. "A house might feel lonelier than an apartment when I'm there alone..." Her eyes widen suddenly, and she trails off. "Um, yeah, so I'm okay with us moving in."

"Some cosmetic repairs have been done, like the floors, and the walls have been painted, but we can change anything. We can do whatever we want inside. Bella has a spot for us, I asked her just in case, so she can help us with the interior design if we want."

"Considering I love what she did for Angie's house, and for Drake's, where Layla lives now, I'm totally on board." My wife narrows her eyes at me. "I know I don't make nearly as much as you, but I want you to let me pay for something. Anything. Movers? Bella's help? Some furni—"

I press my mouth to hers, shutting her up immediately. My tongue slips between her lips, tangling around hers as I deepen our kiss. My fingers entangle in her locks, then I fist my hand around her hair and tug lightly. The hum of my body sets my skin on fire; my heart beats fast against my rib cage. Anything I do with her feels like it's not enough, like my life turned upside down and the whole world stopped—like time stopped, and there's just us. High on our love for each other. High on us.

It still makes me speechless on some days. How she feels about me.

Nevaeh loves me.

All of me.

The good and the bad, the broken and the sad.

She doesn't care if I'm moody, doesn't care if I'm distant on days when the pain of my brother's death returns. She's just there for me whenever I need her, even when I feel like I'll be fine on my own.

She's mine.

Just like I'm hers.

Always.

Pressing my forehead to hers, I inhale deeply. Her sweet scent fills my nostrils, and I smile broadly.

"Ready to see our house for the first time?" I ask.

"Absolutely."

I give her a peck, then I take her hand in mine and make her follow me. I pull the keys out of my pocket, open the door, and let Nevaeh go in first. She steps inside but halts in her tracks pretty quickly. Then she turns around, putting her hands on her hips, and her eyebrows pinch together. She studies me with her eyes slightly narrowed as I close the door and lock it.

"You have the keys, and there's no one here to show us around," she states.

"I might have had the contract prepared, but I warned them that I wasn't going to finalize anything without talking to you first." I run my fingers through my hair, still holding her gaze. "I'll show you the contract once we get back in the car. And, Nevaeh—remember that if you don't like this house, we can always look for another one. I mean it."

Nevaeh rolls her lips together, as if she's annoyed with me. I wait, inwardly cursing myself in Russian. If she says no—

"You and your surprises lately," she says again. Then she turns on her heel and walks into the house.

Grinning, I follow her. "I honestly don't get why you were so surprised when I said I wanted to tattoo 'Malyshka' on my arm. What better way to celebrate the woman I love and winning my first Stanley Cup than with her by my side?"

"I have plenty of opinions, Roman. You should've asked me," she says, looking around the house.

The white walls leave a room for imagination. We can paint them any color we want, even her favorite pastel pink—I don't really care, because I'd do absolutely anything to make her happy. And damn if I don't intend to be the happiest here with her.

"What if we put the couch here?" Nevaeh points at an empty space in the living room. "And a huge TV on the wall here?" She turns around and points at the wall. "And you and Maks's jerseys here?"

I prop my shoulder against the wall, hiding my hands in my shorts pockets. "Sounds great," I say. "We can also use the empty space for bookshelves."

"You think we'll need floor lamps, or will the chandelier be enough?" Nevaeh wheels around, the skirt of her dress flowing seamlessly. "With these floor-to-ceiling windows, we might not need much light."

"Even at night?"

My wife rolls her eyes and heads to the kitchen, putting her hand on a little alcove and tracing her fingers over it. "When do you think we can start working with Bella? Because even just looking around I have so many ideas—for example, doing the kitchen in metallic colors, with just a bit of wood here and there. And maybe buying a rug for our living room? Or—"

"Next week. Bella has a spot for us next week."

"Really?" Nevaeh stops and stares at me with her lips parted. I nod, coming closer to her, my fingertips itching to touch her, to feel her skin against mine. Something about hearing her talk about our life in this house makes me unreasonably horny. "Oh, I know that look."

"What look?" I lick my lips and reach out for her, but she walks backward, avoiding getting caught.

"The one you get when you want me."

"I always want you," I confess, stepping into her, and she moves away again. "What are you doing?"

Nevaeh puts her hands behind her back. Her tits stick out, and the deep cleavage of her dress makes them absolutely mouthwatering. "Let's play a game."

"I'm all ears."

"You stay here and count to fifty, while I go upstairs and hide in one of the rooms. If you find me within seven minutes—you'll get a reward."

"A reward?" I step in front of her, wrap my arm around her waist, and pull her against my chest. "What will it be?"

"An orgasm," Nevaeh whispers, rising onto her tiptoes. "And your surprise."

"What if I don't find you in seven minutes?"

"Then no orgasm for you, husband." She puts her hands on my chest and pushes me away. "Start counting."

Laughing to myself, I turn around and do as I'm told. Her steps are loud and hurried at first, becoming quieter and quieter with each number I say until I don't hear her at all.

"Fifty," I announce loudly, pulling my phone out of my pocket and setting a timer. Seven minutes starts now. "Ready or not, here I come, Malyshka."

I veer to my right and walk out of the kitchen, through the living room and straight to the stairs. When I get to the second floor, I pause, looking around. There are three bedrooms and one bathroom; this should be easy, especially since there's no furniture at all. I don't know what she expects...unless she wants to be found.

Opening the first door on my left, I walk into a spacious bathroom. There's no sight of my wife, but I can easily imagine what we might do with this room—blue and white tiles, a big tub, a mirror on the wall, and...*Roman, focus.* Shaking my head, I step out of the bathroom and close the door.

The next one is the first bedroom. It's not the biggest one, from what I remember, so we can totally use it as a guest room—or maybe a nursery, in the future, when we're ready. Or it can be Nevaeh's office, where she works on her articles or the book she's started to outline. A smile blooms on my face as I walk out and close the door.

Two more rooms. I take my phone out of my pocket and realize that I have only two minutes left. Taking a deep breath, I rush to the second bedroom, stepping inside and looking around. This one is bigger than the previous one, and it has a walk-in closet. That's exactly where I go first, finding it empty a moment later. Dammit.

Rushing out of the bedroom, I don't bother closing the door. I swing open the door of the third bedroom and stalk inside. The scent of her perfume hits my nostrils, and a satisfied smile crosses my lips. She still smells like vanilla and marshmallows with a dash of cinnamon, and probably caramel.

"Come out, come out, wherever you are," I say, moving forward into the room and straight to the walk-in closet. My eyes land on Nevaeh the second I step into the space; her back is pressed to the wall. "Here you are, Malyshka."

"You weren't in a hurry," she replies, tossing a candy into her mouth and hiding the rest of the pack in her purse. "I almost ate all of my Sour Patch Kids."

"I was thinking about what we can do with all of these rooms."

"And?"

"One of the bedrooms we can use as your office. Another one might be a guest room, or a nursery whenever it's time." I smile at her, and she smiles back. "And this one? This one will be ours."

"I don't even want to pretend to be surprised that we think the same," she murmurs as I shift to her, caging her in my embrace. "What's next?"

"I was promised an orgasm, and a surprise. I think I earned them both."

"You did." Nevaeh slides her hands under my tee, feeling my muscles flex under her touch. "What do you want first?"

"My surprise."

Her hands move up until she pinches my nipples between her fingers. A seductive grin appears on her lips when she notices me wince.

"I have a doctor's appointment on Thursday," she tells me. "I'm going to talk with her about going off the pill." A harsh tug on my nipples makes me hiss, and I furrow my brows. "And anything else I might need to know about getting pregnant once I'm off birth control."

My chest feels a bit too tight as I croak out words. "You really want that? When I mentioned wanting a kid a few months ago, I didn't mean we had to start trying now. Not unless it's something—"

"Goodness, stop talking," Nevaeh scolds me. Taking her hands out from under my tee, she reaches around the back of my neck and pulls my face down to her. "If I didn't want it, I wouldn't even think about going off the pill."

I search her face, my eyes roaming over her beautiful features. "*Bozhe, kak ya tebya lyublyu*[1]."

"And I love you," she says with a timid smile on her face. "More than anything in the world."

Smashing my lips onto hers, I kiss her hungrily. Her mouth is soft and inviting, and the sour taste of her candies erupts on my tongue once I curl mine around hers. I press my body to hers, feeling a heat that has nothing to do with the summer weather spread all over my skin. It's all her, only her.

Nevaeh tugs on my tee, and I take it off, throwing it to the ground immediately. Her hands slip around my shoulders and move down to my torso. She hooks a finger over the waistband of my shorts, pulling me even closer to her. My dick grows hard as she starts to grind over it, her hips moving frantically. So greedy for my cock. My wife is my fucking undoing.

I place my hands on her waist and move them up until I have a handful of her tits. I squeeze, sinking my teeth into her bottom lip at the same time. Pulling down the bodice of her dress, I release her breasts, in a lacy pink bra, groaning from how perfect she looks.

"So fucking beautiful." I dip my head and bury my face between her breasts. I lick and suck on her skin, leaving a hickey on her right tit —and instantly getting a smack on my forearm.

"That hurts!"

I palm her tits and pop them free from her bra, tugging it down too. Massaging her breasts, rubbing her nipples between my fingers, I make my way up her throat, leaving open-mouthed kisses along the way. Wet and hot, I drag my teeth over her skin and suck again, leaving a hickey there too.

"Roman!" Nevaeh hisses, but the sound quickly drowns in her

1. Боже, как я тебя люблю. — God, how much I love you.

moans. She wiggles against me; her nipples are puckered and hard, looking almost red in contrast to her pink buds. “Please...Roman.”

“Please what?” I ask her teasingly, my mouth hovering over hers.

Instead of answering, she fists my hair and tilts my head to the side. We’re both panting, our chests rising and falling rapidly. I feel pre-cum on my cock, and I know how desperately I want to bury it inside her. To give her pleasure. But I also love playing by her rules... when she’s in control.

“Be a good boy for me,” she whispers, “and fuck me against this wall.”

Nevaeh lets go of my hair, her hands dangling at her sides. I drape an arm around her waist, pulling her to my chest. The smile playing on her lips sends my thoughts into turmoil. I push my hands down her hips, lifting the skirt of her dress and palming her ass cheeks.

“Not wearing any panties?” I ask, digging my nails into her ass.

“I love the ones that go with this bra,” she mewls. “I didn’t want you to rip them apart, as you so often do, so I didn’t even wear them.”

“So you knew I was going to fuck you at some point today?”

“I was counting on it.” Nevaeh fists my cock and slides my pre-cum all over it. She slowly pumps, and I start to lose it. My vision blurs; the heat of our bodies mixing together sets my whole being on fucking fire.

Pushing down my shorts with one hand, I snake my other around her waist. I lift her, making her wrap her legs around my hips. Her scent. Her taste. The softness of her skin. It’s never enough, no matter how many times I taste her. If anything, it just makes me crave her even more.

Nevaeh winds her hands around my neck, our breaths mingling together. I sneak my hand between us, my finger brushing her clit and feeling her wetness. Growling, I fist my cock and press it to her opening. I push my length inside her slowly, my lips devouring hers. I grip her ass with my palms, pulling her up and down my cock.

“So good,” I murmur against her lips, sinking deeper and deeper inside her as she adjusts to my size.

My eyes find hers in the dimness of the room, and I’m drowning.

The lust I feel for her, my love and my desire to protect her and make her happy, tangle together. It's powerful, breathtaking. Nothing compares to being with her, not even winning the title I've been dreaming about since I was a little boy. Nevaeh is everything for me. My whole world. My universe.

"Right there...Roman, please, right there," she begs, her breath hitching.

Picking up speed, I fuck her long and hard, squeezing her ass roughly. Her tits bounce, and my name spills over her lips, along with her begging for more. And, like the good boy I am, I fucking obey.

"Oh God," she screams, her walls suffocating me. Her orgasm hits her strongly, and her body trembles in my arms. She shuts her eyes; her mouth is open. I move inside her, prolonging her pleasure for as long as I can while still controlling my own release.

I'm not done with her yet.

When Nevaeh opens her eyes, she looks disoriented. A puff of air blows out of her mouth as she focuses on me. I grin, pulling my cock out of her and lowering her to her feet.

"You didn't come," she scolds me, her voice sounding weak.

"I have time."

"Wh—" Her question dies in her throat as I turn her around and make her face the wall. Her dress is around her waist.

"Put your hands on the wall," I order her, pushing her hair to the side. I press my lips to her ear and slide them down the back of her neck. Then I bite her shoulder, my teeth leaving a mark. "And give me your perfect ass."

Nevaeh listens to me. She puts her hands on the wall and arches her back for me. So fucking flexible, *moya Malyshka*[2]. I sneak my hand around her and rub her clit between my thumb and index finger. She bucks into me, aching for more friction as the sexiest sounds come out of her mouth.

"More...please..."

I smirk and place my hand on her lower back, making her arch her

2. Моя малышка — My baby girl

back even more. My cock throbs, longing to be inside her little cunt again. I glide my hands down her hips and press my cock to her ass. Just to tease her. Last time we tried anal, she said it was one of the strongest orgasms she'd ever had, but how she felt after wasn't something she wanted to repeat. At least for now.

Your cock is too fucking big for that. No way I'm letting you fuck my ass ever again.

Her words flash in my head, and I can't help but grin. I'm so smitten with her, it's unreal.

I slide the tip of my cock inside her and pull out. Next time, I go a bit deeper then pull out again. Her frustrated groan makes me chuckle. I bury myself deeper in her, and she rotates her hips, not letting me move away this time. Fucking her steadily, I reach over and cup her tit, playing with her nipple. Her moans mix with mine, filling the walk-in closet with our sounds and our scent. I'm not sure I'll ever be able to come in here without thinking about this moment.

"You're taking me so well," I praise her. My forehead is sweaty, and my hair sticks to it. "So fucking well...Your pussy was made for me, Nevaeh."

I can feel my approaching release in my bones. It's hot and barely controllable, but I want her to come first. My hand finds her clit again, circling it with my fingers. I thrust into her from behind, harder and faster as my fingers relentlessly rub her sweet spot.

"I'm gonna...I'm gonna come..." Nevaeh moans.

Her cunt starts strangling my dick, and my eyes roll back in my head. I choke on my words; only a low growl escapes my lips when I come. I shoot my cum deep inside her, rocking against her as she moves her ass to meet me.

Only when I'm spent do I take a step back and pull out my cock. Nevaeh twirls around, cupping my cheeks and bringing my face to hers. Her lips collide with mine, and she kisses me as if I'm her fucking oxygen. It's teeth and tongues battling together. Nothing gentle, pure passion consuming us both.

"I love the way you fuck me," she says against my lips. "As if you own me."

I sneak my hand between her legs as my cum drips down her thigh.

"My cum is leaking out of your cunt, Malyshka. I do own you," I say with conviction. Nevaeh rears back, her eyes narrowed. "But don't forget that you own me too."

The corner of her mouth trembles as she tries to fight her smile—unsuccessfully, as her lips ease into a broad grin that lights up her face.

"That's better," she states and starts fixing her clothes. I pull up my shorts and help her, and once she's ready, I lift my tee from the floor and put it on. "Where to now?"

"I need to sign the contract, and then we can go somewhere to celebrate."

Nevaeh stops, staring at me from under pinched eyebrows.

"What?" I ask.

"Your cum is still dripping out of me, Roman. I need to go home so I can pee, take a shower, and change my clothes. And I also want to talk to Bella before we go anywhere."

"Whatever you need." I extend my hand to her. "You can call Bella on our way home. We have a lot to do in less than two weeks, before we leave, so it would be great to start decorating as soon as possible."

With a sigh, my wife comes to me, and I take her hand in mine.

"Did you really need to remind me about our trip to Minsk? I'm still worried I'll feel like an outcast since I don't understand anything in Russian."

"I'll always be by your side," I tell her as we descend the stairs. "And you're lying. You know some words already."

She laughs, letting me pull her along. "I know when you curse, when you call me 'Malyshka,' and when you tell me that you love me. Though I highly doubt you'll be okay with anyone cursing me or telling me that they love me."

"They can try; you know I can fight."

We walk out the door smiling from ear to ear. As we approach my car, I stop and turn to look at Nevaeh. Her disheveled hair and the glimmer in her eyes scream happiness. And love—so much love that it overwhelms us, knocks us both off our feet. It came absolutely unexpectedly, and it's the best thing ever.

I will never stop falling in love with Nevaeh, because our love has no expiration date. It's forever.

THANK YOU SO MUCH FOR READING!

If you enjoyed **BREAKAWAY**, I'd be immensely grateful if you can leave a review.

Stay tuned for **POWER PLAY**, the last book in the *Sinners on the Ice* series. Layla and Clay's book will be released by the end of 2024.

For exclusive bonus content and new releases make sure to sign up for my newsletter via my website. Follow me on my socials for news, announcements and giveaways.

about the author

Anastasija is an indie author who spends her days creating swoon-worthy and steamy stories that will make your heart race. Her writing is filled with flawed and relatable characters that you'll find yourself rooting for. Whether you're in the mood for angsty drama or steamy romance, her stories take you on a rollercoaster ride of emotions with guaranteed happy endings.

When she's not writing, she loves to lose herself in reading books, rewatching her favorite tv-shows and spending time with her son. She loves traveling and exploring the world, and then including places she visited in her novels.

If you're a fan of romance that leaves you breathless and begging for more, Anastasija is the author for you. Connect with her on Instagram and TikTok, where she loves to hear from her readers and share sneak peeks of her books and upcoming projects.

also by anastasija white

SIN-BIN: An Enemies to Lovers College Hockey Romance

BARN BURNER: A Fake Dating Hockey Romance

HALE: A Single Dad Sports Romance

BREAKAWAY: An Accidental Marriage Hockey Romance

POWER PLAY: A Second Chance Hockey Romance (Fall, 2024)

Title TBD (Rules Duet, book 1, 2025)

Title TBD (Rules Duet, book 2, 2025)

HADE: A Rockstar Romance (2025)

DOMINIC: A Stepbrother Romance (2025)

Printed by Amazon Italia Logistica S.r.l.
Torrazza Piemonte (TO), Italy

62828515R00197